THE CASE OF

The Cautious Coquette

THE CASE OF

The Cautious Coquette

The Case of the Crimson Kiss
The Case of the Crying Swallow

BY

ERLE STANLEY GARDNER

WILLIAM MORROW & COMPANY

NEW YORK

THE CASE OF

The Cautious Coquette

1

PROMPTLY at nine o'clock, Perry Mason joined Paul Drake for breakfast.

The tall detective, head of the Drake Detective Agency, grinned at the lawyer, said, "You're thirty seconds late, Perry."

Mason shook his head. "Your watch is thirty seconds fast. Have you ordered?"

"I've ordered," Drake said. "Double pineapple juice, ham and eggs, toast and coffee. It'll be coming right up. Have you seen my ad in the paper?"

"No," Mason said. "What ad?"

"In that Finchley case."

"I was going to ask you about that."

"I have an ad in the morning papers. I also have one that came out in the *Blade* yesterday afternoon."

The waiter, entering the booth with the pineapple juice, said, "Good morning, Mr. Mason. Mr. Drake told me to go right ahead and put your order on the stove. The ham and eggs will be right up. He said you'd be here."

"I'm here."

Drake took a long drink of the pineapple juice, then put down the half empty glass, reached in his brief case and took out a newspaper. "Here it is," he said.

Mason looked at the classified ad indicated by the detective.

ONE HUNDRED DOLLARS REWARD!! If the parties who were changing a tire on an automobile at the intersection of Hickman Avenue and Vermesillo Drive at about five o'clock on the afternoon of the third will communicate with the Drake Detective Agency and give a description sufficient to identify the black sedan which was speeding east on Vermesillo Drive and crashed into the Ford going north on Hickman Avenue they will receive one hundred dollars, cash. Bystanders think the young woman in this parked car jotted down the license number of the speeding sedan but left the scene before the ambulance arrived. Any information from anyone leading to an identification of this hit-and-run driver will result in the prompt payment of one hundred dollars. Address all communications Drake Detective Agency, Box 624.

"That should produce some results," Mason said, putting down the folded newspaper. "That Finchley kid was badly hurt . . . I hate a hit-and-run driver."

"Probably he'd had a few cocktails and didn't dare to stick around," Drake said. "Of course the people in that parked automobile may not have seen anything."

"As I get the story, they did," Mason told him. "There were a man and a woman in the car. It was a light-colored sedan fairly new. They'd evidently just finished changing a tire. The man was putting the flat tire back in the trunk when the accident happened. The woman wrote something down in a notebook. Apparently it was the license number of the automobile that speeded away from the scene of the accident after slamming the Finchley Ford over against the lamppost."

The waiter brought ham and eggs, coffee, golden brown toast.

"Suppose their testimony should be adverse to your clients?" Drake asked.

"It can't be if they're telling the truth. I want to know who they are, anyhow. I don't want them held in the background where they might show up someday as surprise witnesses, testifying on behalf of the defendant."

The waiter popped his head back into the booth and said apologetically, "Your office is on the line, Mr. Drake. Your secretary said I was to tell you there'd been a reply to that ad in the paper, and that you'd want to know about it while you were breakfasting with Mr. Mason."

"Have someone bring the reply down here," Drake said. "Tell my secretary to put a messenger in a taxicab and rush it down here."

Mason grinned. "Shows what advertising will do, Paul."

"Shows what *money* will do," Drake commented.

"That Finchley boy has a broken hip," Mason said. "He was planning on graduating from college. I'd sure like to stick the driver of that car."

Drake sipped coffee, and said wearily, "It probably won't work out that way, Perry. The driver of the other car was drunk. If you could have nabbed him at the scene of the accident, you could have proved he was drunk. The way it is now, he'll have a beautiful fairy story about how the Finchley car crashed into him, that he looked back and felt certain there was no damage done . . ."

"And then I'll tear into him on a hit-and-run charge," Mason said.

Drake grinned. "You just *think* you will. You'll find that the chap has an influential friend or two who has rung up the district attorney. You'll find influential people all over town who'll get busy on the telephone telling what a fine chap he is, good to his family, considerate of his dogs and cats, a person who makes substantial donations to religious causes—and to the right political party."

"Nevertheless, I'll tear into him," Mason said. "I'll get him on the witness stand and rip him wide open."

"You won't even get to do that," Drake said. "A representative of some insurance company will get around to Bob Finchley and say, 'Look, if you go to court, even if you recover a big judgment, you'll have a lot of lawyers' bills to pay, and by the time you get done, you'll have all the uncertainty of a lawsuit, you'll have to fight clean through to the Supreme Court, and the net result to you wouldn't be half as good as though we took over and paid all the doctor and hospital bills and gave you a little money that you could put into a new car. In fact, by using connections we have, we can get you one of the late models . . .'"

"Shut up," Mason interrupted, grinning. "You're spoiling my breakfast."

"I was just telling you how it'll go," Drake said.

"I know how it'll go," Mason told him, "but you let me find out who was driving that black sedan and I'll give him something to think about, anyway."

They ate for a while in silence. The waiter appeared once more. "A messenger from your office, Mr. Drake. He said I was to give you this envelope and ask you if he should wait for any instructions."

"No," Drake said. "This letter should speak for itself."

Drake slit open the Manila envelope, which had been sent through the mail addressed to the Drake Detective Agency, said, "There's something heavy in it, Perry."

Drake shook the envelope over the table. A key fell out on the tablecloth.

Drake looked at it with surprise.

"Probably the key to the situation," Mason said.

"*Don't* do that so early in the morning!" Drake told him, wincing.

"What's the letter?" Mason asked.

Leaving the key on the tablecloth, Drake pulled out the letter, typewritten in elite type on a good grade of tinted stationery.

"It's dated yesterday," Drake said, "and is addressed to the Drake Detective Agency. Here's the letter, Perry:

Gentlemen:

The party whose aid you are requesting in your ad in this evening's *Blade* will never get in touch with you voluntarily. Because I am interested in fair play, I am going to give you the following information. At the time of that accident yesterday afternoon at the intersection of Hickman Avenue and Vermesillo Drive, Lucille Barton and a man, whose name I do not know, had just finished changing a tire on Miss Barton's automobile, a light tan sedan. This automobile was parked on the south side of Vermesillo Drive immediately east of the intersection with Hickman Avenue. Miss Barton saw the accident and with great presence of mind wrote down the license number of the sedan which was speeding away to the east on Vermesillo Drive.

Later on she told her companion what she had done.

The man became panic-stricken, explaining to her that it would ruin him if it should be known he was with her at that time. (I have been unable to find out who this man is, or the reason he is so afraid of having his identity known.) However, I am a very good friend of Lucille's. I know that this is a matter which is bothering her conscience. Under the circumstances, she cannot give you the information you wish, nor can she ever admit that she was anywhere near the scene of the accident.

I have, however, obtained a duplicate key to her apartment which is at 719 South Gondola. (She is living in Apartment 208.) This is a small apartment house with an outer door, the latch of which can be released by tenants of any of the apartments by means of a button. The key to any of the apartments in the house will fit the outer door. If you will use the enclosed key and go to that apartment sometime between the hours of two o'clock and five o'clock in the afternoon of the fifth, you will find no one in the apartment. There is a writing desk in the northeast corner of the sitting room. If you will look in the upper right-hand pigeonhole of that desk you will find a leather-backed notebook. On the next to the last page of that notebook you will find the license number of the automobile that you want. After you have fully satisfied yourself that this is correct and have determined that this automobile is indeed the one you want, I will make arrangements to get in touch with you, redeem the key and will then expect to be reimbursed in the amount of the one hundred dollars which you have offered for a reward.

Very sincerely yours,
A FRIEND"

Drake looked at Mason, said, "Of all the cockeyed things."

"Any handwriting at all?" Mason asked.

"Not a bit. The signature is in typewriting, the same as the letter."

"Let me take a look at it," Mason said.

Drake passed Mason the letter.

"That's a ragged job of typing, Paul," Mason said. "The letters are spaced irregularly, the keys weren't struck with a uniform touch, there are a couple of strikeovers—altogether, I would say, the work of an amateur typist."

Drake nodded. "It looks like a two-finger job. Lots of speed though. That's where the skips and uneven spacing come from. What do you make of it?"

"I'm darned if I know," Mason told him. "It looks like a trap to me. We'll let Della Street cast her feminine eye over it and see what she thinks."

Mason picked up the key, inspected it, saw the number "208" stamped on it, dropped it into his vest pocket and said, "However, it's a lead we can't afford to pass up."

Drake said, with sudden apprehension, "Don't go messing around that apartment, Perry. That's dangerous. If anyone should catch you snooping around in there they could . . ."

"Could what?" Mason asked, smiling. "In order to constitute a burglary, the entrance must be made for a felonious purpose, or . . ."

"Or," Drake said, significantly, "someone could mistake you for a housebreaker, shoot first, and ask questions afterwards."

"But," Mason told him, "you certainly don't expect me to pass up this lead, do you?"

Drake pushed back his plate and picked up the check. "Hell, no," he said. "Do you want to pay the exact amount of this check at the present time, Perry, or have it presented on my expense account later on and take a chance that the amount will be about ten per cent higher at that time?"

Mason took the check, said with a grin, "I think it will be a damn sight smarter to pay it now. That letter bothers me, Paul. If it were on the up-and-up the writer would have copied the license number from the notebook and asked for the hundred bucks."

"It's a trap of some sort," Drake said.

"Well the bait interests me, Paul."

"That's the theory on which traps are constructed," Drake said.

2

DELLA STREET, Perry Mason's confidential secretary, had placed mail in three piles on the lawyer's desk. The *"important"* pile was squarely and suggestively in the middle of the blotter.

Mason, entering through the door which led directly to his private office, removed his latchkey, grinned at Della Street and then frowned at the position of the mail on the desk.

"Hi, Della."

"Good morning," she said. "You've seen Paul Drake?"

"Yes."

"His office was trying to get in touch with us. I knew you were having breakfast with him."

Mason hung up his hat, regarded the pile of mail, and said, "I take it those are letters which can't be put off any longer."

She nodded.

Mason said, "Add this. Put it on top of the *'important'* pile."

"What is it?"

"A letter Paul Drake received."

"About that witness?"

"Yes."

"What does it say?"

"Read it."

Della Street took the letter, started skimming swiftly through it, then her eyes narrowed as she began to read more slowly and carefully. "Where's the key?" she asked at length.

Mason took it from his vest pocket.

Della Street looked at the key for a moment, then returned to the letter and read it entirely through once more.

"What do you make of it?" Mason asked.

"I don't know."

"A trap?"

"For whom?" she asked.

Mason said, "Now, there, Della, you've got me."

"If someone thought Drake would turn this letter over to you and that you would go there personally, I would say that it might be a trap for almost anything, but in view of the ad in the paper, the natural assumption would be that Paul Drake would send one of his men—just any one of his men."

Again Mason nodded.

"So," Della Street said, "if we rule out a trap, then what?"

"Could it have been written by the woman herself?" Mason asked.

"Why?"

"Perhaps an attempt to sell out the mysterious boy friend who didn't want to be recognized, and then get the hundred dollars for herself later on?"

"Now that could be," Della Street said.

"I wanted to get the feminine angle," Mason said.

She laughed. "There aren't any feminine angles, they're curves."

"Then this is a *fast* curve. What's your guess?"

"I don't like to stick my neck out, but I'd say your theory is the right one. It's a girl who wants a hundred dollars. She wants the Drake Detective Agency to discover the license number, find out it's the car that's wanted, and then she'll call for the reward. She'll do it all very surreptitiously so that the boy friend who was in the car with her doesn't know she's furnished the tip. . . . Can you *prove* it's the car once you find it?"

"I think so," Mason said. "The car was going plenty fast. It shot in ahead of the Finchley Ford. Mrs. Finchley tried to stop, couldn't, and hit the hind end of this mysterious black sedan. Evidently the bumper on the black sedan hooked under her front bumper, swung her car completely around. She lost control and slammed into the lamppost, her twenty-two-year-old son was thrown out against the lamppost and smashed his hip."

"Then technically," Della Street said, "she ran into the black car instead of the black car running into her."

"That's what the driver of the black car will probably try to claim," Mason said, "but having speeded away from the scene of the accident, he'll hardly be in the position to make any defense that can't be torn to pieces."

"Can he say he didn't know he'd hit anything?"

"There must have been too much of an impact for him to get by with that. We can tell more when we see his car—if we ever do."

"What are you going to do about your mysterious Lucille Barton?"

"I'm going to go see her."

"Use the key and enter her apartment?" Della Street asked. "You'd better be sure you have witnesses and . . ."

Mason shook his had. "There's no reason to enter the apartment while she's away. If she's the witness we want, we can find out by talking with her. At least we *should* be able to."

"Between the hours of two and five?"

"Nope. That's when she'll be gone," Mason said, looking at his watch and grinning. "Between the hours of ten and eleven is the time I'm picking."

"Want a witness?"

"I don't think so, Della. I think I can do more by just dropping in and talking with her."

"Going to say anything about this letter?"

"No, I don't think so."

Della Street looked ruefully at the pile of important mail in the middle of Mason's blotter.

"You go ahead and answer it," Mason said, following her glance. "Figure out whatever needs to be done, and . . ."

"Chief, those are letters that simply must have your personal attention."

"I know," Mason said, "but think of Lucille Barton, probably sleeping late, the license number of the car that is responsible for Bob Finchley's broken hip in the upper right-hand pigeonhole of the desk in the living room. . . . Sounds like rather an elaborate apartment for a working girl. What do you suppose Lucille Barton does?"

"Who said she worked?" Della asked.

Mason said to Della Street, "Make a copy of this letter, Della. I'm going to take a copy along with me and leave the original here. I may want to show her the letter but I see no reason for showing her the original."

Della Street nodded, moved over to her secretarial desk, ratcheted paper into the typewriter, and Mason watched while her skilled fingers flew over the keyboard.

Mason surveyed the finished results, said, "That looks a lot better than the original, Della."

"The original," she said, "was written by someone who had a hunt-and-peck system, but was awfully good at it, someone who had developed a lot of speed."

"That's the way I doped it out," Mason said.

"Probably on a portable typewriter."

Mason folded the copy of the letter Della Street had made, returned the key to his vest pocket, said, "I'm on my way."

"If you get arrested," Della Street observed smilingly, "let me know and I'll be down with the checkbook and bail."

"Thanks."

"And if she isn't home," Della said, ceasing to smile, "please *don't use that key.*"

"Why not?"

"I don't know. There's something about it I don't like."

"There's a *lot* about it I don't like," Mason said. "What do you bet I don't walk in on a corpse, Della?"

"No takers."

"You keep that letter and the original envelope with the postmark in the safe," Mason told her. "I may have to square myself with the police."

"Meaning you're going to walk in if she isn't home?"

"Shucks," Mason said, grinning, "I never know just *what* I'm going to do."

THE address on South Gondola Avenue was a relatively small apartment house. The list of names on the left of the door indicated there were some thirty-five tenants.

Mason found without difficulty the name which had been clipped from the center of a visiting card, "Lucille Storla Barton." The figure opposite was "208" and there was a worn push button to the right and a speaking tube.

Mason deliberated for a few seconds over the push button, but curiosity about the key got the better of him. He fitted the key to the lock in the outer door and twisted it. The lock immediately clicked back and the door opened.

Mason found himself in a narrow lobby where a few uncomfortable chairs had been placed uninvitingly in a cold, symmetrical design. There was a public pay-station telephone in one corner and a cubbyhole office, separated by a low counter from the rest of the lobby. Back of this was a door marked "Manager" and on the counter was a placard reading, PRESS THIS BUTTON FOR THE MANAGER. Mason walked through the narrow lobby, into a corridor flanked with the doors of apartments. The elevator was lighted and back some thirty feet down the corridor. The building had three floors and Lucille Barton evidently lived on the second.

Mason pushed the button on the automatic elevator and when the lighted cage slid to a stop, opened the door, got in and pushed the button for the second floor.

Rattling upward, the lawyer realized it well might have been quicker had he climbed the stairs.

Apartment 208 was toward the rear of the building. Mason followed the doors back until he came to the one he wanted. He pressed a bell button and waited. There was no sound from within the apartment. Mason tried his knuckles on the door and again had no luck.

Surreptitiously, the lawyer inserted the key and twisted with thumb and forefinger.

The latch came smoothly back. The door opened.

Through the open crack in the door, Mason could look through a dark living room into a bedroom lighted by an overhead electric light. The bed had not been made and a feminine nightgown lay across it where it had been thrown. The lawyer could hear the sound of water running in a bathroom.

Mason gently closed the door, removed the key, waited in the corridor for some two minutes, then pressed the button again.

This time he heard sounds of motion and a feminine voice on the other side of the door asked, "What is it, please?"

"Is this Miss Barton?"

"Yes."

"I want to talk with you. My name is Mason. I'm a lawyer."

The door opened a cautious crack. He saw laughing, saucy blue eyes, molasses-taffy hair, and a hand holding a robe tightly at the neck. Even, white teeth flashed in a smile. "I'm sorry, Mr. Mason," she said, "but I'm not presentable. I'm just getting up. You'll have to . . . to wait or come back."

"I'll wait," Mason said.

"I'm afraid I don't know you, Mr. Mason. I . . ." She looked him over from head to foot, then her eyes widened. "You're not *the* Perry Mason?"

"Perhaps you'd better say that I'm *a* Perry Mason."

She said, "*Honestly*, Mr. Mason!"

There was a moment of silence. Then she said, "Look, Mr. Mason, it will only take me a second or two to get into some clothes. Things are in sort of a mess, but if you'll just step into the living room, please, and—you can raise the shades and make yourself comfortable—I'll be with you in just a few seconds."

"Or," Mason said, "I can come back, and . . ."

"No, no, come on in and sit down. It'll only take me a minute to make myself presentable."

She held the door open.

Mason entered the dark living room.

"If you don't mind raising the curtains, Mr. Mason, and—well, just sit down and make yourself at home."

"Thanks," Mason told her.

She moved swiftly across the sitting room to the bedroom and closed the door.

Mason walked over to the windows, raised the shades, and let in the morning sunlight.

Mason saw to his surprise that the apartment represented an incongruous clash of the cheap and the costly. A small but exquisite Oriental rug made the larger drab rug beside it seem hopelessly shoddy. The furniture was for the most part expensive, comfortable and had been selected with taste. Against this note of quiet luxury a few pieces of cheap furniture, their mediocrity emphasized by the aristocratic articles surrounding them, gave a jarring note.

On the table an ash tray was still well filled with cigarette stubs. Some of them had lipstick, some did not. A small kitchenette disclosed an empty bottle of Scotch on the sink, a couple of glasses, and two empty soda bottles. A magnificent, antique walnut writing desk was over in the corner. Mason hesitated for a moment, then swiftly walked over toward it, inserted his fingers in the ornamental metal handle on the top of the door and pulled. The desk was firmly locked.

Mason returned to a chair by the table in the center of the room, picked up an old magazine, settled himself, crossed his legs and waited.

He had to wait about five minutes. Then the young woman came out of the bedroom wearing a chambray housedress which looked simple and domestic, but which had been carefully cut for the purpose of showing various curves and contours. She was wearing well-shaped shoes with medium high heels. Her legs were smoothly stockinged and very visible.

She said, "I'm not human in the morning until I've had my coffee, Mr. Mason. If you'll pardon me, I'll put a percolator on the stove. I suppose you've had breakfast."

"Oh, yes."

"You make me sound hopelessly lazy," she laughed, "but . . . how about a cup of coffee with me?"

"Thanks. Put my name in the pot and I'll join you."

She went into the kitchen, busied herself with the coffeepot.

"Nice apartment you have here," Mason said, getting up and strolling around the room.

"It's large," she said, "and I get the morning sun. The building

is old-fashioned, but the way things are now that's very conveni-
ent. I have lots of elbow room and there's a private garage which
goes with the apartment—and that's more than I'd have in a more
modern apartment."

"I see you have a portable typewriter. Do you write?"

She laughed. "I pound out a letter once in a while. There *was* a
time when I thought I was going to write the great American novel.
I'm not only too dumb, I'm also too lazy."

Mason lifted the cover from the portable typewriter, said, "I
want to make a memo. A matter has been bothering me. Would
you mind if I used this typewriter for a minute? It's something that
had escaped my mind until just now and . . ."

"Not at all," she said. "Go right ahead. There's some stationery
in the drawer there in the table. I'll be with you in a minute. I'm
going to put on some toast and a soft-boiled egg. How about you?"

"No thanks. I've had breakfast. Just a cup of coffee for me,
please."

Mason opened the drawer in the table. There were two piles of
stationery, one the conventional full letter-size sheets such as are
used in preparing manuscripts, the other a pink tinted stationery,
apparently matching the stationery on which the letter that had
been received by the Drake Detective Agency had been typed.

Mason fed a sheet of this paper into the machine and hurriedly
wrote out a memo dealing with an imaginary witness in a fictitious
case, involving the validity of a will, a witness who must be questioned along certain lines. When he had completed the memo, he
put the cover back on the machine.

The aroma of coffee came from the kitchenette.

A few moments later Lucille Barton appeared with a tray and
two coffee cups. There was toast on a plate, a small bottle of cream,
a sugar bowl, a soft-boiled egg in a cup.

"Sure you won't have anything except coffee?"

"That's all, thanks," Mason said.

She put the tray on the table, said, "Just make yourself at home,
Mr. Mason. I'm honored by this visit, but I'm also just a little bit
frightened."

"Why frightened?"

She said, "I don't know. There's something about having a lawyer call on you, particularly a famous lawyer such as you are. I
suppose—well, why suppose? Let me drink my coffee, and *then*
tell me what it is."

She sipped her coffee, added cream and sugar, poured cream into Mason's coffee, and handed him the sugar bowl. After a few seconds she said, "Well, here's hoping it isn't too serious. What have I done, Mr. Mason?"

"Nothing as far as I know," Mason said. "That's delicious coffee."

"Thanks."

"Mind if I smoke?" Mason asked.

"Of course not."

Mason took his cigarette case from his pocket, lit a cigarette.

Lucille Barton munched on toast, watched him with speculative eyes, smiled easily and naturally whenever she caught him looking at her.

She was, Mason decided, in the late twenties, and evidently a young woman who knew her way around, but there was nothing hard about her. She seemed as naturally naïve and as spontaneous with her friendship as a young puppy, anxious to make friends with everyone in a joyful world.

"Well," she asked, "when do we start?"

"Now," Mason said. "Where were you on the afternoon of the third—day before yesterday?"

"Oh, good heavens," she said, and then laughed throatily.

"Where *were* you?"

"Is that a gag?" she asked, cocking a quizzical eyebrow. "Tell me, are you really serious?"

"Yes."

"The third—let me see. . . . Heavens, I can't tell you, Mr. Mason."

"Do you keep a diary?"

"Come, come, Mr. Mason. Do I look *that* dumb?"

Mason said, "I'll put it another way. Were you near the intersection of Hickman Avenue and Vermesillo Drive?"

She puckered her forehead in an attempt to search her recollection. "On the third?"

"On the third."

Slowly, she shook her head. "I don't believe I was."

Mason said, "Let's go at it again from a slightly different angle. I have reason to believe that you were with some man in a light-colored sedan. You had had a flat tire and had pulled into the curb to fix it. There was an accident there at the intersection just as you were getting ready to drive away, and you noticed something about the car, or about one of the cars that had been in the accident. It was a dark sedan and . . ."

She was shaking her head vigorously now. "Mr. Mason, I'm *quite* certain there's some mistake. At the moment I can't recall where I was, but I do know very definitely that I haven't seen any accident within the past few weeks and I certainly wasn't riding in any car which had a punctured tire. That's something a person wouldn't forget in a hurry, don't you think?"

"It would certainly seem so."

"I'm sure I wouldn't forget a thing like that. . . . Why are you interested, Mr. Mason?"

Mason said, "I'm representing the occupants of the car that was hit. There was a young man, Bob Finchley, a chap twenty-two years old, who has a broken hip. We hope it will heal up all right so he won't be crippled, but it's a serious injury, and it's certainly going to take some time, even with the best of luck, before he can . . ."

"Oh, that's too bad!" she interrupted. "I can't imagine anything worse than a young man being smashed up. I *do* hope there is no permanent trouble."

"We'll hope for the best," Mason agreed.

She finished the egg and toast, reached for a cigarette. Mason held a light and she placed her hands over his. She guided the match to the end of the cigarette. Her hands were warm, vital, and her touch was not too firm, not too delicate, just close enough to let the softness of her fingertips register for a moment on Mason's hand. Then, as she moved her own hand away, she slid the fingertips along the lawyer's fingers. "Thanks," she said, looking up at him with eyes that were suddenly serious. "I suppose you know, Mr. Mason, that I admire you tremendously."

"Do you?"

"I most certainly do. I've followed many of your cases. I think you're—well, you're brilliant and magnetic and powerful, and you're willing to stand up and fight for the underdog. I like that."

"Well, that's certainly gratifying," Mason said. "I try to do the best I can when I'm working on a case. Is there any way that you have of finding out where you were on the afternoon of the third?"

"Why, yes, Mr. Mason. I'm quite certain I can check back over daily events and puzzle it out. But I'm afraid I can't do it now. Having such a famous personage sharing coffee with me in my apartment is a little *too* much of a thrill. I don't suppose you know it but I'm as nervous as can be. This is something I'll remember for a long time, Mr. Mason."

"When do you suppose you can let me know where you were on the afternoon of the third?"

"I don't know. It may be—oh, it may come to me within an hour or two. Do you want me to telephone you?"

"If you will, please."

"I'll cudgel my wits—although it's very difficult for me to think back and remember just where I was on any given date. I mean even yesterday. Of course, if I keep thinking long enough, I'll remember some little thing and then that will pave the way for something else. Let's see . . . day before yesterday . . ."

"I take it you're not working at any regular job."

She smiled. "I have an allowance."

Mason impaled her eyes with his. "Alimony?"

She quickly averted her glance, then suddenly turned defiant eyes back to his. "Anything wrong with that?" she asked.

"Nothing," Mason said.

"And does it make any difference—in the matter you're investigating?"

Mason laughed, and said, "That would seem to be a nice way of asking me if it's any of my business."

"Well, I was just wondering what—well, whether you were investigating me and this story about the automobile accident was something to sort of pave the way."

"No," Mason said. "I'm telling you very frankly that I'm interested in you because I'm trying to uncover witnesses to that automobile accident."

"Well, I'm quite certain that I didn't see any automobile accident, and I'm quite certain that wherever I was on the afternoon of the third, I wasn't at the intersection of Hickman Avenue and— what was that other street?"

"Vermesillo Drive."

She said, "I know where Hickman Avenue is, but I don't even know where Vermesillo Drive is, Mr. Mason."

"You own a car?"

"Well, it's transportation. It's a good-looking car, but the engine is in bad shape."

"What color?"

"A light tan sedan."

"Well, of course," Mason interrupted, "that's primarily the point I'm interested in, but I *would* like to know just where you were at that time."

"How did you happen to come here in the first place, Mr. Mason?"

Mason smiled. "I can't divulge the source of my information, but I had reason to believe you might be the person I was looking for. You certainly answer the description."

"But you can't tell me how you got my description—who gave it to you?"

"No."

She said, "Mr. Mason, I wonder—do you believe in Fate?"

"Why not?" Mason asked with a swift glance of appraisal.

She said, "It just happens, Mr. Mason, that I'm in need of someone to—to do something for me—a lawyer."

Mason instantly became cautious. "I'm not in a position to take on any more responsibilities. I have a desk piled up with mail now and I . . ."

"But you took on this accident case and *that* only occurred day before yesterday."

"That's different. There was an element of urgency about it and, frankly, the case appealed to me."

She said, "Mr. Mason, let me tell you something about my case. I think *it* will appeal to you."

"I warn you, I can't handle it."

"Well, let me tell you anyway. I've been married twice. The first time was simply tragic. The last time I was—well, I was more cautious."

"And it worked out all right?" Mason asked.

"It didn't. My second husband was wealthy. That's one thing that helped. I had made up my mind I'd never marry again, but then he came along and he had money and—well, I married him."

"And the marriage broke up?"

"Yes, but I'm getting alimony."

"How much?"

"Two hundred dollars a week," she said.

Mason whistled.

"Well?" she asked defiantly. "Do you think that's too much? You should see how much money he makes!"

"I take it you weren't married very long."

"Five years, and during that time he made a lot of his money."

"That, of course, makes it different," Mason admitted.

"And now he's going into court trying to do something about my alimony, trying to get it reduced."

"You can't blame him for that."

"I thought perhaps you could talk to him and . . ."

Mason shook his head emphatically. "In the first place it wouldn't be ethical for me even to talk to him. Your husband has a lawyer representing him and . . ."

"No, he doesn't, Mr. Mason."

"You mean he's taking the matter up with the Court by himself?"

"No, he . . . well, I'll explain it this way. He had a lawyer who made an application to have alimony reduced about six months ago and the Court refused to do it. The judge intimated he thought my husband had got slightly the best of the property settlement. You see, I worked with my husband in his business, and I really made a lot of that money for him. My husband got peeved at the lawyer he had and swears that when he takes the matter up in court again he'll do it himself."

"He'll probably wind up with some lawyer representing him, however," Mason said.

"I don't think so. Willard Allison Barton is a very determined, very ingenious individual. I think I'd be more afraid of him in a court than I would of any lawyer—except you, of course, Mr. Mason."

Mason said, "I don't do much work involving domestic relations."

"Mr. Mason, will you *please* listen?"

"All right," Mason said, settling back in his chair.

She said, "I'm going to marry again, and this time I *really* know it's going to work out all right. This man is an older man and a wiser man. He's very understanding. I feel differently about him than I have about the others."

"Well," Mason said, "that should dispose of the alimony matter. As soon as you get married again, your alimony will cease."

"But can't you see, Mr. Mason, I don't want to burn my bridges. I'm really entitled to this alimony. If you should warn Willard Barton that *you* were going to ask for an *increase* if he dragged me into court again, it would keep him from making a move."

"But if all alimony is going to cease within a few months, why not . . . ?"

She said bitterly, "I'm not going to let *him* off. I'd go to him and offer to settle the whole business for twenty-five thousand cash. He'd jump at that."

Mason said coldly, "And you want me to engineer that deal for you, is that it?"

She started balancing the spoon on the edge of the coffee cup.

"Well?" Mason asked.

She said, "You think I'm terribly scheming and designing. I'm only cautious. I want to protect my interests."

"So it would seem."

"Mr. Mason, look at it from a business viewpoint. Think of what a fool I'd be to give up two hundred dollars a week for any man, *any* man."

"If you were sure of having the alimony continue," Mason pointed out.

"Mr. Hollister wants to fix things so marrying him won't entail a financial sacrifice on my part. You *do* think I'm a golddigger, don't you, Mr. Mason?"

"You're certainly not madly in love."

"Well, Mr. Mason, it isn't as bad as it sounds. I've really been unfair to myself. As a matter of fact, it was Ross Hollister's own idea—I *did* tell him that I had finished with marriage, that I wasn't going to make any more matrimonial ventures, and then he asked me why and kept probing. You just have to see him to understand the sort of man he is. He's very understanding and sympathetic, but he's always probing. He has ways of working right into the back of your mind and pulling out ideas that you yourself hardly knew that you had."

"So he found out that you were worried about giving up two hundred dollars a week and a perfectly satisfactory alimony for a husband. Is that right?"

"That's right, and I'll tell you what he did, Mr. Mason, all of his own accord. He put some property in trust so that it will be mine as soon as I marry him. He has already given me an insurance policy for twenty thousand dollars on his life and he's agreed to see that I have an allowance of seven hundred and fifty dollars a month just for my own clothes and spending money and things—you know, my own personal expenses, quite outside of running the household, and he has a very swank convertible roadster ordered that he's going to give me for my very own as a wedding present."

"Well," Mason asked, and then added dryly, "what more do you want?"

"I want his love and respect!" she blazed at him. "He's already made these arrangements. The papers have even been signed. The insurance has gone through—and if my husband comes into court and asks to have the alimony reduced, Ross Hollister will never *say* a word, but all of our married life he'll think I knew my financial boat was about to spring a leak and that I was looking for a transfer. *Can't* you see the thing from my position?"

"You're afraid that if your ex-husband starts a move to reduce the alimony Mr. Hollister will feel you knew that was coming, were afraid of the outcome and manipulated things so he . . ."

"Exactly!" she interrupted.

"When is your wedding going to take place?" Mason asked. "Why not hurry it up a little?"

She said, "Well, there's a little trouble about that. Mr. Hollister has been married before and there's some technicality—something about his divorce that's holding things up temporarily."

"I see," Mason said.

"Mr. Mason, can't you *please* go and talk with Willard Barton? He's at the Broadway Athletic Club. He lives there . . . but you mustn't give him any inkling, not even the faintest inkling as to the *name* of the man I'm going to marry."

"Does he know Hollister?"

"Of course he knows him. Mr. Hollister is a member of the club, although he lives in Santa del Barra. Good heavens, Mr. Mason, they've even played poker together. Willard would die, just simply die, if he knew. In fact, you'll have to be very tactful in talking to him. He's inclined to be insanely jealous as far as I'm concerned— I guess that's one of the troubles—one of the reasons our marriage didn't work out better. He was always bringing my other husband into the conversation, wanting to know if I still didn't care for him, and . . ."

"Your first husband is alive?" Mason asked.

She went back to balancing the spoon on the cup.

"Is he?"

"Yes."

"And you have seen him recently?"

"Mr. Mason, *why* do you ask that question?"

"I don't know. I'm simply trying to get information."

"But I don't see why you . . ."

Abruptly Mason threw back his head and laughed, said, "You're a very ingenious young lady, Lucille. I have to give you a medal for ingenuity, but I'm not interested in your case, although I will admit that the unconventional approach intrigues me."

"What do you mean, the unconventional approach?"

Mason said, "You saw the ad in the paper. You evidently had some way of knowing that I was representing the Finchleys. You thought that if you could get me here and get me in a rather disadvantageous position, you . . ."

She pushed back the chair, her eyes were blazing. "Mr. Mason, that's absolutely uncalled for! That's entirely untrue. I don't even know what ad you're talking about! And there's certainly been no attempt to get you into what you are pleased to refer to as a 'disadvantageous position'! What do you think I am, anyway?"

"Well, what *are* you?" Mason asked.

"I'm a woman. I'm human and I've been disappointed in love. And I don't want to have my alimony reduced. I know you can scare my ex-husband to death. If he only thought I knew you, and that *you* were interested in me—in my case, I mean . . ."

Mason pushed back his chair, got to his feet, bowed and said, "I'm sorry, but I just don't believe you, and I can't waste any more time. It was a good attempt. I'm sorry that I can't fall for it. Perhaps if I had been *caught* in your apartment between two and five I might have been forced to take your case. Thanks for the coffee."

Mason picked up his hat, walked to the door. "And that business of pretending you can't remember where you were day before yesterday is just a little too crude. Bait another trap and try another lawyer, Mrs. Barton."

And Mason pulled the door shut, leaving her standing there, her face flushed and angry.

4

"Come on," Della Street said, "give."

Mason grinned. "A very nice girl with wheat-colored hair, laughing blue eyes, a luscious strawberry mouth with white, pearly teeth."

"Oh, my Lord," Della Street said. "He's in love."

Paul Drake said, "How old, Perry?"

"Somewhere between twenty-five and thirty."

Della Street brought a thesaurus and placed it on Mason's desk.

"Thank you, Della," Mason said. "Now let's see, Paul. How do I find exactly the words with which to describe her?"

Mason turned the pages, said, "Ah, yes, here we are, Paul—virtuous, maidenly, virginal, vestal, upright, moral, worthy, honorable . . ."

"What does she do for a living?" Drake asked.

"You would ask that," Mason told him.

"Come on," Della Street insisted, laughing, "let's have the story."

Mason walked over and sat on the corner of his desk, the left foot on the floor, the right foot swinging in an arc in much embarrassment at their kidding.

"He's *afraid* to tell," Drake said.

"I do believe he's blushing," Della charged.

Mason said, "Well, if you want to know the truth, it *was* a trap."

"Badger game?" Drake asked.

"Don't be silly," Mason told him. "Apparently this girl read the ad in the *Blade* and decided that while a detective agency was after the information, a lawyer must be in back of the detective agency."

"Go ahead," Drake said, "tell me about what happened when you opened the door."

"Apparently," Mason said, "she was in the bathtub."

"Oh, oh!" Drake observed.

"So," Mason said virtuously, "I noiselessly withdrew to the corridor, waited two minutes, then knocked on the door. She let me in. You'd get a kick out of her apartment, a lot of perfectly grand furniture, which must have come from a settlement when her marriage broke up, mixed with some terrible junk which could have been part of the furniture in the place.

"There's an Oriental rug that's worth a lot of money. It's a beauty, and the desk is an antique that's in perfect condition. The ash tray and glasses show she was entertaining a man last night and didn't even bother to empty the ash tray when she went to bed—and they didn't break up the party until the Scotch was all gone.

"But she's clever. She seems almost naïve in her excessive friendliness, but back of it all she must be a scheming, cautious golddigger. She was *very* friendly. Having lured me into close quarters, she sized me up before planning the kill."

"What's the catch?" Drake asked.

"The catch," Mason said, "is that she wants some attorney to handle an alimony matter with her ex-husband. Having used the bait to lure me into the apartment, she proceeded to use her eyes, teeth, and her figure to hold my personal and undivided attention while she tried to interest me in a project to keep her ex-husband, one Willard Barton, who, I understand, is a rather practical, hardened, and exceedingly ingenious individual, from reducing her alimony to a figure materially less than the two hundred dollars a week which it costs her to live."

"Did she say anything about a retainer?" Della Street asked.

Mason grinned, and said, "Not a word."

"You're sure the thing was a plant?" Drake asked.

Mason said, "Judge for yourself."

He took from his pocket the sheet of pink stationery. "Here's some stationery that I mooched from the drawer in the table, Della. You might compare it with the stationery of the letter which we received. I also used the typewriter. We can check to see if this same machine was used in writing that letter."

Della Street hurried to the files, brought out the original letter, held the two sheets of stationery side by side, and said, "The paper's the same."

"How about the typewriter?" Drake asked.

They bent over the desk studying the alignment of the type. "It's the same," Mason said. "Notice that 'g' is a little out of alignment, and the 'i' has dropped down a little and is canted over to the right."

"Well, that settles it," Drake said. "Hang it, I was hoping we had a lead. The hundred-dollar reward offer *should* get some action."

"Give it time," Mason said. "Remember the paper was hardly off the presses when this woman had her brain storm."

"Well," Della Street said, "since you have now spent most of the morning in a romantic adventure, I take it there'll be no objection on your part to tackling that pile of mail that's marked 'important.'"

Mason dismissed Drake with a gesture. "My nose, Paul, is being held to the grindstone. . . . Let me know if you get any answers to the ad."

Drake nodded.

When he had left the office, Mason and Della Street settled down to work. Coffee and sandwiches were brought in at noon, and by one-fifteen they had most of the mail out of the way.

Gertie, the office receptionist, appeared with a letter. "A letter for you, Mr. Mason," she said. "It came by messenger. I thought you'd want to see it."

Mason groaned. "That, Della, is the reward of virtue. We try to get this pile of mail whittled down and what happens? More comes pouring in."

Della Street picked up a paper knife and slit the edge of the envelope, saying as she did so, "A plain stamped envelope with a special delivery stamp put on it, and—there's something in here, chief, something heavy."

"Probably another key," Mason said.

Della Street's voice showed surprise. "The paper that's in here, the stationery—chief, it's the same pink colored stationery, and it *is* another key."

She shook the envelope and a key fell out on the blotter. The key had an ornamental design at the end, was about two and a half inches long, hollow at the end of the shaft, with an intricate design of square-faced grooves on the part which was intended to actuate the lock.

"Looks like the key to a piece of furniture," Della Street said.

Mason, grinning, unfolded the letter. Della Street came to look over his shoulder.

Dear Mr. Mason:
I'm sorry that the desk was locked, so that you couldn't get the information you wanted this morning. I'm enclosing the key to that desk. The information you want is in a little leather notebook in the upper right-hand pigeonhole. You will find it on the next to the last page of the notebook—the license number of the car which collided with the Finchley automobile.
When it has been established quite to your satisfaction that this is the license number of the car you want, I will do something about collecting the hundred-dollar reward.

Very truly yours,
A FRIEND

Mason opened the drawer of his desk, reached for the magnifying glass, said, "Well, I suppose we may as well make a routine check of the typing."

Della Street's quick eyes caught the letters which were out of alignment.

"It's the same typewriter, chief," she said, "and the same stationery."

Mason nodded.

Della Street regarded Mason with brows that were knit together, causing two furrows in the otherwise smooth contours of her forehead. "Will you tell me what's the answer?"

Mason said, "I'm darned if I know. I have an uneasy feeling that I'm being played for a sucker."

"But surely, chief, she's smart enough, realizing you know it's a trap, not to expect you to walk into it a second time. And you simply can't expect her to be so dumb as to write this second letter on a typewriter that she knows by this time you have seen."

"Of course," Mason pointed out dubiously, "there are many people who don't realize that typing is as individual as handwriting. Not only does the type face tell the make and model of the typewriter on which a message is written, but the alignment gives a definite answer as to whether a document was or was not written upon a certain machine. However, it is surprising how many people fail to realize that."

"But, even so," Della Street pointed out, "that pink stationery. She *must* have known that you used some of it this morning."

"The thing gets me," Mason admitted, studying the letter.

Gertie, after a perfunctory knock on the door, pushed her head in and said, "A Lucille Barton is here, Mr. Mason. She said it would only take a minute and that she knew you'd want to see her."

Della Street smiled. "I'll have to have that thesaurus, chief. What were the words? Virginal, maidenly, sweet, attractive, charming, naïve . . ."

Mason grabbed up the letter and envelope, pushed them down into a drawer in his desk. He hastily dropped the ornamental key into the side pocket of his vest where it rubbed against the key to the apartment, said, "I'll see her, Gertie."

"There's a man with her."

"What's his name?"

"Mr. Arthur Colson."

Mason said, "Show them in, Gertie."

As Gertie nodded and closed the door, Mason turned to Della Street and said with swift decision, "Della, if I give you something to be typed for these people to sign before they leave the office, I want you to hold them here under one pretext or another. Be sure they don't get away."

"I don't get it," Della said.

"It will be a stall, Della. I want you to hold them so I can get down to her apartment and look in that desk."

"But, chief, isn't that just what . . ."

"I can't help it," Mason said. "My curiosity is aroused now. I'm going to find out what this is all about."

"But suppose she has . . ."

The door opened. Gertie, with an air of formality, said, "Miss Lucille Barton and Mr. Arthur Colson."

Lucille Barton came gliding across the office. Her tight dress emphasized her voluptuous figure, but the laughing candor of her eyes, the freshness of her face, and the spontaneous smile gave her an appearance of wholesome frankness.

"Mr. Mason, I couldn't understand the insinuations you made this morning. You thought I was lying about where I was on the afternoon of the third, trying to hold you up or something. And you mentioned an ad in the paper, so I read the ads, and found the one you must have been referring to. So I decided to come and *prove* to you how wrong you were. Mr. Mason, I want you to meet Mr. Colson."

Arthur Colson, a slender individual, slightly stooped, with eyes

that peered out studiously from under straight eyebrows, extended
a thin, muscular hand with an air of preoccupation. "How do you
do, Mr. Mason?" he said, in a voice cultured almost to the point
of affectation. "I suppose you wonder what I'm doing here. I do
myself, but Lucille insisted. Impetuous as ever. Something about
being a witness, I believe."

"Miss Street, my secretary," Mason introduced them.

They both bowed.

"How do you do?" Della Street said.

"Will you be seated?" Mason asked.

Della Street picked up a pencil, held it poised over her notebook
as she seated herself at her secretarial desk.

Lucille Barton went on hurriedly, "I feel that I owe this to you
and to myself. You know, Mr. Mason, when I told you that I was
no good at remembering what takes place from one day to another, I was fibbing a little. I was with Arthur on the third, but I
wasn't certain he'd want to be—well—have his name mentioned. So
I waited until I could get in touch with him and get his permission
to tell you.

"You see I am working with Arthur. It's just a part time job, two
to five. But the third was his day off, so we went to see *The Gay
Prince.*"

"A play?" Mason asked.

"A movie. It's a swell picture, Mr. Mason. One of those things
that makes you feel sort of churned up inside."

Arthur Colson contented himself with a nod.

"Where was it showing?" Mason asked.

"At the Alhambra. It's a second-run picture, but we both missed
it when it first came out and I've been wanting to see it. Arthur is
terribly, terribly busy, but I've persuaded him to take one day a
week off, even if he is working for himself. As I told him, 'All work
and no play . . .'"

"Did you," Mason interrupted, "after leaving the theater, go to
the vicinity of Hickman Avenue and Vermesillo Drive?"

Colson shook his head in positive negation.

"Heavens, no," Lucille said, laughing. "The Alhambra theater
is way out at the other end of town, Mr. Mason. The show lasted
until almost five o'clock and when we got out we . . ."

"Went to a cocktail lounge at a hotel near the theater," Colson
observed.

The man had an almost dreamy air of abstraction, as though his mind, immersed in books, had somehow become imprisoned between the printed covers of some text book and had failed to emerge. With him, life might well be a series of dim experiences lived in a state of half consciousness similar to that of a waking dream.

Lucille evidently noticed Mason's appraisal.

"Arthur's a chemist," she interpolated hastily and enthusiastically. "He's working on an invention of a new type of film that will react to infra-red rays of light so that . . ."

Colson suddenly came to life. The absent-minded air of studious preoccupation dropped from him abruptly. He said sharply, "We won't discuss it now, Lucille."

"Oh, I just wanted Mr. Mason to know what you're doing, how successful you've been with inventions. And I wanted you to understand the relationship, Mr. Mason. I've invested a little money in financing him, and I work with him from two to five, doing his typing and things like that. Not that I'm too hot as a typist, but I can get by. And Arthur couldn't trust any regular stenographer with the things he's doing. He's so ingenious! This new invention is . . ."

"We haven't translated that invention into money yet," Colson warned. "It's better not to discuss these things."

Mason said, "I don't want to pry into your business, Mr. Colson, but I *am* interested in knowing what happened on the afternoon of third. Now, as I understand it, you went to a cocktail lounge."

"That's right."

"And how long were you there?"

"Oh, I'd say an hour or so. We sat and drank cocktails and talked about the picture."

"And then we went to Murphy's for dinner," Lucille supplemented.

"And then?" Mason asked.

"Then we went home and—well, Arthur stopped up at the apartment for a drink or two—and we sat and talked some more."

"Until how late?" Mason asked.

They exchanged glances. Neither answered the question.

Mason raised inquiring eyebrows.

Both suddenly answered the question at the same time.

"Eleven o'clock," Lucille Barton said positively.

"Half past twelve," Colson said, the two answers being almost simultaneous.

Lucille recovered her composure first. "What *am* I thinking about?" she said. "Of course, it was the week *before* that you had to leave early. It must have been just about half past twelve. . . . You see, Mr. Mason, Arthur takes one day a week off. The rest of the time he limits himself to a rigid schedule."

Mason said, "I'm very sorry to inconvenience you people, but this is very, very important. Would you mind dictating to my secretary a statement covering what you have just told me, and then waiting until she's typed it, and after that affix your signatures?"

"But, Mr. Mason," Lucille Barton protested, "if we *weren't* there, what difference does it make if . . ."

"It's a matter of form," Mason interrupted. "Of course you don't *have* to do it. If you have any objection . . ."

"Not at all," Arthur Colson said. "We'll be glad to. In fact, Mr. Mason, there's a book I've been trying to get hold of, one which you probably have available here in your law library. I could be reading while your secretary is typing."

"What's the book?" Mason asked.

"Wellman, on the art of cross-examination."

"Indeed, yes," Mason said. "You may wait in the law library. How about you, Miss Barton?"

She surrendered reluctantly. "Very well, if Arthur wants to, I will. You might give me some of those magazines from the table in the outer office to look at while Arthur's reading. How long will it take?"

Mason said, "I suppose about half an hour. It should take you about ten minutes to dictate a complete statement, and then about twenty minutes for Miss Street to have it typed and ready for your signature. Now, if you'll excuse me, I have an appointment which I simply must keep. I'm very pleased I met you, and I'm certainly sorry if I am causing you any trouble."

"Not at all," Colson said. "There's something in that book I wanted to look up. I'll be very happy. After we've dictated the statement I take it that we may wait . . ."

"In the law library," Mason interrupted. "Della, you'll be as quick as you can, won't you?"

She caught and held his eyes. Her own eyes were apprehensive.

"Yes," she said.

5

MASON stopped his car in front of the apartment house on South Gondola Avenue. A near-by cigar stand gave him access to a public phone.

Mason dropped a nickel and dialed the number of his office.

He heard Gertie's voice saying, "Hello, Mr. Mason's office," and said, "This is Mr. Mason. Go into my private office, tell Della Street she's wanted for a moment and then put her on a phone where no one can hear her talk. Get it?"

"Just a minute," Gertie said. "I'll have you connected."

A moment later Mason heard Della Street's voice. "Okay," she said, keeping her voice low.

"How's everything coming?" Mason asked.

"Okay."

"Are they getting impatient?"

"Not particularly. How much more time do you need?"

"I'd say ten minutes," Mason said.

"I think I can safely promise you fifteen from here."

"Okay," Mason told her. "I just wanted to know the coast was clear."

"Be careful," she warned.

"I can't. I'm going to have to break an egg to make an omelet," Mason told her, and hung up.

He crossed the street, entered the apartment house, using the key he had received earlier in the day. This time he didn't bother with the elevator but climbed the stairs and walked rapidly to "208."

Mason took the precaution of sounding the buzzer some two or three times to make certain there was no one in the apartment. Then he tried the key. The lock clicked back.

Mason entered the apartment and closed the door behind him.

The place had been made tidy. The ash trays had been cleaned and polished. The bed was made. Dishes had been cleaned up in the kitchen and the sink was spotlessly white.

Mason called out, "Hello. Anyone home?"

His voice echoed back from the empty apartment.

The lawyer took the desk key from his pocket, crossed to the desk and fitted the key to the lock. He twisted his wrist and the bolt clicked back.

Mason lowered the lid of the writing desk.

The interior was a miscellaneous assortment of confusion. There were letters lying about in the lower partitions. The upper pigeon-holes were crammed with canceled checks, bank statements, more correspondence and memos.

The upper right-hand corner pigeonhole contained a small leather-covered notebook and a revolver.

Mason thumbed through the notebook. On the next to the last page on which there was writing, the lawyer found the figure of a license number, apparently hastily scrawled in pencil.

For the rest, the various notations were models of neatness—names, dates, telephone numbers, and mysterious figures evidently relating to some form of cash accounting in a code which Mason had neither the time nor the inclination to figure out.

Swiftly he copied the license number from the book, started to replace the book, then on impulse decided to take a look at the revolver.

Using a handkerchief over his fingertips so that he would leave no prints on the gun, Mason eased it out of the receptacle.

It was, he noted, a businesslike Smith and Wesson .38 caliber revolver. On the tang across the handle appeared the number "S65088."

Mason made a note of the number on the revolver, then replaced it, gently closed the desk, twisted the key in the lock, put the key back in his pocket and, using his handkerchief so that he would leave no fingerprints on the knob of the door, opened the apartment door.

The lawyer took the stairs two at a time, hurried across to his automobile, jumped in, and drove rapidly away.

He drove half a dozen blocks before he stopped in front of a drugstore, entered a telephone booth, dropped a coin and dialed his office.

"Hello, Gertie," he said, when he heard her voice on the line. "Get Della Street to come to the phone. Don't ring her telephone. Get her . . ."

"I understand," Gertie interrupted. "Just a minute."

A few moments later, Mason heard Della Street's anxious voice. "Hello, chief."

"Everything's okay," Mason said.

"Did you get it?"

"Yes. What's happening?"

"We still have five minutes to go at this end."

"It's okay. Get rid of them at any time now."

"Okay."

"Be as casual as possible about it," Mason said.

"No trouble?" she asked.

"I'm not certain, Della, and I may have to revise my appraisal. She may want the hundred bucks but wants to make the chap with her feel she's on the up-and-up."

"You mean that he's her boy friend who . . ."

"I don't know," Mason said. "But whatever he is, I have a license number. It may be bait for a trap, in which event it's a more complicated trap than I thought. But if it should be the real thing, she'll be back sometime within the next day or two and want her hundred bucks. Don't worry, Della. Everything's okay."

Mason hung up and telephoned Paul Drake.

"Paul," he said, "I have a license number. I want the record of ownership on the automobile. Rush it through for me."

"What's the license number?" Drake asked.

Mason read the license number over the telephone, "9Y6370."

"Where are you now?"

"Hillcrest 67492," Mason said. "It's a pay station. I'll be sticking around. Make time on it, Paul, and call me back."

Mason had a coke at the counter, smoked a cigarette, then as the phone rang, he entered the phone booth.

Drake said, "It's a Stephen Argyle, living at 938 West Casino Boulevard—that's a swank neighborhood, Perry."

"Okay," Mason told him. "I'm going to gamble an hour's time."

"The car's a Buick sedan," Drake said. "No data on color. How did you get the license number, Perry?"

"That lead you had this morning. I can't talk about it now. Della can tell you all about it in ten or fifteen minutes. The parties are in my office now."

"Okay," Drake said. "I'll be sticking around. If there's anything you want, give me a ring. You have that address all right?"

"I have it," Mason said.

The lawyer left the drugstore, climbed into his car and drove out to the address on Casino Boulevard.

The house was a huge white stucco affair with red tile roof, porches, awnings, a well-kept lawn, hedges closely and neatly trimmed on each side, a driveway leading to a triple garage in the rear. A black Buick sedan was parked in the driveway.

Mason parked his own car at the curb, walked calmly up the driveway and began examining the Buick.

A fender on the rear had been straightened. There were a few places on the rear of the body where it looked as though the paint had been skillfully matched and rubbed. The tire on the right rear wheel was brand-new.

Mason was looking at the rear bumper when the door opened. A man with broad shoulders, heavy square jaw and belligerent manner said, "What's the idea?"

Mason looked up and said without smiling, "Mr. Argyle?"

"No."

"Is he in?"

"What's that got to do with the way you're prowling around that car?"

"I'm not prowling. I'm examining it. Are you related to Mr. Argyle?"

"Not me. I work here."

"Indeed? What capacity?"

"Chauffeur and butler."

"In that event," Mason said, taking a cardcase from his pocket, "you may assume a more respectful attitude, take my card to Mr. Argyle, and tell him that I want to see him about a matter of the gravest importance—to him."

The chauffeur took the card, looked at it, said, "Very well," and started up the steps to the house.

Mason followed.

"Just a minute," the chauffeur said. "*You* wait here."

He went inside, closing the door behind him, reappeared after a few moments and said, "Yes, sir. You may come in."

The interior of the house was steeped in an atmosphere of quiet luxury. The aroma of an expensive cigar came from the room on the right. The chauffeur indicated this door, said, "In there. Mr. Argyle will see you."

The room was a combined den and library, with guns, books, comfortable leather chairs, hunting prints, photographs and an air of having been lived in. The portable bar in one corner was open, disclosing rows of bottles. A glass of Scotch and soda reposed on a smoking stand near the leather chair in which a man in the early fifties was seated.

He arose as Mason entered the room, said, "Mr. Mason, the lawyer?"

"That's right."

The man extended his hand. "I'm Stephen Argyle. I'm very glad to meet you. I have heard about you. Won't you sit down and join me in a drink?"

He was thin to the point of being bony, with long fingers, high cheekbones, bleached out eyes, thin hair which was well shot with gray. He wore glasses which clamped on the bridge of a high nose with a black ribbon hanging from the side, giving him an expression of austere power.

Mason said, "Thank you. I'll have a Scotch and soda, please."

Argyle nodded to the butler, who walked over to the portable bar, dropped ice cubes in a glass, mixed a Scotch and soda, wordlessly handed it to Mason.

"Nice room you have here," Mason said. "It's comfortable, has the feeling of being lived in."

"I spend much of my time here. Would you care for a cigar?"

"I'll have one of my cigarettes, if you don't mind." Mason opened his cigarette case.

As he tapped the cigarette on the side of the cigarette case, he saw that the butler and chauffeur had no intention of leaving.

"You'll pardon me," Mason said, striking a match, "if I'm rather abrupt. My time is somewhat limited."

He lit the cigarette, blew out the match and dropped it in an ash tray.

"Go right ahead," Argyle said.

Mason glanced at the chauffeur who was standing by the bar.

Argyle made no move to dismiss the man.

"On the afternoon of the third of this month," Mason said, with complete assurance, "at about five o'clock, your Buick out there was involved in an accident at the intersection of Hickman Avenue and Vermesillo Drive. Who was driving it, you or your chauffeur?"

"That's a question?" Argyle asked, raising his eyebrows.

"A question about who was driving it," Mason said. "The part about the accident isn't a question. It's an assertion."

"Really, Mr. Mason, I'm surprised! Surprised beyond words."

"I take it, then, *you* weren't driving it?"

Argyle hesitated for a minute, then said, "No."

Mason glanced at the chauffeur, whose eyes had suddenly become as intent as those of a cat stalking a bird.

"As a matter of fact," Argyle said, carefully weighing his words, "you are bringing information which confirms my worst fears. I trust the accident was not serious."

"It was serious," Mason said. "What about your fears?"

"My car was stolen on the afternoon of the third. The police recovered it later on that evening, parked in front of a fireplug in the downtown district. The gasoline tank was half empty and the car had been driven over a hundred miles."

"Quick work," Mason said.

"On the part of the police?" Argyle asked.

Mason smiled.

Argyle frowned.

Mason said, "I'm representing Bob Finchley. His mother was driving the car. She was badly shaken up. The car was pretty well wrecked. Bob Finchley sustained a broken hip. It's too early yet to tell whether there will be complications."

"Indeed. That's too bad," Argyle said. "I will have to consult my lawyers. As I understand it, Mr. Mason, in the event I let anyone use my car *with my permission* I am responsible for damages, but, of course, in the event of theft . . ."

Argyle shrugged his shoulders, tapped ash from the end of his cigar.

Mason said, "Let's quit beating around the bush. That stall about the stolen car is two years older than Moses. In addition to which, it stinks."

The chauffeur took a step forward.

Argyle waved him back.

"Now, Mr. Mason," Argyle said, "I'm satisfied that as an attorney you wouldn't want to make any insinuations."

"All right," Mason said, "I'll go at it the long way round. *When* was the car stolen?"

"Sometime around three o'clock in the afternoon."

Mason smiled. "When was the car *reported* stolen?"

"I didn't miss it until around seven o'clock," Argyle said. "I had left it parked at the curb in front of my club. I went out to get in the car and it was gone."

"And you immediately reported it to the police?"

"Yes, sir."

"Using the club telephone?"

"Yes, sir."

"And how far away from the place where the car was stolen was it recovered?"

"I would say not over eight or ten blocks."

Mason said, "The boy's pretty badly injured. He's going to be laid up for a while and the mother has of course suffered nervous shock. Then there's the matter of the car."

"Surely, Mr. Mason, you don't think I'm liable."

"Why not?"

"I tell you the car was stolen."

Mason grinned. "As you so aptly stated, as a lawyer, I'm too smart to make any accusations—in front of witnesses. You'll have a lo' of fun listening to what I tell a jury, however."

"*Surely*, Mr. Mason, you don't doubt my word. Good heavens, I'm a responsible citizen! My car is fully insured. If there were any question of liability on my part, I would be only too glad to make an adjustment. As it is, my insurance company will handle things."

"All right," Mason said. "If that's the way you want it, I'll do business with your insurance company."

"Provided, of course, there's any liability."

"Oh, certainly," Mason said. "What's the name of the club where you spent the afternoon?"

"The Broadway Athletic Club."

Mason got to his feet. "Nice to have met you," he said, and started for the door.

Argyle arose, hesitated, then sat down again.

The chauffeur saw Mason to the door.

"Good afternoon, sir," he said.

A moment later the door slammed.

CHAPTER NUMBER

6

THE office of the Drake Detective Agency was on the same floor as Mason's offices. Mason stopped in hurriedly for a few words with Paul Drake.

"By gosh, Perry, we hit the jack pot. I can't figure out how it happened, but it's the jack pot!"

"I want men on the job immediately, Paul. Men who can really do an intelligent job. I want Stephen Argyle checked for the afternoon of the third. He was probably at the Broadway Athletic Club. I want to know how much he drank. I want to know how long he was there. I want to know whether people who were there with him noticed any break in the continuity of his visit. I want to find out everything we can from the doorman. I think the doorman may have been bribed. I don't think we have enough money to compete with Stephen Argyle, on bribery, so we're going to have to throw a scare into the doorman. I want a man who can *really* scare the guy.

"I want to find out all about the records of Argyle's car, which was supposed to have been stolen on the afternoon of the third, when it was reported stolen, when it was recovered, all about it. I particularly want to find out if Stephen Argyle didn't drive up to the Broadway Athletic Club in a taxicab sometime between five and six. At that hour people were dropping in for cocktails and you should be able to find some club member who saw him arrive in a taxi. You're going to have to work fast."

"Okay," Drake said, "I'm on the job. How many men shall I put out?"

"As many as it takes," Mason said. "We're going to get the dope and when we get it, we're going to send the bill to Stephen Argyle and make him pay it and like it."

"He's the man all right?"

"It was his car," Mason said, "and I think he's the man. Incidentally, I want to find out everything I can about him. I have an idea his wife is dead or has recently left him."

"What gives you that idea?"

"He has a butler and chauffeur," Mason said, "who certainly wouldn't get along for five minutes in a house where there was a woman. Yet the house on Casino Boulevard is a great big place and apparently Stephen Argyle does most of his living in one room, a room which fairly reeks of tobacco."

Drake said, "Okay, Perry, I'll put men on the job right away. By the way, Perry, you were right about that flirtatious young grass widow. She sent her little playmate in to collect the hundred bucks."

"Well, she's entitled to it. Hang it, I can't figure that one out. She certainly had me fooled. When did this dame come in for the reward?"

"Not over five minutes ago," Drake said. "I sent her down to your office and told her Della Street, your secretary, would take care of it."

"Who is she?" Mason asked.

"A cute little number, name of Carlotta Boone. She was very coy about it and, of course, wouldn't let on that she knew anything at all about Lucille Barton. She simply said she'd come to collect the hundred dollars' reward."

"I'll go see her," Mason said. "You rush men out to get the dope on Argyle. I'm *really* going to shake him down for a settlement—we'll give that Finchley kid a chance to finish his college education in return for the inconvenience of a broken hip."

"Don't let Argyle off the hook too easy," Drake warned. "I detest these hit-and-run boys who try to get away with it, and who probably have enough political pull to help them out in case the going gets tough."

"I'll stick him," Mason grinned. "And now I'll go pay Lucille her hundred dollars. It's going to be interesting to listen to the way Carlotta Boone tries to get the hundred without betraying Lucille's frame-up. Okay, Paul, I'm on my way."

Drake said, "I'll have men on the job within five minutes."

Mason walked down the corridor to his own office, whistling a little tune. He unlocked the door of his private office, entered, grinned at Della Street, sailed his hat over to the shelf in the coat closet and said, "Well, Della, I understand Lucille has sent a stooge for the hundred dollars."

Della Street's face was a mask of perplexity. "Wait until you hear *her* story."

"I want to," Mason grinned. "Is it good?"

"I haven't had time to get all of it," Della Street said, "but it's one that's going to knock you for a loop."

"What's the name again?" Mason asked.

"Carlotta Boone."

"What sort, Della?"

"Brunette, slender, shrewdly calculating, probably a golddigger, reticent about herself. She resents me, wants to talk with you, says she came to give information and get a hundred dollars, and doesn't want a run-around."

Mason grinned, said, "Well, let's get her in, Della, listen to her story, give her the hundred bucks, and send Lucille's keys back. Maybe this kid shares the apartment with Lucille. Anyway, bring her in."

Della Street said, "Just don't jump to conclusions, chief. The talk I've had with her indicates it may be something entirely different."

"Oh well, get her in," Mason said, "and we'll find out what it's all about."

Della Street picked up the telephone, said, "Send Carlotta Boone in, Gertie."

Then Della went to the door of the private office to open it and usher the visitor across the threshold.

She had black lacquered eyes which were for the most part utterly devoid of expression but glistened with vigilance. Her hair was a deep glossy black. She was about two inches taller than the average woman and about ten pounds lighter, and there was a peculiar, wary tension about her.

"Well, how do you do, Miss Boone?" Mason said. "I understand you came to collect a hundred dollars."

"That's right."

"How did you happen to get the information?" Mason asked. "How did you know so much about where the number was written down?" He winked at Della Street.

"You mean the license number?"

"Yes."

"Because I'm the one who wrote it down."

"Oh I see," Mason said. "And then you placed it in the desk?"

"I placed it in my purse," she said. "How do we fix it up about paying the hundred dollars? Of course, I understand that you can't afford simply to dish out a hundred bucks to every girl who comes in here with a plausible story and a license number."

Mason, grinning amiably, said, "Certainly not. However, I think we've pretty well established our point in the present case."

Della Street coughed warningly.

Mason glanced at her, frowned, then became cautiously on guard.

Carlotta Boone settled herself in the chair, took pains to cross her legs so that she showed a good expanse of stocking. Her legs, while thin, were well streamlined.

She said, "I suppose I can trust you."

"I suppose you'll have to," Mason said.

She had started to reach into her purse. Now she stopped and regarded Mason with an appraisal that indicated her inherent suspicion. "How do *I* know you're not going to double-cross me?"

Mason said, "After all, young lady, *I've* been in business some time. And before I pay you the money I want all the details of the story."

"Oh, all right," she said wearily, "here's your number."

She pulled a slip of paper from her purse and handed it to Mason.

Mason glanced at the number, then frowned, looked at it again and said, "I'm sorry, Miss Boone, but I think it's only fair to tell you in advance that this is the wrong license number."

"How do you know?"

"Because I already have the information I wanted. I have not only the license number of the automobile, but I have inspected the automobile, and have talked to the owner. Quite obviously this is the wrong number."

"It's not the wrong number," she said with firm determination. "What are you trying to do? Talk me out of the hundred dollars? Don't think I'm *that* easy."

Mason frowned.

She said angrily and defiantly, "I was with my boy friend. We'd been out for a rendezvous at one of the cocktail bars. We'd done a little dancing. He was driving me home. We had a flat tire. I got out and was standing around looking ornamental and giving a little help here and there. He got the tire changed. We were just finishing with it, when there was a terrific crash at the intersection. I saw this big black sedan roaring and swerving down Vermesillo Drive. Behind it there was a Ford coupe that was skidding all over the road. It smashed into a telephone post just as I looked up. A woman and a man were in it. The man seemed to be pinned between the door and the post. The woman who was driving had bumped her head. I thought there might be an opportunity for—well, frankly, Mr. Mason, I thought I could make some money. I saw the big black car was going to make a run for it. I pulled out my notebook and jotted down the license number. All right, I didn't give it to the police, I waited for a reward to be offered. I kept looking at the ads."

Mason, frowning, regarded her.

"And why not?" she went on defiantly. "You'll get plenty out of this case. You aren't working for nothing. Why should I? I need money a lot more than you do, Mr. Perry Mason!"

Mason turned to Della Street. "Get Drake on the phone," he said.

A moment later, when Paul Drake was on the phone, Mason said wearily, "Paul, here's another license number for you—49X176."

"What about it?" Drake asked.

Mason said, "Find out who owns the car, the address and the type of car."

Mason hung up the phone, said to Carlotta Boone, "This is a new development. It's an unexpected development. I thought we had the license number we wanted."

"I can readily understand," she said, "that with an ad such as you have placed in the paper you must have been deluged with girls who were willing to tell a good story and give a license number in return for a hundred dollars. However, *I'm* giving you the straight goods. The question is, do you want it or don't you?"

"What do you mean by that?"

She said, "You're not kidding me. The man who was driving that sedan is in a jam. He's mixed up in a hit-and-run case. If I wanted to, I could go to him and shake him down for ten times what I can get out of you."

"Why don't you do it, then?"

"Because it's too risky. It's blackmail. *You* could do it as a lawyer. I can't."

"So what do you want?"

She said, "I put myself in your hands. I want you to investigate

that license number. When you're convinced that that's the car, you
can give me the hundred dollars."

"All right," Mason said. "What's your address? How do I get in
touch with you?"

"You can't, and you don't," she said. "*I'll* get in touch with *you*,
and of course I don't want my name mentioned. The boy friend I
was with is married. He'd have a fit if he knew I had come to you.
But, after all, a girl has to live!"

"And when will you get in touch with me?" Mason asked.

"Sometime before noon tomorrow. You should know by then.
Good night."

With complete assurance, she arose from the chair, marched to
the exit door, jerked it open and walked out.

Mason looked at Della Street, scratched his head, and said, "If
you'd like to go in for a slight understatement, Della, this is what
might be called a complicating factor."

"You don't suppose that that's some ruse this man has worked
out to throw you off the trail, do you?" she asked.

"Probably," Mason said, "but it's not going to throw me off the
trail. I'll now go out and chase after the red herring, but Paul
Drake is going to keep after the real quarry."

The telephone rang. Drake said, "Your man is Daniel Caffee. The
car's a Packard sedan; the address is 1017 Beachnut Street. What
about him?"

Mason said, "You getting your men on the Argyle job?"

"They're on. Four men are out right now, and two more are on
their way."

Mason nodded to Della Street, said, "Get your hat and a notebook, Della. We'll leave Paul here to handle this end of the business. You and I are going to chase a red herring."

Into the phone he said, "That's fine, Paul, you stay on the job.
I'm going out to take a look at Mr. Daniel Caffee."

"Okay, Perry, I'll get all the dope on Argyle. However, he'll know
that we're investigating him. I can't have my men contact these
club members without some of them getting in touch with Argyle
and telling him what's going on."

"That's all right," Mason said. "That's the way I want it. Let's
let him know we're on the job."

Mason hung up the phone, said, "Come on, Della, let's go."

7

DRIVING along Beachnut Street, Della Street said, "Why do you suppose a girl would pull a trick like that?"

"Probably to get a hundred bucks," Mason said. "But, hang it, Della, there's something about that girl which impresses me."

"She's a golddigger."

"I know she's a golddigger. She took down the license number, intending to use it for blackmail. Then for some reason she didn't. She saw the ad in the paper offering a hundred dollars. She couldn't resist the temptation of cleaning up a hundred dollars where her action would be entirely within the law. Somehow or other the girl gives me the impression of telling the truth, and yet—well, hang it, Della, I've already seen Argyle's automobile. It has dents on the back end; it's been in a collision, the right rear wheel is brand-new, and . . ."

"And, of course," Della Street said, "his story about the car having been stolen *could* have been true."

"Just about one chance in a hundred, Della. Well, we'll soon find out. Here's 1017."

Mason brought his car to a stop in front of a good-looking apartment house, quite obviously of the better class.

"What do we do?" Della Street asked. "Barge on in?"

"No," Mason told her. "We look around a bit first. There's a private garage down here in the basement. There'll be someone in charge. Let's park the car and take a look."

Mason found a parking place for his car, then he and Della Street walked down the sharply inclined ramp to the garage.

The man in charge was parking cars.

Mason looked around the place, said to his secretary, "Keep looking for a big black Packard, Della. You take the left side, I'll take the right. Let's go."

The man finished parking the car, called out, "Hey, you!"

Mason turned and waved his hand reassuringly.

Della said, "Here's a Packard over here on the left."

Mason took a quick look at the license number, said, "That's the one, Della. Okay, let's give it a once-over."

The man who ran the garage was walking toward them now. "What do you folks want?" he called.

Mason, moving toward the rear of the Packard, said, "You talk with him, Della. Tell him we understand the car is for sale."

The light was dim there in the back of the garage, but Mason could see that a new fender assembly had been put on the back of the car, that there was still a dent in the trunk and that the left rear tire bore marks of a deep gouge.

Mason heard Della Street explain that they understood the car was for sale and then heard the garage man insisting that they'd have to talk with Mr. Caffee about it.

Mason completed his hurried inspection, handed the garage man ten dollars and said, "Mr. Caffee is the one who offered the car to a friend of mine. I wanted to get the low-down on it."

"Yes, sir," the garage attendant said, instantly mollified.

"Now, as I understand it," Mason said, "the car was in some sort of a wreck."

"Oh no, sir, not a wreck. The car's in wonderful shape. Just a minor traffic collision that made it necessary to put on a new fender. That is, the old fender *could* have been fixed up but Mr. Caffee's very particular about the car, keeps it running like a watch."

"I see," Mason said. "When was this accident?"

"Oh, not very long ago—a couple of days. Mr. Caffee just got the car back. He has some sort of a pull with the car agency here. I don't think the agency did the installation for him, though. I know he got the fender through them. Anyhow, the car wasn't hurt a bit. It was just a little sideswipe. The rear bumper got most of the damage. It was torn loose from its supports, but that's all been fixed up now."

"I see," Mason said. "Well, thanks a lot. I suppose Caffee is in now?"

"Oh yes, sir. Sure. When his car's here, he's here. He always drives when he goes out."

"Married?"

"Yes. His wife has her own little coupe. She doesn't like the big car. Mr. Caffee says he likes weight and power and speed—he's that sort."

"I see," Mason said. "What's the number of his apartment, by the way?"

"22-B."

"Could you describe him to me?" Mason asked. "I always like to know the sort of chap I'm doing business with."

"Why yes, sir. He's—oh, I should say he was around fifty-five, rather slender, a quiet sort of man who always dresses in good taste, smokes cigars, wears double-breasted gray suits, nearly always gray. I don't think I've ever seen him in any other color."

"Okay, thanks," Mason said. "We'll go see him. The car looks to me like a pretty good buy."

"I didn't have any idea he intended to sell it. He's only had it a few months, and I know he likes it very much."

"Can we take an elevator here?"

"Yes, sir. You can ring and the elevator comes right down here. As visitors, you're supposed, of course, to stop by the desk and be announced."

"I know," Mason said, "but that's a useless formality, under the circumstances. What floor is Apartment 22-B on?"

"The fifth floor."

Mason said to Della Street, "Come on, Della. We'll at least make Mr. Caffee an offer."

The garage attendant pushed the buzzer which brought the elevator down to the basement.

Mason closed the door, punched the button for the fifth floor.

"Well?" Della Street asked.

Mason shook his head. "I'm going around in circles. This whole business is completely cockeyed."

The elevator lurched to a stop at the fifth floor.

Mason pushed a mother-of-pearl button by the side of the door numbered 22-B, and within a few seconds the door was opened by a man with thin gray hair who was in the late fifties. He was attired in a double-breasted gray suit and was smoking a cigar.

"Mr. Caffee?" Mason asked.

"Yes, sir."

Mason shoved a card at Caffee, said, "I'm Perry Mason, the lawyer. I want to talk with you about your automobile."

"What about it?"

Mason pushed forward.

Caffee instinctively fell back. Mason and Della Street walked into the apartment.

"What about my automobile?" Caffee asked.

"I want to know about the accident you had on the third."

Caffee stood rigid for a moment, then his lip began to quiver, the cigar almost fell from his mouth. Caffee clutched at it hurriedly, cleared his throat, said, "What do you mean?"

"You know what I mean," Mason charged, his manner radiating positive assurance. "Your automobile smashed into a Ford coupe at the intersection of Hickman Avenue and Vermesillo Drive. I suppose you'd had a few drinks, were afraid to stay and take the rap, and decided you could escape undetected. A look in the rear-view mirror showed you that all eyes were focused on the car that was crashing into the lamppost. You were going fast and you kept on going fast."

"Oh, my God!" Caffee exclaimed, and collapsed into a chair. His face seemed suddenly to be made of bread dough. His lips trembled.

"Well?" Mason demanded.

"You've got me," Caffee said pathetically. "Why in the world did I ever do it?"

Della Street dropped into a chair, opened a shorthand book, balanced it on her knee, and started taking notes.

"You admit it?" Mason asked.

"Yes," Caffee said, "I admit it. You've caught me. You've caught me dead to rights. I supposed at the time there was just property damage. . . . Tell me . . . was anyone hurt, Mr. Mason?"

"Two people were hurt," Mason said. "The woman who was driving the car was shaken up. The son sustained a broken hip. He was slammed against the lamppost when the door of the car jerked itself open and spilled him out. It's a wonder he didn't crack his head and die."

Daniel Caffee put long, bony hands to his head, moaned.

"Well," Mason said, "what about it?"

"You've caught me," Caffee repeated in abject contrition. "I suppose I'll have to take my medicine. Mr. Mason, I give you my word, I didn't know anyone had been hurt. I kept hoping it was just a question of property damage and I was trying to find some way of paying off . . . I was a coward. I'd had a few drinks too many. You see, I'd met an old friend and we'd stopped in a cocktail lounge. Ordinarily I never drink if I'm going to drive. My wife was expecting me and I—well, I was late and I was trying to make time. I was going fast. I hit that intersection and honestly I didn't see that other car until it was right on top of me. I thought I could give my car the gun and get by. I pushed the throttle down to the floor boards. My car has a marvelous pickup. It shot ahead and all but missed that other car, but that other car couldn't seem to stop. It seemed to me to keep right on coming. It hit the rear end of my car and I guess my rear bumper snagged the front wheel and jerked the other car around and into the ornamental lighting pole.

"At first I thought I'd stop. Then I looked in the rearview mirror and, just as you say, I saw that everyone was running toward the other car. The street was clear ahead, and I knew that there were no traffic signals for half a dozen blocks, so I just kept the car rolling. I felt sure that no one had seen me well enough to recognize the car, and my car had suffered relatively little damage. If it hadn't been for those drinks I'd never have even considered any such crazy idea."

"What time was this?" Mason asked.

"I guess it must have been shortly after five o'clock, Mr. Mason."

"Where?"

"Right there at the intersection of Hickman Avenue and Vermesillo Drive. I was traveling east on Vermesillo Drive and, as I say, I was hurrying right along."

Mason glanced at Della Street's busy pen.

"And the date?"

"The third of the month. Mr. Mason, I know that I'm in bad, but let's do what we can to square it. I'm covered by insurance. I'll get in touch with the insurance company and I know that they'll make a generous settlement. In addition to that, I'll make your clients a check for ten thousand dollars on my personal account. I suppose technically I'm guilty of hit-and-run and I'll have to take my medicine there. And I *do* hope we can handle this without my wife finding out about it."

"Your wife's home now?"

"No, I'm expecting her in about thirty minutes."

Mason narrowed his eyes, thinking the situation over.

He said, "Write out a brief statement of what you've just told me. Sign it and make a check for ten thousand dollars, payable to Robert L. Finchley.

"The hit-and-run angle you'll have to handle with the police. I suppose under the circumstances, and in view of the payment, you may get probation. Now, while you're writing out that statement and the check, do you have a telephone I can use?"

"Yes, sir, right over there on the table."

Mason walked over to the telephone, asked for an outside line, gave the number of Drake's office.

When he had Drake on the phone he said, "Paul, that Argyle thing was a false alarm. Call off your men."

"The hell it's a false alarm," Drake said indignantly. "One of my men has a signed statement from the doorman at the Broadway Athletic Club. He says Argyle showed up in a taxicab about seven o'clock. He seemed all upset and nervous. He told the doorman he was going to report his car as having been stolen, and gave the guy a hundred bucks to swear Argyle had been there ever since noon. The doorman would have stayed put if my man hadn't pulled everything in the quiver and told the guy he was going to the pen for compounding a felony."

Mason remained silent.

"You there?" Drake asked.

"I'm here."

"Argyle's wife left him about six months ago. He's a speculator in oil leases. He has two associates, Dudley Gates and Ross P. Hollister. Hollister lives in Santa del Barra and has the dough. Since Argyle's wife left him Argyle has been living alone in his big house, only the chauffeur with him and a maid who comes in by the day. Argyle is well thought of at the club. He's considered to have made a nice nest egg in that new oil field up north. He'd been drinking and was still a little woozy when he slipped the doorman at the club the hundred bucks. Now what more do you want than that, Perry? He's your man."

"He *can't* be!"

"I take it you're where you can't talk without someone hearing you?"

"That's right."

"Well, don't let him flimflam you, whoever he may be," Drake said. "He's giving you a run-around. Argyle's the man you want."

"He's giving me a written confession and his personal check for ten thousand bucks," Mason said in a low voice, and hung up the telephone just as he heard Paul Drake's gasp of astonishment.

8

MASON, driving his car rapidly along Beachnut Street, said to Della Street, "All right, Della, I'm going to take you down to the Ketterling Hotel. You'll be able to get a taxi there. Go see Paul Drake, tell him about these new developments, then go to my office and wait for me to call you.

"I'm going back to talk with Argyle, then I'm going to that South Gondola Street address."

"You be careful. I think that whole thing is a trap."

"I know," Mason said, "but someone is playing games and I want to find out who."

Mason drove rapidly and in silence to the Ketterling Hotel.

Della said, "Now, as I understand it, I'm to contact Paul Drake, fill him in with what's happened, and then go to the office and wait?"

"Right."

"I'll be there," she told him, jumping out of the car. "Good luck to you."

He grinned. "That's the trouble, we're shot with luck. We have two guilty drivers and only one smashup."

He drove to Argyle's house at 938 West Casino Boulevard. The big Buick was no longer in the driveway. Nor did Mason get any answer when he rang the bell on the front door.

He returned to his car and, driving more rapidly now, went at once to South Gondola Street, where he took the precaution of parking his car a couple of blocks from Lucille Barton's address. Then, having walked to the apartment house, he circled around to the rear, to inspect the garages.

Without much difficulty he found the garage bearing the number "208." The doors were closed, and a padlock was snapped shut.

The curve of the padlock and the loose hasp gave the doors

enough leeway so Mason could open the door for a scant half inch, enabling him to see far enough into the dark interior of the garage to tell there was no automobile behind the closed, locked doors.

Having satisfied himself on that point, Mason crossed the street and walked down to the corner to a cigar store where there was a public telephone.

Dialing the unlisted number of his private office, he waited until he heard Della Street's voice.

"Hello, Della," he said in a low voice. "I've looked the place over. She's out somewhere in her car. I'm going to try and find that notebook."

"I was afraid you'd do something like that. How long will you be?"

"Not long."

She lowered her voice and said, "Mr. Argyle's in the waiting room. He's having kittens."

"What's happening?"

"Apparently his conscience is bothering him."

"You don't think he wants to retract any of the statements he made?"

"Apparently not."

"How long has he been there?"

"He says he left his place immediately after you talked with him. He's really worried about something. He tells me he couldn't talk freely with you when you were there and he's very anxious to see you now."

"Why couldn't he talk freely?"

"He didn't say."

"There's only one reason I can think of, his chauffeur and butler was present."

"Well, why didn't he simply send the man out?"

"I don't know. There's something strange about that relationship."

Della said, "The chauffeur was down there sitting at the wheel of the Buick when I came in. Mr. Argyle went down right afterwards to tell him he needn't wait. That was when I told him I didn't know when you'd be in. Argyle says he's going to wait, no matter how long it is."

"Okay," Mason said. "I'm on my way, Della. Try and hold Argyle there."

Mason hung up the phone, walked rapidly up the street to the entrance of the apartment house, used his key to open the outer door, ran up the stairs to the second floor, made certain that the second floor corridor was empty, and then walked rapidly back to apartment 208.

Mason knocked, and received no answer.

He made another quick survey of the corridor, then quietly inserted his key in the door, clicked back the lock and, opening the door, stepped swiftly inside the apartment.

Lights were on in the apartment. The desk was open. The upper right-hand pigeonhole was empty. Both the notebook and the gun had disappeared.

Mason gave an exclamation of annoyance, took two steps toward the bedroom, then stopped.

From where he was then standing, he could look through the half-open bedroom door, across the lighted bedroom and through an open door into a bathroom.

A girl was standing in the bathtub behind a shower curtain, and evidently had just shut off the water.

A white enameled bathroom stool was standing beside the bathtub. On this stool was a blued-steel revolver, squat, ominous and ugly.

As Mason stood watching the silhouette of the woman against the shower curtain, a naked arm dripping with water reached around the end of the curtain.

The wet hand closed about the gun.

Mason swiftly stepped back out of the range of vision.

"Hello," he called. "Anybody home?"

"Who . . . who's there?"

"Hello," Mason called. "This is Perry Mason."

"Oh . . . are you alone?"

"Yes."

"I was taking a shower. How did you get in?"

"I rang the doorbell. No one answered. I pushed against the door and it came open."

"Oh," she said, "sometimes that latch doesn't click. Just sit down, Mr. Mason, and make yourself at home for a few minutes, but you'd better close that door into the bedroom. I'm definitely not decent."

"I have to see you," Mason said, "right away."

She laughed. "Not *right* away."

"There isn't any time to waste," Mason told her.

"My, but you're terribly impatient. Close that outer door, will you please, Mr. Mason, and make sure it's locked this time. And now the bedroom door, please. I'll be with you in a second or two, just as soon as I dry myself and put on a housecoat."

He closed the bedroom door, made certain the outer door was locked, then went over to the desk. After going through the contents for some ten seconds, he could find no sign of the notebook he had seen earlier in the day.

He crossed back to the chair by the table and waited.

After some four or five minutes the door from the bedroom opened. Lucille Barton, wearing a housecoat of dark velvety material which outlined the curves of her figure, came gliding toward him.

Mason arose to meet her.

She hesitated a moment, then, smiling a full-lipped smile, gave him her hand.

Mason drew her to him and put his arm around her.

"Why, *Mister* Mason, I didn't expect this of *you*."

Mason's hands moved swiftly.

"Why, Mr. Mason, *what* are you looking for?"

"At the moment," Mason said, "I'm looking for a gun."

"Oh." Her voice showed a very definite change of expression.

"Where is it?" Mason asked.

She said, "You saw me, didn't you, Mr. Mason? You saw me through the shower curtain."

"I saw the gun on the bath stool," Mason said. "Where is it?"

"In my bedroom in my handbag."

"Let's go take a look at it."

"I'll get it."

"*We'll* get it."

"What's the matter, Mr. Mason? Don't you trust me?"

"No."

"Why, Mr. Mason, what's come over you?"

Mason said, "I'm getting cautious, that's all."

"Why, Mr. Mason," she said laughing, "that's what Arthur Colson says about me. He says I'm *too* cautious."

"And what," Mason asked, "brought up that subject of conversation when you were talking with him?"

Her light laughter was her only answer. She opened the door, led the way into the bedroom and said, "Honestly, Mr. Mason, this is *terribly* unconventional."

She moved over toward the bed, suddenly grabbed for the handbag.

Mason beat her to it.

She said sharply, "Mr. Mason, don't you take that gun away from me. Don't you try to . . ."

"What do you want a gun for?" Mason asked.

"For protection."

Mason took the gun out of the handbag, pulled the catch which enabled him to open the cylinder and slipped the cartridges into his pocket. Having done that, he snapped the cylinder back into place, returned the empty gun to her purse.

"Why, Mr. Mason, you mustn't do that."

Mason said, "Let's talk."

"But we *are* talking—you're not listening."

"Where did you get this gun?"

"It was given to me."

"By whom?"

"Mr. Hollister . . . No, I can't tell you. Please don't ask me."

"How long have you had it?"

"For two or three weeks."

"Why did Hollister think you needed it?"

"That's—that's something I can't tell you, Mr. Mason."

Mason said, "Let's start getting a few things straight, Lucille. I don't like to have anyone try to slip something over on me."

"No," she said, "I presume not."

"You told me that you were engaged to Mr. Hollister."

"Yes, I'm going to marry him."

"Where is he now?"

"You mean *right* now?"

"Yes."

"I don't know. Up in the northern part of the state somewhere."

"You don't know where? He doesn't call you?"

"No. You see I don't have a telephone, Mr. Mason. That's the bad part of this old-fashioned apartment house. There's no way he *can* call me. He'll drop me a letter. There's probably one in the mail now."

"You love him?"

"Mr. Mason, *why* are you prying into my private affairs this way?"

"Because I want to find out something about you and about some of the things that are going on."

She said, "Mr. Hollister is a gentleman. I care for him very deeply. I certainly respect him. He's a speculator who deals in oil properties. He'll take business trips for a week or two at a time, then he'll be back here in the city for perhaps—oh, sometimes as long as a month."

"And when he's gone, you start playing around with Arthur Colson?"

"Why, *Mister* Mason!"

"Well?" Mason asked.

She shook her head, and said, "No, it's not that way. Arthur's just a business partner, but why are you so curious?"

"Because I want to find out. I have to know what's going on."

"Why?"

"Because I think it concerns me, and I think there may be more to this than you know about—or else you're trying to slip a fast one over on me."

"Why, *Mister* Mason! I don't know what you're talking about. You've acted in the *most* mysterious manner ever since you came in here this morning. I . . . I would like very much to have you negotiate this alimony matter with my ex-husband, Willard Barton, but I'm not going to permit you to make a lot of nasty insinuations just because I want you to do that for me. Of course, naturally, I respect you."

"All right," Mason said. "Under those circumstances tell me more about Arthur Colson."

"What about him?"

"I want to know all about him. Not the business part, the other."

"Heavens, he's just a friend. He's more a friend of Anita's than he is of mine."

"Who's Anita?"

"Anita Jordon, a girl that I know."

"Describe her."

"She's small, with very dark eyes, and nice dark hair. She likes to dress smartly and—you'd like her. She's just as cute as can be."

"All right. Now we've talked about everything else, let's come back to the question, and talk about Arthur Colson."

"What about him?"

"How long have you known him?"

"Not very long. He—he's an inventor. Sort of the dreamy, studious type. We have difficulty getting him to relax and do any—well, any playing around. He likes to read. He'll spend nights in research work at the library, reading. Then he'll go home and make plans and pound away on his typewriter."

"What does he invent?"

"Oh, lots of little gadgets. He's made money out of some of them."

"What sort of gadgets?"

"Well, right now he's working on something in connection with infra-red rays. Before that, he worked out a device that opens and closes doors and does things like that."

"What do you mean?"

"It works with invisible light, what I think they call a black light. A beam runs across the room and as soon as some object crosses that beam it closes a circuit and does things—oh, for instance, like making electrical contacts so that the minute you walk into the house the electric stove clicks on and starts cooking, the radio turns on, and lights come on, and . . . I don't know, Mr. Mason, I think it's just a gadget. So many of his things are scientifically fine, but impractical when you want to work with them."

"And what's your interest in him?"

"It's just as I told you. I'm financing him."

"And why did you put up money for his inventions?"

"Because I think it's good business."

"And he's here until after midnight at times?"

"Well, sometimes when Mr. Hollister isn't here, and I . . . oh, Arthur gets blue and lonely. You see, he makes it a rule to take only one day a week for relaxation. I'm trying to get him to take his evenings off. He's definitely not the type that knows *how* to play. He's dreamy and abstract, and sometimes he can be something of a bore."

"But he likes Anita Jordon?"

"Yes."

"And she likes him?"

"I guess so. Anita's—well, Anita's selfish in a way. You know, she wants security. I think she'd like very much to have someone marry her and settle down. I've tried to tell her that marriage doesn't mean security, but you can't argue with a girl about a thing like that."

"No," Mason said, "you can't. Now, suppose you quit lying, Lucille, and tell me who bought this gun for you."

"I think you're attaching a perfectly exaggerated importance to that gun, Mr. Mason."

Mason said, "When a woman takes a bath and has a gun on a stool right beside the bathtub, I feel that she's the one who's attaching an exaggerated importance to the weapon."

"Someone has sworn he's going to kill me. Arthur is afraid and I'm afraid."

"Who's that someone?"

"You wouldn't know him."

"You can't be certain," Mason said. "I know lots of people. What's his name?"

"His name is Pitkin—Hartwell L. Pitkin. He's a tough, coarse, uncouth individual. I made a mistake and married him when I was just a kid. I was only eighteen at the time, not old enough to have any sense about men. He had batted around and I felt he was a man of the world who could give me everything I wanted. I'd lived more or less of an isolated existence in a small town and . . ."

"How long did you live together?"

"Between two and three years."

"Then what?"

"Then I ran away."

"What do you mean, you ran away?"

"Just that."

"Did you get a divorce?"

"Eventually, but at the time I left him, I just ran away."

"With someone?" Mason asked.

"You're terribly direct, aren't you, Mr. Mason?"

"Were you with someone?" Mason repeated.

"Yes," she said, meeting his eyes.

"So what happened?" Mason asked.

"Hartwell swore that he'd follow us, find us and kill us both. He couldn't find me. He never did. I changed my name and then I got a divorce in Reno and . . ."

"And what happened to the man you ran away with?"

"He was killed in the war. I loved him."

"And then what?"

"He left me some insurance and—well, I married Willard Barton."

"All right, now tell me about Hartwell Pitkin."

"He . . . he's found out I'm in the city. Not the address yet."

"He's here in the city?"

"Yes."

"Where? What's he doing?"

"He's working for a man by the name of Stephen Argyle. He lives at 938 West Casino Boulevard. He doesn't know that I know where he is, but I found that out—and the worst of it is, Mr. Mason, that Ross Hollister and this man, Argyle, belong to the same club, play cards together and all that.

"Now you can see my predicament. Even if I should marry Ross Hollister it wouldn't really *solve* anything. You can imagine how a a man like Ross would feel if he realized he'd married the ex-wife of his friend's chauffeur. It would humiliate Ross, and his friends would laugh at him . . . and Hartwell Pitkin is crazy jealous.

"Oh, Mr. Mason, it's a mess!"

"Now," Mason said, "I am beginning to understand."

"What do you mean by that?"

Mason gently but firmly pushed her toward the door of the bedroom. "Get some clothes on, Lucille. We're going places."

"Mr. Mason, why are you so . . . so grim?"

"Because you've been trying to slip something over."

"I have not!"

"Did you get all this furniture as spoils from your last marriage?"

"Don't be silly. It's a furnished apartment."

"Oh, I see. They furnish Oriental rugs, antique desks, and . . ."

"All right. If you *have* to know, I'll tell you about those. I saw you stretching your neck when you came in here this morning. Ross Hollister likes the good things of life. He intends to keep his place in Santa del Barra after we're married, but he wants to keep this place up too. He's an expert on furniture and interior decorating, and gradually he's bringing down bits of furniture he can spare from his place in Santa del Barra.

"That rug, for instance, came in Sunday. And his snooty old housekeeper had to wire me yesterday morning asking if he'd given me an Oriental rug. As though it's any of *her* business! She comes in by the day and goes home at four-thirty. Ross takes his dinners out, but he pays her just as much as if she were there all the time. I can tell you one thing, when we're married that woman is going to go— *fast!*"

"Why did she wire *you?* Why not ask *him?*"

"Because he left Santa del Barra at six o'clock Monday to secretly lease some lands on which he has a very confidential report from a geologist. He's a whiz at . . ."

"All right," Mason interrupted. "We'll hear more about him later. Right now go get some clothes on. You're going places"

9

Mason held the door open for her and they walked down the steps together.

"I wish you'd tell me where we're——" She stopped abruptly.

"What's the matter?" Mason asked.

"That's my car!" she exclaimed.

"Where?"

"That sedan over there."

"You're certain?"

"Of course I'm not absolutely certain. It *looks* like my car."

"Just which one is it?"

"Right across the street, the one parked down next to the alley. The light brown sedan with the red wheels and the white side-walls."

"All right," Mason said, "let's go take a look and see if it's yours."

They crossed the street. Lucille walked around to the left-hand side of the car, opened the door, and said, "Good heavens, yes! This is my car *and my keys are in it.*"

"Don't you usually leave your keys in it?"

"In the garage, yes. I leave the garage door locked and my keys are in it then, but whenever it's parked on the street I *always* take the keys out."

"Didn't you use the car today?"

"No."

"How did you get to my office?"

"In Arthur's car."

"All right, what do you want to do with your car—take the keys out and leave it here, or . . . ?"

"I want to drive it right back into the garage where it belongs."

She climbed in behind the steering wheel, angrily twisted the ignition keys, and jabbed her foot on the starter.

The starter whirred, the motor caught, raced for a moment, backfired, sputtered, raced and backfired again.

"Perhaps you have your choke too far out," Mason said.

"The choke isn't out," she said.

"I'll walk around to the garage," Mason told her, "and open the doors. Do you have your garage key?"

She let the motor idle while she opened her purse, silently handed Mason a key.

Mason said, "That motor certainly doesn't sound right."

"Well, it doesn't *feel* right. I don't know whether someone's playing a joke on me or what, but—Arthur's a good mechanic. He was supposed to put new wiring on the car and—I don't know *what* he did. It was running all right, only the wiring was a little worn."

"It's probably connected wrong," Mason said. "You can drive across through the alley and up to your garage. I'll walk over and open the door. I guess you can get the car that far. Then we'll look under the hood and see what's wrong."

He walked across the street and up the alley.

Behind him, he could hear the car sputtering, banging and backfiring as Lucille Barton nursed it across the street. Then the shaft of her headlights illuminated the garage doors. Mason fitted the key to the padlock, removed the hook of the padlock from the hasp on the door, flung back the right-hand door, groped on the inside for the catch which held the garage door, then suddenly paused in mid-motion.

The beam of headlights from Lucille Barton's car illuminated the legs of a sprawled figure which was stretched out on the floor of the garage. The shadow of the door hid the rest of the man's body.

Abruptly the motor slowed and almost instantly sputtered and died.

Lucille Barton, jerking open the left-hand car door, came out from behind the wheel with one swift, leg-revealing motion. She dashed over to Mason's side. "What's that?" she demanded. "Who's in there?"

Mason said, "That seems to be a man who's either sleeping, drunk or dead. Suppose we take a look."

He found the chain catch on the inside of the door, pulled it down far enough to release the door, swung it open a few inches, then stopped as reflected light from the headlights gleamed on the sinister red pool which had welled out from the bullet hole in the man's head.

"Apparently," Mason said, "he's dead."

She took a tentative step forward, then suddenly drew back. Mason could hear the hissing intake of her breath.

"Well?" Mason asked.

"What kind of a frame-up is this?" she demanded. "What have you been doing? What kind of a deal are you trying to rig up on me?"

Mason, moving so that he could look down on the features of the dead man, said, "I think, Lucille, we'll put the question the other way. What sort of a deal have *you* been trying to frame on *me?*"

She said, "I'm beginning to see it all now—this whole business, this . . . all this stall about the gun and the car and the garage, and . . . so *that's* why you wanted to go in the garage."

Mason frowned, said nothing, but stood looking down on the body of Hartwell Pitkin who, by Lucille Barton's own admission, had been her first husband. He was now very evidently quite dead.

Lucille, looking past him, suddenly recognized the man. "Oh, my God!" she exclaimed, and flung her arms around Mason's shoulders to steady herself.

10

Mason said, "Lucille, you're going to have to notify the police."

She stood looking at him with startled, suspicious eyes.

"Now, then," Mason went on, "when you tell your story to the police, try and make a better job than you did when you told it to me."

"What do you mean?"

Mason said, "Let's look at it from the police viewpoint. The man who is lying dead on the floor of that garage stood between you and everything you wanted in life. You had a chance to marry Ross Hollister. You couldn't do it as long as Pitkin was alive. It took his death to clear the way for you to proceed with that marriage. Why beat around the bush about it?"

"Are you trying to insinuate that I'm—that I'm responsible for—for this?"

"I'm not," Mason said, "the police will."

"Oh, Mr. Mason," she said, clutching his arm, "why did this have to happen to *me?*"

"It hasn't happened to you yet," Mason told her. "It's happened to Pitkin. Now leave the car here. Come on in and telephone the police. You'd better switch off the lights on your car. Aside from that, leave everything just the way we found it. Come on now, we'll go in and telephone the police."

He took her arm, gently pulled her away from the vicinity of the body, then escorted her down the alley and up the steps of the apartment house.

"You have your key?" he asked.

"Yes."

She fitted the key into the outer door, opened it and entered the lobby.

"There's the phone booth over there," Mason said. "You have a nickel?"

"No, I don't think that . . ."

"Here's one. Call police headquarters. Tell them you want to report finding a body in your garage."

"You're going to stay with me?"

"No, I can't."

"I'll have to tell the police you were with me when we found him."

"That's right—when we found him. Now go telephone."

She walked a half a dozen steps toward the booth, then hesitated, turned, saw Mason's eyes were on her, and reluctantly walked the rest of the way to the booth.

Mason watched until she had dropped the coin and started dialing, then he hastily stepped back through the door, dashed down the short flight of steps to the street, and walked as rapidly as he could to where his own car was parked.

He drove to a drugstore, parked his car, called the unlisted telephone in his office.

"Hello," Della Street said.

"Argyle still there?" Mason asked.

"He went out to telephone and hasn't returned."

"How long ago?"

"About five minutes."

"When you got there you saw his Buick and the chauffeur waiting?"

"Yes."

"How long ago?"

"It was just after five o'clock, about an hour ago."

"How did you know it was Argyle's car?"

She laughed. "I noticed the license number. This case has made me license-number-conscious. I find myself constantly peering at numbers."

"Argyle's been there up until five minutes ago?"

"Yes. He went down and dismissed the chauffeur right after I came in, then came right back."

"How long was he gone?"

"Not over a couple of minutes. Why?"

"I can't tell you over the phone, Della. When Argyle comes back get rid of him. Tell him I won't be back any more tonight."

"But I thought you wanted to see him."

"I did, but I don't. I can't tell you details. Wait there for me."

"Okay, anything else?"

"No. That's all. Be seeing you. 'By now."

11

DELLA STREET said, "Good heavens, what's the hurry, chief. What . . ."

"Where's Argyle? Did you get rid of him?"

"I didn't have to. He went out to telephone and didn't come back. What's all the excitement about, chief?"

Mason said, "The chauffeur's name is Hartwell Pitkin. It now turns out that he was Lucille Barton's first husband. They were married some seven or eight years ago. She ran off with a man and later divorced Pitkin. Now then, apparently as soon as Argyle dismissed Pitkin and while I was out at Argyle's house, Pitkin went to the address of Lucille Barton. His body is now in her garage. He was shot in the front of the forehead. Judging from the evidence, the shooting took place right where he fell in Lucille's garage."

"And you're going to . . . represent this Lucille Barton?"

Mason grinned, "Not on your life, Della."

"That's fine," she said, relief in her voice.

"For once in my life, Della, when I talk with the police, I'm going to put the cards absolutely and squarely on the table. Lucille Barton isn't my client in any sense of the word. I advised her to tell the police the truth. *I'm* going to tell the police the truth."

"About the keys? About your search and . . . ?"

"About everything," Mason said. "Get those letters out that we received in answer to the ad in the paper. Here are the keys, Della. You can put the keys right with the letters. We'll tell the police about the call this afternoon, about the license number in the notebook, about everything. You know, Della, I *could* be in a spot on this thing and I want to get out of it."

"How soon will the police be here?"

"That depends."

"On what?"

"On how many questions they ask Lucille Barton. Let's get this stuff out and then go have some dinner. After that, we'll come back here and wait for the cops. In the meantime, I want to start Paul Drake doing some work."

"What?"

"I'll show you," he said.

Mason picked up the telephone, dialed the number of Drake's office and when he had Drake on the line, said, "All right, Paul, here's a rush job for you. I want you to find out about a Smith and Wesson .38 revolver number S65088. Find out when it was sold, who bought it, and everything you can about it. I also want you to find out something about Argyle's chauffeur. A man by the name of Hartwell Pitkin."

"Why the gun?" Drake asked.

Mason grinned into the telephone and said, "Because, sweetheart, it looks as if someone had tried to get Perry Mason all tangled up in something."

"And you don't want to get tangled?"

"I not only don't want to get tangled," Mason said, "but I don't intend to get tangled. I like to pick my cases rather than have them thrust upon me. Get the information and relay it to me just as soon as you can. Della and I are going out to dinner. When we return we'll probably have a date with the police."

"Want to tell me about it?" Drake asked.

"No. It's better for you to remain entirely innocent."

He hung up the telephone, said to Della Street, "Come on, Della, we're going out and eat. At least we won't be facing the police on an empty stomach."

"And for once," Della Street said, relief in her voice, "we can face them with a clear conscience."

"Oh, that's a cinch," Mason said. "Our conscience is *always* clear. Sometimes our motives are a little obscure and at times I have to hold out something."

"Yes. Quite a lot," Della Street observed. "Where do we eat?"

"Some place not too near here," Mason said. "Some place where the police won't find us in the middle of the meal and make us leave a half-finished filet mignon."

They walked down the corridor, passed Paul Drake's lighted office, took the elevator to the street and Mason hailed a taxi.

"We'll leave my car in the parking lot," he explained, "then the police will know we intend to be back. That will save them wasting a lot of time and energy."

They went to a quiet restaurant more than a dozen blocks from the office, a place where there were curtained booths, an atmosphere of quiet seclusion, and good food.

More than an hour later, Mason finished his last cup of coffee, said to Della Street, "Well, how about it? Do you feel up to facing the police?"

"I feel up to facing anything."

"Okay, let's go."

They found a taxi, returned to the office building, and Mason said casually to the night operator of the elevator as they were whisked up to his floor, "Anybody looking for me, Sam?"

"No, sir, not a soul," Sam said.

Mason exchanged swift glances with Della Street, said, "I guess we'll take a look in Paul Drake's office, Della"

They found Paul Drake sitting in the little cubbyhole which was his private office, a desk littered with telephones in front of him.

"How are you coming, Paul?" Mason asked.

"Okay," Drake said. "I found out the dope on that gun for you. It was sold to a jobber here in the city and by the jobber sold to a dealer out in the mountains about a hundred and thirty miles. The Rushing Creek Mercantile Company."

"To whom did the Mercantile Company sell it?" Mason asked.

"Don't know. It's a little place up there, and they fold up the sidewalks. I can't get any action on the phone."

Mason said, "Hang it, I need that information. Rushing Creek? That's a little resort and lumbering village, isn't it?"

"That's right. Quite a few trout fishermen go up there. It's also the gateway to some nice picnic and camping grounds back in the mountains."

"Well," Mason said, "keep after them. See if you can find out anything. You haven't heard anything more about Argyle—or that chauffeur of his?"

"Argyle's house is dark," Drake said. "I have a couple of men on the job. I'm working on the chauffeur's background."

Mason said, "Okay, stay with it, Paul. Let me know as soon as you find out anything."

He walked down to his office with Della Street, said, "Gosh, Della, the police must be *really* giving her a third-degree."

"Would she tell them about you?"

"I told her to."

"Do you think she did?"

"She had to. I was with her when she discovered the body."

Mason unlocked the door of his office, switched on the lights, sat down at his desk, started drumming with his fingertips . . . "I'll tell you what, Della. *You* wait here. Hold the fort. I'll take a quick run out to the hospital and tell Bob Finchley that we're coming along all right. You stay right here and if the police come, tell them you're waiting for me, that I'm out working on a personal injury case. And you can pave the way for a series of very pleasant relations with the police by showing them the ad we put in the *Blade*, telling them about the accident case, and showing them the letters we've received, and then giving them the keys."

"And tell them about Argyle?"

"Sure, the whole thing."

"Okay," she said, "I'll wait here and do my stuff with the police. Will it be the men from Homicide?"

"That's right, Homicide—probably Lieutenant Tragg."

"I like him."

"Don't make any mistake about him," Mason said. "He's smart."

"What difference does it make, if we're going to tell him everything we know?"

"I guess it won't make any," Mason said, grinning. "It's simply that I'm not accustomed to all of this law-abiding frankness. They'll be as puzzled as I am. They'll feel we're holding out something and have a nervous breakdown trying to find out what it is . . . Okay, Della, I'm on my way."

12

MASON walked down the linoleum-covered hallway of the hospital.

Nurses had begun to quiet the patients down for the evening. The lights were dim and the hospital quiet was broken only by the occasional rustle of starched uniforms as nurses on rubber-soled shoes moved swiftly and efficiently about their business.

Mason, feeling embarrassingly healthy, tiptoed awkwardly down the corridor.

The supervising nurse frowned at him, said, "No visitors after . . . " then, recognizing him, smiled and said, "I think your patient is feeling very *very* fine this evening, Mr. Mason."

"How come?" Mason asked.

"This afternoon he was worrying about the hospital bills, wondering how he was ever going to pay them, and . . ."

"I told him I'd take care of all those," Mason said.

"I know, but he didn't want you to do that, Mr. Mason. You've been terribly good to him, and of course he didn't have the faintest idea of who'd hit him. Those hit-and-run cases are really terrible things."

"And what happened to make him feel good this evening?" Mason asked.

She smiled. "The man who hit him came up and acknowledged the fault and was just ready to do anything on earth."

"Man by the name of Caffee?" Mason asked, frowning.

"I don't know what his name was."

"A man with thin features, gray hair, a gray double-breasted suit, about fifty-five or fifty-six . . ."

"That's the one," she said.

"Humph," Mason grunted. "I hope he didn't slip anything over on Bob Finchley. I'd warned that boy not to make any . . . oh well, let's go take a look."

The lawyer forgot to tiptoe. His heels were pounding belligerently on the corridor as he pushed open the door of Room 309. Bob Finchley, lying flat, with an elaborate system of pulleys holding his leg and hip in position, looked up, saw Mason, and a big grin engulfed his features.

"Hello, counselor."

"Hello, Bob. How's it coming?"

"Fine, Mr. Mason. Gosh, we're all out of the woods! You know what happened?"

"What?"

"The man that hit me came in. He's really a swell guy. He had a young fellow with him from the insurance company, a chap about my age, who was really swell."

Mason said, "You should have called me."

"Gosh, I tried to, Mr. Mason, but your office was closed."

Mason frowned. "All right, Bob. What happened?"

"Well, this man told me that there was no need of my going to court. He wanted to know what I thought it was going to cost me for doctors and hospital bills and then the man from the insurance company said they felt pretty bad about it and—do you know what they did, Mr. Mason?"

Mason drew up a chair. "Look here, Bob. Did you sign anything?"

"Why, sure. I had to in order to get the settlement."

Mason's face darkened. "You mean you sold me out, Bob? You settled without me?"

"No, no, Mr. Mason, I fixed it so everything was all right for you. They really paid off."

"What happened?"

"The insurance adjuster said that he'd pay me five thousand dollars; that they'd pay all of my hospital bills, all of my doctor's bills, and that they'd agree to pay you a reasonable sum as an attorney's fee."

"A *reasonable* sum," Mason said.

"That's what they agreed."

"Of course," Mason said, "my idea of what's reasonable and their idea of what's reasonable might be very far apart under the circumstances."

"And in addition to that," Bob said, "the man gave me his personal check for a thousand dollars over and above what the insurance company would pay."

"A man by the name of Caffee?" Mason asked.

Bob's face showed surprise. "No, not Caffee—Stephen Argyle."

"What!" Mason exclaimed.

"That's right."

Mason said, "Begin at the beginning. Tell me the whole thing. Make it quick, Bob. Get it out just as fast as you can. Did they give you a copy of the document you signed?"

"Yes, sir."

"Let me see it," Mason said.

Mason glanced through the document. A slow grin came over his features. "All right, Bob. Now tell me what happened."

"Well, they came in here about an hour and a half ago, Mr. Mason. It seems that Mr. Argyle was very very much upset. He said he couldn't talk about the accident, because the insurance company wouldn't let him, but he was just terribly sorry about everything. He was a nice guy."

"Go ahead," Mason said.

"Mr. Argyle is really trying to do the right thing, Mr. Mason. He told me he'd been waiting at your office for you to come in because he wanted to have you with him when he talked with me. He said your office was closed but your confidential secretary was there and that she wasn't certain you'd be back any more this evening.

"He tried to call you from the hospital here two or three times but there was no answer."

Mason frowned. "We don't answer the phone after the office closes. I have an unlisted phone in my private office. I had no idea of what Argyle wanted. I was out on another case."

"Gee, Mr. Mason, I hope I didn't do anything wrong."

Mason shook his head and smiled. "On the contrary, Bob, you did just right."

"Gosh, I'm glad of that! The way you acted at first . . . well, I wasn't sure."

Mason pocketed the signed copy of the release, said, "Usually whenever anything like this happens, we tell the client not to make any independent settlement, because the lawyer can make a better settlement than the client can ever hope to. But this time, because we didn't know who had hit you, and it didn't look as though there'd ever be much chance of finding out, I neglected to give you the usual warnings. How's your head? Hurting much?"

"No, it's feeling swell. . . . Gosh Mr. Mason, I hope I didn't . . . hope I didn't . . ."

"Not a bit," Mason said, grinning. "That signed receipt you have releases Stephen Argyle for any and all claims you may have against him for his own acts and/or those of his agents from the beginning of the world to date."

"Well, isn't that receipt all right?"

"Sure, it's all right," Mason said, "but now remember, Bob, don't sign anything else. No matter who comes to you with anything, or what offer is made to you, don't sign anything. Understand?"

"Why, yes, sir."

"Now the insurance company gave you a check, and Argyle gave you a check?"

"Yes, sir. That's right."

"And what about your mother?"

"They're going to see her. They had me telephone her. They asked me if I thought a thousand dollars would cover the effect of her shock. . . . I knew Mom would be tickled to death with that settlement, but I looked thoughtful, and then Mr. Argyle said, 'And I'll raise that another five hundred dollars by my personal check.' So I guess they're making a settlement with Mom."

Mason said, "That's fine, Bob. Now I want you to endorse those checks and give them to me. I'm going to see that they're deposited to you first thing in the morning. You have an account?"

"Just a small one. Just a few dollars that I'd been saving up for my next year in college, in the Farmers and Mechanics National."

"All right," Mason said. "Write on the back of those checks 'Endorsed for deposit to my account,' then sign your name on them, give them to me, and I'll have my secretary take them down and deposit them to your account first thing in the morning."

"Gee, Mr. Mason, that'll be swell! Tell me, honestly, did I do wrong in making this settlement?"

"Under the circumstances," Mason said, "you did all right, but don't do it again. If anybody comes with anything for you to sign, no matter what it is, just tell them you're not signing a thing. Can you do that?"

"Yes, sir. I think so."

Mason took out his fountain pen. "All right now, endorse those checks. Be sure to endorse them only for deposit so that in that way nothing can be done with them except to put them to your account."

"Well, Mr. Mason, how about your fee? Are they going to . . ."

"You're damm right they are," Mason said, handing him the fountain pen. "They usually think they're pulling a fast one when they tell an injured party they'll pay a 'reasonable' attorney's fee. They offer the lawyer some absurdly small amount and then point out he'll have to sue to get any more. By the time they get done they whittle the thing down until . . ."

"Gosh, Mr. Mason," Finchley exclaimed in dismay, "they aren't going to do that to you, are they?"

"No," Mason said, smiling, "they aren't going to do that to me. You see, Bob, the insurance people were so afraid they'd admit liability that they made these releases read that they still denied their policy holder had actually inflicted the injury, but were making a settlement just to avoid litigation."

"Well, isn't that all right?" Finchley asked.

"Sure, it's all right," Mason grinned, "particularly because their policy holder really *didn't* inflict the injury. Tomorrow we'll make another settlement with the man who *really* hit you. And in the meantime we'll deposit these checks.

"And *that* should teach the insurance company not to sneak around behind a lawyer's back.

"Now you go to sleep, Bob."

And Mason gently closed the door to the patient's room.

13

WHISTLING a tune, his hat pushed jauntily to the back of his head, Mason opened the door of his office and found Della Street pounding away at her typewriter.

"For heaven's sake," Mason exclaimed, "you do enough work during office hours. When I leave you here like this at night to keep an eye on things, don't try to ruin your nervous system by pounding away at that typewriter."

"This was some stuff that's important, and . . ."

"And your health is important too," Mason said. "This job isn't particularly easy on the nerves. What happened to the police, Della?"

"I don't know. I haven't heard a peep out of them."

Mason frowned. "*That's* something I can't understand. They should have been here hours ago."

"You didn't hear anything?"

"No, I've been out at the hospital."

"How's Bob Finchley?"

Mason grinned and perched himself on the edge of his desk. "Now there, Della," he said, "we have the bright spot of my entire legal career."

"Tell me about it."

Mason said, "The better class of insurance companies are always willing to deal with a lawyer, but there's a certain type of adjuster who loves to cut a lawyer's throat."

Della Street nodded.

"Obviously," Mason went on, "they figure they can settle with a client a lot cheaper than they can with a lawyer, and if they can get the client to make a settlement by assuring him that they'll agree to pay his lawyer 'a reasonable fee' the client thinks that's all there is to it. He doesn't realize that the insurance company will then offer the lawyer a nominal fee and tell him to file suit if he wants to get any more.

"That puts the lawyer in the position of having to throw in a lawsuit in order to get what's really coming to him and even then a jury is usually inclined to look at the thing from a layman's viewpoint, so he takes the offer and grits his teeth.

"A lawyer has a lot of overhead. He has to keep his office running and when he handles a personal injury case, he has to get a pretty good fee from the ones he wins in order to compensate for all of the time, energy and money spent in connection with the ones he loses."

"Are *you* trying to tell *me* the financial problems of running a law office?" Della demanded. "If you could see the bookkeeping headaches I have with five people on your payroll   "

Mason grinned. "No, Della, I'm simply feeling so darned good that I have to begin from scratch."

"Well, then," she told him, smiling, "by all means proceed from scratch." She pushed her chair back and came over to sit on the desk beside Mason. "All right, what happened?"

"The long arm of coincidence is playing right into our hands, Della."

"How come?"

"Evidently Argyle's chauffeur must have had the car out on the third and hit someone. He went to Argyle and without telling him any details let Argyle know he was in a mess. So Argyle decided to be smart, took the car out, parked it in front of a fireplug and then went to the club and reported it as being stolen. And to make his story stand up, bribed the doorman to say he hadn't been out all afternoon."

Della frowned. "Then Argyle's chauffeur was the one who was driving the car that hit . ."

Mason grinned. "Don't be silly. It was Daniel Caffee, but Argyle *thought* his chauffeur was guilty."

"So what happened?"

Mason said gleefully, "I can see by the twinkle in your eye that you know what happened, but you don't want to rob me of the pleasure of telling you about it. And believe me this is a *real* pleasure."

"Go ahead," she said, smiling, "tell me all the sordid details."

"Well," Mason said, "Argyle evidently got in touch with his insurance carrier and some young adjuster came out. This young adjuster was full of vim, vigor and vitality, and anxious to make a record with the main office. So he put the idea in Argyle's head. They consulted records of traffic accidents, found out the name and address of the victim, learned what hospital he was in, and went out there."

"When did they do all this?"

"Apparently," Mason said, "we can make a pretty good pattern. Almost immediately after I talked with Argyle he jumped in his car and came up to my office. He was waiting here for me when you arrived. Then he went down and dismissed his chauffeur. His chauffeur proceeded to go out and get himself murdered, and . . ."

"Yes," Della Street prompted, as Mason came to a frowning stop.

"Damn it," Mason said, "I'm so tickled about that insurance business that I'm letting my mind get away from the murder."

She placed her hand on his, gave a firm, steady pressure. "Go on, chief. The murder doesn't mean anything to *us*, but this insurance business does."

Mason pushed back his chair. "It's beginning to worry me. Why the deuce do you suppose the police haven't been in touch with me?"

"I can't guess."

"Well," Mason said, getting to his feet. "We're going to find out. We'll just drive casually down South Gondola Avenue and see how much excitement is going on, how many police cars are parked there, and so forth. If the police cars are still there, we'll know they're grilling Lucille Barton in her apartment. If the police cars have gone, we'll find a crowd of curious people still standing around in doorways, and we can get out and walk around and pick up enough from bits of conversation to know what happened."

"Let's go," Della Street said.

Mason held her coat for her. She put on her hat in front of the mirror, and Mason, putting on hat and topcoat, switched off the office lights.

Mason stopped in Drake's office long enough to say, "Okay, Paul, we're leaving now. You haven't found out anything new?"

"Yes, I have, Perry."

"What?"

"I have a hunch your friend, the chauffeur, Hartwell L. Pitkin, is a blackmailer."

"The devil!"

"Nothing a hundred per cent definite at this time," Drake said, "but one of my men has uncovered an associate of Pitkin's, a friend who is a little more than a casual friend, and that chap intimated that Pitkin is making money from some source, that it's cash money, that it comes in in large quantities and that Pitkin doesn't need to hold his job as chauffeur unless he wants to, that he's only holding that job as sort of a blind to divert suspicion from himself."

Mason gave a low whistle.

"So," Drake said, "my operative put the screws on this chap and found out as much as the fellow knew, which wasn't a great deal, but it indicates Pitkin may be shaking someone down."

Mason exchanged significant glances with Della Street. "A woman?" he asked.

"I wouldn't know," Drake said. "If it's a woman, she must be someone who has a reasonable amount of money, because Pitkin seems to be pretty well heeled with cash—that is, no really *big* money, but he can always pull out a roll with two or three hundred dollars in it."

Mason said, "Well, keep on working, Paul, but don't lose any sleep over it. If you've got your men out, let them do the work."

"I'm about ready to knock off," Drake said. "Getting a bunch of men out on an investigation is a job. What about Argyle? Do you want me to keep on him?"

"No," Mason said. "I've changed my mind about Argyle. You can take your men off the house and let Argyle do whatever he wants. I'll drop in and see him sometime within the next two or three days, and after he recovers from my visit, he'll know he's had a shock."

"You certainly seem to be sitting on a cloud," Drake said.

"I'm sitting on a cloud and the cloud's right on top of the world," Mason grinned. "You might find out something about Pitkin—anything you can—hell, Paul, there must be *something* . . . oh well, never mind. Want to hear what happened?"

Drake said hurriedly, "Don't tell me. I don't want to know."

"Well," Mason said, "call your men off Argyle. He isn't important any more. I'd like to find out a little more about Pitkin, and in the morning you can find out about that gun. I wish you could have found out about it tonight."

"I think I can get something on that," Drake said. "I have a man who does work for me who lives in Santa del Barra. It's about eighty miles from there to Rushing Creek and I got hold of this chap and told him to go up to Rushing Creek and see if he couldn't get hold of the proprietor of the Rushing Creek Mercantile Company. It's probably a one-man concern."

"Okay," Mason said. "Let me know if you hear anything. Come on, Della. I'll take you home. Don't lose any sleep, Paul. It's not that important."

"Okay," Drake said. "I'll keep in touch with the office by telephone and let you know if I get anything."

"Don't call me if it's later than an hour from now," Mason said. "I'm going to roll in. Good night, Paul."

"Good night."

Mason escorted Della out of the office, down to his waiting automobile, said, "Well, let's just drive by the neighborhood and see what's doing, Della."

"You want me to drive?"

"No, I'll drive."

Mason slid in behind the wheel of the automobile, nodded to the parking station attendant, gunned the car, and rolled out of the parking station to the street. He piloted the car with deft skill through the late traffic and swung into South Gondola Avenue.

Mason said, "Okay, Della, keep your eyes open. I'll drive slowly. You see how many police cars you can spot."

"Which place is the apartment house?"

"The one at 719. It's in the middle of the next block on the left-hand side, and . . ."

"Oh, yes, I have it spotted now."

"Quite a few cars around there," Mason said.

He drove slowly across the intersection.

Della said, "They seem to be private cars. I don't notice any police cars. Would they have red spotlights on them?"

"That's right, and long radio antennas. Gosh, Della, I don't see a one."

"Well, they've probably taken Lucille down to Headquarters for questioning and . . ."

"But the neighborhood would hardly have quieted down this soon," Mason said. "I'm going to drive very slowly. As I pass the entrance to the alley we'll take a good look at the garage and see what's around there."

Mason slowed the car almost to a stop.

They looked up the alley. The row of garages was dark and silent, illuminated only by such light as filtered in from the street lamps.

"Hey, wait a minute," Mason said, "something's wrong."

"What?" Della Street asked.

Mason braked his car to an abrupt stop. "Sit over behind the steering wheel, Della," he said. "Here, give me the flashlight out of that glove compartment. No, wait a minute. I'm going to drive in there. I think we can drive in and then back and turn around."

"Chief, what's wrong? What do you think . . ."

"I don't know," Mason said. "There's something fishy about the whole business."

"If there is, hadn't you better keep out and . . ."

"I have to find out what it is," Mason said.

He looked back to make certain the road was clear, backed a few feet, then turned the car so it was headed toward the garages, and slowly entered the alleyway.

He drove to the garage bearing the figures 208, said, "Okay, Della, you sit here. Give me that flashlight."

Mason took the flashlight, jumped out of the car, approached the garage, saw that the doors were closed but unlocked. Mason eased the right-hand door back a few inches, and flashed the beam of the light into the interior of the garage.

Abruptly, he ran back to the car, jumped in, threw the flashlight over on the back seat, backed the car swiftly, and turned it around.

"What's the matter?" Della Street asked.

"Everything," Mason said grimly. "We're hooked!"

14

DELLA STREET said nothing until Mason had gained the street once more, turned the car sharply to the right, and urged the motor into speed.

"What is it?" Della Street asked.

"That little devil!" Mason said. "That double-crossing little devil!"

"You mean she didn't report to the police?"

"She didn't report to the police," Mason said. "The body is lying in there on the floor just as I saw it, only *now*, there's a nice shiny gun lying right beside his right hand."

"So it will look like suicide?"

"So it will look like suicide."

"Well?" Della Street asked.

Mason said, "I've got to find a place where I can park this car and do a little thinking, Della."

"Can't we just forget about the whole thing?"

"That's what I'm trying to figure. Let's . . . here's a parking place. Let's stop here for a minute."

Mason eased the car into the parking place and switched off the motor and the headlights.

They sat for a while in silence.

"After all," Della Street said, after two or three minutes, "no one *knows* that you were there except Lucille Barton, and *she* certainly can't talk."

Mason said thoughtfully, "Someone is masterminding this thing. Someone has talked her into playing smart."

"Well, *you* told her what to do."

"I told her what to do," Mason said, "but remember I also have a responsibility. I saw the body. And when I saw the body there was no gun near it."

They were silent for another few minutes, then Mason said suddenly, "Start asking me questions, Della."

"What about?"

"About this darned case. Let's try and clarify it."

"Well," Della Street said, "suppose you *don't* tell the police? Then what will happen?"

"Then," Mason said, "the police will find the body—that is, *someone* will find the body and report it to the police."

"Who?"

"Probably Lucille Barton."

"I don't get you."

"She'll come driving home with some witness, probably her girl friend, Anita Jordon."

"Why not the boy friend?"

"Because she's engaged, and if she's going to get her name in the papers she wants it to appear she spent the evening with a girl friend."

"I see. Go on. Then what?"

"Then," Mason said, "Lucille Barton will hand Anita the key to the padlock and ask her to open the garage. Anita will find the doors unlocked, the padlock missing. She'll open the doors, the headlights from the automobile will illuminate the interior, Anita will scream, Lucille will scream, they'll have mutual hysterics, notify the police, and put on an act for the benefit of spectators and officers."

"Can they get away with it?"

"I don't know," Mason said. "It depends on how good a job they've done."

"You mean Anita and Lucille?"

"No, Lucille and whatever person was acting as mastermind— probably Arthur Colson."

"You want me to ask questions about him?"

"About anything. Just throw questions at me."

"Won't the police ask her if she knows this dead man?"

Mason thought that over. "Yes. And she'll have to admit that she does. She'll have to admit that he was her ex-husband. Then police will want to know why he picked her garage as a place in which to commit suicide. They'll immediately become suspicious about whether the death is or is not a suicide, and . . . Then, of course, later on they'll fire a test bullet through the gun and compare it with the fatal bullet—if they can find the fatal bullet. Then they'll know the gun in the garage was a planted gun. That won't look good."

"All right," Della Street said. "Now, I'll take the opposite approach. Suppose you *do* tell the police."

"Then," Mason said, "I'm in a jam."

"Why?"

"Because I told Lucille to report it, but I didn't stick around long enough to make sure that she followed my instructions."

"Are you responsible for her?"

"No," Mason said, "but I'm an attorney. I'm an officer of the court. I know I'm supposed to report any bodies I find. I found one and simply told Lucille to report it."

"And what will Lucille say?"

"That's the hell of it," Mason said. "Lucille will have to insist that we didn't find any body, and that I'm now trying to protect some client by making her the fall guy."

"Will the police believe her?"

"If they do I'm in a jam. If they don't they'll raise hell with me because I didn't make certain the body was reported, and because I didn't check later when police didn't contact me."

"Well, why didn't you?"

"Because," Mason said, "of that damned insurance business. I was so tickled with what had happened and the way Argyle had slipped one over on himself that I didn't pay enough attention to the fact police hadn't called on us. Hang it, Della, if I'd had my wits about me I'd have known what must have happened. Well, the logical thing to do, the only thing I can do as a law-abiding citizen and as an officer of the court, is to report to the police."

"Well, why don't you do it then?"

"Because," Mason said, "the police are laying for me. They wouldn't want anything better than an opportunity to trip me up, and I have a feeling I'm fighting someone who is in a position to trip me up if I do make such a report."

"I'm running out of questions, chief," Della Street said.

"I've already run out of answers, Della."

They sat for a while in silence, then Mason started the car.

"Well?" Della asked.

"I'm hooked," Mason said. "I have the answer now."

"What is it?"

"Whoever is directing this thing is smart. There's only one way I can save myself."

"What's that?"

"We've got a client."

"Who?"

"Lucille Barton."

"I don't get it."

Mason said, "As her attorney anything she said to me would be privileged. They can't ask her about it and they can't ask me about it."

"What about what you *saw?*"

"If she tells the police about it she'll be acting on my advice. If she doesn't, there's no way of proving I was there."

"I don't like it," Della Street said.

"*Like* it!" Mason exclaimed, "I *hate* it, but I'm hooked with a client, Della. Show on the books I'm representing her on a question of alimony with her last husband, one Willard Barton.

"And now, I'm going to drive you home."

15

PAUL DRAKE was waiting in Mason's office the next morning when Mason came in.

Della Street flashed Mason a warning glance and took his overcoat and hat.

Paul Drake studiously avoided Mason's eyes, said, "I've been trying to call you, Perry. Della thought you might be in early this morning so I decided to wait. It's about this man, Hartwell L. Pitkin, you wanted me to look up."

"Oh, yes," Mason said. "I saw the papers this morning. Seems he committed suicide in the garage of Lucille Barton's apartment house."

"That's what the papers said, Perry."

"Strange coincidence, isn't it, Paul."

"Certainly is. She'd been married to him years ago."

"To Argyle's chauffeur, Paul? Good heavens, you mean that . . ."

"That's right," Drake interposed, still refusing to meet Mason's eyes.

"What other details do you have, Paul?"

Drake said, "Sometimes, Perry, you get so damn smart that you have us all running around in circles and meeting ourselves coming back."

"I don't get it," Mason said.

"There are lots of goofy things about the case. The police received a report from Lucille Barton. She was hysterical. She'd opened the garage door to put her car away for the night and found the body. She had a girl friend who was going to spend the night with her. They didn't touch anything but left the car right there with the motor running and beat it to the telephone in the apartment house. They notified the police."

"I see," Mason said.

"Hartwell L. Pitkin had been shot with a .38 caliber revolver," Drake went on, methodically. "The gun was found by his right hand."

"So I saw in the paper, Paul. No question but what it's suicide?"

"The police are investigating."

"What do they think?"

"They aren't taking me into their confidence."

"No, I suppose not."

"Now then," Drake said, "I have some other information for you."

"What?"

"That gun you wanted to know about, the Smith and Wesson .38 number S65088."

"Oh yes, what about it, Paul?"

"Well, that gun was sold, just as I told you, to a jobber who in turn sold it to the Rushing Creek Mercantile Company.

"A chap by the name of Roscoe R. Hansom is the proprietor of the Rushing Creek Mercantile Company. The revolver was sold about a month ago to a man who signed the gun register as Ross P. Hollister."

Mason said, "That's interesting."

"You don't know the half of it," Drake went on.

"No?" Mason asked, settling himself back in his swivel chair. "What's the other half, Paul?"

Drake said, "I got that information last night. You remember you were in a hurry, and I had a man from Santa del Barra drive up to Rushing Creek. He managed to get Hansom out of bed and talked him into going down to the store and looking at the records. Of course you were in a hurry to get the information, and—well, that's the way it is. When you want things in a hurry, you want them."

"Right you are," Mason said, grinning. "No use dilly-dallying around. So you got the information. Thanks a lot, Paul. That's good work."

"And," Drake went on, "naturally the fact that we were in such a hurry for the information impressed Mr. Hansom."

"Well, naturally," Mason said. "However, I fail to see what connection *that* has with the matter. If he wants to live out in the country and go to bed with the cows and chickens he'll have to realize that *we* can't gear *ourselves* to *his* schedule."

"Oh, sure, sure," Drake said, "but I just thought you should know."

"Why, Paul?"

"Because," Drake said, "when the body of Hartwell L. Pitkin was found, the gun with which he had either shot himself, or had been shot, was lying by his right hand. Someone who had a nice little emery wheel had ground every number off the gun, the number on the tang, the number on the inside of the cylinder mechanism, the numbers that are on the little concealed places, everywhere."

"Well, well," Mason said, his voice showing relief. "Then they couldn't trace the gun, Paul?"

Drake kept his eyes averted. "But the guy who had filed off the numbers didn't know too much about guns. On that model of gun, the Smith and Wesson, the number of the gun is also stamped on the inside of the wooden grip. You have to take a screw driver and remove one of the wooden grips to see it."

"Go on," Mason said.

"The police did that. They found the number. It was S65088.

"Of course, the police got busy and started tracing the number. When they got Roscoe Hansom out of bed for the second time to find out about the sale of the gun, naturally Hansom wanted to know if it had become a habit, and . . ."

"The devil!" Mason said, straightening himself abruptly in his swivel chair, and frowning.

"Exactly," Drake said. "Of course, Hansom didn't know the name of my operative from Santa del Barra, but he has a pretty good description and putting two and two together, the police are apt to make four at any moment. When they do, you're going to have some explaining to do.

"Now, then," Drake went on, still avoiding Mason's eyes, "there are two or three other things you should know about."

"Okay, Paul," Mason said, his voice sharp with anxiety, "let's hear them. Spill em fast. I may have to start moving."

Drake said, "Naturally, police wondered why no one had heard the sound of the shot. Quite evidently the shot had been fired there in the garage. The nature and extent of the hemorrhage shows the man dropped almost immediately when the shot entered his brain."

"Go ahead, Paul."

"They made inquiry around and found that one of the automobiles was doing a lot of skipping, backfiring, and banging. It caused some annoyance on the part of the occupant of the building across the alley. He looked out of the window. It was beginning to get dark, but he saw a man and a woman standing in front of the garage at 208. The man was a tall, distinguished-looking gentleman with a light topcoat. The woman was wearing a plaid coat, had a dark hat. They were opening the door of the garage. They had some conversation and then the motor was shut off and they walked away and left the car there. The car had been making a terrific noise from a series of backfires, and police think the shot must have been fired at about that time. If that's true, of course, that would make it murder. A man would hardly have committed suicide in the presence of two witnesses; and if he had, and the witnesses didn't report it—well, you can see the police reasoning."

"Go ahead," Mason said.

"Now then," Drake went on, "when the police answered Lucille Barton's call, they found she was wearing a plaid coat and a black hat. On the strength of those garments, the witness now makes an identification of Lucille Barton as being the woman he saw. Lucille denies that she was anywhere near the garage at that time."

"What time?"

"Somewhere around six o'clock. The witness isn't positive as to the time."

"What about the man?" Mason asked.

Drake said, "So far, they have only a general description of the man, but when police fingerprinted the gun they found a print on the inside of the gun where someone had probably been holding it while he tried to remove the numbers, or it *could* have been in ejecting shells. They think it's the print of a man's right index finger. It's a pretty good print."

"I see," Mason said.

Drake said, "By pulling a lot of wires with the newspaper boys I was able to get a photographic copy of that print."

He reached in his pocket, pulled out a wallet, took out a small photograph of a fingerprint, handed it to Mason, and said, "That's enlarged about three times, Perry."

"Any other fingerprints?"

"No. The outside of the gun had been wiped clean of fingerprints, but apparently the person who had been handling it forgot to remove the fingerprint on the inside."

"I see. Anything else?"

"Some other stuff," Drake said, "but I don't know what it is. The police are suspicious about the whole setup. They're particularly suspicious about Lucille Barton. She was out with a girl friend named Anita Jordon. Anita knows Lucille, and she knew Hartwell Pitkin. She gives Lucille an alibi, but for some reason she isn't too happy about it. Police have an idea she's going to weaken on her alibi before they get done with her."

"A lot of commotion," Mason said, "over the mere finding of a body under circumstances which would indicate suicide."

"The trouble is," Drake said, "that when they went through the pockets they found around five thousand dollars in nice crisp currency. There was a package of hundred-dollar bills which still had the sticker from the bank wrapped around them, and the initials of a cashier. The police traced that money and found it had been drawn out a few days ago by a Mr. Dudley Gates. Dudley Gates is a business associate of the Stephen Argyle who employed Pitkin as his chauffeur. He's also a friend of this Ross P. Hollister, who seems to have bought the gun and then gone out on a business trip and neglected to communicate with any of his friends telling them where he'd be. Dudley Gates apparently accompanied Hollister."

Mason pinched out his cigarette, drummed nervously on the edge of the desk.

"That's probably all right, Paul. I happen to know something about Ross Hollister. He's a sharpshooter who handles oil leases and investments of that sort. He's on a business trip and he'll communicate with his friends by mail. His girl friend doesn't have a telephone so he usually drops her a line as soon as he gets located, or sends her a telegram and lets her know where he is."

Drake said, "Well, I got a little stuff on Hollister. He lives at Santa del Barra, divorced, decree not final for a couple of months yet. Has a nice place there, a housekeeper comes in by the day. She comes early to get breakfast, goes home at four-thirty. Hollister was there Monday when she left at four-thirty, but was expecting to leave at six that night. She hasn't seen him since. His business trips usually take about ten days. She never hears from him while he's gone. That oil lease business is secretive."

"And Dudley Gates is with Hollister?"

"That's right. Argyle, Gates and Hollister are partners of a sort. Hollister is the big shot. The other two guys are yes men."

"It's all tied in with that damn apartment of Lucille Barton's," Mason said.

Drake said, "Well, that's the general situation. Of course, finding all that money on a corpse is bound to attract attention, and naturally police are going to wonder about the cash transaction between Dudley Gates and Hartwell Pitkin."

"And police are interviewing Stephen Argyle?"

"Yes, they got Argyle up out of bed early this morning and started talking with him. Argyle says the last time he saw his chauffeur was out here in front of your office. He says he had driven to your office to see you and left his car outside. Then when he realized you weren't in the office, and weren't apt to come in within the next few minutes, he went down and told the chauffeur to take the car and drive it back to the house, put it in the garage, and then Pitkin could have the night off."

"Well?" Mason asked.

"Apparently Pitkin did just that. He must have driven the car out to the house and put it in the garage. It was there this morning when Argyle went out to look for it after the police had got him out of bed. By the police time schedule that would have put Pitkin back in Lucille's garage at just about the time the witness heard the car doing all the backfiring. The man must have been talked into entering that garage—and he was killed as soon as he walked in."

Drake got up out of the chair. "Keep that photograph of the fingerprint if you want, Perry. I'll let you know about new developments."

"Thanks, Paul."

Drake said, "So long, Della."

"So long, Paul."

The detective left the office. Mason glanced at Della Street, said, "Hand me that ink pad from the rubber stamp outfit, will you, Della?"

She wordlessly placed it on the desk. Mason pressed his right index finger on the pad, then on a blank sheet of paper.

Della Street came to look over his shoulder and compare his fingerprint with the photograph of the fingerprint police had found on the gun which had been responsible for the death of Hartwell Pitkin.

"Good Lord, chief," Della Street gasped, her fingers digging into his arm.

"Take it easy, Della," Mason said. He pushed back his chair,

walked over to the washstand, carefully soaped his hands, and removed all traces of the ink. "And I thought the guy who was masterminding this business was crude!"

Della Street picked up the inked impression of Mason's fingerprint, struck a match, burned the paper, and then crumpled the
ashes in the ash tray.

"Where does all this leave *you*, chief?" she asked.

"Right behind the eight ball," Mason told her thoughtfully. "But
that doesn't mean I have to *stay* there."

16

MASON had just finished drying his hands when Gertie, the receptionist, announced that Daniel Caffee and the representative of his insurance company, Frank P. Ingle, were waiting to see Mason.

Mason hesitated, then said to Della Street, "Have Gertie show them in, Della."

Frank P. Ingle, a grizzled, gray-eyed, shrewd individual, shook hands with Mason, turned to Caffee and said, "If you don't mind, Mr. Caffee, I'll do the talking."

"Not at all," Caffee said.

"I take it you're willing to talk this over, Mr. Mason," Ingle said, seating himself and smiling cordially.

"Certainly. Go ahead and talk."

"Perhaps you'd better *start* the talk, Mr. Mason."

Mason said, "Money talks, gentlemen."

"I know, I know," Ingle said hastily, "but the question is, Mr. Mason, how are we going to work out any standard for . . ."

Mason interrupted. "This boy's been seriously injured. I want three thousand dollars for doctors and medical expenses; I want five thousand dollars' compensation; I want two thousand dollars' attorney's fees; that ten thousand dollars in the boy's case. I want two thousand dollars for the mother, fifteen hundred for a new car, and one thousand dollars' attorney's fees; that's a total of fourteen thousand five hundred dollars. I have Caffee's check for ten thousand. The insurance carrier can give me its check for the balance."

Ingle smiled. "Well, of course, Mr. Mason, one can understand that you *want* these things, but we, of course, have a duty to our stockholders. It is, of course, unfortunate that the accident happened, but we must look at it as practical businessmen. How about the earning capacity of this boy? If *you* had been the one who had been the victim of this accident, while the pain and suffering would not have been any more intense, nevertheless our liability would have been greater because *you* have a greater earning capacity.

"As a practical man, as a practicing attorney, Mr. Mason, you will recognize that the monetary limit of our responsibility is the loss of earning capacity, plus some *reasonable* amount which will compensate for pain and suffering. Now I would say that with a young, vigorous boy of this kind, fifteen hundred would be a *very* adequate compensation for pain and suffering. Statistics show that within ninety days at the outside he'll be back at work with his earning capacity unimpaired. Even if we were to consider he could make three hundred dollars a month, let us say, from that amount he would have to pay room and board which are furnished him in the hospital, and . . ."

Mason interrupted, "I've heard all that line before."

"Doubtless you have," Ingle said.

Mason said, "I don't want to hear it again."

"Surely, Mr. Mason, you're not going to be arbitrary."

Mason met Caffee's eyes. "I'm going to be arbitrary."

Caffee coughed, said, "After all, Mr. Ingle, there are circumstances in this case which . . ."

"Now let's not misunderstand each other," Ingle said hastily. "Whatever the responsibility may be for having failed to stop and render assistance, we are now discussing only the property damage."

"That's right," Mason said. "We're not compounding a felony or conspiring to conceal a crime."

There was a moment's uncomfortable silence.

Mason said, "However, in the event any action should be taken against Mr. Caffee, he would doubtless want to apply to the Court for probation, and the Court would be very much influenced by the sort of settlement which had been made."

Ingle said, "Well, of course . . ."

Caffee said, eagerly, "Why do you say *in the event* there should be any criminal action?"

Mason stretched and yawned. "Well, of course, someone would have to sign a complaint in order to start a criminal prosecution. I don't *know* that anyone's going to sign a complaint. On the other hand, I don't know that anyone is going to fail to sign one, so I said, 'in the event.'"

Caffee looked at Ingle. Ingle looked at Caffee.

Ingle said, "Well, of course, as far as the insurance company is concerned, we can't consider these extraneous matters. We have . . ."

"You can consider the circumstances in a case, can't you?"

"What do you mean?"

"The bearing they'd have on a jury?"

Caffee coughed nervously. "I wonder if I could speak with Mr. Ingle privately, Mr. Mason. I think . . ."

"Sure," Mason said. "Della, show the gentlemen into the law library. Take your time, gentlemen."

Della Street arose and, crossing the room, opened the door into the law library.

Ingle and Caffee filed out of the office.

Mason closed his right eye in a wink at Della Street.

She closed the door, came back and said, "What's going to happen when they find out there have been *two* settlements, chief?"

"Damned if I know," Mason said. "After all, we don't have much in the line of a precedent in such matters. It's usually hard enough to get one settlement, let alone two.

"Right now, Della, the important thing is to get this settlement cleaned up while we're free to work on it."

"You mean while we're *free?*"

"That's right," Mason said. "Ingle thinks I'm pretty crude, but if he could only look under my hair and see what's going on in my mind, he'd probably faint."

"I'll say he would!"

Mason said, "We're practicing law with a stop watch in one hand and a time bomb in the other—a hand grenade with the pin pulled."

Mason started pacing the floor.

Della Street's eyes, sympathetic, loyal and understanding, followed him.

The door from the law library opened. The two men returned to the room. This time Caffee was in the lead, and Caffee did the talking.

"We'll make that settlement, Mr. Mason," he said. "The insurance company doesn't care to establish a precedent in such matters. It's angry with me for having given you that check and statement last night. I'll give you my check for the balance, and I'll make an adjustment with the insurance company later."

"Just so we get the money," Mason said.

Caffee whipped out a checkbook.

Mason said, "Let me look at those releases, please, Mr. Ingle."

While Caffee was making out checks, Mason looked over the releases. "These seem to be all right," he said.

Mason signed the releases, accepted the checks.

Caffee said, "I hope we understand each other, Mr. Mason."

"I think we do."

"You . . . well, Mr. Ingle says it will be better if I don't have any *definite* understanding."

"Exactly," Mason said, and shook hands.

Caffee said, "I can't begin to tell you how sorry I am this happened. It's been a lesson to me."

"I know," Mason said. "You probably didn't sleep any last night."

"Frankly, I didn't, Mr. Mason."

"We live and learn," Mason told him, arising and ushering them to the door. "I have sleepless nights myself."

Ingle said over his shoulder, "You're a fast worker, Mr. Mason."

Mason said, "Well, there's no use dillydallying around."

"No," Ingle said, as he was being all but pushed out into the corridor, "you don't dally, but you certainly are a dilly, Mr. Mason. *Good* morning!"

"Good morning," Mason said, closing the door.

17

"Do you want me to run down and deposit those checks?" Della Street asked.

"No," Mason said. "I'm going to do that job myself. It'll give me a legitimate excuse to be out of the office for a while."

"And after that?" she asked.

"And after that," he said, "I'm going to have to think up another one. If I can't think of a legitimate excuse, I'll think of an illegitimate one and have to make it sound legitimate."

"Bad as that?"

"It may be."

The unlisted telephone rang. Della Street picked up the receiver, listened, said, "It's Paul Drake, chief. He wants to talk with you."

Mason walked over, picked up the receiver, and said, "Okay, Paul, let's have it."

Drake said, "You remember I was telling you about this man Hansom who's the proprietor of the Rushing Creek . . ."

"I remember," Mason interrupted.

"Well, the police decided they'd talk with him. Apparently they had a hunch somewhere, so they brought him down here and went over his gun register with him, and they don't like the looks of what they find."

"What do they find, Paul?"

"Well, in the first place, while the signature purports to be that of Ross P. Hollister, and the address and everything matches, the name on the gun register apparently was written by someone else. The specimens don't agree with Hollister's handwriting."

"What else?"

"And among other things, the police found that Lucille Barton was playing around a bit with a man by the name of Arthur Colson. Exactly what his relationship is isn't clear, but in any event, when

Hansom was confronted with Arthur Colson, he made an immediate and positive identification. He says that's the man who
bought the gun."

Drake quit talking, and Mason was silent for a while.

"You there?" Drake asked abruptly.

"I'm here," Mason said. "I'm doing a little thinking. Anything
else, Paul?"

"That's all at present."

"What does Arthur Colson say?" Mason asked after a moment.

"Arthur Colson says it's a case of mistaken identification. He's
squawking his head off. He said that if the police wanted to make
any sort of an identification they should have put him in a line-up,
and let this man Hansom identify him. Of course, the police realize
that he has a point there. The police were simply exploring around
when they stumbled on to this. However, they don't like what
they're finding, and they're going to keep digging."

"Any chance it is a false identification, Paul?"

"Not a chance in the world. As I get the story, this fellow Hansom
is a pretty shrewd old duck. He knows most of the customers who
come in the store, that is, the regular customers. Along during the
fishing season, there's quite an influx of people buying fishing
licenses and all that, but this was off season. He remembers the
transaction and he's absolutely positive of his identification. He
certainly impressed the police."

"That makes it look a little different," Mason said.

"Moreover," Drake went on, "they made a paraffin test on Pitkin's
hands. That, of course, isn't as conclusive as it might be, but nevertheless it means a lot where they get an absolutely negative reaction within such a short time after a gun has been fired."

"There was no reaction?"

"Not at all. Police did a good job on that one. They made the
test even before the body was moved. Something about the case
made them a little suspicious."

"Do you know what it was, Paul?"

"I think I do, Perry."

"What?"

"You're not going to like this."

"Hell, I don't like any of it," Mason said.

"Well, there was quite a little spot of blood on the garage floor
directly *underneath* the gun. Now of course it *could* have hap-

pened that way, but police are inclined to think it didn't. The man *could* have shot himself, then remained on his feet for a second or two, and blood *could* have spilled, and then he *could* have fallen over and dropped the gun. But you know how Lieutenant Tragg is, he's a thorough worker and a smooth worker."

"Yes," Mason said, "I know how he is. You aren't holding anything else back on the theory that you want to give me this stuff in small doses, are you, Paul?"

"That's all of it to date."

"Well, it sounds like enough," Mason said, and hung up the phone.

"What is it?" Della Street asked.

Mason said, "Whoever pulled off that job last night wasn't half as clever as I'd thought. But it's too late to worry now, Della. If Carlotta Boone, who gave us the tip on Caffee's license number, comes in, give her a check for one hundred dollars. Be sure it's a check and not cash. Tell her we need the canceled check for our accounting."

"So we can see where she cashes it and perhaps trace her if we have to?"

"That's right. Hold the fort, Della. I'm on my way."

18

Iᴛ was eleven o'clock when Mason returned to the office building.

One of Drake's men who had been lounging unostentatiously by the cigar counter casually moved forward so that he entered the same elevator with Perry Mason.

"Good morning, Mr. Mason," he said. "How's everything this morning?"

Mason glanced sharply at him, said, "Okay. You're one of Drake's men, aren't you?"

"That's right. Just going up to report."

Mason felt the man's hand brush against his and a card was deftly inserted between the lawyer's thumb and forefinger.

Mason pocketed the card, then said, "Hang it, there was a telephone number I was supposed to call. What the deuce did I do with it?"

He made a show of searching his pockets, then finally drew out the card which Drake's operative had just given him. He said, "Here it is," and held it in his hand so that he could read the message which had been written on it.

The card was in Della Street's handwriting and said, C.B. CAME IN. GOT CHECK $100. LOTS OF VISITORS—OFFICIAL— WAITING.

"Oh, well," Mason said, "I guess it's not too late. I'll call as soon as I get to my office."

The elevator stopped at his floor. Drake's detective entered the office of the Drake Detective Agency without a word, and Mason walked down the corridor and fitted his key to the lock of the door to his private office.

"Well, Della," he said, "I guess we've . . . hello," he exclaimed abruptly, as he saw the office was filled with people.

Lieutenant Tragg removed a cigar from his mouth, said, "Hello, Mason."

"Well, well, hello, Lieutenant! How are you? You seem to have quite a gathering here."

"Yes," Tragg said, "I think you know Lucille Barton and Arthur Colson. This is one of my plain-clothes men here. Come in and sit down, Mason. We want to talk with you."

"Fine," Mason said. "How have you been, Tragg?"

"Sit down," Tragg said. "Make yourself comfortable. This may be a long session. I'm going to warn you, Mason, that you're not going to like this."

Mason smiled at Lucille Barton, who looked as though she hadn't slept all night. "How are you, Lucille? I see by the morning papers that you've had quite a shock."

"Yes," she said, her eyes avoiding Mason.

"How are *you* today?" Mason said to Arthur Colson.

"Fine," Arthur Colson said, keeping his eyes concentrated on the carpet.

"Where were you about six o'clock last night, Mason?" Tragg asked.

Mason smiled, shook his head, and said, "I can't remember off-hand, Tragg."

"Well, start thinking."

"All right."

"Keep thinking."

"How long do you want me to keep thinking?" Mason asked.

"Until you think of the answer."

Mason frowned, settled himself behind his office desk, noticed Della Street's apprehensive eyes.

"Well?" Tragg said, after some two minutes.

"Haven't thought of it yet," Mason grinned.

Tragg's face showed concern. "Look, Mason, I like you. I want to give you the breaks, but I'm going to tell you something. This is murder, and you're in a different position than you usually occupy in a murder case."

"Indeed," Mason said. "Well, I'll have a cigarette. I notice you're smoking, Tragg. How about you people, want a cigarette?"

Two heads shook in silent unison.

"How about you?" Mason asked the plain-clothes officer.

"No, thanks."

Mason lit up, settled back once more in his chair.

"All right," Tragg said, "if you're going to take time to think, we'll make a record of how long you think." He took his watch out from his pocket, said, "Now then, Mason, I'm going to ask you for the second time. Where were you about six o'clock last night?"

Mason watched Tragg's eyes glued to the face of the watch, said, "I can't tell you, Tragg."

"Keep thinking," Tragg said.

"I *know* now where I was," Mason said, "but I can't tell you."

"Why not?"

"It would be violating a professional confidence."

"Having to do with what clients?"

Mason smilingly shook his head. "After all, Lieutenant, there are some things we can't discuss, you know. A lawyer has a certain obligation to his client."

Tragg, with a gesture of exasperation, put the watch away, said, "You were interested last night in a gun. A Smith and Wesson having the number S65088."

"Was I?" Mason asked.

"You know you were. You had a detective from Santa del Barra get in touch with Roscoe Hansom who runs the Rushing Creek Mercantile Company and inquire about the sale of that gun."

"Well," Mason said, "if you want to make positive statements like that, Lieutenant, I certainly don't want to contradict you."

Tragg said, "I became interested in that same gun a short time later. I roused the telephone operator at Rushing Creek out of bed and got her to get Roscoe Hansom out of his bed. Your man had just left about half an hour before with the information."

"Indeed."

"*Why* were you interested in that gun?"

"I wanted to find out who had purchased it."

"Why?"

"For various reasons."

Tragg said, "That gun was involved in a murder. The murder was committed around six o'clock. The body wasn't found until around ten-thirty. Now then, Mason, *how did you know the gun was going to figure in a murder case as early as nine o'clock?*"

"I didn't," Mason said, his voice and manner showing complete surprise.

"Your man must have left Santa del Barra even before nine o'clock."

"Probably considerably before," Mason said. "If I had been interested in the gun, and right at the present time I'm not prepared to admit that I was, Lieutenant, it would have been because of its importance as evidence in a civil matter. And I, of course, had no inkling that it had been used in a murder."

"Oh, certainly *not*," Tragg said, sarcastically, "but just what *was* your interest in the gun?"

"I'm sorry, Lieutenant, I can't tell you that."

Tragg's face showed concern. "This is a lot more serious than you think it is, Mason. I've got a whole fist full of cards that aren't on the table yet. It'll be a lot better if you come clean."

"Well, I'll answer any question I can," Mason said.

"When did you first become acquainted with Lucille Barton?"

"Yesterday," Mason said instantly.

"Did she get in touch with you, or did you get in touch with her?"

Mason said, "I'm glad you're now asking me something I *can* answer. Della, where's that issue of the *Blade*? The one I had the ad in?"

Della Street arose, silently went to the files, opened one of the drawers, took out a folder, and handed Mason a copy of the ad in the *Blade*.

"Take it over to Lieutenant Tragg," Mason said.

Tragg regarded the ad, frowned and said, "What's *that* got to do with it?"

"Get that letter out of the file, Della," Mason said. "The one that came to the Drake Detective Agency, the one that had a key in it."

"A key?" Tragg said.

"A key!" Lucille Barton exclaimed.

"A key," Mason repeated, smilingly. "A key—one you open doors with, you know."

Della Street brought the letter from the file.

"Give it to the Lieutenant, Della."

Lieutenant Tragg took the letter, read it and frowned.

"We may just as well give it to Miss Barton," Mason said. "She wrote it you know, Lieutenant."

"The hell she did," Tragg said, chewing on his cigar.

Della Street handed the letter to Lucille Barton, who read it, then passed it across to Arthur Colson.

"And what did you do about that letter?" Tragg said. "You

waited until the hour mentioned when she was out of her apartment and then went to . . ."

"Don't be silly, Lieutenant," Mason interrupted. "You don't think *I'd* use a key to open the door of a person's apartment without permission, do you? I immediately went to Miss Barton's apartment. I knocked on the door, rang the doorbell, and found that I'd caught her at rather an inopportune moment. However, she invited me to come in and make myself at home while she retired to the bedroom and finished dressing. Then she came out and we had a delightful talk and *that*," Mason said, glancing meaningly at Lucille Barton, "was where the relationship of *attorney and client* began. She requested me to represent her in a certain matter."

"*Oh*," Lucille Barton said.

"So you're representing Mrs. Barton?"

"Oh, yes," Mason said. "I believe she prefers to go under the name Miss Barton,' Lieutenant."

"So you're representing her," Tragg said.

"Why, yes."

"And what are you doing for her?"

Mason smiled and shook his head.

Tragg said, "Your activities yesterday, Mason, were rather peculiar."

"Why, I didn't think so, Lieutenant."

"You had a busy day, didn't you?"

"Fairly so. I usually keep pretty busy."

"You went out to 938 West Casino Boulevard. You met Stephen Argyle, and accused him of driving a car in a hit-and-run accident, didn't you?"

"I believe I suggested to him that his car might have been involved in an accident, yes."

"And while you were there you met Hartwell L. Pitkin?"

"Are you referring to Mr. Argyle's chauffeur?"

"Yes."

"He was there," Mason said.

"Now then," Tragg said, "when did you first see that gun—that Smith and Wesson Number S65088, and why did you become interested in tracing it?"

"I'm sorry, Lieutenant. We were getting along fine, but *now* you're asking something I can't tell you about."

"Why not?"

"A privileged communication."

"Now then," Tragg went on, "the numbers on this gun had been ground off with a nice little emery wheel. One number had been overlooked, but it took a screw driver to get at it. The grinding of the metal looks like a very fresh job."

"Indeed?" Mason said courteously.

"Now when you became interested in this gun, how did you know the number?"

Mason smiled and shook his head.

"Was it before the numbers had been ground off, or afterwards?"

"I'm sorry," Mason said, smiling affably.

"It *must* have been before they were ground off, Mason, because that screw hadn't been loosened since the gun left the factory. I'm wondering if perhaps *you* weren't the one who removed the numbers."

Mason merely smiled, then stifled a yawn behind his hand.

Tragg nodded to the officer, said, "All right, bring in that witness."

The officer pushed through the door toward Mason's reception room.

Tragg said, "I'm going to put it right on the line with you, Mason. I think that at six o'clock you were out in front of Mrs. Barton's garage at 719 South Gondola. I think a shooting took place there in that garage and I think you're trying to cover up that shooting. I think I have a witness who can identify you."

Mason tapped ashes from the end of his cigarette. "I feel quite certain you haven't any such witness, Lieutenant."

"This witness positively identifies Lucille Barton here."

Before Mason could say anything, the door was jerked open. The plain-clothes officer stood to one side and a tall man with a high forehead, high cheekbones, thin lips, a long neck, entered the office in an apologetic manner as though ashamed of the intrusion.

Tragg pointed to Perry Mason, and said, "Is that the man?"

"I . . . I don't know until he stands up," the man said. "You see, I never saw his face real clear."

Mason smiled at him and said, "I'm Perry Mason. What's your name?"

"Goshen—G-O-S-H-E-N," the man said, "Carl Ebert Goshen. I

live next door to the place where the murder was committed and . . ."

"Never mind," Tragg said, "I just want to know whether that's the man."

"I can't tell until he stands up and walks around. I can tell you then."

"Stand up," Tragg said to Mason.

Mason grinned. "That's a hell of a way to make an identification, Lieutenant. You'd better have some sort of a line-up if you want to have an identification that's worth anything."

"I can't get you in a line-up without arresting you," Tragg said. "I don't particularly care about doing that until I'm certain of my ground. If this witness identifies you, then I'm certain of my ground."

"That's not only getting the cart before the horse," Mason said, "but it's putting him in circular shafts and letting him chase the tailboard."

"Shut up," Tragg said. "I'm doing this."

"Indeed you are," Mason said.

"Get up," Tragg insisted. "If you're innocent you have nothing to fear."

Mason tilted back in his swivel chair, smiling at Tragg.

"How was he dressed?" Tragg asked Goshen.

"Just like I told you, he had on a light topcoat, tan-colored, and a gray hat."

Tragg said to the officer, "There's the coat closet there. Get out his coat and hat."

Mason said, "Now, wait a minute, Tragg. You know you haven't any right to do that. You can't . . ."

"The hell I can't," Tragg said, and then, turning to Goshen, said, "When this witness gets up to try and stop the officer, you notice particularly the way he walks, the way he moves . . ."

Mason said, "I'm telling you, Lieutenant, this is an invasion of my rights as a citizen."

The officer opened the door of the coat closet, suddenly stopped, hesitated for a moment, then turned back to face Tragg.

"Go on," Tragg said impatiently, "get out the coat and hat. We'll put it on him, if we have to. He's going to stand up and . . ."

"I'm sorry, Lieutenant, but . . ."

"Get that coat out!" Tragg said.

The officer brought out the topcoat. It was a heavy black coat Mason had never seen before.

"Get out the tan one," Tragg said.

"That's the only one in here, Lieutenant."

Mason flashed a glance at Della Street. She was cherubic in her innocence.

"That's not the coat," Goshen said, positively.

Tragg said suspiciously to Mason, "Where did you get that coat?"

"I didn't get it. You did."

"Well, then, where did you get that lead to Stephen Argyle? How did you know it was *his* car that was mixed up in the accident?"

Mason merely smiled and shook his head. "Lieutenant, you keep asking questions which are predicated on false premises. I'm sorry, but Argyle's car really *wasn't* mixed up in the accident."

"I thought you . . ."

"I really thought it was," Mason said, smiling, "but you know how it is, Lieutenant. Lots of times you'll think you have all the evidence in a case and start making charges, accusations and wild assertions, and then suddenly find out, much to your chagrin, that the facts were entirely different, and . . ."

"Never mind all that," Tragg said. "I want to know where you got the information, why you went out and told Argyle his car had been in the accident, how you knew it."

Mason said, "As a matter of fact, Lieutenant, the man who was involved in the accident is a gentleman by the name of Caffee—Mr. Daniel Caffee, 1017 Beachnut Street, Apartment 22-B. I located him yesterday evening and I'm quite satisfied that it was purely a mistake on Mr. Caffee's part. When Mr. Caffee learned that my client had been injured he was only too glad to make adjustments."

"What do you mean—adjustments?"

"He paid off."

"When?"

"This morning, after making a partial payment yesterday."

"I'll be damned," Tragg blurted.

"Of course," Mason told him, "I don't care to have that information noised about, Lieutenant. I'm merely trying to help you clean up a case in which you seem to be interested. I understand that Mr. Pitkin committed suicide in Miss Barton's garage."

"He was murdered in Miss Barton's garage."

Mason made clicking noises with his tongue against the roof of his mouth.

Tragg said, "You weren't in your office last night between five and six. Della Street showed up in a taxicab. Stephen Argyle was waiting here for you. His chauffeur was waiting down in front. Shortly after five o'clock, Argyle went down and told the chauffeur there was no need for him to wait. Argyle came back and waited here until almost six o'clock. Then he telephoned his insurance carrier and made an appointment to meet an adjuster in front of the building. He can account for every minute of his time, and he also knows that *you* weren't here in your office."

"I'm seldom in the office after five o'clock," Mason said. "I try to close up and get out. Of course, occasionally I do night work but I don't like to see clients after five o'clock. It establishes a bad precedent and . . ."

"And," Tragg went on, "the reason you weren't here is because you were with Lucille Barton. When Pitkin entered that garage, you were there. At any rate, you were there shortly after he entered. Now I'm willing to be fair about the thing, Mason. I think the evidence indicates that probably Pitkin was there for no good purpose. He may have attacked you or Miss Barton. One of you had a gun and pulled the trigger. That stopped the career of Mr. Hartwell L. Pitkin, and I'm perfectly willing to concede that it wasn't the career of an exemplary citizen. It was the career of a blackmailer, an opportunist, and a crook. If he was waiting there in that garage, I'm satisfied he was waiting for no good purpose, but I'm only going to give you this one chance to come clean privately. After this it will have to be publicly. I'm going to tell you frankly that, if it was self-defense, I'm willing to make allowances for that, but I want to clean this case up fast."

"Yes, I can understand that," Mason said. "And I know you want to be fair."

"Now, then," Tragg went on, "Lucille Barton says she was with you."

"She does?"

"That's right. At first she said she was with Anita Jordon, and Anita Jordon was to give her an alibi for the entire evening, but when we started getting right down to brass tacks that alibi blew up."

Lucille Barton said hurriedly, "I didn't say I was with Mr. Mason at six o'clock. At first I said I was with him until just before I met Anita and . . ."

"Now *I'm* doing the talking," Tragg said.

"He doesn't want you to talk," Mason said meaningly to Lucille Barton. "Therefore, *as your attorney,* I would advise you to keep quiet."

"None of that," Tragg said to Mason. "I'm talking to you."

"And I'm talking to my client, Lieutenant."

"When were you with Mrs. Barton yesterday?"

"I told you I saw her sometime in the morning."

"When did you see her after that?"

"I'm sure I can't tell you the time, Lieutenant."

"But you *did* see her after that?"

"Oh, yes."

Tragg said, "All right, we'll quit beating around the bush, Mason. I want to take your fingerprints."

"Certainly," Mason said, "go right ahead I'll be only too glad to co-operate in every way I can, Lieutenant; but of course you understand I can't betray the confidences of a client."

Tragg nodded to the officer, who produced a small fingerprint outfit from his pocket and approached the desk.

"Stand up," Tragg said.

"Oh, I'll do it sitting down," Mason told him smiling, extending his hand to the officer.

Goshen suddenly said, "I don't think that's the man. The man that I saw was not quite so heavy and . . ."

"Just step outside for a minute," Tragg said. "I want you to see this man with his overcoat on and I want you to see him standing up and walking. You can't make any identification while he's sitting down there behind the desk."

Mason said, "And I warn you, Lieutenant, he can't make an identification that's worth a damn unless he picks me out of a line-up."

Goshen arose, paused uncertainly, then walked out through the door to the reception room.

Tragg said, "You can be tough about it if you want to, Mason, but there's an easy way of doing this and there's a hard way. If I can't do it the easy way, I'll do it the hard way."

"That's very logical," Mason said. "Now, where is it you want my prints, officer—on this piece of paper? Oh, yes, now I believe I'm supposed to roll each finger across the white paper."

Lucille Barton was regarding Mason with fixed intensity. Arthur Colson glanced at Mason, then hastily averted his eyes.

Silently, the officer took Mason's fingerprints.

"You can get up and wash the ink off your hands now," Tragg said.

Mason grinned. "No, thanks. Your witness might come popping in. Della, I think you have some cleaning tissues in your desk. You might bring them to me and I'll wipe the ink off my hands with those. No need to get the washbowl all smeared with ink."

Tragg said, "Try sitting there if you want to, but you can't stay there forever. You're going to have to leave this office sometime. I'll have the witness watch you walk through the foyer. I'll have him watch you at various places and if this fingerprint evidence comes out the way I think it's going to I may have him watch you in a shadow box."

Della Street handed Mason a box of cleaning tissue, and some cleansing cream. "Put the cream on your fingers, chief," she said. "Rub it in. That will clean off the ink."

"Thanks," Mason said.

The officer handed Tragg the fingerprints. Tragg took a photograph from his pocket, compared the fingerprints one at a time, then suddenly gave an exclamation of satisfaction. He whipped a magnifying glass from his pocket and began examining the prints more closely, comparing one of them with the print on the photograph.

Suddenly he said, "Mason, that's your fingerprint on that murder weapon!"

"Is it indeed?" Mason said.

"What have you to say to that?"

"Nothing."

"Mason, I'm going to tell you officially that gun was used to murder Hartwell L. Pitkin. I can now establish definitely that gun has your fingerprint on it. Now, then, in the face of that evidence, what have you to say?"

"Nothing," Mason told him. "I'm protecting the confidence of a client."

"You can't protect the confidence of a client to the extent of failing to explain your fingerprint on a murder weapon."

"There seems to be a difference of opinion about that," Mason said. "By the way, Della, Lieutenant Tragg didn't ask about that second letter. Miss Barton didn't tell him anything about that because she didn't know anything about it. *She* wrote the first letter to me, but that second letter must have been written by someone else without her knowledge."

"What letter are you referring to?" Tragg asked.

"Get that second letter, Della. The one that enclosed the key to the desk in her apartment."

Della Street once more went to the files, brought out the second letter, and handed it to Lieutenant Tragg.

"This letter came special delivery," Mason explained.

Tragg read the letter, asked ominously, "There was a key in it?"

"Oh, yes," Mason said, "a key to the desk."

"Where is it?"

Mason said, "I have both keys right here, Lieutenant. Would you like them?"

Tragg took the keys which Mason handed across the desk, regarded them in frowning concentration.

"So you see," Mason said, "I quite naturally felt that Miss Barton wanted me to get the evidence, but didn't want to take the responsibility of being the one who gave it to me. So when she and Arthur Colson over there came to my office yesterday afternoon I took advantage of her presence here to slip down to her apartment and open the desk. Sure enough, the key fitted the desk and in the upper right-hand pigeonhole was a notebook and a gun. Now, Lieutenant, if you can find the person who wrote that *second* letter, you can go a long ways toward discovering the murderer of this man Pitkin, in the event your premise is correct and the man was murdered."

Tragg said, "By gosh, if you entered that apartment and started messing around in it, I can . . ."

Mason interrupted sharply, "Come, come, Lieutenant. Once more you're getting your cart and your horse all mixed up. I didn't enter the *apartment* without permission. Lucille Barton wrote that first letter and sent me the key. That certainly gave me permission to enter her apartment by using the key, which she had so conveniently placed at my disposal. But that second letter, that must have been a trap, Lieutenant. That . . ."

"You opened that desk," Tragg said. "Was that gun in there?"

"I will go so far as to say this, Lieutenant—*a* gun was in there. Now you can see what that means. The desk was kept locked. Someone had a key to that desk, a duplicate key. Someone sent me that key. Now, quite obviously, Lieutenant, since Miss Barton was here at the office at that time, and the gun was there in the desk at that time, Miss Barton *couldn't have been carrying that gun.* And if you didn't find her fingerprints on the gun you can't prove that she *ever* had it. But I really can't tell you anything more, Lieutenant. I've given you some hints. In fact, I think I've stretched a point in giving you some hints."

Lieutenant Tragg said suddenly to the officer, "Take Colson and this Barton woman out of here. He isn't talking to me. He's using me as a sounding board to tell these two what he wants them to say."

The officer rose abruptly. "Come on," he said to the others.

Mason said, "My advice to you, Miss Barton, under the circumstances, is to *say absolutely nothing.* In view of the hostile attitude of the police I suggest you refuse to answer any questions on the advice of counsel."

"On the advice of counsel!" Tragg said. "Wait a minute. Are you going to represent her in this murder case?"

"Is she accused of murder?"

"She may be."

"Well, as I pointed out to you," Mason said, "when I went to call on her at her apartment yesterday, she retained me to act as her attorney."

"For what?"

"That I can't tell you."

Tragg turned to Lucille Barton and said, "You didn't tell me that."

"You didn't ask me specifically," she answered evasively.

"Well, what was it you wanted him to do?"

"Tut, tut, Lucille," Mason said, wagging a warning finger. "Not a word, remember now, not a word."

She turned to Tragg. Her face showed relief. "You heard what my lawyer just told me," she said.

Tragg said to the officer, "Get them out of here," and then chewed angrily on his cigar while the officer herded the pair out into the reception office.

Tragg scraped a match into flame on the sole of his shoe, lit his cigar once more, turned to Mason, said, "Mason, I don't want to drag you into this unless I have to."

"Thanks."

"But the way you're doing things, I'm afraid I'm going to have to."

"Yes, I can see that."

"You know what it will look like in the newspaper—LAWYER'S FINGERPRINT FOUND ON MURDER WEAPON."

"You feel you should release that information to the newspapers?"

"I'll have to."

"Yes," Mason said, "that certainly will make headlines."

"Then there'll be another headline, LAWYER REFUSES TO EXPLAIN."

"Yes, I can see where that will make sensational newspaper reading."

"Hang it, Mason," Tragg said, "you and I are on opposite sides of the fence, but I don't want to crucify you. I'm not certain that you were the one who was with her when Goshen looked across there at the garage. If you were with her, I think it was because she'd got hold of you and dragged you out there to show you something and you didn't have any idea what it was. If you can explain that, for heaven's sake go ahead and explain it."

Mason said, "Let's follow that thought a little farther, Lieutenant. Suppose that's what did happen. Would that relieve me of responsibility?"

Tragg said, "I'm not prepared to give you a definite and final answer on that."

"Well, give me an indefinite and temporary answer."

Tragg said, "The time of death is particularly important. We can fix the time of death within an hour or so the way things are now, but if we'd been notified, say at six o'clock, we could have fixed the time of death almost to the minute. You had a duty to notify police."

"Yes, I understand."

"Therefore," Tragg went on, "you'd have to take your medicine on that. Now, was the body in the garage when you were called there at six o'clock?"

Mason said, "I've told you, Lieutenant, I can't tell you where I was at six o'clock."

"And if this man Caffee was the fellow who hit Finchley's car, how does it happen you strong-armed a settlement out of Stephen Argyle?"

"I didn't."

"He made a settlement last night with Finchley."

"That's right."

"That is something I checked up on rather carefully," Lieutenant Tragg said, "because naturally I was interested in accounting for his time during the afternoon and evening."

"And you were able to do it?"

"Sure. He was out at his house. You came out there and accused him of a hit-and-run. Naturally, he doesn't want to discuss the hit-and-run charge."

"I daresay he doesn't."

"But immediately after you'd left him," Tragg went on, "Argyle did some thinking and decided he'd better buy his way out. He rushed to your office. He had the chauffeur wait downstairs. Then, when it looked as though you weren't going to be in for a while, and Argyle remembered it was Pitkin's night out, he went back down to let the chauffeur go. He told him to take the car back to the house."

"I see."

"Argyle waited until around six o'clock, then telephoned the insurance people and told them where he was, and what he was doing. The insurance adjuster had kittens, told him to stay away from you and under no circumstances to talk with you. The adjuster said he was on his way up to the office just as quick as he could get there, so Argyle waited in the lobby. The man at the cigar counter remembers him distinctly. Argyle waited about five or ten minutes in the lobby, and then the insurance adjuster came up and took him in tow."

Tragg studied Mason, added, "Of course, if Argyle's car didn't hit this guy, Argyle and the insurance company will naturally want a return of the money they paid."

"I'm quite certain they will," Mason said.

Tragg looked at him sharply. "You aren't saying specifically you're going to give it back?"

"That's right. I didn't say that. I'm not."

"What!"

"I'm going to hang on to it."

"Look," Tragg said, "why don't you take your hair down and come clean, Mason?"

"I don't like to take my hair down. It might get in my eyes."

"Well *something's* in your eyes now. Look, Mason, this woman didn't think you were her attorney when she came in here."

"The deuce she didn't!" Mason exclaimed apparently in surprise.

Tragg said, "If you come clean I'll do everything I can to see that you get a square deal, not only with the press but at Headquarters."

"And the district attorney?" Mason asked.

"And with the district attorney," Tragg said, but his voice suddenly lacked conviction.

Mason grinned. "You know as well as I do, Tragg, that if you could get anything on me, the district attorney would welcome you with open arms. The case against Lucille Barton would pale into insignificance."

"Well," Tragg said, "what do you think he's got against you now? He's got enough to throw the book at you."

"Let him throw," Mason said. "Just so he throws it across the plate. And you can tell him for me I'll knock it over the fence for a home run."

"Not with that fingerprint on that gun you're not going to," Tragg said. "That gun was the one that killed Pitkin. I have a report from our expert in ballistics."

"Indeed?"

Tragg got to his feet. "Well, I gave you your chance, Mason."

"You sure did," Mason said. "Pardon me if I don't get up, Tragg. That man Goshen might come running in the door and put the finger on me. I don't like to be identified in that way. I always prefer to have some sort of a line-up. At least the witness should have *some* choice."

Tragg said, "Don't be a fool, Mason. You can't spend the next two weeks sitting down. We'll identify you sometime and when we do it's going to look like hell—the asinine way you tried to dodge."

Tragg stalked through the door of Mason's office out to the entrance room.

Mason exchanged glances with Della Street. "Good Lord, Della, that gun *was* the murder weapon!"

She nodded mutely.

"I'd felt certain that when they examined the fatal bullet they'd find it had been fired from another gun and . . . Della, where the devil did you get that topcoat?"

"It's Paul Drake's," she said in a low voice. "Gertie heard them talking while they were waiting in the reception room. I slipped down to Drake's office, borrowed his overcoat and left yours there with him."

Mason grinned. "Did Drake know what you wanted it for?"

"He didn't ask any questions—he was careful not to."

Mason said, "Della, raise your salary a hundred dollars a month, and come over here by my desk. *I* can't get up at the moment because Tragg may come busting in here again with that popeyed witness."

19

MASON spread out the newspaper on his desk, said, "Well, they certainly did a job, didn't they, Della?"

Della Street nodded.

"Nice headlines," Mason said, reading them, LAWYER'S FINGER-PRINT FOUND ON MURDER WEAPON—ATTORNEY REFUSES TO STAND SO WITNESS CAN MAKE IDENTIFICATION . . . BEAUTIFUL DIVORCEE ARRESTED IN MYSTERIOUS MURDER . . . . LAWYER POSSESSED KEY TO SUSPECT'S APARTMENT.

Mason looked up. "That sure is quite a smear, Della."

"'Smear' is no word for it. Incidentally, I've been wondering, why did you tell Lieutenant Tragg about those letters and give him the keys?"

"It was the only way I could tip off Lucille Barton to what I wanted her to say."

"I don't get it."

Mason said, "Suppose someone else had written *both* of those letters."

"Well?"

"Sooner or later," Mason said, "it was bound to come out that a key to the apartment had been sent to Paul Drake and that Paul Drake had turned that key over to me. Now then, if anyone else had sent that key and I used it to enter the apartment I was a lawbreaker. But if Lucille Barton herself had sent that key then I was entering the apartment with her permission."

Della Street nodded. "I see now. I wonder if she did."

"Once in the apartment with her permission," Mason went on, "the situation was entirely different. So if I can get the idea across to her that *someone else* sent the key to the desk, and that the gun was kept in the desk, I've given Tragg something to worry about."

"Suppose she had sense enough to get it?"

"Darned if I know," Mason said, "but I wasn't trying to give her

an out. I was giving Tragg something to worry about, also Colson.
I wonder if Colson . . ."

Mason was interrupted by Drake's code knock on the door.

"Let Paul in, Della."

Della Street opened the door.

Paul Drake, carrying an afternoon paper under his arm, said,
"Did you see what they had to say in . . . Oh, I see you have
one."

"Sit down, Paul," Mason said. "Quite a smear, isn't it?"

"I'll say it's a smear."

Mason said, "This witness, Goshen, will identify me if he has a
half a chance. I don't want him to have that chance."

"You can't prevent it," Drake said. "Why didn't you let him do
it in the first place? It's going to look like hell when he does it now."

Mason grinned. "You talk like Tragg, Paul. What does Hollister
look like? You must have his description."

"He's around forty-seven or forty-eight, tall, raw-boned, brunet,
bushy eyebrows. I've picked up a fair description and am trying to
get a photograph."

Mason seemed surprised. "Well, well, there's another tall man
who enters the picture. Perhaps Goshen saw him. And this Dudley
Gates, who got some money out of a bank and turned it over to
Pitkin. What does *he* look like?"

"He's a younger man, about thirty-three, medium height, stocky,
blond, blue-eyed . . ."

"Well," Mason said, "we can probably cross him out of the picture, but Goshen certainly should see this man Hollister."

Drake's face lightened. "You *may* have something there, Perry.
Was it Hollister?"

Mason said nothing.

The hope which had been on the detective's face faded. He said,
"I'll withdraw the question."

"Okay," Mason told him. "How about Dudley Gates? Have
they found him? What does he say about the money?"

Drake said, "Dudley Gates is with Hollister. They're partners,
and they left Monday night to look over some oil properties."

"Where are these properties?"

"Up north somewhere. Naturally the location would be something they'd keep secret."

Mason said musingly, "This is Thursday, the sixth. They left

on Monday. They've had three days. . . . What time Monday
night, Paul?"

"Probably right at six o'clock. Hollister's housekeeper left at
four-thirty. Hollister was waiting to see a man, then Gates was
joining him, and he was leaving at six o'clock.

"The housekeeper heard him talking to Gates on the phone, and
saying he was leaving on the dot at six, and Hollister was a stickler
for punctuality.

"It would have taken Gates a little over an hour to get up there
from here."

Mason said, "Paul, I've got to get out of this building without
anyone seeing me."

"You can't do it," Drake said. "Tragg has this witness, Goshen,
planted in a car with a police escort, waiting for you to walk out.
Newspaper reporters and photographers are sprinkled all around
the place."

"Paul, *you* keep *your* offices open twenty-four hours a day?"

Drake nodded.

"You have the only office in the building that is open all night?"

"Well?" Drake asked.

"I'm coming down and live with you, Paul."

"I don't get it."

"We're going to close up this office. Della is going to scout the
corridors and make certain that there's no one between here and
your office. Then I'm going down to your office. Della will lock up
this place and start home. Naturally newspapermen will intercept
her. She'll smile sweetly at them and tell them that Mr. Mason left
the office about half an hour before, that he made arrangements
to leave the office in such a way he could work on the case without
interruption."

"You think they'll take her word for that?" Drake asked.

"Hell, no," Mason said grinning. "They'll come up here, though,
and find the office dark."

"And be satisfied you're still in it."

"Sure they will, but they'll then get a brilliant idea, and get
hold of the janitor and when the scrubwomen come in to clean up
the office the newshawks will be snooping around—illegal, but
they'll do it just the same. They'll want pictures and interviews."

Drake seemed dubious. "Then they'll know that you're in my
office. They'll simply watch *it*."

Mason said, "We'll make them think I managed to get out through the basement."

"How?"

"There again is where you come in," Mason said, grinning. "You are going to ship a big packing case by truck. You're going to be very particular about it, and the packing case which is supposed to contain evidence is to go to the garage in my apartment house. It will be plenty heavy when you ship it. There will be a few holes bored in the lid. You'll have an operative you can trust go out to the garage, receive the package and promise to unpack it. By the time the newspaper reporters find it it will be empty."

"What makes you think they'll find it?"

"As soon as they get the idea that I may have left the office they'll start asking questions of the janitor to find out whether I could possibly have gone out the back way. They'll also start questioning you and your office girl to find out if I'm in your office. You'll let the cat out of the bag by telling them about the packing case."

"Don't be silly," Drake said. "They've got a reporter, a photographer and a plain-clothesman covering the back way."

"That's fine," Mason said. "They'll all remember seeing the big box go out."

"Suppose they get suspicious and look in the box?"

"If they look in the box we'll try something else. If they don't, we'll make them think I went out that way."

"But all this isn't going to do you any good," Drake said irritably. "You're simply crucifying yourself. Figure what the papers will do when they—why, hang it, Perry, it will put your neck right in a noose. Evidence of flight is evidence of guilt."

"That's right," Mason said.

"Well, it seems to me you're playing right into Tragg's hands. You can't live in my office indefinitely, Perry."

"Of course I can't," Mason said. "That's where we use psychology. No one watches the empty barn for the stolen horse.

"Della, run out and scout the corridor. Let me know if it's clear."

Della Street nodded, opened the door, walked out into the corridor, returned and said, "It's all clear now, chief."

"Come on, Paul," Mason laughed, "you have a guest."

Drake said, wearily, "Okay, here we go again."

20

MASON, comfortably seated in Paul Drake's office, his feet on the edge of Drake's desk, the back of his chair propped against the wall, held a cup of coffee in his right hand, a sandwich in his left.

Paul Drake, sitting at the desk with three telephones in front of him, munched on a sandwich between incoming calls. One of the telephones rang. Drake swallowed hastily, answered the phone.

When he had finished talking and dropped the receiver into place, he said, "Well, I guess that does it, Perry."

"What happened?" Mason asked.

"That packing-case clue started the reporters off like a pack of hounds. They traced the packing case to your garage, where they found the empty case with holes bored in the lid. The newspapermen are sore and Tragg's having kittens."

"What about Goshen?"

Drake said, "At last reports Goshen was still waiting down there. He . . ."

A telephone rang.

Paul Drake picked up the receiver, placed it to his ear, said, "Okay, Drake talking . . . he did . . . Okay . . . tell you what you'd better do. You'd better be absolutely certain about that. It may be a trap. We have Goshen's address. Beat it down there, cover the place. See if Goshen actually goes home . . . Okay, call me back."

Drake dropped the receiver into place. "Goshen's gone."

"I guess that does it, Paul."

"It may be a trap," Drake pointed out. "We'll check and see if he shows up at his home. He's been waiting for hours. He'll be sore."

A telephone made noise. Drake picked up the receiver, said, "Hello, Drake talking . . . yes . . . what the hell! . . . You sure . . . ? that may be important. Hold the phone a minute—just stay on the line now. Don't let anyone disconnect you. Stay right on there."

Drake cupped his hand over the mouthpiece of the telephone and said to Mason, "They've found Hollister's car. It had been driven over a grade and wrecked."

"Any trace of Hollister?"

"No trace. Just the empty car."

"Where?" Mason asked.

"Ten and two-tenths miles above Santa del Barra on the Canyon road. Apparently it had been deliberately driven off the grade."

"What makes you think so?"

"My man's reporting. He's been in touch with the highway patrol. They discovered the car about an hour ago. The car was in low gear, the ignition switch was on."

"How did they happen to find it?"

"One of the highway patrol just happened to notice very faint tracks. It was just luck he did, because the tracks were almost obliterated. They were at a wide place in the road where there's a lot of rock, and then a cliff goes straight down for something over a hundred feet into a canyon."

Mason said, "Where's your man now?"

"He's reporting from Santa del Barra."

Mason said, "Tell him to examine the car as much as the police will let him. I want to know exactly what's in it, and exactly what isn't in it."

Drake relayed instructions into the telephone, then said, "Okay, wait a minute, just hold on a second."

Once more he cupped his hand over the mouthpiece, said to Mason, "The police are going up there with a hoist. They've phoned Tragg, and Tragg has ordered the car to be hoisted back to the road. It's going to be quite a job. They'll take out a wrecking car and they'll literally have to lift the car as a dead weight up the side of the cliff."

"Okay. Tell your man to stay with the police, Paul."

Drake said into the telephone, "Stay with the police. Examine the car. Call back as soon as you have anything."

He dropped the receiver back into place, said, "Hollister didn't get very far before ditching his car."

"He got ten miles, five of it up a mountain road. Isn't that the road to Rushing Creek, Paul?"

"Good heavens, so it is!" Drake said. "Would that mean anything, Perry?"

"I don't know."

Mason started pacing the floor. "Damn it, Paul, I wish you'd get a bigger office."

"Can't afford it," Drake said. "I only need an office as headquarters. I don't have to impress clients the way you do."

Mason said, "The trouble is you have no place to walk. About the time you get started pacing the floor in this cubbyhole you run up against a wall. How the heck do you ever do any thinking?"

Drake said, "I sit in a chair when I think."

"You sure have to in this dump," Mason told him.

"What are you thinking about?"

"Goshen."

"You should have let him put the finger on you and then yelled it was a frame-up," Drake said. "He'll get you sooner or later and then it'll look like hell because you ran away."

Mason kept pacing the floor.

"You can't squirm out of that situation," Drake said. "The guy's going to identify you."

"He didn't get a good look at the man's face," Mason said.

"He's had a good look at yours now. Tragg saw to that."

Mason said, "With the recovery of that car in Santa del Barra, Tragg will be tearing up there in order to see what he can find. Now Lieutenant Tragg is the brains on the homicide squad. The other boys aren't particularly smart. On the other hand, Tragg is fair, and the other chaps are inclined to take every advantage . . . And Sergeant Holcomb would welcome a chance to knife Tragg in the back. . . . I'll tell you what let's do, Paul. Do you have an operative who's about my size and build? One whom you can trust?"

Drake looked Mason over thoughtfully, said, "Will he get into trouble?"

"Not if he does exactly as I say," Mason said.

"There's Jerry Lando. He's just about your build, and about your age."

"Can you trust him?"

"You can trust Jerry anywhere. He's been around. He's a smart cookie."

Mason said, "I remember you told me once that lots of times a camera and a flash gun would get a detective in places when no other scheme would do the work, Paul."

"That's right. Whenever anyone sees a chap carrying a press camera and a flash gun they take him for a newspaper photographer and very seldom even bother to ask questions."

"Therefore I take it you keep a camera on hand?"

"Yes."

"Okay, I want it."

"You do?"

"Yes. Also I want you to round up some good photographers. Can you get them?"

"How many?"

"Five or six."

"There's a night school in journalistic photography. I could probably hire some of the advanced students."

"Okay. Get this Jerry Lando up here. Does he have a car?"

"Yes."

"Okay," Mason said. "We'll use his car. Tell him to bring a suitcase and I'll want that tan topcoat Della left here. Tell him to rush. We've got to make it fast if we pull the stunt I have in mind."

"What stunt do you have in mind?" Drake asked, reaching for the telephone.

Mason grinned, "Do *you* want to know?"

"Hell no," Drake said hastily. He spun the dial with nervous fingers.

21

JERRY LANDO, tall, athletic, good-natured, but with a devil-may-care glint in his dark eyes, put his suitcase in the corner and said, "Okay, Mr. Drake, I have my car downstairs. It's full of gas and I'm ready for anything."

"You know Mr. Mason?" Drake asked. "Perry Mason, the lawyer?"

"How are you, Mr. Mason," Lando said, shaking hands. "I've heard a lot about you," and then grinning, he added, "and read a lot about you."

"You're going to read more," Mason told him. "We're paving the way for a story in tomorrow morning's papers."

"What do we do?" Lando asked.

Mason said, "We go to an automobile court. We pick one where the arrangement of the cabins is just the way I want it. Then you put on this tan topcoat. Let's see how it fits."

Mason held the topcoat. Lando put his arms in the sleeves, pulled it up over his shoulders.

"Just like my own coat," Lando said.

Mason said, "Paul, get your photographers. Have them bring press cameras, flash guns and lots of bulbs. How soon can you have them here?"

"Oh, give me an hour."

"I'll give you thirty minutes," Mason told him. "I'll phone in instructions. Come on, Lando, let's go."

Lando picked up his suitcase.

Mason slipped the strap of the big camera case over his shoulder.

"Have a heart, Perry," Drake pleaded. "I can't get these men on the job . . ."

"Thirty minutes is the deadline," Mason said. "Come on, Lando."

They started through the door.

Drake said hastily, "Remember you're working out of this office, Jerry. Don't let this guy get you in any trouble."

"As far as I'm concerned," Lando said, "when I'm with Mr. Mason, I'm acting under my attorney's advice."

At the elevator, the night janitor looked at Mason in open-mouthed surprise. "Why I thought you . . . Why you were supposed to have sneaked out . . ."

"Nonsense," Mason said. "I was working late."

"But you . . . you weren't in your office."

"Of course not," Mason said. "I was in conference with Paul Drake."

"Well, I'll be darned," the janitor said. "You should have seen all the trouble they made about that packing case I shipped out. Why, I'm just going to tell those boys . . ."

"Don't tell them anything for a while," Mason said. "Let them find out their own mistakes. After all, you're not responsible for what they put in the papers."

And Mason opened his wallet, selected a crisp ten-dollar bill, folded it, and slipped it into the hand of the grinning janitor.

"Your car's outside?" he asked Lando.

"Right in front of the place," Lando said.

"Okay," Mason told him. "We make a sprint for it in case anyone should be watching, but I don't think they will be."

"The place was clear as a bell when I came in," Lando said. "Everyone had cleared out."

"That's fine."

They crossed the lobby without incident, entered Lando's automobile.

"Where do we go?"

"Drive up the main highway north," Mason said. "Keep an eye out for auto courts. I want to get one that's arranged just the way I want it."

After a few miles Mason said, "Here's a place that looks about right and I see it has a sign saying 'vacancy' so I guess we're okay."

"What accommodations do we want?"

"We want a two-room bungalow if we can get one," Mason said. "Otherwise we'll take a one-room. But it has to be at the extreme rear of the lot. Simply register as Lando and party. Give them the license number of the automobile. That's all they'll want. Do you get me?"

"I get you," Lando said.

Lando brought the car to a stop in front of the bungalow marked "Office," left the motor running and went in.

Within a couple of minutes he reappeared, accompanied by a stout woman carrying a key.

Lando beckoned, and Mason, sliding over into the driver's seat, put the car into low gear and drove slowly along until the landlady fitted a key to the door of one of the cabins in the rear.

The woman went in, followed by Lando, lights were switched on, and after a moment, Lando appeared in the doorway and nodded.

After the landlady started back to the office, Mason got out and inspected the cabin.

"Okay?" Lando asked.

"Okay," Mason said. "Now let's go telephone Paul Drake."

"There's a phone in the office."

"We don't want that," Mason said. "There's a service station down the street that has a phone. We'll use that."

"Okay," Lando said. "You want me to drive?"

"That's right. Get started and I'll tell you what you're to do while we're traveling."

Lando left the lights on, locked the door, climbed in behind the steering wheel.

Mason said, "Now, when you get Paul Drake give him the address and tell him to rush his men with the cameras out here."

"Okay."

"Then," Mason said, "wait ten minutes. Then call up police headquarters. You'll ask for Sergeant Holcomb at Homicide. You'll tell Holcomb that you're a representative of the *Blade.* Tell him that you'll give him a tip that will enable him to scoop the whole force if he'll absolutely protect you and see that the other papers don't get it."

"Suppose he says he won't?"

Mason grinned and said, "Sergeant Holcomb will promise anybody anything in order to steal a march on the other guys on the force."

"Okay, what do I tell him?"

"Tell him that your reporters have located Perry Mason out here in this auto court. Give him the number of the cabin, give him the address of the auto court, and tell him that Mason is not registered personally, but that he's with a representative of the Drake Detective Agency by the name of Lando, driving an automobile of a certain make and license number, and give him all the data. Tell him to rush Goshen out here to make an identification. Tell him your paper wants a scoop on the identification, inasmuch as you're giving him the exclusive tip."

"Okay," Lando said. "What else?"

"Then," Mason said, "we ring up the city editor at the *Blade*. Tell him you're giving *him* an exclusive tip. That if it pans out you'll call on him later for a five-spot. Tell him that Homicide is sending Goshen out here to make a surprise identification."

Lando studied Mason's guileless countenance with shrewd eyes. "This guy Holcomb knows you, doesn't he?"

"Sure he knows me," Mason said.

"Isn't that going to wreck things?"

Mason said, "Holcomb is a fiend for publicity. He's always trying to make it appear he's done something Tragg has been unable to do."

Lando said, "I still don't get it."

Mason said, "Holcomb believes in results and doesn't care how he gets them. He'll force Goshen to make an identification. Tragg wouldn't go that far."

"What I'm getting at is what Holcomb will say when he sees *you*."

Mason said, "When Holcomb drives in here he's not going to see anything."

"What do you mean?"

"Have you ever tried looking at something in the dark, just after half a dozen flash bulbs backed by silvered reflectors have popped into your eyes?"

Lando said, "I'll be damned," and his voice held admiration. He went into the service station, and started putting through calls.

22

MASON, wearing Paul Drake's black overcoat, met the car containing Drake's men, gave them careful instructions, and assigned them to positions as carefully as a football coach working out a play.

From the highway, came the sound of brakes as a car swung into the driveway leading to the auto court. The long antenna and red spotlight characterized it as a police car.

Mason said, "Okay, boys, this is it."

The car came to a stop as Drake's men converged on it.

Flash bulbs blazed into brilliance, blinding the eyes of the driver and his passenger.

"Hey," Sergeant Holcomb growled, "what's the idea?"

"Just a picture for the press, Lieutenant Tragg," one of the men said.

"It ain't Lieutenant Tragg. It's Sergeant Holcomb. Be sure you get that name right now, will you? H-O-L-C-O-M-B."

"Okay, we've got it," one of the men said. "How about another picture?"

Again flashlights popped.

Mason, taking advantage of the dazzled eyes of the officer, moved forward to stand by the running board, holding the Speed Graphic in his hand. Sergeant Holcomb reached for the ignition switch, then the dash panel switch. "Is Mason really in there?"

One of the men said, "He's there. We checked the register. He's with one of Drake's men."

More flashlights blazed.

"Say, wait a minute," Holcomb protested, "you're making this look like the Fourth of July."

"Here he comes!" one of the men shouted. "He's seen the flash bulbs and he's breaking cover. He knows we've located him now."

"Here he is," Holcomb said to Goshen.

The figure which came running out of the door of the cabin, attired in a tan overcoat and holding a hat in front of his face, ran up the gravel driveway directly toward the police car.

The photographers deployed into a semicircle. Flashlights blazed into brilliance.

The figure hesitated, stopped, turned, put on the hat, and with the dignity of surrender strode back toward the cabin.

Cameramen ran along beside the figure snapping more pictures. Mason remained at the side of the police car.

"Okay," Sergeant Holcomb growled to the man at his side. "You seen him. That's him, ain't it?"

There was a silence.

"Well?" Holcomb asked.

"That's him," Goshen said.

Sergeant Holcomb chuckled, turned on the ignition, and backed the car. "Hope those pictures turn out good," he called out. "So long, boys."

As the police car drove away, Mason said to the other operatives, "All right, boys, rush back and get those pictures developed. I want each man to keep track of his own pictures he took so we can identify them."

Mason watched them drive away, then went back into the cabin and grinned at Lando.

"How did I do?" Lando asked.

"Okay," Mason said.

"It was a lot of action there for a minute. Those flashlights certainly do blind a man."

"We'll change overcoats now," Mason said. "This black one isn't *quite* as good a fit. The tan one, I think, will be more comfortable. The car from the *Blade* should be here. . . . Let's see what this one is."

Headlights shone down the long driveway, as a car approached the cabin.

Lando went to the door and looked out.

A man's voice said, "We're from the *Blade*. We want to interview Mr. Mason."

"What are you talking about?" Lando asked.

"Oh, let them come in," Mason said. "If they've located me here they're entitled to an interview. We can't dodge them."

A newspaper reporter and a photographer entered the cabin.

"Hello, Mr. Mason," the reporter said.

"Hello," Mason said, grinning.

"You've been leading the cops quite a chase, haven't you?"

The photographer raised his camera, a flash blazed into brilliance.

Mason said, "I'm working on a case. I'm not letting everyone know where I am, but I'm not dodging the police. In fact, the police were here not over ten minutes ago. You want another picture? Sergeant Holcomb was out here—with Goshen."

They wanted more pictures and then asked Mason to pose in the doorway.

"And also coming out of the cabin," the photographer said.

The photographer stood in the yard. Mason opened the door, emerged from the cabin, holding his hat slightly to one side of his face.

"That's swell," the photographer said. "Looks as though you'd been trying to dodge a picture and I'd slipped around to the side and got a good one."

The reporter said, "We'd like to know more about this case, Mr. Mason, and . . ."

"Sorry, I have no comment to make on the case."

The reporter looked at his watch. "I guess that does it. Come on, Jack, let's rush these pictures back and get them developed. You say Holcomb was out here?"

"That's right. He'll give you details on the phone."

23

AT NOON the next day, Mason, working casually and unconcernedly in his office, received word that Lieutenant Tragg was once more a visitor.

Tragg followed on the heels of Gertie as she made the announcement.

"Pardon me for not waiting in the outer office," Tragg said, "but you have such a habit of slipping out of doors and things, and hiding in packing cases . . ."

Mason, a stack of morning papers on his desk, said irritably, "Damn it, Tragg, I don't know how that rumor got started."

"Well, the *Blade* certainly had a scoop," Tragg said. "Guess you had quite a time out there, didn't you?"

"Oh, so-so."

"You knew that Goshen identified you?"

"Did he?"

"Absolutely. He saw you walk and he saw you run."

Tragg settled himself comfortably in the chair. "Now look, Mason," he said, "you have a lot at stake. Don't let this two-timing little bitch get you into a position where your professional career is ruined."

"I'll try not to."

"Well, then, come clean."

Mason said, "It's just as I've told you, Tragg. You're a square shooter, but there are people in the district attorney's office who have been laying for me. They'd do anything on earth to get me."

"Well, they've got you now."

"Then let them prove it."

"They just might surprise you."

"On the other hand, I might surprise them. How did Sergeant Holcomb find out where I was last night?"

"I don't know," Tragg said. "Frankly, that was what I wanted to ask you about. Holcomb claims it was the result of some damn fine detective work. I had an idea it might—just *might*, you understand, have been the result of a tip-off."

"The *Blade* had a clean scoop. You don't suppose . . ."

"No. Holcomb's sore as hell at the *Blade*."

"Why?"

"Well, they didn't use pictures of him. They only had pictures of you giving an interview in the cottage after he'd left, and pictures of you coming out of the door trying to hold your hat in front of your face."

"I know exactly how he feels," Mason said. "Only I don't care about having my picture in the paper."

Tragg grinned. "Holcomb does."

"Is that so?"

"You know damn well it's so. He's been all over town buying papers, and he's intimating he made good on the job after I fell down."

Mason said, "That's leading with his chin."

Tragg looked long and searchingly at Perry Mason. "There's something about Holcomb's account of that thing that doesn't jibe."

"Is that particularly unusual?"

"I'm not commenting about what he says about his detective work. I'm referring to what he says about the photographers."

"Oh?"

"According to Holcomb there were photographers all over the place."

Mason lit a cigarette. "Well," he said, "Sergeant Holcomb is a trained observer. He should know."

"But no reporters," Tragg went on, "only photographers. Now when you stop to think of it, that's peculiar."

Mason blew smoke at the ceiling.

"Moreover, with that number of photographers every newspaper in town should have had a picture. Only the *Blade* carried the story."

"The trouble with Sergeant Holcomb," Mason observed, his eyes following the spiral of smoke which eddied up from his cigarette, "is that he hypnotizes himself, because he always wants the facts to be his way. I don't know whether you've ever noticed it, Lieutenant, but Sergeant Holcomb will get an idea, then he tries to make the facts fit that idea."

Tragg studied Mason with cautious, speculative eyes. He took a cigar from his pocket, bit off the end, lit the cigar, and said, "I'm sorry I can't promise you immunity all the way through the D. A.'s office."

"I know," Mason said.

"The way things look now," Tragg said, "they've already charged Lucille Barton with murder. They'll rush her up for a preliminary, and hold everything else in abeyance."

"Uh huh."

"Ready to close in on the others," Tragg went on, "when the situation becomes a little more clarified, as it will at the preliminary hearing. You probably know you're the one they're laying for."

"I thought they'd take me in this morning," Mason said. "In fact, I thought that was why you were coming here. I was getting my business cleaned up a bit and . . ."

"There have been complicating circumstances," Tragg said, grinning.

"What are they?"

"Hollister's automobile, for one."

"No trace of Hollister?"

"Not so far. It's only due to luck we found the car. It could have stayed there for a month or two."

"No trace of Dudley Gates?"

"Dudley Gates heard we were looking for him and telephoned us. He's in Honolulu. He'd rushed over by plane on a business deal. He tells a straightforward story, but it deepens the mystery on Hollister. Gates was planning to go with Hollister on Monday afternoon, but he had to change his plans on a few minutes' notice. He says he was supposed to go with Hollister leaving at six o'clock Monday night, but that afternoon an urgent matter came up and he suddenly decided to fly to San Francisco, and then take a plane to Honolulu. He says he'd previously advised Hollister and Hollister had talked with him in San Francisco at about quarter of five. A check of Hollister's phone records shows that's right. He called Gates at the airport in San Francisco and had him paged. Gates said Hollister told him he was going to leave Santa del Barra within an hour."

"Very interesting," Mason said.

"That changes the whole setup. You can probably see it from the D. A.'s viewpoint."

"Anything else on Hollister's movements that afternoon?"

"At four-thirty Monday when the housekeeper left the place, Hollister was just about ready to leave. His car was in the driveway. He told her six o'clock was the absolute deadline. We haven't been able to locate him."

"What does the housekeeper look like?"

"Not bad. About forty. She says he was playing around with Lucille and that Lucille had nicked him for furniture. Oriental rugs, an antique desk and a lot of other stuff."

"She evidently doesn't like Lucille?"

"Definitely not."

Mason nodded. "She wouldn't. Which direction was the car headed when it was run off the grade, Lieutenant—upgrade or downgrade?"

"It's hard to tell from the tracks. There's a wide place there, then the drop. The tracks are very faint and almost at right angles with the road. But the car must have been driven *up* from Santa del Barra.

"Someone pulled the usual stunt of locking the car in low gear, easing it off the road over to the edge, then jerking open the hand throttle and jumping from the running board to the ground "

"Then, of course, you're looking on all of the steep turns and sharp drops farther *up* the grade?"

"*Up* the grade?"

"That's right. If someone had wanted to dispose of something in the car, and then wanted to dispose of the car, he'd find the place to run the car over the cliff, and he'd naturally dispose of the object *after* he'd located the place."

"Then it would be *down* the grade. The car must have been driven up from Santa del Barra."

"That's right. The driver would *first* spot the place to dispose of the car."

Tragg thought that over.

"But the heavy object would have to be disposed of while he still had the car."

Tragg arose hurriedly. "I'd better be going."

"Well, drop in any time," Mason said.

Tragg shook hands. "Thanks, I will."

When he had left the office Mason winked at Della Street over the circling wisp of cigarette smoke.

She said, "You virtually promised him you'd make Sergeant Holcomb wish he hadn't boasted about that identification, chief."

"Did you get that impression, Della?"

"Well, in a way, yes."

"Then Tragg must have got it."

Della frowned as she studied Mason's face. "He likes you, doesn't he?—I mean personally, not officially."

"He should," Mason said.

24

AT NOON on Sunday, the ninth, Paul Drake called up Perry Mason on the unlisted telephone at the lawyer's apartment. "News for you, Perry."

"Okay," Mason said, stretching himself out luxuriously in the reclining chair, and propping the telephone to his ear, "let's have it."

"They've discovered Hollister's body."

"Where?"

"About a mile and a half *up* the grade from where Hollister's car was found."

"Well, well," Mason said, "that's very interesting."

"And he too had been shot in the head, but with a .45 caliber automatic."

"Death instantaneous, I suppose?"

"Practically."

"Where was the body?"

"It had been thrown over a cliff and then someone had gone down, rolled the body against the steep face of the bank and pushed dirt over it, a rather effective but very hasty burial."

Mason said, "Now get this, Paul. It's important. Was there anything unusual about that body—its position?"

"Yes. It was wrapped in canvas and trussed up with the knees pulled up across the chest, the head drawn forward, and the shoulders tied to the knees."

"Anything to show time?"

"Hollister's smashed wrist watch had stopped at 5:55. The clock on the dash of the car at 6:21. Police think Hollister must have been shot by a hitchhiker who drove the car up a side road, went through Hollister's pockets and tied him in a bundle so he could be rolled down the cliff. Then twenty-six minutes later got rid of the car. Hollister usually carried a good roll. There wasn't a dime in the pockets.

"But, of course, the police aren't at all certain. Because of his connection with Lucille Barton, they're moving very slowly."

"In other words, the police are pretty badly confused?"

"Well, they're starting to clarify the situation. They're filing a complaint charging Lucille Barton with murder, and they'll hold a preliminary hearing just as soon as they can rush it through."

"That's fine," Mason said. "How did they happen to find the body, Paul?"

"Well, Lieutenant Tragg evidently doped it out. He felt that Hollister's car had been ditched by someone who had wanted to conceal the body of the owner, that the car had been taken up the grade from Santa del Barra, then turned around and headed back down. He felt certain the body must have been ditched above the place where the car turned around, so he found a wide place in the road where it was possible to make a turn, then started looking for steep cliffs. Starting from there, he began to look for freshly dug ground and—well, he found it—incidentally he's taking a lot of kudos for some damn good detective work."

"I'm glad of that," Mason said. "He's certainly entitled to it. Didn't say anything about how he happened to get that hunch, did he, Paul?"

"No, it was just clever detective work on his part."

"I see," Mason said. "And what else did they find other than the body?"

"Nothing. Isn't that enough?"

"No."

"What do you mean?"

"If Hollister was starting out on a trip, he'd have had . . ."

"Oh, you mean baggage?"

"Yes."

Drake was silent for a few seconds, then said, "It's a good point, Perry. I don't think there was any."

"Well, thanks a lot for calling, Paul. I don't think they'll try to arrest anyone else until after Lucille Barton's preliminary. You should see a lot of action there, Paul."

"Heaven help us both if I don't," Drake said wearily as he hung up the telephone.

25

PERRY MASON, surveying the crowded courtroom, walked over to engage in a whispered conference with Paul Drake and Della Street.

"Hamilton Burger, the district attorney, is going to take charge of the preliminary personally," Mason said in a low voice. "That means he's gunning for me. He . . ."

The door from the judge's chambers opened and Judge Osborn walked into the courtroom and took his place on the bench.

"People versus Lucille Barton," he said. "This is the time fixed for the preliminary hearing. Are you ready, gentlemen?"

Hamilton Burger, big, ponderous, dignified, built like some huge bear, was on his feet, his voice suave, plausible, his manner radiating a synthetic impartiality, which was deadly in its effect on jurors.

"Your Honor," he said, "we are ready. Now I am going to state to the Court frankly that the death of Hartwell L. Pitkin is to some extent shrouded in mystery, but at this preliminary hearing it is only necessary for us to show that a crime was committed and to show that there is reasonable cause to believe the defendant committed that crime.

"I am very frank to state to Your Honor that I am hoping the evidence in this case will clear up some elements of the mystery and I will further add that before the case is done, we will quite probably ask for a warrant to be issued for at least one other person."

And Hamilton Burger turned meaningly toward Perry Mason.

"We're quite ready to proceed, Your Honor," Mason said. "All we ask is an opportunity to meet the issues and cross-examine the People's witnesses."

"I may say," Hamilton Burger snapped, "that our investigation in this case has been somewhat handicapped by the fact that counsel for the defendant has apparently been active in this case from its inception, *even before* the murder of Hartwell Pitkin."

"Go on with your proof," Mason said. "Don't try to prejudice the Court."

"I'm not trying to prejudice the Court," Burger snapped, his voice and manner showing the seething anger which raged within him. "I'm merely trying to explain to the Court that we have been handicapped in this case from its inception. Our witnesses have been unable to make proper identifications because of tactics used by counsel for the defense."

"What tactics?" Mason asked in surprise.

"Refusing to stand up so that a witness could identify you, for one thing," Burger said, raising his voice so that the volume of sound reverberated through the courtroom. "And following that, Your Honor, counsel permitted himself to be secreted in a packing case so that he could be spirited out of his office building through the freight exit in order to thwart the attempts of . . ."

"That's not true," Mason said cheerfully.

"Gentlemen, gentlemen," Judge Osborn said. "This is neither the time nor the place for such a discussion. If you have evidence, Mr. District Attorney, put it on."

"He hasn't any, and he can't get any," Mason said.

"Don't tell me I haven't and can't!" Burger shouted, his face darkening. "I'll show you whether or not I have any such evidence. You give me half a chance, and I'll prove that you were spirited out of your office building in a packing case so a witness by the name of Carl Evert Goshen couldn't identify you; that you then went to the Sleepwell Auto Court with a bodyguard, where you tried to hide until the witness found you and made an absolute identification."

"Go ahead and prove it," Mason said.

"And the minute I try to prove *that* in *this* case you'll start objecting that it's not within the issues," Burger said contemptuously. "*Our* hands are tied, and you know it."

Mason said, "If you have witnesses who can prove any such thing, I won't make a single objection."

"Come, come, gentlemen," Judge Osborn said. "The Court has to be considered in this matter. We have a crowded calendar. This is merely a preliminary examination and . . ."

"If Your Honor will permit me to take up counsel's offer," Hamilton Burger said, "I'll convince the Court that the time consumed by putting on that evidence is the most important time Your Honor has ever spent on the bench. I'll blast the subterfuge of this scheming attorney wide open. I'll show him in his true colors. I'll . . ."

Judge Osborn's gavel banged on the desk. "You'll refrain from these insulting personalities, Mr. District Attorney."

"I beg the Court's pardon," Burger said, controlling himself with difficulty. "I have been led to lose some measure of my self-control by the tactics I've encountered in this case. Counsel has made an offer. He's made it publicly. I don't think he dares to stand by that offer, but I would like to . . ."

"You go ahead and put on your proof," Judge Osborn said. "The Court will not permit its time to be taken up with extraneous matters, but I think you know this Court well enough to know that any legitimate attempt to get at the truth will be welcome."

"Very well," Hamilton Burger sneered. "Counsel has stated he won't object. I'll lay the preliminary proof of the *corpus delicti* by showing that Hartwell L. Pitkin was employed by Stephen Argyle as a chauffeur and butler; that on the fifth of this month he was murdered, having been shot with a Smith and Wesson revolver, Number S65088. I'll call Lieutenant Tragg as a witness."

Tragg took the witness stand, testified to his official connection with the police and the fact that he was on the homicide squad; that on the fifth he had been called to a garage in the back of an apartment house at number 19 South Gondola; that there he had found the body of Hartwell L. Pitkin.

Tragg then went on to describe the body, the manner in which it had been found, and what had been done.

"There was a gun lying near the right hand of the body?" Burger asked.

"That's right," Tragg said. "It was a .38 caliber Smith and Wesson, number S65088. An attempt had been made to remove all the numbers but one number had been overlooked and was still intact. The cylinder contained five loaded shells and one empty shell."

"Is this the weapon?" Burger asked, producing the gun.

"It is, yes, sir."

"I ask that it be marked for identification, Your Honor."

"Very well. It will be so marked."

"Now, Lieutenant, you say this gun was found near the body?"

"Yes, sir, but a paraffin test showed the decedent had not fired a gun. Also there had been an extensive hemorrhage from a wound in the head. We found this gun lying *on top of the pool of blood.* There was no blood on the gun except on the *under* side. There were blood spatters on the hand of the decedent. There were no spatters on the gun and no fingerprints whatever on the outside of the gun."

"How about the inside of the gun?" Burger asked.

"On the *inside* of the gun," Tragg said, "we found a fingerprint which was subsequently identified as being the print of a man's right index finger."

"Whose finger?" Burger asked.

"Perry Mason's finger," Tragg said.

"You have those fingerprints here?"

"I have them here."

"Your Honor," Burger said apologetically, "this is perhaps the wrong way to introduce this evidence. I should technically have produced a photograph of the fingerprint and then prints of Mr. Mason's fingers and compared them, but in view of the fact that there can't be any question about the identification of the print, and in view of . . ."

"I'm not going to object," Mason interrupted. "Go right ahead. Handle it any way you want to, Mr. District Attorney."

"Thank you," Burger said sarcastically. "Now, Lieutenant Tragg, if you have those fingerprints, we'll introduce them in evidence. People's Exhibit A, the fingerprint that was found on the inside of the gun. People's Exhibit B, a print that was taken from Mr. Mason's right index finger. Now, will you describe the circumstances under which you took that fingerprint of Mr. Mason's right index finger?"

Tragg said, "That was on Thursday, the sixth. I went to Mr. Mason's office with a Mr. Goshen . . ."

"His full name?"

"Carl Evert Goshen."

"You had there some conversation with Mr. Mason?"

"Isn't this entirely outside of the issues, Mr. District Attorney?"

"I think I can connect it up," Burger said. "Mr. Mason is not objecting."

"I understand Mr. Mason's position. However, I don't care to hear a lot of extraneous or hearsay evidence."

"This isn't hearsay. This gets right down to the gist of the case."

"All right, go ahead."

Burger said, "Mr. Goshen was there with you, Lieutenant Tragg. Who else?"

"The defendant in the case, Lucille Barton, a gentleman by the name of Arthur Colson, who had apparently been interested in the purchase of the gun, and a plain-clothes officer."

"Mr. Mason permitted you to take his fingerprints?"

"Yes."

"Did he make any comment about his fingerprint being on the inside of the gun?"

"He admitted that he had used a key which he said he had received in the mail to enter the apartment of Lucille Barton on the day of the murder . . ."

"Come, come, gentlemen," Judge Osborn interrupted. "Despite the fact that there isn't any objection from the attorney for the defense, I feel that . . ."

"But he admitted seeing the gun in the defendant's apartment," Burger said.

"A gun," Mason corrected.

"Well, *a* gun similar to this gun," Burger retorted. "That certainly is significant and it's relevant."

"Yes, I suppose so," Judge Osborn said. "Go right ahead."

Lieutenant Tragg said, "At that time I pointed out to Mr. Mason that Mr. Goshen was a witness who had seen two people at the garage where the body was found at about the time the murder must have been committed. One of these persons Goshen had previously identified as the defendant. She was accompanied by a man who answered the description of Mr. Perry Mason. I asked Mr. Mason to stand up so that Mr. Goshen could see if he were the same person. Mr. Mason refused to do so."

"You mean he refused to get up?" Mr. Burger said, his voice for dramatic emphasis showing a synthetic incredulity. "You mean that Mr. Mason, an attorney at law, refused to let a witness look at him to see if he could be identified as a man who had accompanied . . ."

"I think that question's argumentative and has already been asked and answered in effect," Judge Osborn said. "The Court is going to try to keep this examination somewhere within the limits of the legal rules. It is, of course, a peculiar situation where an attorney for the defense refuses to object." And Judge Osborn frowned disapprovingly at Perry Mason.

"Your Honor," Mason said, "quite obviously the district attorney is preparing to attack my reputation by insinuation and innuendo. He knows, of course, that the press is represented at this hearing. I am fully aware that by pretending to be balked by technical objections on my part he can leave the impression that I am fighting to suppress the real facts. Therefore, I am throwing the doors wide open. If he has any facts, I want them brought out."

"Well," Judge Osborn said, "I guess, on second thought, I can appreciate your position, Mr. Mason. However, of course, the court can't be used as a place for trying personalities."

"There aren't personalities, Your Honor," Hamilton Burger said. "This gets right down to the meat of the situation."

"All right, go ahead, start carving," Judge Osborn said.

"Now then, did you subsequently make an attempt to have Mr. Mason identified by Mr. Goshen?"

"I most certainly did."

"What did you do?"

"I had Mr. Goshen in my car with me, waiting in front of the exit of Mr. Mason's office building. I was working in co-operation with reporters who were also covering the freight exit of the building and who were prepared to signal me in the event Mr. Mason left the building by that entrance."

"And what did Mr. Mason do?"

Tragg grinned and said, "He had himself put in a packing case and shipped out of the back door as merchandise."

There was a ripple of merriment through the courtroom.

"Did Goshen subsequently identify Mr. Mason?"

"I wasn't there at the time," Tragg said. "One of my associates, Sergeant Holcomb, was there when that happened."

"Cross-examine," Burger said triumphantly.

Mason said smilingly, "How do *you* know that I left the building in a packing case, Lieutenant?"

"Well, now," Tragg said hurriedly, "perhaps I should correct that. As a matter of fact, I only knew it from what I read in the papers and what I was told. I didn't *see* you leave the building in the packing case. If I had . . ." He broke off and grinned.

"Did you talk with anyone who saw me in that packing case, Lieutenant?"

"No, sir."

"You have any reason to believe I was in that packing case?"

"Yes, sir."

"What makes you think so?"

"It was the only way you could have got out of the building without having been observed."

"Permit me to correct you, Lieutenant. You probably don't realize it, but as a matter of fact I was in Paul Drake's office until late that evening, until long after the packing case had been shipped. If you had talked with the janitor of the building you would have found that I left and went down in the elevator with him, accompanied by one of Paul Drake's men, a Mr. Jerry Lando, a man, incidentally, who is here in court and who can be questioned by you at any time."

Tragg's face showed surprise. "You mean . . ."

"I mean exactly what I say, Lieutenant. I'd suggest that you have a talk with Mr. Lando before you make any more accusations based on hearsay. Now, thank you very much, Lieutenant Tragg. I have no further questions on cross-examination."

Tragg and Burger exchanged glances. Tragg stepped down from the witness stand, turned when he was halfway across the courtroom, and said, "Where is this Jerry Lando?"

"Right here," Jerry Lando said, standing up.

"Never mind," Hamilton Burger said, hiding embarrassment behind a new belligerency. "I'll call Sergeant Holcomb to the witness stand and we'll clear *that* matter up very rapidly."

Sergeant Holcomb came striding forward, raised his hand, took the oath, and with a satisfied anticipatory grin, settled himself in the witness chair.

Hamilton Burger asked a few preliminary questions as to name, age, residence, occupation, and then plunged into the evidence. "Sergeant, where were you on the evening of the sixth—that was Thursday, you'll remember."

"I remember," Sergeant Holcomb grinned. "I located Perry Mason at the Sleepwell Auto Court and got a witness by the name of Carl Goshen to accompany me. We went out to make an identification. We made it."

Sergeant Holcomb grinned gleefully as he thought over the events of the evening.

"What happened while you were there and in your presence?" Burger asked.

"Well, we drove into the auto court and in some way the word got around to newspapers. A bunch of newspaper photographers were out there. They took pictures of us when we drove in. They did that before I could stop them."

"And then what happened?"

"Well, when the flash bulbs started popping, Mason, who was in Cabin Number 6, evidently accompanied by this Jerry Lando because Jerry Lando had signed the register and given the license number of his car, well, Mr. Mason came running out, and when he saw all the newspaper photographers he put his hat up in front of his face to try and keep them from getting his picture; but they started shooting flash bulbs anyway. Then he saw he was trapped, so he turned around and walked back to the cabin."

"Did you follow him into the cabin?"

"No, sir."

"Why not?"

Sergeant Holcomb grinned and said, "Because it wasn't necessary. I'd done all I wanted to do. The witness Goshen, who was with me, had seen Mason come out of the cabin, had seen him walk and run, had seen his size and build, and he identified him absolutely as the man he'd seen in front of that garage about the time the murder was being committed. He'd previously identified the defendant, Lucille Barton."

"This is a highly irregular manner of receiving evidence," Judge Osborn snapped. "The witness Goshen should speak for himself."

"He will," Hamilton Burger promised. "I'm simply taking up Mason's challenge and proving that I had the evidence I said I had. The Court will observe that it has only taken some twenty minutes of the Court's time."

"Very well," Judge Osborn said. "It is of course a most unusual situation, the defendant's counsel permitting all this hearsay evidence without objection."

Sergeant Holcomb said, "It isn't hearsay, Your Honor. I was sitting right there when Goshen made the identification. I heard what he said."

"That's *exactly* what is meant by hearsay," Judge Osborn said. "You don't know whether the man at the garage was Perry Mason. *You* only know what the witness said. The witness should speak for himself."

"Well, he will," Hamilton Burger interposed hastily. "He'll be my next witness, if the Court please."

"Very well, finish with this witness," Judge Osborn said.

"I'm finished with him now," Burger announced triumphantly.

Sergeant Holcomb started to leave the stand.

"Just a minute," Mason said. "I want to ask you a few questions about that identification at the Sleepwell Auto Court, Sergeant. Now, *you've* known me for some time?"

"Yes, sir."

"You recognized me when I ran out of the cabin and you said to Goshen, 'There he is. There's Mason now,' or words to that effect?"

"I don't think I had to say anything like that. He recognized you as soon as he saw you."

"You may not have thought you *had* to say it, but you *did* say it."

"I may have."

"The man who ran out had his hat in front of his face?"

"*You* had *your* hat in front of *your* face, trying to keep people from taking *your* picture."

"Then this man turned his back and walked back to the cabin?"

"That's right. That's exactly what *you* did."

"How far did the man run from the cabin before he turned around and ran back?"

"Oh, some thirty or forty feet."

"There were several newspaper photographers there?"

"Yes, sir."

"How do you know they were newspaper photographers?"

"Well, I . . . I . . ."

"In other words, you just *assumed* they must have been newspaper photographers, is that right?"

Holcomb said angrily and sarcastically, "That's right. I'm just a dumb cop, but when a newspaper gives me a tip, when I see a bunch of guys carrying press cameras with flash bulbs fixed in reflectors, I just get credulous enough to think they're newspaper men. It's careless of me!"

"Oh, so you had a tip from a newspaper?"

"Well, I used methods of my own."

"How did you know I was there at this auto court?"

Holcomb grinned. "A little bird told me."

"And when you got there, there were some half dozen photographers there?"

"Right."

"Some of them took your picture?"

"Yes, sir."

"Can you remember any of them? Would you know them if you saw them again?"

"Why, I don't know," Sergeant Holcomb said. "I . . ."

"If you can identify the man you saw running out of the cabin, why couldn't you identify some of the photographers?"

"Well, as a matter of fact, that's sort of hard to do when those flash bulbs are popping in your eyes. I . . ."

"Oh, so you were dazzled by flash bulbs?" Mason said.

"Not enough so I couldn't recognize *you*," Sergeant Holcomb shouted.

"I see," Mason said, smiling. "The flash bulbs dazzled you so you couldn't see any of the other men, but they didn't dazzle you enough so you couldn't see me."

"I didn't say that."

"Well, how about those other men—can you describe them?"

"I can describe some of them."

"Well, go ahead."

"Well," Sergeant Holcomb said, "there was a photographer right next to me, the man who came up and took my picture at the first. He was wearing a black overcoat."

"About how old?"

"I couldn't tell how old he was from looking at him out of the corner of my eye. He was a youngish man."

"About how tall?"

"Oh . . . fairly tall, perhaps about as tall as you are."

"About how heavy?"

Holcomb looked Mason over thoughtfully and said, "Somewhat your build."

"Did you talk with this man?"

"I don't think so. I tell you I was looking at you when you ran out of the cabin. I had my headlights on and you ran right into those headlights and put up your hat to shield your face, and—acted just like a shyster lawyer caught in a web of his own trickery, and . . ."

"That will do!" Judge Osborn shouted, pounding with his gavel. "That is absolutely uncalled for, Sergeant Holcomb! You know better than that."

Sergeant Holcomb said angrily, "Well, he's trying to insinuate I couldn't see him."

"Nevertheless, these personalities are uncalled for. Now, while you're in this court, Sergeant, you confine yourself to answering questions. Otherwise the Court is going to have to take some disciplinary action. Do you understand?"

"Yes, sir," Sergeant Holcomb said sullenly.

"Now, you say this man who was standing next to you took your picture as you drove up?" Mason asked.

"That's right."

"What were you doing when the picture was taken? Do you remember?"

"I remember exactly," Sergeant Holcomb said. "I was leaning forward to turn off the ignition, and also the switch on the dashboard which controlled the dash and panel lights, so this man Goshen could get a better view; that is, so he could look through the windshield without having lights in his eyes."

Mason said, "I'll show you a photograph, Sergeant Holcomb, and ask you if that's the photograph which was taken of you at that moment by this photographer who was standing beside your car. You'll notice it shows the witness Goshen sitting in the car and you're leaning forward to . . ."

"That's the picture," Sergeant Holcomb said. "That's the one that was taken at that moment."

"That was the only time you leaned forward, when you turned off the ignition and the dash and panel lights?"

"That's right. That's the picture that was taken by that photographer who was standing right next to me."

"And that flashlight didn't dazzle your eyes?"

"Not mine," Sergeant Holcomb said. "My eyes are good. I'm accustomed to driving a lot at night and headlights don't bother me. I can look right past a glare and . . . No, sir, those flashlights didn't bother me at all. They didn't keep me from seeing everything that was going on."

"Now, at about that time," Mason said, "there was another photographer directly in front of the automobile who took a photograph right through the windshield, wasn't there?"

"I believe so, yes, but you can't mix me up by making the claim that those flashlight bulbs blinded us, because they didn't."

"No, no," Mason said, "I'm not making that claim. I'm simply trying to identify the order in which the photographs were taken. Now, here is another photograph which shows you leaning forward in the automobile and apparently was taken immediately before, or immediately after the photographer who was on your left had taken his picture. This, however, is taken from the front of the car, looking through the windshield."

"That's right," Sergeant Holcomb said. "That's the picture."

"That picture shows you, shows Mr. Goshen, and shows the photographer who had just taken this first picture. Is that right?"

"That's right."

"All right," Mason said. "Let's have these photographs marked for identification as Defendant's Exhibit One and Defendant's Exhibit Two."

The clerk marked the photographs.

"Now, then," Mason said, "at about that time, there were other photographers taking pictures of the man who ran out of the cabin?"

"You hadn't run out of the cabin then," Sergeant Holcomb said. "You can't trap me that way, Mr. Mason. The photographers all clustered around and took our pictures when I first drove up. Then the flashing of those bulbs made you realize something was wrong. You broke cover and came dashing out of that cabin just like a rabbit breaking cover and running away. When you saw all that gang in front of you, you turned around and scuttled right back into the cabin, but not until Goshen had had plenty of opportunity to identify you."

"And as that figure came running out, the photographers took pictures of him?"

"That's right, pictures of you."

"Holding his hat up?"

"That's right, holding *your* hat up."

"Now, then," Mason said, "I'll show you a photograph which I would like to have marked for identification as Defendant's Exhibit Number Three, and which shows a figure running out from this cabin with a hat held in front of his face." •

"That's the one," Sergeant Holcomb said. "That's a good picture. That shows *you* running out with a hat up in front of *your* face."

"Exactly," Mason said. "We'll have that as Defendant's Exhibit for identification Number Three. Now, I'll show you Defendant's Exhibit for identification Number Four, Sergeant Holcomb, and you will notice that that shows the running man, but slightly from a side view. It also shows the photographer who has just taken picture Number Three."

Holcomb studied the picture, said, "That's right. That seems to be the way the picture was taken. That's it, all right."

"But," Mason said, "you will notice that in this picture which 's marked Number Four for identification, Sergeant, the angle of the camera was a little to one side so that the features of the man ar ; a little more plainly visible than this photograph Number Three."

"Yes, I guess they are," Holcomb admitted.

"Now, then," Mason said, "I'll show you a photograph, Exhibit Number Five, which shows the running figure with the hat held in front of his face, and also shows the photographers who took pictures in Three and Four."

"That's right," Sergeant Holcomb said mechanically.

"That's right?"

"That's right."

"Better take another look at that picture," Mason said. "You can see the man's profile in it quite clearly. Do you think that is my picture, Sergeant?"

Sergeant Holcomb suddenly grabbed at the picture, said, "Wait a minute. I'd better get my glasses on here." He reached in his pocket, adjusted spectacles, studied the picture, said suddenly, "No, this isn't you. There's some sort of flimflam work here! *That's* another man!"

"Exactly," Mason said. "Now, if you will look at the photograph marked for identification as Exhibit Number Two, Sergeant, and look at the man standing with the camera just to the side of your automobile, the man who took picture Number One, just as you were leaning forward, you may recognize the features of that man."

"Just a minute—just a minute," Hamilton Burger said. "I want to see those pictures. What's happening here?"

"Come up and take a look at them," Mason invited.

Sergeant Holcomb, studying the picture, said suddenly, "That isn't right. This is fake photography."

Mason smiled. "What makes you think it's fake photography, Sergeant?"

"Because that isn't the way it happened. This is another one of your slick flimflams."

Mason said, "Better be careful with your accusations, Sergeant. We have six reputable witnesses to testify as to what happened there. Now, do you see any signs on that photograph that indicate it's a fake photograph?"

"I don't know enough about photography to tell," Sergeant Holcomb said.

"Then how do you know it's a fake?"

"Because it isn't—it isn't the way things happened."

"Oh, yes it is," Mason said. "Now, as a matter of fact, Sergeant, let's remember you're under oath here. When you first drove up to that cabin, photographers came and clustered around the automobile and took a whole series of flashlight pictures of you, didn't they?"

"I've told you they did."

"And let's remember our oath, now," Mason said. "Isn't it a fact, Sergeant, that the effect of those flashlights blinded your eyes so that you were temporarily incapable of seeing clearly—particularly objects in the semi-darkness on the side of the car?"

"Well, I tell you I wasn't looking at those objects. I was looking at that house because right at that time the door popped open and . . . and . . ."

"Go on," Mason said, smiling, "and remember you're under oath, Sergeant, and that there are six reputable witnesses to testify what took place there."

"Well," Sergeant Holcomb said lamely, "the door popped open and this running man came out."

"Holding his hat in front of his face?"

"Yes."

"So you couldn't see his face?"

"Well, I . . ."

"Did you or didn't you see his face?" Mason asked.

"Well, I didn't see his face, no."

"Then how could you tell who he was?"

"Well, I—I thought I recognized him by his walk and the way he ran, and . . . Well, I'd been told Perry Mason was hiding in that cabin, and . . ."

"Exactly," Mason said. "You *expected* me to run out. Therefore, when a figure ran out and acted as you expected I might act under the circumstances you . . ."

"Oh, Your Honor, I object to this," Hamilton Burger said. "This is incompetent, irrelevant and immaterial. It's argumentative. It's not proper cross-examination."

"Well, well," Mason said, smiling. "Look who's objecting now!"

"I think the pictures speak for themselves," Judge Osborn said.

"Well, if the Court please," Hamilton Burger announced, "this is manifestly an unfair advantage to take of a witness. It is quite on a par with the trickery for which counsel is noted. It's . . ."

"Sure, it's trickery," Mason said, "but it's a trickery which wouldn't confuse an honest witness. As a matter of fact, Sergeant Holcomb's eyes were blinded by those flash bulbs just as I expected they'd be. He isn't frank enough nor honest enough to admit it, but he is sitting here under oath on this witness stand and he's going to tell the truth or he's going to be guilty of perjury. There are six witnesses who took these pictures and will identify them. Now, I want to know from Sergeant Holcomb right here and now and on cross-examination whether *I* was the person who ran out of that cabin, or whether *I* was the person standing within four foot of his left elbow holding a camera focused on his face and taking a flashlight picture. Now which was it, Sergeant?"

Sergeant Holcomb's face was a picture of dismay.

"Oh, Your Honor," Hamilton Burger said, "that's an unfair question. That . . ."

"Objection is overruled," Judge Osborn snapped. "Let the witness answer the question."

"Which was it?" Mason asked, grinning cheerfully at the discomfited officer. "And remember we have both photographs and photographers to refute any false testimony."

"I don't know," Sergeant Holcomb blurted.

"Thank you," Mason said. "That concludes my cross-examination, Sergeant. And now I believe, Mr. District Attorney, you said you wanted to put Mr. Goshen on the stand as your next witness. Put him on. Let's hear what Mr. Goshen has to say."

Hamilton Burger said, "Your Honor, I dislike these personalities . . ."

"Counsel is merely repeating a promise which you made," Judge Osborn said, fighting back a smile. "Of course, I will admit that his manner is perhaps more dramatic than the situation calls for, but . . . in any event, proceed with your case, Mr. Burger."

Hamilton Burger said, "I would like to ask the Court at this time for a five-minute recess. I would like to confer briefly with one of my associates. This situation has take me somewhat by surprise."

"And I submit, Your Honor," Mason said, "that counsel has re-

peatedly promised to put the witness Goshen on the stand. I'd like
to have him go on the stand now before there's been any opportunity to coach him."

"I resent that!" Burger shouted. "I have no intention of coaching the witness. He doesn't need any coaching."

"Put him on then," Mason challenged.

"I have made a motion for a five-minute recess."

"I've opposed it," Mason said.

"The motion is denied," Judge Osborn ruled. "The Court sees
no reason for a recess at this time."

"Very well, then, I'll call Roscoe R. Hansom to the stand."

"I thought you were going to call Goshen," Mason said.

"I don't have to follow your instructions or the instructions of
anyone else in putting on my case. I can put it on any way I please!"
Burger shouted.

Mason said, "You were hurling challenges at me a few moments
ago, Mr. District Attorney, now I'll hurl one right back at you. I
dare you to put Mr. Goshen on the stand *as you promised,* and
before you've had an opportunity to talk with him about this new
development."

Hamilton Burger sullenly said, "I asked for Roscoe R. Hansom.
Mr. Hansom, will you come forward please?"

Mason grinned.

Judge Osborn clamped his lips together in a firm, thin line.

Hansom identified himself as the proprietor of the Rushing
Creek Mercantile Company, told of selling the gun, and of the general description of the man who had purchased the gun. He then
produced the gun register, and the signature of the man who had
signed for that gun on the register. The gun, which had been previously marked for identification, was received in evidence as
People's Exhibit C.

"Have you subsequently seen that man?" Burger asked.

"Yes, sir."

"Who was he?"

"His name is Arthur Colson. I saw him at your office on the
morning of the sixth."

"Cross-examine," Burger snapped.

"No questions," Mason said, gleefully. "Do you want to call Mr.
Goshen now?"

"Your Honor," Burger said, "I resent this continual nagging by
counsel."

"You've invited it," Judge Osborn said.

"Nevertheless, Your Honor, I feel that it is improper."

"It is improper," the Court said. "However, I can tell you this much, Mr. District Attorney. You can stall around if you want to. You've a perfect right to put on your case in any way that you see fit. But when it comes to a showdown, your proof is going to be addressed to the discretion of the Court. Now I take it there's a matter of identification of this defendant by the witness, Goshen, which is material. Very material to your case."

"Yes, Your Honor."

"And you promised, in fact, you threatened, I may say you bragged, that you were going to put this witness on the stand in order to prove certain statements you made in your opening address to the Court. Now the judge of this court wasn't born yesterday, and I know that if you stall matters along until the Court takes its usual adjournment for recess that there's a reason for doing it. And in the mind of the Court such tactics are going to greatly weaken the testimony of the witness Goshen. Now that's plain talk, Mr. District Attorney, but it's because of a situation which you yourself invited. I'm speaking my mind. There's no jury here. This is a preliminary hearing. It's a matter addressed entirely to the discretion of the Court and that's the way the Court feels about it. Now proceed with your case."

Hamilton Burger cleared his throat, stood for a moment undecided, then blurted out, "Carl Evert Goshen, take the stand."

Goshen took the witness stand, and, after the preliminary questions, stated that he lived next door to the apartment house at 719 South Gondola. He had occasion to remember the evening of the fifth and in particular was annoyed by an automobile which had sputtered and backfired with a series of explosions which indicated the carburetor or the timing, or both, were badly out of adjustment.

"What did you do?" Burger asked.

"I opened the window, intending to call to the people across the way, asking them to shut off that motor, or do something about it," Goshen said.

"Did you do so?"

"No, sir, I didn't."

"Why?"

"Because they shut off the motor at right about that time."

"And did you see the car and the people?"

"Yes, sir."

"How far away were they?"

"Well, they were across an alley which leads to the garage. Oh, I'd say they were perhaps seventy-five feet."

"Were the figures illuminated?"

"Well, sir, the headlights were on on the automobile and I could see these figures moving around. They were looking in the garage and—well, I saw their backs and saw how they were dressed."

"Now can you describe those figures?"

"Yes, sir. One of them was Lucille Barton, the defendant in this case. She was wearing a plaid coat and a black hat with a little red feather. A hat that was close-fitting and slanted down on her head over to the right. She had those same clothes on when the police showed her to me."

"And the other figure?"

"Well, now," Goshen said, crossing his legs and running his hand over the top of his partially bald head, "now you've got me guessing."

The courtroom broke into laughter.

Hamilton Burger frowned, and said, "You have your two eyes, don't you know what you saw?"

Goshen rubbed his head, "And I've got my two ears, and I know what I've just heard."

Even Judge Osborn joined in the laughter which rocked the courtroom.

When order had been restored, Burger said, sullenly, "Well, tell us what you saw as best you can."

"Well, I saw a tall man. I never did see his face. He was a tall, athletic looking fellow, apparently sort of young, from the way he moved, not real young, but moving around sort of easy like. He took long strides, had long legs, and he was wearing a gray hat and a tan overcoat."

"Have you ever seen that man again? Can you identify him?"

"Well, now," Goshen said, hesitating and rubbing his hand over his head, "I just don't rightly know."

The courtroom tittered and Judge Osborn pounded it to silence.

"But you can positively identify the defendant?" Hamilton Burger asked.

"Objected to as leading and suggestive, assuming a fact not in evidence, argumentative, and putting words in the mouth of the defendant," Mason said.

"The objection is sustained."

"Well," Hamilton Burger said, "you definitely know how she was dressed?"

"Yes, sir."

"And her height, weight, age, and general build?"

"Yes, sir."

"All the same as this defendant?"

"Yes, sir."

"And the man. Was he about the same height as anyone you are now looking at?"

"Objected to as leading and suggestive."

"Objection sustained."

"Well, how can you describe him?"

"Objected to as already asked and answered."

"Objection sustained."

"Cross-examine," Hamilton Burger snapped, with exasperation.

Mason said, "You *thought* you saw that same person again, didn't you?"

"I certainly thought I did, Mr. Mason, yes, sir. It was just the way Sergeant Holcomb has described it."

"In other words, the figure you saw at the garage that night was a man of just about the same height, build, and wearing about the same colored garments as the man you saw emerging from the auto court?"

"That's right."

"But you never did see the man's face?"

"No, sir."

"When you saw him at the garage you saw only his back?"

"Yes, sir."

"So all you know is that you saw a rather tall man with a tan-colored topcoat and a gray hat."

"Yes, sir."

"And any tall man of approximately the same build, wearing those garments, would look just about the same to you as the man you saw at that time?"

"Well, I . . . no I don't think so. I think probably I could identify him."

Mason said, "You *did* identify him, didn't you?"

"What do you mean?"

"You heard the Sergeant's testimony that you pointed out the man who ran out of that cabin."

"Well, I guess I made a mistake there," Goshen admitted, gulping in embarrassment.

"What makes you think you made a mistake?"

"Well, that man evidently was someone who had been planted there."

"What makes you think you made a mistake?"

"Well . . . my gosh, Mr. Mason, you've just proved it wasn't you."

"In other words," Mason said, "you had been told that the man you had seen at the garage was none other than Perry Mason?"

"Well, that's what the police seemed to think."

"You'd been told that?"

"Yes."

"And when you saw that man run out of the cabin you said to Sergeant Holcomb, 'that's the man,' didn't you?"

"Well, I guess I did."

"And you saw that figure running toward the headlights of an automobile, and you saw it turn around and run back?"

"Yes, sir."

"You saw it as plainly as you saw the figure that you were looking at across the alley?"

"Well, I . . . as a matter of fact, those flashlights popping in my eyes certainly did make everything seem all sort of black to me, sort of hard to look at."

"But you saw the figure well enough so that you were willing to identify him?"

"Well, yes."

"And did identify him?"

"Yes."

"And now think you were mistaken?"

"Well, I guess I must have been."

"Simply because the figure was not that of the man police had told you you must have seen at the garage, is that right?"

"Well . . . I . . . I just don't rightly know how to say it, Mr. Mason, but I guess I walked into a trap and . . . and I guess," he added ruefully, "I've got my fingers caught."

Even Judge Osborn smiled.

"And this woman whom you saw across the alley was with a man?"

"Yes."

"And you saw her at the same time and place as the man?"

"Yes, sir."

"Under the same conditions?"

"Yes, sir."

"And if you can't identify the man, how do you expect to identify the woman?"

"Well—well, I really could have identified that man if I hadn't made a mistake."

"You did identify *a* man?"

"Yes."

"And now you think it was the wrong man?"

"It must have been."

"And you saw the woman there at the garage no more distinctly than you saw the man?"

"Well, no."

"Thank you," Mason said. "That's all."

"And *now*," Judge Osborn said, cocking a stern eye at Hamilton Burger, "the Court will take a ten-minute recess."

26

As soon as Judge Osborn had left the bench, Lucille Barton turned to Perry Mason, placed her gloved hand over his wrist, squeezed so hard the leather of the glove stretched taut over her knuckles.

"Mr. Mason, you're wonderful!" she whispered.

Mason said, "This is just the opening round, Lucille, we've shaken the witness in his identification of me; but don't overlook the fact that his identification of you will stand up unless we can find some way of showing you weren't there."

"Yes, that's so," she admitted in a whisper.

"And," Mason said, "the gun with which Pitkin was killed was a gun that quite evidently had been given you by Arthur Colson. And incidentally, Ross Hollister was also murdered, and you had twenty thousand dollars' insurance on Hollister's life."

"But, Mr. Mason, can't you understand? I loved Ross. His death is a great blow to me. We were going to be married. He represented security, affection, a home, everything a woman wants."

"Unless, perhaps, she happened to have been in love with Arthur Colson, who showed her a way of collecting twenty thousand dollars' insurance so she could marry *him*."

"Mr. Mason, don't be silly! You were so nice, and now you're talking just like that district attorney."

"You don't know the half of it," Mason said. "Wait until you hear the way he's *going* to talk! You never have told me why you didn't take my advice and telephone the police when that body was discovered, and when that gun was still in your purse."

"Mr. Mason, I can't. I simply can't. I can't tell you that story. I can't tell anyone."

"All right," Mason said, "I can put on all sorts of a grandstand here, but you're going to be bound over for murder, and later on, unless you can tell some satisfactory story to a jury, you're going to be convicted of murder."

"Mr. Mason, can't *you* get me off?"

"Not unless I know what happened, and unless it's a good story."

"Other women shoot people and get off. Lawyers . . ."

"I know," Mason said, "but you're up against a different situation. Colson started masterminding this thing, and two men have been murdered. The revolver which killed one of them was in your possession both before and after the murders were committed. You're going to have one hell of a time explaining that it wasn't in your possession *while they were being committed.*"

"Mr. Mason, Arthur Colson wasn't the one who did what you call masterminding that."

"No?" Mason said skeptically. "He's never done anything, or said anything that convinced me of his sincerity."

She said impulsively, "He's simply trying to stand by me, Mr. Mason. You must believe that. You *must* understand that."

Mason merely smiled.

"The man who did what you call masterminding the thing," she said, "was someone whom you haven't even talked to."

"Who?"

"Willard Barton," she blurted, and then suddenly removed her gloved hand to press it against her lips. "There, I've said too much! He'd be furious if he knew that."

Mason watched her with coldly cynical eyes. "Was that an act?" he asked.

"What?"

"Letting that information slip out."

"No, I . . . I'm sorry I said it."

Mason said, "You're a damn smart little actress. I don't know what sort of trap you're setting for me now, but I'm not going to walk into it."

She said, "They can never *prove* that gun was in my possession if *you* keep quiet."

"What makes you think so?"

"Arthur Colson told me that."

Mason said angrily, "That dreamy-eyed goof!"

"He's smart, Mr. Mason. He's terribly clever."

"I daresay," Mason said sarcastically.

"And he says he won't ever let them trace that gun into my possession."

Mason said, "You were engaged to Hollister. He planned to

leave on a business trip Monday night. You knew that and you spent that evening with Arthur Colson. I don't like that story, and a jury won't like it."

She said, "It's the truth. Arthur is just like a brother to me."

"Did Hollister know Arthur Colson?"

"No. They'd never met."

Mason said, "I don't like Arthur's presence in the case."

"You just wait," she flared. "He'll . . ."

"Yes?" Mason prompted as she paused, he'll do what?"

"Nothing."

Mason studied her for a few seconds, then said, "That gun has my fingerprint on it. You're going to have to explain that eventually."

A cunning smile twitched the corners of her mouth. "Arthur Colson told me something about that. Don't worry, I'll explain it."

27

As COURT reconvened, Hamilton Burger, still flushed and angry, but having regained some of his composure, said, "Call Willard Barton to the stand."

Lucille Barton, sitting at Mason's side, said under her breath in a whisper, "No, no. Don't let him do *that*."

Mason casually swung around in his chair. "Smile," he said.

There was panic in her eyes, her lips were trembling.

"Smile," Mason ordered. "They're looking at you."

She twisted her lips in a quivering travesty of a smile.

Willard Barton, a well-groomed, chunky man with a profusion of dark, wavy hair which furnished a contrast with steel-gray eyes, settled himself in the witness chair in the manner of a substantial businessman who is more accustomed to giving orders than receiving them, and who is quite accustomed to being the center of attention.

In a firm, incisive tone he stated his name and address, gave his occupation as that of an investor in potential oil-bearing properties, and then flashed Lucille the first quick glance he had given her since he had taken the stand. It was a glance of swift appraisal that held no emotion whatever. Then his eyes turned back to Hamilton Burger as he waited for the next question.

"You have the same name as the defendant in this case?"

"She has *my* name, yes, sir."

"You were married to her at one time?"

"Yes, sir."

"And divorced?"

"Yes."

"When were you divorced?"

"About eighteen months ago."

"The decree has become final?"

"It has."

"You are paying her alimony?"

"Yes, sir."

"Did you see her on the evening of the fifth of this month?"

"I did, yes, sir."

"What time?"

"About half-past six, perhaps a little later."

"Where?"

"I was at the Broadway Athletic Club. She telephoned me and asked if she could see me. I told her I'd see her for a moment in the lobby, but I warned her that if she tried to make any scene . . ."

"Objected to," Mason said. "Not responsive to the question which has already been asked and answered."

"Very well," Burger said irritably. "You saw her there in the lobby of the club?"

"I did, yes, sir."

"Who was present?"

"Just Lucille and I."

"What did she say?"

"She told me that something terrible had happened. That she was going to have to get out of the country. She wanted to know if I would give her fifteen thousand dollars in cash as a complete settlement if she'd waive any claims to future alimony payments and give me a complete release."

"You were paying her alimony?"

"Yes, sir."

"How much?"

"Two hundred dollars a week."

"Did she tell you why she wanted to leave the country?"

"Yes, sir."

"Why?"

"She said a man had been found dead in her garage. She finally admitted to me the body was that of her first husband, and said the exposure of that fact would ruin her."

"What did you tell her?"

"Well, naturally, I was trying to get out of paying any more than I had to. I told her I couldn't raise fifteen thousand dollars in cash. I told her I'd have to put her proposition up to my attorneys to see whether or not she could make a valid agreement under the circumstances. I told her I didn't think too much of the idea, and I thought the amount was too high."

"And did she accept that answer as final?"

"No, sir. She told me I'd have to do something fast. She said the offer wouldn't be open later than midnight. She said she would call me at a little before midnight. That she wanted to take a plane that night. Then, finally, she lowered her figure to ten thousand spot cash."

"Did she call you again?"

"No, sir. I had seen my attorneys and had made arrangements to accept her proposition, and I had the ten thousand dollars in cash, together with a proper release ready for her to sign. She didn't get in touch with me."

"And no one was with her when you saw her?"

"No, sir."

"Do you know a woman named Anita Jordon?"

"I have met her."

"Was she with the defendant when this conversation took place?"

"No, sir. The defendant was alone."

"Cross-examine," Burger said, hurling the words at Perry Mason as though they were a challenge.

"You were paying her two hundred dollars a week alimony?" Mason asked.

"Yes, sir."

"And you want the Court to believe that you hesitated about the advisability of settling such weekly payments for fifteen thousand dollars?"

"Well, no, sir, I let *her* think I was hesitating."

"In other words, you told her you were hesitating, is that it?"

"I wanted to convey that impression, yes."

"But you actually were eager to make the settlement?"

"Naturally."

"But as a good business trader you tried to keep her from seeing that was your attitude."

"Yes, sir."

"So you told her that you didn't know whether you wanted to do it or not?"

"That's right."

"In other words, you lied to her."

Barton flushed.

Burger, on his feet, said, "Your Honor, I object to that. That's an insulting statement to the witness."

"Oh, I'll put it this way," Mason said, "if you'd like a softer term for the same thing. In other words, Mr. Barton, you told your wife a falsehood. Is that correct?"

Barton's eyes glinted angrily.

"Same objection," Burger said.

"It can be answered yes or no," Mason said.

Barton glared angrily at him.

"The question," Mason said, "is whether you told your wife a falsehood. It can be answered yes or no."

"About what?"

"About your willingness to make a settlement."

"I don't think that's material."

"I do," Mason said.

"Well, I don't," Hamilton Burger said. "I want to interpose an objection on that ground. It's not proper cross-examination."

"Overruled," Judge Osborn said.

"You told her a falsehood?" Mason asked.

"Yes," Barton shouted angrily.

"How long have *you* known Pitkin?"

"Well, I'd seen him but I didn't know who he was. That is, I had no idea he had ever been married to Lucille. It came as a shock to me when I realized that."

"But you had seen Pitkin?"

"I had known him as Mr. Argyle's chauffeur. Mr. Argyle is a member of the club to which I belong. Many oil men join it."

"And because you were interested in oil speculations, and Mr. Argyle, Mr. Ross P. Hollister, and Mr. Dudley Gates were all interested in similar transactions, and all members of the same club, you saw quite a bit of each other?"

"No, sir. Argyle, Hollister, and Gates had some sort of a partnership arrangement. They had pooled their interest in certain leases. While I was in the same general line of business, my own interests were adverse. I didn't want them to find out what I was doing. They didn't want me to find out what they were doing. We spoke when we met and occasionally would discuss general conditions, but we had very little in common."

"Had you ever spoken to Pitkin?"

"I had, but it was purely a personal matter."

"Trying to get Pitkin to tell you something about the business activities of the other three men?"

Burger shouted angrily, "Your Honor, that's another insulting question. It's utterly uncalled for."

"Do you have any evidence indicating such is the case, Mr. Mason?" Judge Osborn asked.

"No, Your Honor," Mason said, smoothly, "that question is merely part of a fishing expedition."

"The objection is sustained," Judge Osborn said. "You can, however, ask him what he discussed with Pitkin."

"What did you discuss with Pitkin? What was your reason for talking to him?"

Barton, thoroughly angry, said, "I wanted to hire a chauffeur by the day. I understood there was an association, sort of an employment agency, which specialized in that sort of stuff. I asked Pitkin about it because I knew he was Argyle's chauffeur. I happened to see him waiting out in front of the building. I asked him if he knew of such an association."

"Did he?"

"He did. He told me where it was. It was the Chauffeurs' Exchange. I believe it's listed in the telephone book. It's composed of chauffeurs who are willing to work on their days off. It's some sort of a mutual co-operative affair. They rotate jobs, and a person can nearly always get a chauffeur by the hour, or by the day, by calling up."

"Did Mr. Pitkin belong to that association?"

"He said he did. I don't know. He told me Thursday was his regular day off, that he was off duty at six o'clock Wednesday evening, and didn't have to come back until Friday morning. He said he'd be glad to take care of my needs himself on his days off, or I could get a chauffeur through the association on other days."

Mason said, "You have no affection left for your ex-wife, the defendant in this case?"

"I am very fond of Lucille in a way."

"And, trying to be clever, you advised her to plant a gun by the body of this man so it would look like suicide and say nothing to anyone, didn't you?"

"I did not. You have no proof of that. The defendant might make such a claim, but it's preposterous. Your accusation, sir, is entirely false, and is resented as such."

"Didn't you offer her *any* suggestion by which she might get out of the scrape in which she found herself?"

"Certainly not."

"Yet you say you are fond of her?"

"Yes."

"But you regarded that alimony settlement as a purely cold-blooded business transaction?"

"No, sir. I take an interest in Lucille. I wanted to be certain that she wasn't trying to raise money just to throw it away."

Mason said suavely, "Yet the affection which you bore for your ex-wife, the friendship, the regard, and the desire to see that she wasn't fleeced by some designing person, didn't prevent you from attempting to fleece her by deceiving her so that you could get a five-thousand-dollar advantage?"

"I don't think I had any idea of deceiving her."

"Then why did you try to conceal your eagerness to make a cash settlement such as she proposed?"

Barton thought that over, then said, "Well, just as a matter of habit I guess. Just as a matter of business policy."

"Come, come," Mason said. "You knew what you were doing. You deliberately concealed your eagerness to make the settlement."

"That's been gone over a dozen different times," Hamilton Burger said.

Judge Osborn said, "Well, I think counsel is entitled to make his point. It indicates the motivation of the witness and enables the Court to make an appraisal of the witness's character."

"All right," Barton suddenly shouted, "I lied to her! I saw a chance to make a good business deal. I tried to put it across. Now what's wrong with that?"

"Not a thing," Mason said, "and thank you very much for your commendable frankness, Mr. Barton. Now there's one other matter. As I understand your testimony, you say the defendant finally admitted the body was that of her first husband?"

"I don't think I said that."

Mason said, "I'll ask the court reporter to consult his notes and see what was said."

There followed a period of restless silence while the court reporter thumbed through the pages of his notes. Willard Barton changed his position on the witness stand.

"Here it is," the court reporter said. " '*Question:* Did she tell you why she wanted to leave the country? *Answer:* Yes, sir. *Question:* Why? *Answer:* She said a man had been found dead in her garage. She finally admitted to me the body was that of her first husband and said the exposure of that fact would ruin her.' "

Mason said, "Thank you, Mr. Court Reporter. I'll now ask you, Mr. Barton, what you meant when you said she '*finally admitted*' the body was that of her first husband?"

"Well, she finally admitted it, that's all."

"Not at first?"

"No."

"After searching questions on your part?"

"Yes, I guess so."

"So you discussed the matter and you felt she was trying to hold something back and kept questioning her?"

"I presume so."

"And in order to get her to '*finally admit*' what she did, you had to use some pressure?"

"Well, in a way."

"And you told her you couldn't help her unless she told you the truth, or words to that effect?"

"Yes, I guess so."

"So she told you the truth—finally?"

"Yes."

"So then you set about helping her?"

"I did not!"

"But you've already said you told her you couldn't help her unless she told the truth, and that because of your promise she '*finally admitted*' the truth. Now am I to understand *you* then failed to fulfill *your* part of the bargain?"

Barton hesitated, crossed his legs, glanced pleadingly at Burger.

"Well?" Mason demanded.

"I didn't *help* her," Barton blurted.

"That's what I thought," Mason said scornfully. "That's all, Mr. Barton."

Barton came down off the witness stand, swung over toward Mason's table, caught the cold, stony glint of the lawyer's eyes, thought better of what he had in mind, and veered away.

"Call Arthur Colson," Burger said, ignoring Barton.

Arthur Colson marched to the witness stand. His eyes moved restlessly around, appraising the courtroom, carefully avoiding, however, the eyes of the district attorney and the table behind which Mason and Lucille Barton sat.

He gave his name, age, occupation, and residence.

Hamilton Burger produced the gun. "I show you a .38 caliber Smith and Wesson revolver, Number S65088, and ask you if you ever saw that gun before?"

Colson took a sheet of paper from his pocket and reading from it, said, "I refuse to answer that question upon the ground that the answer might tend to incriminate me."

"Did you buy that gun from the Rushing Creek Mercantile Company?"

"I refuse to answer on the ground that the answer might tend to incriminate me."

"Did you sign the name Ross P. Hollister on the register?"

"I refuse to answer, same ground."

"Did you kill Hartwell L. Pitkin?"

"No."

"Did you know him?"

"No, sir. I didn't know him."

"Did you place this gun by the body of Hartwell L. Pitkin in the garage at number 719 South Gondola on the fifth of this month?"

"No, sir."

"Or at any other time?"

"No, sir."

"That's all," Hamilton Burger said.

"Just a minute," Mason said. "One more question on cross-examination. Did you ever have this gun in your possession?"

"I refuse to answer on the ground that the answer might incriminate me."

"Did you ever take it when Lucille Barton didn't know you had taken it?"

"I refuse to answer on the ground that the answer might incriminate me."

"Did you ever have a key to Lucille Barton's apartment?"

"No, sir."

Mason said, "I show you two letters, both typewritten, one of them addressed to the Drake Detective Agency, the other addressed to me. The first letter refers to a key to the apartment of Lucille Barton. The second letter refers to a key to the desk of that apartment. I ask you if you wrote either of those letters."

"No, sir. I did not."

"That's all," Mason said.

"That's all," Burger announced.

Judge Osborn said, "In view of the very unsatisfactory answers given upon such a vital point by this witness, the Court feels that the district attorney's office should take steps to clarify the situation."

"Yes, Your Honor," Burger said, wearily. "We are fully aware of the possibilities."

"And the implications," Judge Osborn said.

"And the implications," Burger repeated.

"Very well," Judge Osborn said. "Do you have one more witness you wish to put on before the hour of adjournment?"

"If the Court please, Your Honor, I'd like to wait until . . ."

"Very well. Court will now take a recess until two o'clock this afternoon. The defendant is remanded to the custody of the sheriff. Witnesses under subpoena are instructed to return here at two o'clock this afternoon."

As the spectators arose to leave the courtroom, Mason beckoned Paul Drake over to him. "Afraid I can't join you for lunch, Paul."

"Why, Perry?"

"I'm going to have to spend a couple of hours on the telephone. You take Della to lunch and get her a nice steak."

"Have a heart," Drake protested, grinning.

"I have," Mason told him, "and it's been in my mouth so long that I won't feel right when it drops back to where it belongs."

28

AT TWO o'clock when court reconvened, Hamilton Burger, apparently worried, said, "Your Honor, a peculiar situation has developed in this case. I had every reason to believe that it would be possible to connect this murder weapon with Mr. Perry Mason by reason of his fingerprint, and with the defendant by reason of the fact that I expected to be able to show Mr. Mason was with her at the garage at about the hour the man must have been murdered. That identification evidence has been made a football because of certain ingenious legal trickery, but I want to call to the Court's attention that it is merely an ingenious legal trickery. The witness ordinarily would have made an absolute identification."

"Well, of course," Judge Osborn said, "that's the vice of identification evidence. The witness saw a tall man wearing a light tan topcoat and a gray hat. He didn't see the man's face except vaguely and at a distance. A great number of men would answer that description. The description of the woman, because of the identification of her wearing apparel, which is more unusual, is, of course, much more persuasive; but there were probably thousands of tall men wearing light topcoats in the city at the hour the witness, Goshen, saw the couple at the garage."

"But there's only one Perry Mason who could have left a fingerprint on the inside of that gun belonging to his client," Burger said.

"You haven't proved the weapon belonged to his client yet," Judge Osborn said.

Hamilton Burger said, "I admit, Your Honor, the case has become somewhat complicated, but if the Court will bear with me I think the Court should appreciate the trickery by which the identification witness was confused."

Judge Osborn smiled. "The Court will bear with you as long as you're putting on proof, Mr. Burger."

"Very well. Call Sadie Milford."

Sadie Milford, a well-upholstered woman in the early forties proved to be the manager of the apartment house where Lucille Barton had her apartment. She testified that the garages went with the apartments. That they were kept locked. That the apartment at 208 was entitled to a garage. That duplicate keys to the apartment and to the garage had been given Lucille Barton when she moved in.

"Who had these keys?"

"Lucille Barton."

"Do you have any receipt showing that to be the case?"

"Yes, sir."

"Was that signed by Lucille Barton?"

"Yes, sir."

"In your presence?"

"Yes, sir."

"I want it introduced in evidence," Hamilton Burger said.

"No objection," Mason said.

"Do you care to cross-examine?"

"Yes."

Mason took the receipt, said, "And you did deliver Lucille Barton these four keys, two to the apartment, and two to the garage?"

"Yes."

"Thank you," Mason said. "That's all."

Burger's next witness was a service-station operator who testified that at a little after six o'clock on the evening of the fifth Lucille Barton had driven her automobile into the service station. It was a Chevrolet sedan with a light brown body. He had found the timing so out of adjustment that the car constantly skipped and backfired. He had changed the adjustment of the timing device, and while with the time and the tools available he hadn't been able to make a thoroughly workmanlike job of it, he had smoothed the car out so that it ran without backfiring.

"What time did she drive the car in there?" Hamilton Burger asked.

"About six-fifteen, or six-twenty."

"Who was driving it?"

"Miss Barton."

"Had you seen her before?"

"Yes, she buys gasoline from me regularly."

"And by Miss Barton you mean the defendant sitting there at the counsel table with Mr. Mason?"

"Yes, sir."

"That's all," Burger said.

"That's all," Mason announced, smiling. "No questions."

"Call Stephen Argyle," Burger said.

Argyle took the stand, gave his residence as 938 West Casino Boulevard, his age as fifty-five, stated that he had employed Hartwell L. Pitkin during his lifetime as chauffeur. That Pitkin had been in his employ on the day of his death.

"When was the last time you saw Mr. Pitkin?" Burger asked.

"Shortly after five o'clock."

"Where was he at that time?"

"In front of the office of Mr. Perry Mason. That is, in front of the building where Mr. Mason has his office. I was waiting to see Perry Mason. I suddenly remembered that it was Hartwell's night off. Despite the fact that I was thoroughly annoyed with him, I went down and told him he could take the car and go home."

"And do you know what happened after that?"

"I only know that I found the car at my residence when I returned there."

"What time?"

"Sometime . . . oh, it was after I got back from calling on a patient in the hospital where I made an adjustment and . . ."

"Never mind anything about *that* case," Hamilton Burger said.

"Well, I was defrauded by Mr. Perry Mason into making a settlement that cost me several thousand dollars," Argyle snapped.

"That's neither here nor there," Burger said, soothingly. "Just try to control yourself and tell us what happened."

"Well, it must have been around nine-thirty or ten o'clock when I returned home. The car was there."

"You may cross-examine," Burger said.

"How do you know it was there?" Mason asked.

"Why it . . . it had to be there. The garage door was closed . . ."

"But you didn't *look* for the car as soon as you returned home."

"No."

"How did you get home, by the way?"

"My companion drove me home, an adjuster for the insurance company which carries my insurance."

"You arrived home when?"

"Somewhere around nine-thirty or ten o'clock."

"And went to bed at what time?"

"Oh, I would say around eleven."

"And when did you have occasion to look in the garage for the car?"

"About two o'clock the next morning. I received a call on the telephone and the police told me about what had happened to my chauffeur. They asked me questions and said they were coming out. I got up and dressed, and was headed for the garage about the time the police arrived."

"Your car was in the garage?"

"That's right."

Mason said, "You evidenced some animosity toward me, Mr. Argyle."

"Personally," Argyle said, "I think you're beneath contempt."

"Why?"

"You knew that I had reason to believe my chauffeur had been in an automobile accident. You talked me into making a settlement of a claim which was entirely spurious. I warn you, Mr. Mason, I am going to sue for fraud and . . ."

"Oh, it was your chauffeur whom you thought was driving the car?"

"Naturally. I knew *I* wasn't driving it. However, I was legally liable for the acts of my employee."

"Is all this material?" Judge Osborn asked.

"I think it shows motivation and bias on the part of the witness," Mason said.

"Let's go into it by all means," Burger announced, rubbing his hands. "I'd like now to show the entire facts."

Mason said, "You shall have the entire facts, Mr. Burger. Suppose you tell your side of the story, Mr. Argyle."

Argyle said, "Around three o'clock on the afternoon of the fifth, Mr. Mason came to my house. Mr. Pitkin was present at the interview. Mr. Mason stated that he had indisputable evidence that my car had been engaged in a hit-and-run accident in which a client of his had been seriously injured. He pointed out that there were bumps on the fenders of my car and . . . well, I thought he was right."

"Why did you think I was right?" Mason asked.

"Because my chauffeur had been in trouble with the car on that date. He'd tried to get rid of it and had reported it as being stolen. He had advised me the car had been stolen and insisted I join him so he could explain the circumstances to the police. I went with him to the place where he said he had left the car. The man had been drinking and seemed terribly nervous about something. I was skeptical but badly worried myself, fearing my man might have been in some scrape which would involve me. I returned to my club and telephoned police my car had been stolen. Actually I don't think the car was ever stolen at all. It was recovered by the police in the downtown business district where it had been parked in front of a fireplug."

Mason said, "And on the strength of what I had told you, you decided that it would be cheaper for you to hunt up Finchley and make a settlement behind his attorney's back, didn't you?"

"I didn't think any such thing."

"But that's exactly what you *did*, isn't it?"

"As soon as I realized a man had been seriously hurt I naturally wanted to do something about it. I felt very much concerned about the whole thing. I went to your office. I kept trying to see you. You were out—apparently calling on your client, Lucille Barton."

"Do you know that?" Mason asked.

"No, I don't know it."

"Have you any reason to think that's where I was?"

"Well, I understood from the police . . . I'll withdraw that. The answer is no, I don't *know*."

"All right," Mason said. "You were at my office and were told I was out."

"Yes."

"And where was your chauffeur then?"

"Sitting in my Buick automobile in front of your office building, waiting."

"You had found a parking place there?"

"My chauffeur had. He had let me out at the entrance to the building. There were no parking places available near the building. I told him to keep driving around the block until he found a parking place right near the entrance of the building. He located one almost immediately."

"So you were waiting for me?"

"Yes, sir, until I telephoned my insurance carrier about six o'clock and told him I was trying to make a settlement with you on a claim for damages. I had suddenly wakened to a realization that I might be negligent in not reporting to my insurance company."

"And the insurance carrier suggested to you that you could make a lot cheaper settlement by going out and making a settlement behind my back."

"My insurance carrier told me to wait there in the lobby and not to talk with you, under any circumstances, until I had seen him. After he arrived, I placed the matter in his hands."

"But you *did* go to the hospital and try to make a settlement with my client behind my back, didn't you?"

"I don't know what you mean by behind your back. You weren't in your office. I certainly tried to communicate with you. I'm not going to wait all day for a lawyer, who's out gallivanting around with a divorcee, to get back to his office. *My* time's valuable!"

"Now, when you made that settlement," Mason said, "you paid out some money of your own in addition to the settlement made by the insurance company, didn't you?"

"Yes, I did."

"Why did you do that?"

"Because I thought the young man was entitled to more money than the insurance company was giving him. I'm not exactly a philanthropist, but on the other hand, I don't have to make my money by capitalizing on the suffering of a young boy."

"Very noble sentiments," Mason said, "but do you want this Court to understand that you not only told your insurance carrier you were liable, but paid out this money of yours purely on the strength of my statement to you that your car had been involved in an accident?"

"Well, I thought you were a reputable attorney. I know different now. At the time, when you said you had proof—well, I thought you had it."

Mason grinned. "Very, very noble and self-righteous, Mr. Argyle. But despite the fact you now consider me beneath contempt, you did go to the doorman of your club and bribe him to swear you hadn't left the club that afternoon so *you* wouldn't be mixed up in anything your chauffeur might have done."

"That's not so!"

"You did give the doorman some money?"

"A tip is all."

"How much?"

"That's neither here nor there."

"How much?"

"Objected to, Your Honor," Burger said, jumping up. "This man was deliberately victimized by . . ."

"Overruled," Judge Osborn snapped.

"How much?" Mason asked.

"Well, I *thought* I was giving him five dollars, but I had had a couple of drinks and it was dark. And later on I was short in my cash, so I may have made a mistake and given him more."

"A hundred dollars?"

"I am afraid so."

"By mistake?"

"By mistake."

"You knew *you* hadn't been driving the car on the afternoon of the third."

"Yes, sir."

"Then you knew then that the only other person who could have done so was your chauffeur."

"Well, the car *could* have been stolen."

"In which event you wouldn't have been liable for an accident," Mason said. "Come, Mr. Argyle, you're a businessman."

"Well," Argyle said, "I see what you're getting at. As a matter of fact, after you left, I put the thing up to my chauffeur and he broke down and virtually admitted that he had been driving the car and had been involved in that hit-and-run case. Then he admitted he had tried to avoid liability by telling me the car had been stolen."

"Exactly," Mason said. "Now you have come to the conclusion that statement was false?"

"You mean your statement to me that my car was involved in the hit-and-run accident?"

"Put it that way if you want to."

"That statement was absolutely and utterly false. A man by the name of Caffee was driving the car that hit that young boy."

Mason said, "By the way, you and the representative of the insurance company went to Mr. Finchley and threatened to prosecute him for obtaining money under false pretenses unless he returned the money you'd paid him, didn't you?"

"Well, we explained to him that he certainly wasn't entitled to the money either by law or equity."

"What did he say?"

"He said that you'd advised him to keep the money. That it was a voluntary payment and that we couldn't get it back. That you were going to teach these insurance adjusters not to suck eggs."

Judge Osborn smiled broadly.

"Exactly," Mason said. "Now why do you suppose Mr. Pitkin admitted to you he had been engaged in this hit-and-run accident if he actually hadn't?"

"I don't know," Argyle said, "and I wish I did. I've been thinking that over, trying to find the answer to it, and I simply can't figure it out. It now would seem the man was a blackmailer. He doubtless had some reason in that warped mind of his."

Mason said, "You were anxious to see that your chauffeur had his night off, despite the fact that he had just confessed to you he had been engaged in a hit-and-run driving accident?"

"I can explain that."

"Go ahead and do so."

"I knew that my chauffeur made money on his days and nights off. He had explained to me that he was a member of this chauffeurs' association and that they worked on their days off, and I knew that it was important that he get up to that association because they make definite bookings. I'm a businessman myself. I knew how I'd feel if I should be waiting for a chauffeur who didn't show up on time. Letting Pitkin go wasn't out of consideration for him, but to his associates in the chauffeurs' association."

"Now then," Mason said, "has it ever occurred to you that that's exactly what did happen, Mr. Argyle?"

"What do you mean?"

"That Pitkin had some definite obligation. Someone for whom he was to work on the evening of the fifth. That in place of taking your car home himself, he made arrangements with some other individual to take it home, and that *he* went out at once to work on this assignment to which he had obligated himself."

Argyle paused to think that over, then said, "It could be that such is the case."

Mason said, "Did *you* ever have occasion to hire any of these chauffeurs on Pitkin's day off?"

"Certainly not. If I had wanted to do that, I'd have simply made arrangements with Pitkin to have charged me the regular rate for working overtime, and kept him."

Mason said, "I'm going to hand you a list of fifteen names and ask you if you know any one of those people, Mr. Argyle."

"Oh, what's the use of this?" Hamilton Burger expostulated.

Mason said, "It may explain the reason the chauffeur, Pitkin, confessed he had been in a hit-and-run accident when he actually hadn't."

"Oh, very well," Burger said. "I don't see the point. It seems to me, Your Honor, we're not only not getting anywhere with this cross-examination, but that it's just a general fishing expedition."

"Fishing in promising waters, however," the Court said, smiling. "I think perhaps Mr. Mason is even getting an occasional nibble."

Argyle adjusted his glasses, looked at the typewritten list, scratched his head, said, "It's going to take me a few minutes to check this list over, Mr. Mason."

"Very well," Judge Osborn said. "The Court will take a fifteen-minute recess. You can look at the list during that time, Mr. Burger, and discuss it with the witness. Court will recess for fifteen minutes."

Judge Osborn returned to chambers.

Mason got up, stretched, yawned with elaborate carelessness, walked over to where Lieutenant Tragg was sitting, and said, "How about stepping over here in the corner for a few minutes, Lieutenant?"

Tragg nodded, and the two men moved over to a corner of the courtroom.

Tragg grinned surreptitiously, and said, "Thanks for your cross-examination of Holcomb. He's been boasting all over about how he trailed you to a place where Goshen could identify you after I'd fallen down on the job. I guess this will cause him to change his tune a little. Not that I am talking to you officially, you understand, Mason, this is just personal."

"Sure," Mason said. "And still talking personally, how'd you like to take a ride, Tragg?"

"Where?"

"Out to the residential district."

"Do you think we have time?"

"I think we have lots of time," Mason said.

"We can't get out there and back inside of fifteen minutes, can we?"

"I think," Mason said, "that when Argyle sees that list he's going to want a little more time. He . . . here comes Burger now."

Hamilton Burger, moving with the ponderous dignity of a man who is forced by business exigencies to consult with someone for whom he has a contemptuous hatred, said, "How important is that list of witnesses, Mason?"

"Quite important."

"Argyle can't possibly check them until he checks a list of some of his stockholders. He says he has a poor memory for names, but he thinks nearly all these men are stockholders in one of his companies. If you want an answer to that question, the case will have to go over until tomorrow morning."

"Suits me," Mason said.

"Well, it doesn't suit me," Burger said.

"I want an answer to the question," Mason insisted.

"Well," Burger announced after some hesitancy, "very well. On your stipulation, we'll let it go over until tomorrow morning."

"Will you explain to the judge?" Mason asked.

"Very well," Burger said, and swung around on his heel.

"Now," Mason said to Tragg, "if you are ready to go, Lieutenant —and I think we'd better take your car."

"Say, do you know what you're doing?" Tragg asked.

"I hope so," Mason told him.

29

TRAGG backed his car into the mouth of the alley Mason indicated.

"We can see the house from here," Mason said.

"Just what are you getting at?" Tragg asked.

Mason said, "Hollister started out on a business trip, didn't he?"

"That's right."

"And intended to be gone for several days?"

"Yes."

"When you found the car and the body," Mason said, "there were certain significant things you didn't find."

"What do you mean?"

"Baggage. When a man intends to go on a trip he takes baggage with him."

"That's right," Tragg said.

"Now, the body was in a peculiar position," Mason pointed out. "What does that position indicate to you, Lieutenant?"

"Only one thing," Tragg said. "The body must have been jammed into the trunk of an automobile."

"That's right. Now was that the trunk of Hollister's automobile?"

"It could have been."

"Here comes Argyle. Driving pretty fast, isn't he, Lieutenant?"

Tragg said, "He probably has a lot of things on his mind. I imagine this trial has disrupted his program."

Mason stretched, yawned, said, "I suppose so."

"What do we do now?" Tragg asked.

"Just wait," Mason said. "You have your radio on here?"

"Yes."

Mason said, "Better make sure it's in working order. Check in to Headquarters and get the time."

Tragg said, "What the devil are you getting at, Mason? What's the idea?"

Mason said, "It suddenly occurred to me I'd taken you away rather unceremoniously. Burger may be trying to get in touch with you. I suppose the blowup of that identification business . . ."

Tragg grinned, and said, "Boy, that *was* pretty! I don't mind telling you, Mason, I wanted to jump up and cheer—personally, you understand, not officially."

Tragg tuned in his radio, checked with police headquarters, settled back and lit a cigar. "Mason, what the devil are we waiting for? If you want to see Argyle why not go over and see him?"

"Oh, let's let him get his records together if that's what he wants. He . . . here he comes now."

Argyle came out of the front door almost on the run, carrying a handbag in one hand, a suitcase in the other. He slammed them in the car and started the motor.

"Now," Mason said, "if you'll start closing in on him, Lieutenant, and use your siren, I think we may get some action."

"*Use the siren!*" Tragg exclaimed. "What's *he* done?"

"Follow him and you'll see what he's *going* to do," Mason said. "He'll at least give you a chance to catch him for speeding."

"Damn it," Tragg said, "I'm not a traffic cop. I . . ."

"Do you want this deal or don't you?" Mason asked.

Tragg looked at him sharply, said, "Okay, I do."

"Better get going then."

Tragg started the motor, eased the police car into gear, slid in the clutch, and started after Argyle's car.

After a moment he poured more throttle into the big police car, said, "That guy certainly is going!"

"What's the limit along here?" Mason asked.

"Thirty-five miles," Tragg said. "He's hitting better than fifty. He shouldn't do that."

"Try giving him the siren," Mason said.

Tragg said, "Well, we'll get alongside of him and . . ."

"Give him the siren," Mason said impatiently, and threw in the switch which started the siren wailing.

Tragg hurriedly kicked the switch out, said, "Damn it, don't do that. I . . ."

Argyle looked back, a startled apprehensive glance, saw the police car coming behind him, and suddenly floorboarded the throttle, sending his car into speed.

"What do you make of that?" Lieutenant Tragg said. "Why, the damn fool, he's . . . hell, Mason, he's trying to get away!"

"Of course he's trying to get away," Mason said. "What are *you* going to do about it?"

"I'll show you," Tragg said grimly. He threw the siren on.

Argyle screamed into a sudden turn to the left, almost upsetting as he skidded around the corner.

"Hold everything," Tragg said, grimly, "you're going to travel."

He slammed the car into second gear, poured the throttle to it and sent the car around the corner in a screaming skid, then snapped it back into high.

"Learned that in the old bootlegging days," he said.

"He's going to try another turn," Mason said.

"We'll cure him of that," Tragg said. "A good cop can take the turns a lot faster than . . . hold your hat, Mason, here we go again."

Tragg sent the car into another screaming turn, which left black tire marks all over the highway.

"I guess he'll try the straightaway now," Mason said. "Better get your gun handy, Tragg. He may want to shoot it out."

"What the hell's he running away from?" Tragg asked.

"The murder of Hartwell L. Pitkin, and the murder of Ross P. Hollister," Mason told him, lighting a cigarette. "How about . . ."

Tragg threw a switch in the radio, said, "Calling Headquarters. Lieutenant Tragg, car number forty-two. I'm chasing a murder suspect in a black Buick sedan, number 9Y6370 north of Hickman Avenue, between Eighty-ninth and Ninetieth Street. Send any available squad cars to help. I have my siren going."

Tragg eased his gun around in his holster, "You got a gun, Mason?" he asked.

"I'm a law-abiding citizen," Mason told him.

"You're deputized," Tragg said tersely. "There's a gun in the glove compartment. Get it. Do you really have the dope on this guy?"

"Of course I have the dope on him," Mason said. "Otherwise we wouldn't be wasting time but I couldn't prove it until he started running. I had to get him stampeded so he'd give himself away."

"He's sure doing it now," Tragg said, gripping the wheel. "We're hitting eighty miles an hour."

"He's going to get away on the straightaway," Mason said.

"My siren is really clearing the way for him," Tragg said, "but if I shut it off, we'll hit somebody and we'll all be killed."

Mason said, "Just keep your siren going, Lieutenant. We can get him sooner or later and this flight is the last nail in his coffin. He . . . *look out!*"

A car shot out of an intersecting street, heard the scream of the siren, saw Argyle's car and Tragg's car rushing along the highway, and tried to swing back to the curb.

Argyle swerved to avoid a collision. His car went into a skid, started rocking dangerously, then suddenly spun completely around, went up on two wheels, shot across the road, over an embankment, and turned over.

Lieutenant Tragg slammed on his brakes.

Mason watched for a moment to see if Argyle emerged from the wreckage, then said, "I guess that does it, Lieutenant. I take it I'm no longer a deputy."

With that he opened the glove compartment and returned the revolver to its holster.

30

PAUL DRAKE, Della Street, and Perry Mason relaxed in Mason's private office. Della Street, perched on a corner of the desk, held one knee in her interlaced fingers. Mason was tilted back in his swivel chair and Drake was sprawled in his customary sideways position in the big clients' chair.

"You mean you knew who it was all along?" Drake asked.

"Of course not," Mason said, "but as soon as I knew that Argyle's car hadn't hit Finchley, I wondered why it was that Argyle would so willingly part with cold, hard cash to settle a claim for which he wasn't responsible. Then I began to wonder if he wasn't buying an alibi."

"Well, of course, it's plain enough now," Drake said, "but I'm darned if I see how you got it at the start."

Mason said, "Here's a pretty good reconstruction of what happened, Paul. Argyle, Hollister and Gates were associated in some oil deals. Hollister furnished most of the capital and took the largest share of the profits. Argyle and Gates started double-crossing Hollister. Hollister either caught them at it, or smelled a rat. He called a conference to take place at his home in Santa del Barra on Monday the third. Argyle and Gates very reluctantly drove up there."

"Did Pitkin drive them up?" Drake asked.

Mason grinned. "No, Pitkin was in San Francisco."

"I don't get it," Drake said.

"Gates and Argyle were in such a spot that they could have been sent to jail for embezzlement. Hollister finally had the goods on them. Gates knew it. Argyle only suspected it. Gates had decided that if it came to a showdown, he'd shoot his way out, if he had half a chance.

"So he'd purchased a plane ticket to Honolulu in his name. Then he paid Pitkin to travel the first leg of the journey *under his name.*

"That gave Gates an alibi in case he had to use one. And he put a .45 automatic in his pocket so he'd be prepared.

"It was as bad as he thought. Hollister served his ultimatum, probably calling on the men to strip themselves of everything. It called for quick decision. Gates made it with his automatic.

"Argyle was almost crazy. Gates had had things all planned for what had to be done in case he killed Hollister. He whipped Argyle into line. They brought in waterproof canvas from the trunk of Gates' car, swiftly rolled the body into a bundle, carried it to the side door and slipped it into the trunk of Hollister's car.

"Then they drove both Argyle's car and Hollister's car up the canyon road. Gates outlined his alibi to Argyle, but Argyle realized he was left without an alibi. Gates told him to rush back to his club and report his car as having been stolen. That was to protect them in case anyone had seen them on the grade. They then smashed Hollister's wrist watch with the hands registering 5:55, and the car clock with the hands at 6:21. Then they parked Argyle's car, drove up to where they could turn Hollister's car around, rolled the body over the bank, shoved earth over it, then sent Hollister's car over a steep ledge and dashed back to Santa del Barra.

"Gates put his alibi into effect by using Hollister's name and calling for Gates at the San Francisco airport from Hollister's phone. Pitkin answered in the name of Gates. That clinched Gates' alibi.

"When Hollister was shot, the body fell on a thick, expensive but small Oriental rug. The two murderers had no time to clean the rug and replace it. So they removed the rug so the bloodstains wouldn't betray them when the housekeeper came to work the next morning. She knew Hollister was intending to take a business trip so she thought nothing of his absence, but she did wonder what had happened to the rug. The day previous, Hollister had mentioned something about giving a rug to Lucille for her apartment. The housekeeper wired Lucille, asking if Hollister had given her the Oriental rug. Lucille became angry, replied that she had the rug Hollister had intended she should have. The housekeeper didn't think much about it until after Hollister's body was found.

"Argyle rushed back here. Pitkin returned by plane. Gates flew to San Francisco, picked up the ticket Pitkin had left for him and went on to Honolulu. Pitkin was smart enough to know he hadn't been paid a large chunk of money to build an alibi for nothing. From that moment he decided to find out why and collect blackmail—and Argyle decided to kill Pitkin.

"Argyle went to his club, reported his car as having been stolen and tried to bribe an alibi. As soon as he calmed down he knew that was a poor way to do it.

"Then Argyle saw our ad in the *Blade* and conceived the idea of buying himself a real alibi by pretending he'd been the hit-and-run driver. He felt he could square that rap and make the insurance company stand most of the expense.

"In searching Hollister's body, Argyle had found keys to Lucille Barton's apartment and garage. He must have known Hollister was going to marry her and what the whole relationship was.

"When Argyle saw your ad in the *Blade* he realized that if he could pose as the driver of the hit-and-run car, he could pay off the claims, mostly with money furnished by the insurance company, and have a perfectly swell alibi. Obviously, if he had been at the intersection of Hickman Avenue and Vermesillo Drive at five P.M. on the evening of the third, he couldn't have been in Santa del Barra at the time the murder was committed. Remember that he *did* have a good alibi for the rest of the evening. He saw to that. Hollister's housekeeper had left at four-thirty on the afternoon of the third. Hollister was alive then and had told the housekeeper he was going to have a short conference and then leave on a business trip.

"Argyle went about killing Pitkin with calm deliberation and considerable shrewdness. He sent a letter to you, enclosing a key to Lucille's apartment. He felt certain that would send someone out to talk with him. He had a new right rear wheel put on his automobile; he dented the fender and had it covered with paint. Then he did the thing which was diabolically clever, the thing by which he intended to give himself an ironclad alibi for Pitkin's murder."

"What?" Drake asked. "If you ask me, he had an ironclad alibi. Hell, Perry, he was sitting in your office at the time the murder was committed."

Mason said, "He went to an employment agency sometime on the fifth, hired a chauffeur, and arranged to pick him up, to have him start work shortly before five o'clock in the afternoon. He explained that this chauffeur would have to go to Detroit by bus in order to pick up a new automobile and drive it down to Mexico to meet him. In that way, the chauffeur would never read any of the papers about Pitkin's death.

"Argyle was smart enough to know that if a man wearing a chauffeur's cap and an overcoat should be seen sitting in his car, witnesses would naturally assume that the chauffeur was Pitkin. At least people who didn't know Pitkin.

"From the attitude Pitkin had toward Argyle, I am assuming Pitkin may have been trying to blackmail Argyle even before Hollister's murder. At any rate, Pitkin had become suspicious of the alibi he'd been building for Gates and wondered if Argyle wasn't in on it too. Argyle evidently had been investigating Pitkin. He'd found out that Pitkin was Lucille's first husband, that she was planning to marry Hollister and that she was out of the apartment from two to five each afternoon. As soon as he got the keys to Lucille's apartment he started planning the murder of Pitkin. My ad in the paper gave him what he doubtless felt was the opportunity of a lifetime. He started prowling in Lucille's apartment and when he found there was a gun in the desk he had everything just the way he wanted it.

"He got Pitkin down to Lucille's garage. Now, the interesting thing is that Pitkin didn't know where Lucille lived. When they went to the garage at 719 South Gondola, it probably meant nothing in the world to Pitkin. He had seen Lucille, knew she was in the city somewhere, and was trying to find her, but he didn't know where she lived.

"On some pretext, Argyle got Pitkin to monkey around with the timing on Lucille's automobile—and it's just possible he knew that Arthur Colson had been rewiring the car. Remember he'd been collecting data on Pitkin, Hollister and Lucille for some time. It was a very sweet setup for Argyle. He waited until the car was sputtering and backfiring so that the noise of the revolver shot would simply sound like one more backfire and wouldn't have any significance whatever to any person who might be listening. He simply pulled the trigger, pocketed the gun, stepped into Lucille's car, drove it across the street, and parked it at the curb. He left the keys in the car, went back to close and lock the garage, then went up to Lucille's apartment and put the gun back in the desk. After that he got in his own car, drove out to pick up his new chauffeur, and was waiting in front of my office by the time Della arrived. He was careful enough to let the man at the cigar stand see *a* chauffeur driving the car around, looking for a parking place and eventually finding one. He had luck in that Della Street also noticed the car and chauffeur.

"He waited around for me as long as he dared. Then he rang up the insurance adjuster, who promptly told him not to have anything to do with me.

"The insurance adjuster came out and picked up Argyle. Argyle told him a story which scared the insurance company to death, offered to stand some of the settlement himself, and they went out to see Bob Finchley."

"How did Argyle know you found the desk locked on that first visit to Lucille's apartment?"

"He must have been waiting where he could watch the apartment. He saw me go in. Probably he'd just found out Lucille kept the desk locked. When I did nothing about hunting him up he knew I hadn't got the license number he'd planted in the notebook, so he sent me a key to the desk, special delivery.

"You see Lucille went out as soon as I'd left so Arthur Colson could tell her what to say. She thought I might be setting a trap for her.

"And when Argyle saw her go out, all dolled up like a million dollars, he felt certain she was going to see Colson. Argyle had previously made himself a duplicate key to the desk just in case.

"He dashed off a special delivery letter and sent me the key.

"There was Argyle's plan and it was a peach. If it hadn't been for the fact that our ad in the paper actually struck pay dirt in having Carlotta Boone come in and put the finger on Caffee, we never would have suspected anything.

"Now, notice the most suspicious circumstance of all, when you come right down to it. When I talked with Argyle on the afternoon of the fifth, he let it appear that *he* had been driving the car. He showed all of the evidences of guilt, and the same was true of the time he went to see Finchley. But after he realized we had found the real hit-and-run driver he started blaming it all on his chauffeur.

"You see he realized what a precarious position he was in, so he extricated himself by reporting a purely fictitious conversation with Pitkin."

"But didn't that leave him wide open?" Drake asked.

"Sure, but there was nothing else he *could* do. Of course once he realized Hollister's housekeeper thought the missing rug had been given Lucille, Argyle felt greatly relieved. If it hadn't been for a mere fluke, Hollister's car might not have been found for months. And if the car hadn't been found the body wouldn't have been found.

"But the breaks went against Argyle on Hollister's death just as they were all in his favor on Pitkin's death.

"You see Lucille didn't want to call the police until she had made a settlement with Willard Barton. He pried the truth out of her and suggested she plant the gun so it would look like suicide. Arthur Colson very agreeably used a small wheel to grind the numbers off the gun. When Lucille saw the body of her ex-husband in the garage, she must have had at least a suspicion someone had taken her gun to do the job. Perhaps she noticed the desk had been ransacked in her absence. I'd emptied shells from the gun. They reloaded it, fired one shell and planted the gun in the garage."

"They must have worked fast on the Hollister job," Drake said.

"Sure. Gates had planned every detail, in case he had to shoot his way out. They arrived at Hollister's house about twenty minutes to five. Hollister was blunt and angry, Gates cold-blooded and deadly. Hollister was killed and rolled in canvas within a few minutes. After that it wasn't too great a job to do the rest of it. Argyle was back here by seven o'clock, and took care to have an alibi for the rest of the evening."

"How did you make Argyle crack?" Drake asked. "That's something I don't get."

"It was when I handed him that list of names," Mason said. "It was a cinch. During the noon hour I rang up every employment agency in town and asked them the names of all persons who had been hired to act as chauffeurs on the fourth or fifth of the month. I had a list of fifteen names which included men who had been hired as butlers and general handymen. I presented that list to Argyle. He saw on there the name of the man whom he had employed and who was even then on a bus, riding to Detroit. That hit him hard. He knew then that I knew."

"How did you ever get that Detroit angle?" Drake asked.

"I didn't have it at the time," Mason said. "At that time it was only a theory. Tragg checked the list after Argyle was removed from the wreck, taken to the hospital, and made a deathbed confession. He found one man—Orville Nettleton—who had given up his room, telling his landlady he had a job for a man who was going to send him to Detroit to pick up a new car and then drive it to Mexico, where his employer would meet him later on. The man was tickled pink over his job and mentioned the name of his new employer, Argyle."

"Well," Della Street said, "it was a nice case, but I don't see any fee in it."

"I'm afraid you won't," Mason said, grinning. "A lawyer occasionally has a case thrust upon him, and this is one we're going to have to charge to profit and loss."

Drake said, "It *should* teach you not to leave your fingerprints on guns."

"And to keep out of girls' apartments," Della Street added.

"You'll notice," Mason told them, grinning, "that I promptly surrendered the key to the apartment to Lieutenant Tragg."

"Gosh, yes," Drake said. "I wonder what Tragg's done with that key."

"Well," Della Street said, "you had *some* compensation, chief. You had a nice tête-à-tête and a breakfast with the much-married Lucille."

"Much-married, but cautious," Mason observed.

Drake winked at Della Street. "I wonder if Mason was also cautious?"

"*I* wonder," Della Street said.

"Keep wondering, both of you," Mason told them, grinning, "and remember that while I missed a fee in a murder case, I certainly made a killing on Finchley's case."

"Darned if you didn't," Drake admitted admiringly. "I certainly had to laugh when I saw Judge Osborn's face when the real nature of that deal dawned on him. Particularly when Argyle quoted Finchley as saying you were going to teach certain insurance adjusters not to suck eggs."

Mason said, "By the way, Paul, I saw your secretary as I came down the corridor. She said if you were in here to let you know that the client in the Emery case was anxious for a report."

Drake came up out of the chair with a sudden bound. "My gosh," he said, "I'd forgotten about Emery! Well, be good."

Mason watched the door slowly close.

"You certainly built a fire under him," Della Street said.

Mason nodded. "I thought," he said, "we could arrange for a

congratulatory dinner, in celebration of squeezing out of a trap through a darn narrow opening, Della."

She glanced at him demurely. "Then why get rid of Paul Drake?"

"Because I didn't think we needed a chaperon."

"Sounds interesting," Della Street said.

THE CASE OF

The Crimson Kiss

1

PREOCCUPATION with her own happiness prevented Fay Allison from seeing the surge of bitter hatred in Anita's eyes.

So Fay, wrapped in the warmth of romantic thoughts, went babbling on to her roommate, her tongue loosened by the double cocktail which Anita had prepared before dinner.

"*I'd* known I loved him for a long time," she said, "but honestly, Anita, it never occurred to me that Dane was the marrying kind. He'd had that one unfortunate affair, and he'd always seemed so detached and objective about things. Of course, underneath all that reserve he's romantic and tender. Anita, I'm getting a break I don't deserve."

Anita Bonsal, having pushed her dinner dishes to one side, toyed with the stem of her empty cocktail glass. Her eyes were pinpricks of black hatred which she was afraid to let Fay Allison see. "You've fixed a date?" she asked, concentrating on the rotating base of the glass.

"Just as soon as Aunt Louise can get here. I want her to be with me. I . . . and, of course, I'll want *you*, dear."

"When will Aunt Louise get here?"

"Tomorrow or next day, I think. I haven't heard from her definitely."

"You've written her?"

"Yes. She'll take the night plane. I mailed her my extra key so she can come right on in whenever she gets here, even if we aren't here."

Anita Bonsal was silent, but Fay Allison wanted to talk. "You know how Dane is. He's always been sort of impersonal. He took *you* out at first as much as he did *me*, and then he began to specialize on me. Of course, you're so popular, you don't mind. It's different with me. Anita, I was afraid to acknowledge even to myself how deeply I felt, because I thought it might lead to heartache."

"All of my congratulations, dear," Anita said.

"Don't you think it will work out, Anita? You don't seem terribly enthusiastic."

"Of course it will work out. I'm not gushing because I'm a selfish devil and it's going to make a lot of difference in my personal life— the apartment and all that. Come on, let's get the dishes done. I'm going out tonight and I presume you'll be having company."

"No, Dane's not coming over. He's going through a ceremony at his bachelors' club—one of those silly things that men belong to. He has to pay a forfeit or something, and there's a lot of horseplay. I'm so excited I'm just walking on air."

"Well," Anita said, "I go away for a three-day week end and a lot seems to happen around here. I'll have to start looking for another roommate. This apartment is too big for me to carry by myself."

"You won't have any trouble. Just pick the person you want. How about one of the girls at the office?"

Anita shook her head, tight-lipped.

"Well, of course, I'll pay until the fifteenth and then ... ."

"Don't worry about that," Anita said lightly. "I'm something of a lone wolf at heart. I don't get along too well with most women, but I'll find someone. It'll take a little time for me to look around. Most of the girls in the office are pretty sappy."

They did the dishes, straightened up the apartment, Fay Allison talking excitedly, laughing with lighthearted merriment, Anita Bonsal moving with the swift efficiency of one who is deftly skillful with her hands, saying but little.

As soon as the dishes had been finished and put away, Anita slipped into a long black evening dress, put on her fur coat, smiled at Fay Allison and said, "You'd better take some of the sleeping pills tonight, dear. You're all wound up."

Fay said somewhat wistfully, "I am afraid I talked you to death, Anita. I wanted someone to listen while I built air castles. I . . . I'll read a book. I'll be waiting up when you get back."

"Don't," Anita said. "It'll be late."

Fay said wistfully, "You're always so mysterious about things, Anita. I really know very little about your friends. Don't you *ever* want to get married and have a home of your own?"

"Not me. I'm too fond of having my own way, and I like life as it is," Anita said, and slipped out through the door, gently pulling it shut behind her.

She walked down the corridor to the elevator, pressed the button, and when the cage came up to the sixth floor, stepped in, pressed the button for the lobby, waited until the elevator was halfway down, then pressed the stop button, then the button for the seventh floor.

The elevator rattled slowly upward, came to a stop.

Anita calmly opened her purse, took out a key, walked down the long corridor, glanced swiftly back toward the elevator, then fitted the key to apartment 702 and opened the door.

Carver L. Clements looked up from his newspaper, removed the cigar from his mouth, regarded Anita Bonsal with eyes that showed swift approval, but kept his voice detached as he said, "It took you long enough to get here."

"I had to throw a little wool in the eyes of my roommate, and listen to her prattle of happiness. She's marrying Dane Grover."

Carver Clements put down the newspaper. "The hell she is!"

"It seems he went overboard in a burst of romance, and his attentions became serious and honorable," Anita said bitterly. "Fay has written her aunt, Louise Marlow, and as soon as the aunt gets here they'll be married."

Carver Clements shifted his position slightly, as though by doing so he could look at the tall brunette from a slightly different angle. He said, "I had it figured out that you were in love with Dane Grover, yourself."

"So that's been the trouble with you lately!"

"Weren't you?"

"Heavens, no!"

"You know, my love," Clements went on, "I'd hate to lose you now."

Anger flared in her eyes. "Don't think you can own me!" she said bitterly. "You only rent me."

"Let's call it a lease," he said.

"It's a tenancy-at-will," she flared. "And kindly get up when I come into the room. After all, you might as well show some manners."

Clements arose from the chair. He was a spidery man with long arms and legs, a thick, short body, a head almost bald, but he spent a small fortune on clothes that were skillfully cut to conceal the chunkiness of his body. He smiled, and said, "My little spitfire! But I like you for it. Remember, Anita, I'm playing for keeps. As soon as I can get my divorce straightened out . . ."

"You and your divorce!" she interrupted. "You've been pulling that line . . ."

"It isn't a line. There are some very intricate property problems. I don't dare to seem too eager, and the thing can't be handled abruptly. You know that. You *should* know that."

She said, "I know that I'm tired of all this pretense. I'm tired of working. If you're playing for keeps, take me off the dole and make *me* a property settlement."

"And have my wife's lawyers suddenly drag me into court for another examination of my assets and start tracing the checks . . ."

"Make it in cash."

"And have the bank withdrawals checked? Don't be silly."

"I'm not going to be. I'm going to be practical. What if I should get dragged into your domestic mess anyway? Look at the chances *I'm* taking."

His eyes were somber in their steady appraisal. "I like you, Anita. I can do a lot for you. I like that fire that you have. But I want it in your heart and not in your tongue. My car's in the parking lot. You go on down, get in the car and wait. I'll be down in five minutes."

She said, "Why don't you take me out as though you weren't ashamed of me? As though . . ."

"And give my wife the opportunity she's looking for? Then you *would* have the fat in the fire. The property settlement will be completed and signed within five or six weeks. Thank heavens, I'll then be free to live my own life in my own way. Until then . . . until then, my darling, we have to be discreet in our indiscretions."

She started to say something, checked herself, turned and stalked out of the apartment.

Carver Clements' automobile was a big, luxurious sedan equipped with every possible convenience, but it was cold sitting there, waiting.

Anita waited for several minutes, then, as she felt the chill creeping through her sheer nylons, turned the ignition switch and pulled out the heater button.

It took a minute or two for warmth to generate in the heater. Then a welcome current of warm air swirled caressingly about her legs.

After ten minutes, which seemed twenty, she grew impatient. She flung open the car door, went to the entrance of the apartment house and angrily pressed the button of 702.

When there was no answer, she knew that Clements must be on his way down in the elevator, so she walked back into the shadows, to stand there, impatient, feeling a strange desire to smash something. But Clements didn't appear.

Anita used her key to enter the apartment house. The elevator was on the ground floor. She made no attempt at concealment this time, but pressed the button for the seventh floor, left the elevator, strode down the corridor, stabbed her key into the metal lock of Clements' apartment, and entered the room.

Carver L. Clements, dressed for the street, was lying sprawled on the floor.

A highball glass lay on its side, two feet from his body. It had apparently fallen from his hand, spilling contents as it rolled along the carpet. Clements' face was a peculiar hue, and there was a sharp, bitter odor which seemed intensified as she bent toward his froth-flecked lips. Since Anita had last seen him he had quite evidently had a caller. The print of half-parted lips flared in gaudy crimson from the front of his bald head.

With the expertness she had learned from a course in first aid, Anita pressed her finger against the wrist, searching for a pulse. There was none.

She opened her handbag, took out the silver cigarette case, held its smoothly polished surface close to the man's lips. There was no faintest sign of moisture which would indicate any breathing.

Quite evidently, Carver L. Clements, wealthy playboy, yachtsman, broker, gambler for high stakes, was quite dead.

In a panic, Anita Bonsal looked through the apartment.

There were all too many signs of her surreptitious and intermittent occupancy of that apartment—nightgowns, lingerie, shoes, stockings, hats, even toothbrushes and her favorite tooth paste.

Anita Bonsal turned back toward the door and quietly left the apartment. She paused in the hallway, making certain there was no one in the corridor. This time she didn't take the elevator, but walked down the fire stairs, as she had done so many times, and returned to her own apartment on the sixth floor.

Fay Allison had been listening to a musical program on the radio. She jumped up with glad surprise as Anita entered.

"Oh, Anita, I'm so glad! I thought—thought you wouldn't be in until real late. What happened? It hasn't been any time since you left."

"I developed a beastly headache," Anita said. "My escort was a trifle intoxicated, so I slapped his face and came home. I'd like to sit up and have you tell me about your plans, but I do have a headache, and you must get a good night's sleep tonight. You'll need to be looking your best tomorrow."

Fay laughed. "I don't want to waste time sleeping. While I'm unconscious I can't revel in my happiness."

"Nevertheless," Anita said firmly, "we're going to get to bed early. Let's undress, put on pajamas, have some hot chocolate, and then we'll sit in front of the electric heater and talk for just exactly twenty minutes."

"Oh, I'm so glad you came back!" Fay said.

"I'll fix the drink," Anita told her. "I'm going to make your chocolate sweet tonight. You can start worrying about your figure tomorrow. After all, you'll be a married woman before this chocolate can put any pounds on you."

She went to the kitchen, opened her purse, took out a bottle of barbiturate tablets, emptied a good half of the pills into a cup, carefully ground them up into powder, then added hot water until they were, for the most part, dissolved.

She placed chocolate on the stove, added milk and melted marshmallows, called out to Fay, "You undress, dear. I'll put on my pajamas after we've had the chocolate."

When she returned to the living room, carrying the two steaming cups frothy with melted marshmallows floating on top, Fay Allison was in her pajamas.

Anita Bonsal raised her cup. "Here's to happiness, darling."

"Lots of happiness," Fay Allison said almost dreamily.

After they had finished the first cup of chocolate, Anita talked Fay into another cup, then let Fay discuss her plans until drowsiness made the words thick, the sentences detached.

"Anita, I'm *so* sleepy all of a sudden. I guess it's the reaction from having been so keyed up. I . . . darling, it's all right if I . . . you don't care if I . . ."

"Not at all, dear," Anita said, and helped Fay into bed, tucked her in carefully, and then gave the situation careful consideration.

The fact that Carver Clements maintained a secret apartment in

that building was known only to a few of Clements' cronies. These
people knew of Carver Clements' domestic difficulties and knew
why he maintained this apartment. Fortunately, however, they
had never seen Anita. That was a big thing in her favor. Anita was
quite certain it hadn't been a heart attack. It had been poison, some
quick-acting, deadly poison. There was no use worrying herself,
trying to figure out how it had been administered, or why. Carver
Clements was a man who had many powerful friends and many
powerful enemies.

The police would search for the woman.

It wouldn't do for Anita merely to remove her things from that
apartment, and, besides, that wouldn't be artistic enough. Anita
had been in love with Dane Grover. If it hadn't been for that dismal
entanglement with Carver Clements . . . However, that was all
past now, and Fay Allison, with her big blue eyes, her sweet, trust-
ing disposition, had turned Dane Grover from a disillusioned wolf
into an ardent suitor. Well, it was a world where the smart ones got
by. Anita had washed the dishes. Fay Allison had dried them. Her
fingerprints would be on glasses and on dishes. The management
of the apartment house very considerately furnished dishes identi-
cal in pattern—and it only needed a little careful work on her part.
She would, of course, put on gloves. The police would find Fay
Allison's nightgowns in Carver Clements' secret apartment. They
would find glasses that had Fay's fingerprints on them. And when
they went to question Fay Allison, they would find she had taken
the easy way out, an overdose of sleeping pills.

Anita would furnish the testimony that would make it all check
into a composite, sordid pattern. A girl who had been the mistress
of a rich playboy, then had met a younger and more attractive man
who had offered her marriage. She had gone to Carver Clements
and wanted to check out, but with Carver Clements one didn't
simply check out. Things weren't as easy as that. So Fay had slipped
the fatal poison into his drink and then had realized she was
trapped when Anita returned home unexpectedly and there had
been no chance for Fay to make surreptitious removal of her wearing apparel from the upstairs apartment. Anita would let the police
do the figuring. Anita would be horrified, simply stunned, but, of
course, co-operative.

Anita Bonsal deliberately waited three hours until things began
to quiet down in the apartment house, then she took a suitcase and

quietly went to work, moving with the smooth efficiency of a woman who has been accustomed to thinking out every smallest detail.

When she had finished, she carefully polished the key to apartment 702 so as to remove any possible fingerprints, and dropped it in Fay Allison's purse. She ground up all but six of the remaining sleeping tablets and mixed the powder with the chocolate which was left in the canister.

Then she donned pajamas, took the remaining six tablets, washed off the label with hot water and tossed the empty bottle out of the back window of the apartment. Then she snuggled·down into her own bed and switched off the lights.

Over in the other twin bed, Fay Allison lay motionless, except for a slight chest motion as her shallow breathing raised and lowered the coverlet.

The maid was due to come at eight the next morning to clean up the apartment. She would find two still figures, one dead, one in a drugged stupor.

Two of the tablets constituted the heaviest prescribed dose. The six tablets Anita had taken began to suck at her consciousness. For a moment there was swift panic. Perhaps she had really taken too many. Could it be that . . . that . . . perhaps . . .

It was too late now. The soothing influence of the drug warmed her consciousness into acquiescence.

She wondered if she could call a drugstore and find out if . . . a moment later she was asleep.

2

LOUISE MARLOW, tired from the long airplane ride, her ears still ringing with the sound of muffled motors, paid off the taxicab in front of the apartment house.

The cab driver surveyed her solicitously. "Want me to wait until you see if your party's home?"

"I have a key," Louise Marlow said.

"How about your bags?"

"Don't worry about them. I'll get them up all right."

He helped her with her bags to the entrance door. Louise Marlow inserted the key which Fay Allison had sent her, smiled her thanks to the cab driver and picked up her bags.

Sixty-five years old, white-headed, steely-eyed, square of shoulder and broad of beam, she had experienced many and varied vicissitudes in life, and from them had extracted a salty philosophy of her own. Her love was big enough to encompass those who were dear to her with a protecting umbrella. Her hatred was bitter enough to goad her enemies into confused retreat.

With casual disregard for the fact that it was now one o'clock in the morning, she marched calmly down the corridor to the elevator, banged her suitcase and overnight bag into the corner of the cage and punched the button for the sixth floor.

The elevator moved slowly upward, then shuddered to a stop. The door slid slowly open and Aunt Louise, picking up her bags, walked down the half-darkened corridor, peering over the tops of her glasses for numbers over the doors.

At length she found the apartment she wanted, inserted her key, opened the door and groped for a light switch.

She found the light switch, clicked it on and called, "It's me, Fay!"

There was no answer.

Aunt Louise dragged her bags in, pushed the door shut, called out cheerfully, "Don't shoot," and then added by way of explanation, "I picked up a cancellation on an earlier plane, Fay."

The continued silence bothered her. She moved over to the bedroom.

"Wake up, Fay. It's your Aunt Louise!"

She clicked on the bedroom light, smiled down at the two sleepers, said, "Well, if you're going to sleep right through everything, I'll make up a bed on the davenport and say hello to you in the morning."

Then something in the color of Fay Allison's face caused the keen eyes to lose their twinkle of friendly humor and become hard with steely concentration.

"Fay!" she said.

The figures slumbered on in complete oblivion.

Aunt Louise went over and shook Fay Allison, then turned to Anita Bonsal and started shaking her.

The motion finally brought Anita back to semi-consciousness from drugged slumber.

"Who is it?" she asked thickly.

"I'm Fay Allison's Aunt Louise. I got here ahead of time. What's happened?"

Anita Bonsal knew in a drowsy manner that this was a complicating circumstance that she had not foreseen, and despite the numbing effect of the drug on her senses, managed to mouth the excuse which was to be her first waking alibi.

"Something happened," she said thickly. "The chocolate . . . we drank chocolate and it felt like . . . I can't remember . . . can't remember . . . I want to go to sleep."

She let her head swing over on a limp neck and became a dead weight in Louise Marlow's arms.

Aunt Louise put her back on the bed, snatched up a telephone directory and thumbed through the pages until she found the name, *Perry Mason, Attorney at Law.*

There was a night number—Westfield 6–59432.

Louise Marlow dialed the number.

The night operator on duty at the switchboard of the Drake Detective Agency, recognizing from the peculiar sound of the buzzing that the ringing phone was that of Mason's night number, picked up the receiver and said, "Night number of Mr. Perry Mason. Who is this talking, please?"

Louise Marlow said in a firm, steady voice, "This is Louise Marlow. I haven't met Perry Mason but I know his secretary, Della Street. I want you to get in touch with her and tell her that I'm at Keystone 97600. I'm in a mess and I want her to call me back here just as quick as she can. Yes, that's right! I know her personally. You tell her it's Louise Marlow talking and she'll get busy. I think I may need Mr. Mason before I get done; but I certainly want to talk with Della Street right now."

Louise Marlow hung up and waited.

Within less than a minute she heard the phone ring and Della Street's voice came over the line as Aunt Louise picked up the receiver and said, "Hello."

"Why, Louise Marlow, whatever are *you* doing in town?"

"I came in to attend the wedding of my niece, Fay Allison," Aunt Louise said. "Now, listen, Della. I'm at Fay's apartment. She's been drugged and I can't wake her up. Her roommate, Anita Bonsal, has also been drugged and I managed to get her awake, but she keeps going back to sleep. Someone's tried to poison them!

"I want to get a doctor who's good, and who can keep his damn trap shut. I don't know what's back of all this, but Fay's getting married tomorrow. Someone's tried to put her under sod, and I propose to find out what's behind it. If anything should get into the newspapers about this, I'll wring someone's neck. The whole business looks fishy to me. I'm at the Mandrake Arms, apartment 604. Rush a doctor up here and then you'd better get hold of Perry Mason and . . ."

Della Street said, "I'll send a good doctor up to you right away, Mrs. Marlow. I just got in. Perry Mason, Paul Drake, the detective who handles his investigations, and I have been out nightclubbing with a client. Mr. Mason brought me home just a few minutes ago and I can catch him at his apartment. You sit tight. I'm getting busy."

3

WHEN Aunt Louise answered the buzzer, Della Street said, "Mrs. Marlow, this is Perry Mason. This is 'Aunt Louise,' chief. She's an old friend from my home town."

Louise Marlow gave the famous lawyer her hand and a smile. She kissed Della, said, "You haven't changed a bit, Della. Come on in. There's a mess here. I can't afford to have a word get in the newspapers. We had to get this sawbones. Now, how do we keep him from blabbing?"

"What does the doctor say?" Mason asked.

"He's working like a house afire. Anita is conscious. Fay is going to pull through all right. Another hour and it would have been too late for her."

"What happened?" Mason asked.

"Someone dumped sleeping medicine in the powdered chocolate, or else in the sugar."

"Any suspicions?" Mason asked.

She said, "Fay was marrying Dane Grover. I gather from her letters he's a wealthy but shy young man who had one bad experience with a jane years ago and had turned bitter and disillusioned, or thought he had. A cynic at twenty-six! Baloney!"

Mason smiled.

"I got here around one o'clock I guess. Fay had sent me a key. The place was closed tight as a miser's purse. I used the key. As soon as I switched on the light and looked at Fay's face, I knew that something was wrong, the color of it and the way she was breathing. I tried to wake her up and couldn't. I finally shook some sense into Anita. She said the chocolate did it. Then I called Della. That's just about all I know about it."

"The cups they drank the chocolate from?" Mason asked. "Where are they?"

"On the kitchen sink—unwashed."

"We may need them for evidence," Mason said.

"Evidence, my eye!" Louise Marlow snorted. "I don't want the police in on this. You can imagine what'll happen if some sob sister spills a lot of printer's ink about a bride-to-be trying to kill herself on the eve of the wedding."

"Let's take a look around," Mason said.

The lawyer moved about the apartment, trying to reconstruct what had happened.

Louise Marlow followed, acting as guide, and Della Street from time to time gave the benefit of a feminine suggestion.

Mason nodded, paused as he came to street coats thrown over the back of a chair, then again as he looked at the two purses.

"Which one is Fay Allison's?" he asked.

"Heavens, I don't know. We'll have to find out," Aunt Louise said.

Mason said, "I'll let you two take the lead. Go through them carefully. See if you can find anything that would indicate whether anyone might have been in the apartment shortly before they started drinking the chocolate. Perhaps there's a letter that will give us a clue, or a card or a note."

The doctor, emerging from the bedroom, said, "I want to boil some water for another hypo."

"How are they coming?" Mason asked, as Mrs. Marlow went to the kitchen.

"The brunette is all right," the doctor said, "and I think the blonde will make it all right."

"When can I question one of them in detail?"

The doctor shook his head. "I wouldn't advise it. Not that it will hurt anything, but you might get thrown off the track. They are still groggy, and there's some evidence that the brunette is rambling and contradictory in her statements. Give her another hour and you can get some facts. Right now she's running around in circles."

The doctor boiled water for his hypo, went back to the bedroom. Della Street moved over to Mason's side, said in a low voice, "Here's something I don't understand, chief."

"What?"

"Notice the keys to the apartment house are stamped with the numbers of the apartments. Both girls have keys to this apartment in their purses. Fay Allison also has a key stamped 702. What would she be doing with the key to another apartment?"

Mason's eyes narrowed for a moment in thoughtful speculation. "What does Aunt Louise say?"

"She doesn't know. I was the one who searched Fay's purse. She went through Anita's."

"Anything else to give a clue?"

"Not the slightest thing anywhere."

Mason said, "Okay, I'm going to take a look at 702. You'd better come along, Della."

Mason made excuses to Louise Marlow. "We want to look around awhile on the outside," he said. "We'll be back in a few minutes."

He and Della took the elevator to the seventh floor, walked down to apartment 702 and Mason pushed his thumb against the bell button.

They could hear the sound of the buzzer in the apartment, but there was no faintest sound of answering motion such as would have been caused by sleepers stirring around.

Mason said, "It's a chance we shouldn't take, but I'm going to take a peek inside, just for luck."

He fitted the key to the door, clicked back the lock, gently opened the door.

The blazing lights of the living room streamed illumination out at them through the open door, showed the sprawled body on the floor, the drinking glass which had rolled from the dead fingers.

The door from an apartment across the hall jerked open. A young woman with disheveled hair, a bathrobe around her, said angrily, "After you've pressed a buzzer for five minutes at this time of the night you should have sense enough to . . ."

"We have," Mason interrupted, pulling Della Street into the apartment and kicking the door shut behind them with a quick jab of his heel.

Della Street, clinging to Mason's arm, saw the sprawled figure on the floor, the crimson lipstick on the forehead, looked at the overturned chair by the table, the glass which had rolled along the carpet, spilling part of its contents, at the other empty glass standing on the table across from the overturned chair.

Her breathing was heavy and fast, as though she had been running, but she said nothing.

"Careful, Della, we mustn't touch anything."

"Who is he?"

"Apparently he's People's Exhibit A. Do you suppose the nosy dame in the opposite apartment is out of the hall by this time? We'll have to take a chance anyway." He wrapped his hand with his handkerchief, turned the knob on the inside of the door, pulled it silently open.

The door of the apartment across the hall was closed.

Mason warned Della Street to silence with a gesture. They tiptoed out into the corridor, pulled the door closed behind them.

As the door clicked shut, the elevator came to a stop at the seventh floor. Three men and a woman came hurrying down the corridor directly toward them.

Mason's voice was low, reassuring. "Perfectly casual, Della. Just friends departing from a late card game."

They caught the curious glances of the four people, moved slightly to one side, then, after the quartet had passed, Mason took Della Street's arm, said, "Don't hurry, Della, take it easy."

"Well," Della Street said, "they'll certainly know us if they ever see us again. The way that woman looked me over . . ."

"I know," Mason said, "but we'll hope that . . . oh, oh!"

"What is it?"

"They're going to 702!"

The four paused in front of the door. One of the men pressed the buzzer button.

Almost immediately the door of the opposite apartment jerked open. The woman with the bathrobe shrilled, "I'm suffering from insomnia. I've been trying to sleep, and this . . ."

She broke off as she saw the strangers.

The man who had been pressing the button grinned and said in a booming voice which carried well down the corridor, "We're sorry, ma'am. I only just gave him one short buzz."

"Well, the other people who went in just before you made enough commotion."

"Other people *in here?*" the man asked, hesitated a moment, then went on. "Well, we won't bother him if he's got company."

Mason pulled Della Street into the elevator, pulled the door shut, pushed the button for the lobby.

"What in the world do we do now?" Della Street asked.

"Now," Mason said, his voice sharp-edged with disappointment, "we ring police headquarters and report a possible homicide. It's the only thing we *can* do. The woman only saw two people she can't identify going *in*, but that quartet will eventually identify us as going out."

There was a phone booth in the lobby. Mason dropped a nickel, dialed police headquarters and reported that he had found a corpse in apartment 702 under circumstances indicating probable homicide. He had, he said, touched nothing, but had backed right out and called the police.

While Mason was in the phone booth, the four people emerged from the elevator. There was a distinct aroma of alcohol as they pushed their way toward the door. The woman, catching sight of Della Street standing beside the phone booth, favored her with a feminine appraisal which swept from head to foot and missed no smallest detail.

Mason called Louise Marlow in apartment 604. "I think you'd better have the doctor take his patients to a sanitarium where they can have complete quiet," he said.

"He seems to think they're doing all right here."

"I distrust doctors who *seem* to think," Mason said. "I would suggest a sanitarium immediately, and *complete quiet.*"

Louise Marlow was silent for a full three seconds.

"Are you there?" Mason asked.

"I'm here," she said. "I'm just trying to get the sketch."

"I think the patients should have *complete quiet,*" Mason said.

"Damn it," Louise Marlow sputtered. "When you said it the first time I missed it. The second time I got it. You don't have to let your needle get stuck on the record! I was just trying to figure it out."

Mason heard her slam up the phone at the other end of the line.

Mason grinned, hung up the phone, took the key to 702 from his pocket, dropped it in an envelope, addressed the envelope to his office, stamped it and dropped it in the mail box by the elevator.

Outside, the four people in the car were having something of an argument. Apparently there was some sharp difference of opinion as to what action was to be taken next, but as a siren sounded they reached a sudden unanimity of decision. They were starting the car as the police car pulled in to the curb. The red beam of the police spotlight pilloried them. The siren blasted a peremptory summons.

The driver of the car looked behind him, then stepped on the throttle.

The police car shot away in angry pursuit and three minutes later, a chastened quartet swung their car back to a stop in front of the apartment house, the police car following them until the machine was safely parked at the curb. One of the radio officers walked over to the other car, took possession of the ignition keys and ushered the four people up to the door of the apartment house.

Mason hurried across the lobby to open the locked door.

The officer said, "I'm looking for a man who reported a body."

"That's right. I did. My name's Mason. The body's in 702."

"A body!" the woman screamed.

"Shut up," the radio officer said.

"But *we* know the . . . why he told you we'd been visiting in 702 . . . we . . ."

"Yeah, you said you'd been visiting a friend in 702, name of Carver Clements. How was he when you left him?"

There was an awkward silence, then the woman said, "We *really* didn't get in. We just went to the door. The woman across the way said he had company, so we left."

"Said he had company?"

"That's right. But *I* think the company had left. It was these two here."

"We'll go take a look," the officer said. "Come on."

4

LIEUTENANT TRAGG, head of the Homicide Squad, finished his examination of the apartment, said wearily to Mason, "I presume by this time you've thought up a good story to explain how it all happened."

Mason said, "As a matter of fact, I don't know this man from Adam. I had never seen him alive."

"I know," Tragg said sarcastically, "wanted him as a witness to an automobile accident or something, and just happened to drop around in the wee small hours of the morning."

Mason said nothing.

"But," Tragg went on, "strange as it may seem, Mason, I'm interested to know how you got in. The woman who has the apartment across the corridor says you stood there and rang the buzzer for as much as two minutes. Then she heard the sound of a clicking bolt just as she opened her door to give you a piece of her mind, thinking you were some drunken bum trying to buzz a girl friend who had cooled off on him."

Mason nodded gravely.

Tragg said, "Either someone opened that door or the door was open. If it was ajar, I don't think you'd have buzzed for two minutes without pushing it open. If someone was in there, I want to know who it was. Now who let you in?"

"I had a key."

"A key! The hell you did!"

Mason nodded.

"Let's take a look at it."

"I'm sorry, I don't have it now."

"Well, now," Tragg said, "*isn't* that interesting! And where did you get the key, Mason?"

"Unfortunately," Mason said, "*that's* something I can't tell you."

"Don't be silly. This is a murder case."

Mason said, "The key came into my possession in a peculiar manner. I found it."

"Phooey! A client gave it to you."

"What makes you think that?"

"It's a reasonable conjecture."

Mason smiled. "Come, come, Lieutenant, if you're going to engage in pure flights of fancy, why not consider the possibility that this client might have taken a sublease on the apartment and wanted me to see that the gentleman lying there on the floor, who was unlawfully withholding possession, was ejected without trouble?"

"So you came to eject him at this time in the morning!"

"Perhaps the sublease didn't become effective until midnight."

Tragg's eyes narrowed. "It's a nice try, Mason, but you're not getting anywhere. That key you have is the dead man's key. When we searched the body we found that stuff on the table there. There's no key to this apartment on him."

Mason sparred for time, said, "And did you notice that despite the fact there's a thermos jar of ice cubes on the table, a bottle of Scotch and a siphon of soda, the fatal drink didn't have any ice in it?"

"How do you know?" Tragg asked, interested.

"Because when this glass fell from his hand and the contents spilled over the floor, it left a single small spot of moisture. If there had been ice cubes in the glass they'd have rolled out for some appreciable distance and then melted, leaving spots of moisture."

"I see," Tragg said sarcastically, "and then, having decided to commit suicide, the guy kissed himself on the forehead and . . ."

He broke off as one of the detectives, walking rapidly down the hallway, said, "We've traced that cleaning mark, Lieutenant."

Tragg glanced significantly toward Mason, said, "I'll talk with you in a minute when . . ."

The man handed Tragg a folded slip of paper.

Tragg unfolded the paper. "Well I'll be damned!" Tragg said.

Mason met Tragg's searching eyes with calm steadiness.

"And I suppose," Tragg said, "you're going to be surprised at this one. Miss Fay Allison, apartment 604, in this same building, is the person who sent the coat that was in the closet to the dry cleaner. Her mark is on it. I think, Mr. Mason, we'll have a little talk with

Fay Allison, and just to see that you don't make any false moves until we get there, we'll take you right along with us. Perhaps you already know the way."

As Tragg started toward the elevator, a smartly dressed woman in the late thirties or early forties stepped out of the elevator and walked down the corridor, looking at the numbers over the doors.

Tragg stepped forward. "Looking for something?"

She started to sweep past him.

Tragg pulled back his coat, showed her his badge.

"I'm looking for apartment 702," she said.

"Who you looking for?"

"Mr. Carver Clements, if it's any of your business."

"I think it is," Tragg said. "Who are you and how do you happen to be here?"

She said, "I am Mrs. Carver L. Clements, and I'm here because I was advised over the telephone that my husband was maintaining a surreptitious apartment here."

"And that was the first you knew of it?"

"Definitely."

"And what," Tragg asked, "did you intend to do?"

"I intend to show him that he isn't getting away with anything," she said. "If you're an officer, you may as well accompany me. I feel certain that . . ."

Tragg said, "702 is down the corridor, at the corner on the right. I just came from there. You'll find a detective there in charge of things. Your husband was killed sometime between seven and nine o'clock tonight."

Dark brown eyes grew wide with surprise. "You . . . you're sure?"

Tragg said, "Dead as a mackerel. Someone slipped him a little cyanide, in his Scotch and soda. I don't suppose you'd know anything about that?"

She said slowly, "If my husband is dead . . . I can't believe it. He hated me too much to die. He was trying to force me to make a property settlement, and in order to make me properly submissive, he'd put me through a softening up process, a period during which I didn't have money enough even to dress decently. His idea was that that would make the settlement he was prepared to offer look practically irresistible to me."

"In other words," Tragg said, "you hated his guts."

She clamped her lips together. "I didn't say that!"

Tragg grinned and said, "Come along with us. We're going down to an apartment on the sixth floor. After that I'm going to take *your* fingerprints and see if they match up with those on the glass which didn't contain the poison."

5

LOUISE MARLOW answered the buzzer.

She glanced at Tragg, then at Mrs. Clements.

Mason, raising his hat, said with grave politeness and the manner of a total stranger, "We're sorry to bother you at this hour, but . . ."

"*I'll* do the talking," Tragg said.

The formality of Mason's manner was not lost on Aunt Louise. She said, as though she had never seen him before, "Well, this is a great time . . ."

Tragg pushed his way forward. "Does Fay Allison live here?"

"That's right," Louise Marlow beamed at him. "She and another girl, Anita Bonsal, share the apartment. They aren't here now, though."

"Where are they?" Tragg asked.

She shook her head. "I'm sure I couldn't tell you."

"And who are you?"

"I'm Louise Marlow, Fay Allison's aunt."

"You're living with them?"

"Heavens, no. I just came up tonight to be here for . . . for a visit with Fay."

"How did you get in, if they weren't here?"

"I had a key, but I didn't say they weren't here then."

"You said, I believe, that they are not here now?"

"That's right."

"What time did you arrive?"

"Around one o'clock."

Tragg said, "Let's cut out the shadow boxing and get down to brass tacks, Mrs. Marlow. I want to see both of those girls."

"I'm sorry, but the girls are both sick. They're in the hospital."

"Who took them there?"

"A doctor."

"What's his name?"

Louise Marlow hesitated a moment, then said, "It's just a simple case of food poisoning. Only . . ."

"What's the doctor's name?"

"Now you listen to me," Louise Marlow said. "I tell you, these girls are too sick to be bothered, and . . ."

Lieutenant Tragg said, "Carver L. Clements, who has an apartment on the floor above here, is dead. It looks like murder. Fay Allison had evidently been living up there in the apartment with him and . . ."

"What are you talking about!" Louise Marlow exclaimed indignantly. "Why, I . . . I . . ."

"Take it easy," Tragg said. "Her clothes were up there. There's a laundry mark that has been traced to her."

"Clothes!" Louise Marlow snorted. "Why it's probably some junk she gave away somewhere, or . . ."

"I'm coming to that," Lieutenant Tragg said patiently. "I don't want to do anyone an injustice. I want to play it on the up-and-up. Now then, there are fingerprints in that apartment, the fingerprints of a woman on a drinking glass, on the handle of a toothbrush, on a tube of tooth paste. I'm not going to get tough unless I have to, but I want to get hold of Fay Allison long enough to take a set of rolled fingerprints from her hands. You try holding out on me, and see what the newspapers have to say tomorrow."

Louise Marlow reached an instant decision. "You'll find her at the Crestview Sanitarium," she said, "and if you want to make a little money, I'll give you odds of a hundred to one, in any amount you want to take, that . . ."

"I'm not a betting man," Tragg said wearily. "I've been in this game too long."

He turned to one of the detectives and said, "Keep Perry Mason and his charming secretary under surveillance and away from a telephone until I get a chance at those fingerprints. Okay, boys, let's go."

6

PAUL DRAKE, head of the Drake Detective Agency, pulled a sheaf of notes from his pocket as he settled down in the big client's chair in Mason's office.

It was ten-thirty in the morning, and the detective's face showed signs of weariness as he assumed his favorite crosswise position in the big leather chair, with his long legs hanging over one overstuffed arm, the small of his back propped against the other.

"It's a mess, Perry," he said.

"Let's have it," Mason said.

Drake said, "Fay Allison and Dane Grover were going to get married today. Last night, Fay and Anita Bonsal, who shares the apartment with her, settled down in front of the fireplace for a nice gabby little hen party. They made chocolate. Both girls had been watching their figures, but this was a celebration. Fay felt she could really let loose. She had two cups of chocolate, Anita had one. Fay evidently got about twice the dose of barbiturate that Anita did. Both girls passed out.

"Next thing Anita knew, Louise Marlow, Fay's aunt, was trying to wake her up. Fay Allison didn't recover consciousness until after she was in the sanitarium.

"The rest of the stuff you know pretty well.

"Anyhow, Tragg went out and took Fay Allison's fingerprints. They check absolutely with those on the glass. What the police call the murder glass is the one that slipped from Carver Clements' fingers and rolled around the floor. It had been carefully wiped clean of all fingerprints. Police can't even find one of Clements' prints on it. The other glass on the table had Fay's prints. It's her toothbrush. The closet was filled with her clothes. She was living there with him. It's a hell of a stink.

"Dane Grover is standing by her, but I personally don't think he can stand the gaff much longer. When a man's engaged to a girl and the newspapers scream the details of her affair with a wealthy playboy all over the front pages, you can't expect the man to appear exactly nonchalant. The aunt, Louise Marlow, tells me he's being faced with terrific pressure to repudiate the girl, publicly break the engagement and take a trip.

"The girls insist it's all part of some sinister over-all plan to frame them, that they were drugged, and all that, but how could anyone have planned it that way? For instance, how could anyone have known they were going to take the chocolate in time to . . ."

"The chocolate was drugged?" Mason asked.

Drake nodded. "They'd used up most of the chocolate, but the small amount left in the package is pretty well doped with barbiturate."

Mason began toying with a lead pencil.

"The police theory," Drake went on, "is that Fay Allison had been playing house with Carver Clements. She wanted to get married. Clements wouldn't let her go. She slipped him a little poison. She intended to return and get her things out of the apartment when it got late enough so she wouldn't meet someone in the corridor if she came walking out of 702 with her arms full of clothes. Anita, who had gone out, unexpectedly returned, and that left Fay Allison trapped. She couldn't go up and get her things out of the apartment upstairs without disturbing Anita. So she tried to drug Anita and something went wrong."

"That's a hell of a theory," Mason said.

"Try and get one that fits the case any better," Drake told him. "One thing is certain, Fay Allison was living up there in that apartment 702. As far as Dane Grover is concerned, that's the thing that will make him throw everything overboard. He's a sensitive chap, from a good family. He doesn't like having his picture in the papers. Neither does his family."

"What about Clements?"

"Successful businessman, broker, speculator, lots of dough, domestic troubles, a wife who was trying to hook him for a bigger property settlement than Clements wanted to pay. Clements has a big apartment he leases by the year, where he lives officially. This place was a playhouse. Only a few people knew he had it. His wife would have given a lot of money to have found out about it."

"What's the wife doing now?"

"Sitting pretty. They don't know yet whether Clements left a will, but she has her community property rights, and Clements' books will be open for inspection now. He'd been juggling things around pretty much, and now a lot of stuff is going to come out—safety deposit boxes and things of that sort."

"How about the four people who met us in the hall?"

"I have all the stuff on them here. The men were Richard P. Nolin, a sort of partner in some of Clements' business, Manley L. Ogden, an income tax specialist, Don B. Ralston, who acted as dummy for Clements in some business transactions, and Vera Payson, who is someone's girl friend, but I'm damned if I can find out whose. Anyhow, those people knew of the hideout apartment and would go up there occasionally for a poker game. Last night as soon as the dame across the hall said Clements had company, they knew what that meant and went away. That's the story. The newspapers are lapping it up. Dane Grover isn't going to stay put much longer. You can't blame him. Pressure's getting pretty strong. All he has is Fay Allison's tearful denial. Louise Marlow says we have to do something fast."

Mason said, "Tragg thinks I had Carver Clements' key."

"Didn't you?"

"No."

"Where *did* you get it?"

Mason shook his head.

"Well," Drake said, "Carver Clements didn't have a key."

Mason nodded. "That is the only break we have in the case, Paul. We know Clements' key is missing. No one else does, because Tragg won't believe me when I tell him Clements hadn't given me his key."

Drake said, "It won't take Tragg long to figure the answer to that one. If Clements didn't give you the key, there's only one other person who could have given it to you."

Mason said, "We won't speculate too much on that, Paul."

"I gathered we wouldn't," Drake said dryly. "Remember this, Perry, you're representing a girl who's going to be faced with a murder rap. You may be able to beat that rap. It's circumstantial evidence. But in doing it, you'll have to think out some explanation that will satisfy an embarrassed lover who's being pitied by his friends, laughed at by his enemies, and ridiculed by the public."

Mason nodded.

"Whatever explanation you're going to make has to be made fast," Drake said. "My best guess is this Grover guy isn't going to stand the gaff much longer."

Mason said, "We'll push things to a quick hearing in the magistrate's court on a preliminary examination. In the meantime, Paul, find out everything you can about Carver Clements' background. Pay particular attention to Clements' wife. See if there isn't a man in her life. If she had known about that apartment . . ."

Drake shook his head dubiously. "I'll give it a once-over, Perry, but if she'd even known about that apartment, that would have been all she needed. If she could have raided that apartment with a photographer and had the deadwood on Carver Clements, she'd have boosted her property settlement another hundred grand and walked out smiling. She wouldn't have needed to use any poison."

Mason's strong, capable fingers were drumming gently on the edge of the desk. "There has to be *some* explanation, Paul."

Drake heaved himself wearily to his feet. "That's right," he said without enthusiasm, "and Tragg thinks he has it."

7

DELLA STREET, her eyes sparkling, entered Mason's private office from the door which led from the reception room, and said, "*He's here, chief.*"

"Who's here?" Mason asked, frowning.

She laughed. "Don't be like that. As far as this office is concerned, there is only one HE."

"Dane Grover?"

"That's right."

"What sort?"

"Tall, sensitive-looking. Wavy, dark brown hair, romantic eyes, with something of the poet about him. He's terribly crushed, of course. You can see he's dying ten thousand deaths every time he meets one of his friends. Gertie, at the switchboard, can't take her eyes off of him."

Mason grinned, and said, "Let's get him in, then, before Gertie either breaks up a romance or dies of unrequited love."

Della Street went out, returned after a few moments, ushering Dane Grover into the office.

Mason shook hands, invited Grover to a seat. Grover glanced dubiously at Della Street. Mason smiled, "She's my right hand, Grover, keeps notes for me, and her thoughts to herself."

Grover said, "I suppose I'm unduly sensitive, but I can't stand it when people patronize me or snub me or pity me."

Mason nodded.

"I've had them do all three ever since the papers came out this morning."

Again, Mason's answer was merely a nod.

"But," Grover went on, "I want you to know that I'll stick."

Mason thought that over for a moment, then held Grover's eyes. "For how long?"

"All the way."

"No matter *what* the evidence shows?"

Grover said, "The *evidence* shows the woman I love was living with Carver Clements as his mistress. The evidence simply can't be right. I love her, and I'm going to stick. I want you to tell her that, and I want you to know that. What you're going to have to do is going to take money. I want it to take *lots* of money. I don't want to leave any stone unturned. I'm here to see that you have what money you need—all you want, in fact."

"That's fine," Mason said. "Primarily, what I need is a little moral support. I want to be able to tell Fay Allison that you're sticking, and I want some facts."

"What facts?"

"How long have you been going with Fay Allison?"

"A matter of three or four months. Before then I was . . . well, sort of squiring both of the girls around."

"You mean Anita Bonsal?"

"Yes. I met Anita first. I went with her for a while. Then I went with both. Then I began to gravitate toward Fay Allison. I thought I was just making dates. Actually I was falling in love."

"And Anita?"

"She's like a sister to both of us. She's been simply grand in this whole thing. She's promised me that she'll do everything she can do."

"Could Fay Allison have been living with Carver Clements?"

"She had the physical opportunity, if that's what you mean."

"You didn't see her every night?"

"No."

"What does Anita say?"

"Anita says the charge is ridiculous, absolutely absurd."

"Do you know of any place where Fay Allison could have had access to cyanide of potassium?"

"That's what I wanted to tell you about, Mr. Mason."

"Go ahead."

"Out at my place the gardener uses it. I don't know just what for, but . . . well, out there the other day, when he was showing Fay around the place . . ."

"Yes, yes," Mason said impatiently, as Grover paused, "go on."

"Well, I know the gardener was explaining to her something about it. He told her to be very careful not to touch that sack because it contained cyanide, and I remember she asked him a few questions about what he used it for, but I wasn't paying much attention. It's the basis of some sort of a spray, and then I believe it's used for the plants."

"Who else was present?"

"Just the three of us."

"Has your gardener read the papers?"

Grover nodded.

"Can you trust him?"

"With my life. He's very devoted to me. He's been with us for twenty years."

"What's his name?"

"Barney Sheff. My mother took an interest in him and . . . well, rehabilitated him."

"He'd been in trouble?"

"Yes."

"In the pen?"

"That's right."

"Then what?"

"Then he was released. He had a chance to get parole if he could get a job. Mother gave him the job. He's been terribly devoted ever since."

"You have a hothouse?"

"Yes."

"I'm wondering if you have fully explored the possibilities of orchid growing."

"We're not interested in orchid growing. We can buy them and . . ."

"I wonder," Mason said in exactly the same tone, and with the same spacing of words, "if you have fully investigated the possibilities of growing orchids."

"I tell you we . . ."

"Fully investigated the possibilities of growing orchids," Mason said again.

"You mean . . . oh, you mean we should send Barney Sheff to . . ."

"Fully investigate the possibilities of growing orchids."

Dane Grover studied Mason silently for a few seconds. Then abruptly he arose from the chair, extended his hand, and said, "I brought you some money. I thought you might need it."

He carelessly tossed an envelope on the table.

"How about your mother?" Mason asked.

Grover touched his tongue to dry lips, clamped his mouth in a straight line. "Mother," he said, "is naturally embarrassed. I don't think *her* feelings need to enter into it."

And with that he marched out of the office.

Mason reached for the envelope Grover had tossed on his desk. It was well filled with hundred-dollar bills.

Della Street came over to take the money. "When I get so interested in a man," she said, "that I neglect to count the money, you know I'm becoming incurably romantic. How much, chief?"

"Plenty," Mason said.

Della Street was counting it when the unlisted telephone on her desk rang stridently.

She picked up the receiver and heard Drake's voice on the line.

"Hi, Paul," she said.

"Hi, Della. Perry there?"

"Yes."

"Okay," Drake said wearily, "I'm making a progress report. Tell him Lieutenant Tragg nabbed the Grover gardener, a chap by the name of Sheff. They're holding him as a material witness, seem to be all worked up about what they've discovered. Can't find out what it is. Think the tip-off to grab him came from Dane's mother, Caroline Manning Grover."

Della Street sat motionless at the desk, holding the receiver.

"Hello, hello," Drake said, "are you there?"

"I'm here," Della said. "I'll tell him." She hung up the phone.

IT WAS after nine o'clock that night when Della Street, signing the register in the elevator, was whisked up to the floor where Perry Mason had his offices.

The offices of the Drake Detective Agency on the same floor, nearer the elevator, were kept open twenty-four hours a day. The innocent-looking entrance door showed merely a single oblong of frosted glass, the illumination back of the glass showing the offices were open, but giving no indication of the unceasing nocturnal activities of the staff which worked in a veritable rabbit warren of offices.

Della Street started to look in on Paul Drake, then changed her mind and kept on walking down the long, dark corridor, the rapid tempo of her heels echoing back at her from the night silence of the door-lined hallway.

She rounded the elbow in the corridor, and saw that lights were on in Mason's office. She fitted her latchkey to the outer door, crossed through the entrance office and opened the door of Mason's private office.

The lawyer was pacing the floor, thumbs pushed in the armholes of his vest, head shoved forward, wrapped in such concentration that he did not even notice the opening of the door.

Della Street stood for a moment watching him.

The desk was littered with photographs. There were numerous sheets of the flimsy which Paul Drake used in making reports to clients.

Della stood quietly in the doorway, watching the tall, lean-waisted man pacing back and forth. He was granite-hard of face, broad-shouldered, flat-stomached; the seething action of his restless mind demanded physical outlet in order to preserve some semblance of internal balance, and this restless pacing was but an unconscious reflex.

After almost a minute, Della Street said, "Hello, chief. Can I help?"

Mason looked up at her with a start. "What are you doing here?"

"I came up to see if you were working and if so, if there was anything I could do to help."

He smiled, said, "I'm not working. I'm like an animal running around his cage trying to find an outlet."

"Had any dinner?" she asked.

He glanced at his wrist watch, said, "Not yet."

"What time is it?" Della Street asked.

He had to look at his wrist watch again in order to tell her. "Nine-forty."

She laughed, "I knew you didn't even look the first time you went through the motions. Come on, chief, you've got to go get something to eat. The case will still be here when you get back."

"How do we know it will?" Mason said. "I've been talking with Louise Marlow on the phone. She's been in touch with Dane Grover and she knows Dane Grover's mother. Dane Grover says he'll stick. How does *he* know what he'll do? He's exploring uncharted depths in his own mind. He doesn't know what he'll find. His friends, his relatives are turning the knife in the wound with their sympathy, the silent accusation of their every glance. How the hell does he know what he's going to do? How can he tell whether he'll stick?"

"Just the same," Della Street insisted, "*I* think he'll do it. It's through situations such as this that character is created."

"You're just talking to keep your courage up," Mason said. "I've pulled that line with a jury once or twice, myself. Soul-seared in a crucible of adversity—the tempering fires of fate—burning away the fat of wealthy complacency as he comes to grips with the fundamentals of life—baloney!"

She smiled faintly.

"The guy's undergoing the tortures of the damned," Mason went on. "He can't help but be influenced by the evidence, by the worldly-wise, cynical skepticism of all his associates. The woman he loves on the night before the wedding having trouble trying to push herself away from the slimy embraces of the man who gave her money and a certain measure of security—until she had an opportunity to trade that security in on a newer and better model."

"Chief, you simply *have* to eat."

Mason walked over to the desk. "Look at 'em," he said, "photographs! And Drake had the devil's own time obtaining them—copies of the police photographs—the body on the floor, glass on the table, an overturned chair, a newspaper half-open by a reading chair, an ordinary, mediocre apartment as drab as the sordid affair for which it was used. And somewhere in those photographs I've got to find the clue that will establish the innocence of a woman, not only innocence of the crime of murder, but innocence of the crime of betraying the man she loved."

Mason crossed over to the desk, picked up the magnifying glass which was on his blotter, started once more examining the pictures. "And, hang it, Della," he said, "I think the thing's here somewhere. That glass on the table, a little Scotch and soda in the bottom, Fay Allison's fingerprints all over it. Then there's that brazen touch of that crimson kiss on the forehead."

"Indicating a woman was with him just before he died?"

"Not necessarily. That lipstick is a perfect imprint of a pair of lips. There was no lipstick on his lips, just there on the forehead. A shrewd man could well have smeared lipstick on his lips, pressed them against Clements' forehead after the poison had taken effect and so directed suspicion away from himself. This could well have happened if the man had known some woman was in the habit of visiting Clements there in that apartment.

"It's a clue that so obviously indicates a woman that I find myself getting suspicious of it. If there were only something to give me a starting point. If we only had a little more time."

Della Street walked over to the desk. The cool tips of her fingers slid over Mason's eyes. She said, "Stop it. Come and get something to eat. Let's talk it over . . ."

"Haven't you had dinner?"

She smiled, and shook her head. "I knew you'd be working, and that if someone didn't rescue you, you'd be pacing the floor until two or three o'clock in the morning. What's Paul Drake found out?"

She picked up the sheets of flimsy, placed them together, folded them, stacked up the photographs, put the flimsy on top of the photographs and anchored everything in place with a paper weight. "Come on, chief, I'm famished."

Mason walked over to the coat closet. Della Street had to stand on tiptoes to help him with his topcoat. The lawyer took his hat, switched out lights, and walked down the corridor with Della Street.

But he didn't really answer her question until after he had become relaxed in one of the booths in their favorite restaurant. Then he pushed back the plates containing the wreckage of a thick steak, shoestring potatoes, golden-brown toasted and buttered French bread, and a lettuce and tomato salad.

He poured more coffee, then said, "Drake hasn't found out much, just background."

"What, for instance?" Della Street asked.

Mason said wearily, "It's the same old seven and six. The wife, Marline Austin Clements, apparently was swept off her feet by Carver Clements' determination to get her, by the sheer power of the man.

"She overlooked the fact that after he had her safely listed as one of his legal chattels, with title in good order, he used that same acquisitive, aggressive tenacity of purpose to get other things he wanted. Marline was left pretty much alone. That's the price one has to pay for marrying men of that type."

"And so?" Della asked.

"And so," Mason said, "in the course of time, Carver Clements turned to other interests. Hang it, Della, we have one thing to work on, only one thing, the fact that Clements had no key on his body.

"You remember the four people who met us in the corridor. They had to get in that apartment house some way. Remember the outer door was locked. Any of the tenants could release the latch by pressing the button of an electric release. But if the tenant of some apartment didn't press the release button, it was necessary for any visitor to have a key in order to get in.

"Now then, those four people got in. How? They must have had a key. Regardless of what they now say, one of them must have had a key."

"The missing key?" Della asked.

"That's what we have to find out."

"What story did they give the police?"

"I don't know. The police have them sewed up tight. I've got to get one of them on the stand and cross-examine him. Then we'll at least have something to go on."

"So we have to try for an immediate hearing and then go it blind?"

"That's about the size of it."

"Was that key in Fay Allison's purse Carver Clements' missing key?"

"It *could* have been. In that case either Fay was playing house, or the key was planted. In that case when was it planted, how, and by whom? I'm inclined to think Clements' key must have been on his body at the time he was murdered. It wasn't there when police arrived. That's the one really significant clue we have to work on."

Della Street shook her head. "It's too deep for me, but I guess you're going to have to wade into it. I can tell you one thing. Louise Marlow is a brick. I've known her since I was a child. If there's anything she can do to help, you can count on her."

Mason lit a cigarette. "Ordinarily I'd spar for time, but in this case I'm afraid Time is our enemy, Della. We're going to have to walk into court with all the assurance in the world and pull a very large rabbit out of a very small hat."

She smiled. "Where do we get the rabbit?"

"Back in the office," he said, "studying those photographs, looking for a clue, and . . ." Suddenly he snapped to startled attention.

"What is it, chief?"

"I was just thinking. The glass on the table in 702, there was a little whiskey and soda in the bottom of it, just a spoonful or two."

"Well?" she asked.

"What happens when you drink Scotch and soda, Della?"

"Why . . . you always have a little. It sticks to the side of the glass and then gradually settles back."

Mason shook his head. His eyes were glowing now. "You leave ice cubes in the glass," he said, "and then after a while they melt and leave an inch or so of water."

She matched his excitement. "Then there was no ice in the woman's glass?"

"And none in Carver Clements'. Yet there was a thermos jar of ice cubes on the table. Come on, Della, we're going back and *really* study those photographs!"

9

JUDGE Randolph Jordan ascended the bench and rapped court to order.

"People versus Fay Allison."

"Ready for the Defendant," Mason said.

"Ready for the Prosecution," Stewart Linn announced.

Linn, one of the best of the trial deputies in the district attorney's office, was a thin-faced, steely-eyed, cautious individual who had the mind of an accountant, the legal knowledge of an encyclopedia, and the cold-blooded mercilessness of a steel trap.

Linn was under no illusions as to the resourcefulness of his adversary, and he had all of the caution of a boxer approaching a heavyweight champion.

"Call Dr. Charles Keene," he said.

Dr. Keene came forward, qualified himself as a physician and surgeon who had had great experience in medical necropsies, particularly in cases of homicide.

"On the tenth of this month did you have occasion to examine a body in apartment 702 at the Mandrake Arms?"

"I did."

"What time was it?"

"It was about two o'clock in the morning."

"What did you find?"

"I found the body of a man of approximately fifty-two years of age, fairly well-fleshed, quite bald, but otherwise very well preserved for a man of his age. The body was lying on the floor, sprawled forward, head toward the door, feet toward the interior of the apartment, the left arm doubled up and lying under him, the right arm flung out, the left side of the face resting on the carpet. The man had been dead for several hours. I fix the time of death as having been during a period between seven o'clock and nine o'clock that evening. I cannot place the time of death any closer than that, but I will swear that it was within those time limits."

"And did you determine the cause of death?"

"Not at that time. I did later."

"What was the cause of death?"

"Poisoning caused by the ingestion of cyanide of potassium."

"Did you notice anything about the physical appearance of the man's body?"

"You mean with reference to lipstick?"

"Yes."

"There was a red smear on the upper part of the forehead, apparently caused by lips that had been heavily coated with lipstick and then pressed against the skin in a somewhat puckered condition."

"You mean the skin was puckered?"

"No," Dr. Linn said, smiling. "I mean the lips were puckered. It was as though some woman had administered a last kiss. The lipstick was deposited at the upper part of the forehead, where the skin across the scalp was stretched tight and smooth. It would have been above the hairline of an individual who was not bald."

"Cross-examine," Linn announced.

"No questions," Mason said.

"Call Benjamin Harlan," Linn said.

Benjamin Harlan, a huge, lumbering giant of a man, took the stand with a good-natured smile, promptly proceeded to qualify himself as a fingerprint and identification expert of some twenty years' experience.

Stewart Linn, by skillful, adroit questions, led him through an account of his activities on the date in question, the finding of the body, the dusting of various things in the apartment, the finding of no latent fingerprints on the glass which the Prosecution referred to as the "murder glass," indicating this glass had been wiped clean of prints, the finding of prints on the glass on the table which the Prosecution referred to as the "decoy glass," on the toothbrush, on the tube of tooth paste, and various other articles. These latent fingerprints had coincided with the rolled fingerprints taken from the hands of Fay Allison, the defendant in the case.

Harlan also identified a whole series of photographs taken by the police showing the position of the body when it was discovered, the furnishings in the apartment, the table, the overturned chair, the so-called murder glass which had rolled along the floor, the so-called decoy glass on the table, which bore unmistakably the fresh fingerprints of Fay Allison, the bottle of Scotch whiskey, the bottle of soda water, the thermos jar containing ice cubes.

"Cross-examine," Linn said triumphantly.

Mason said, "You have had some twenty years' experience as a fingerprint expert, Mr. Harlan?"

"That's right."

"And an identification expert?"

"Yes, sir."

"Now, you have heard Dr. Keene's testimony about the lipstick on the forehead of the dead man?"

"Yes, sir."

"And that lipstick, I believe, shows in this photograph which I now hand you?"

"Yes, sir; not only that, but I have a close-up of that lipstick stain which I myself took with one of the cameras I use for close-up photography. I have an enlargement of that negative, in case you're interested."

"I'm very much interested," Mason said. "Will you produce the enlargement, please?"

Harlan produced the photograph from his brief case, showing a section of the forehead of the dead man, with the stain of lips outlined clearly and in microscopic detail.

"What is the scale of this photograph?" Mason asked.

"Life size," Harlan said. "I have a standard of distances by which I can take photographs to a scale of exactly life size."

"Thank you," Mason said. "I'd like to have this photograph received in evidence."

"No objection," Linn said.

"And it is, is it not, a matter of fact that the little lines shown in this photograph are fully as distinctive as the ridges and whorls of a fingerprint?"

"Just what do you mean?"

"Isn't it a fact well-known to identification experts that the little wrinkles which form in a person's lips are fully as individual as the lines of a fingerprint?"

"It's not a 'well-known' fact."

"But it *is* a fact?"

"Yes, sir, it is."

"So that by measuring the distance between the little lines which are shown on this photograph, indicating the pucker lines of the skin, it would be fully as possible to identify the lips which made this lipstick print as it would be to identify a person who had left a fingerprint upon the scalp of the dead man."

"Yes, sir."

"Now, you have testified to having made rolled imprints of the defendant's fingers and compared those with the fingerprints found on the glass."

"Yes, sir."

"Have you made any attempt to take an imprint of her lips and compare that print with the print of the lipstick on the forehead of the decedent?"

"No, sir," Harlan said, shifting his position uneasily.

"Why not?"

"Well, in the first place, Mr. Mason, the fact that the pucker lines of lips are so highly individualized is not a generally known fact."

"But *you* know it."

"Yes, sir."

"And the more skilled experts in your profession know it?"

"Yes, sir."

"Why didn't you do it then?"

Harlan shifted his position again, crossed his legs, glanced somewhat helplessly at Stewart Linn, the deputy prosecutor.

"Oh, if the Court please," Linn said, promptly taking his cue from that glance, "this hardly seems to be cross-examination. The inquiry is wandering far afield. I will object to the question on the ground that it's incompetent, irrelevant and immaterial, and not proper cross-examination."

"Overruled," Judge Jordan snapped. "Answer the question!"

Harlan cleared his throat. "Well," he said, "I guess I just never thought of it."

"Think of it now," Mason said, with a gesture that was a flourish. "Go ahead and take the imprint right now and right here. Put on plenty of lipstick, Miss Allison. Let's see how your lips compare with those on the dead man's forehead."

"Oh, if the Court please," Linn said wearily, "this hardly seems to be cross-examination. If Mr. Mason wants to make Harlan his own witness and call for this test as a part of the defendant's case, that will be one thing; but this certainly isn't cross-examination."

"It may be cross-examination of Harlan's qualifications as an expert," Judge Jordan ruled.

"Oh, if the Court please! Isn't that stretching a technicality rather far?"

"Your objection was highly technical," Judge Jordan snapped. "It is overruled, and my ruling will stand. Take the impression, Mr. Harlan."

Fay Allison, with trembling hand, daubed lipstick heavily on her mouth. Then, using the makeup mirror in her purse, smoothed off the lipstick with the tip of her little finger.

"Go ahead," Mason said to Harlan, "check on her lips."

Harlan, taking a piece of white paper from his brief case, moved down to where the defendant was sitting beside Perry Mason and pressed the white paper against her lips. He removed the paper and examined the imprint.

"Go ahead," Mason said to Harlan, "make your comparison and announce the result to the Court."

Harlan said, "Of course, I have not the facilities here for making a microscopic comparison, but I can tell from even a superficial examination of the lip lines that these lips did not make that print."

"Thank you," Mason said. "That's all."

Judge Jordan was interested. "These lines appear in the lips only when the lips are puckered, as in giving a kiss?"

"No, Your Honor, they are in the lips all the time, as an examination will show, but when the lips are puckered, the lines are intensified."

"And these lip markings are different with each individual?"

"Yes, Your Honor."

"So that you are now prepared to state to the Court that despite the fingerprints of the defendant on the glass and other objects, her lips definitely could not have left the imprint on the dead man's forehead?"

"Yes, Your Honor."

"That's all," Judge Jordan said.

"Of course," Linn pointed out, "the fact that the defendant did not leave that kiss imprint on the man's forehead doesn't necessarily mean a thing, Your Honor. In fact, he may have met his death *because* the defendant found that lipstick on his forehead. The evidence of the fingerprints is quite conclusive that the defendant was in that apartment."

"The Court understands the evidence. Proceed with your case," Judge Jordan said.

"Furthermore," Linn went on angrily, "I will now show the Court that there was every possibility the print of that lipstick could have been deliberately planted by none other than the attorney for the defendant and his charming and very efficient secretary. I will proceed to prove that by calling Don B. Ralston to the stand."

Ralston came forward and took the stand, his manner that of a man who wishes very much he were many miles away.

"Your name is Don B. Ralston? You reside at 2935 Creelmore Avenue in this city?"

"Yes, sir."

"And you knew Carver L. Clements in his lifetime?"

"Yes."

"Were rather intimately associated with him?"

"Yes, sir."

"In a business way?"

"Yes, sir."

"Now, on the night, or rather, early in the morning of the 10th of this month, did you have occasion to go to Carver L. Clements' apartment, being apartment number 702 in the Mandrake Arms Apartments in this city?"

"I did, yes, sir."

"What time was it?"

"Around . . . well, it was between one and two in the morning . . . I would say somewhere around one-thirty."

"Were you alone?"

"No, sir."

"Who was with you?"

"Richard P. Nolin, who is a business associate, or was a business associate of Mr. Clements; Manley L. Ogden, who handled some of Mr. Clements' income tax work; and a Miss Vera Payson, a friend of—well, a friend of all of us."

"What happened when you went to that apartment? Did you enter it?"

"No, sir."

"Tell us just what happened."

"Well, we left the elevator on the seventh floor, and as we were walking down the corridor, I noticed two people coming down the corridor toward us."

"Now, when you say 'down the corridor,' do you mean from the direction of apartment 702?"

"That's right, yes, sir."

"And who were these people?"

"Mr. Perry Mason and his secretary, Miss Street."

"And did you actually enter the apartment of Carver Clements?"

"I did not."

"Why not?"

"When I got to the door of apartment 702, I pushed the door-bell and heard the sound of the buzzer on the inside of the apartment. Almost instantly the door of an apartment across the hall opened, and a woman who seemed to be somewhat irritated complained that she had been unable to sleep because of people ringing the buzzer of that apartment, and stated in effect that other people were in there with Mr. Clements. So we left immediately."

"Now, then, Your Honor," Stewart Linn said, "I propose to show that the two people referred to by the person living in the apartment across the hallway were none other than Mr. Mason and Miss Street, who had actually entered that apartment and were closeted in there with the dead man and the evidence for an undetermined length of time."

"Go ahead and show it," Judge Jordan said.

"Just a moment," Mason said. "Before you do that, I want to cross-examine this witness."

"Cross-examine him, then."

"When you arrived at the Mandrake Arms, the door to the street was locked, was it not?"

"Yes, sir."

"What did you do?"

"We went up to the seventh floor and . . ."

"I understand that, but how did you get in? How did you get past the entrance door? You had a key, didn't you?"

"No, sir."

"Then how *did* you get in?"

"Why *you* let us in."

"*I* did?"

"Yes."

"Understand," Mason said, "I am not now referring to the time you came up from the street in the custody of the radio officer. I am now referring to the time when you first entered that apartment house on the morning of the tenth of this month—the first time you went in."

"Yes, sir. I understand. You let us in."

"What makes you say that?"

"Well, because you and your secretary were in Carver Clements' apartment, and . . ."

"You, yourself, don't *know* we were in there, do you?"

"Well, I surmise it. We met you just after you had left the apartment. You were hurrying down the hall toward the elevator."

Mason said. "I don't want your surmises. You don't even know I had been in that apartment. I want you to tell us how you got past the locked street door. No surmises now. Just how did you get in? Exactly what did you do?"

"We pressed the button of Carver Clements' apartment, and you—or at any rate someone—answered by pressing the button which released the electric door catch on the outer door. As soon as we heard the sound of buzzing, which indicated the lock was released, we pushed the door open and went in."

"Let's not have any misunderstanding about this," Mason said. "Who was it pushed the button of Carver Clements' apartment?"

"I did."

"I'm talking now about the button in front of the outer door of the apartment house."

"Yes, sir."

"And, having pressed that button, you waited until the buzzer announced the door was being opened?"

"Yes, sir."

"How long?"

"Not over a second or two."

Mason said to the witness, "One more question: did you go right up after you entered the apartment house?"

"We . . . no, sir, not *right* away. We stopped for a few moments there in the lobby to talk about the type of poker we wanted to play. Miss Payson had lost some money on one of these wild poker games where the dealer has the opportunity of calling any kind of game he wants, some of them having the one-eyed jacks wild, and others having seven cards from which five are selected, and things of that sort."

"How long were you talking?"

"Oh, a couple of minutes, perhaps."

"And you decided on the type of poker you wanted to play?"

"Yes."

"And then went right up?"

"Yes."

"Where was the elevator?"

"The elevator was . . . now, wait a minute, I don't remember exactly. It was on one of the upper floors. I remember we pressed the button and it took it a little while to come down to where we were."

"That's all," Mason said.

Della Street's fingers dug into his arm. "Aren't you going to ask him about the key?" she whispered.

"Not yet," Mason said, a light of triumph in his eyes. "I know what happened now, Della. Give us the breaks, and we've got this case in the bag. First, make him prove we were in that apartment."

Linn said, "I will now call Miss Shirley Tanner to the stand."

The young woman who advanced to the stand was very different from the disheveled, sleepless and nervous individual who had been so angry at the time Mason and Della Street had pressed the button of apartment 702.

"Your name is Shirley Tanner, and you reside in apartment 701 of the Mandrake Arms Apartments in this city?"

"Yes, sir."

"And have for how long?"

She smiled, and said, "Not very long. I put in three weeks apartment hunting and finally secured a sublease on apartment 701 on the afternoon of the 8th. I moved in on the 9th, which explains why I was tired almost to the point of having hysterics."

"You had difficulty sleeping?"

"Yes."

"And on the morning of the 10th did you have any experiences which annoyed you—that is, experiences in connection with the ringing of the buzzer in the apartment next door?"

"I most certainly did, yes, sir."

"Tell us exactly what happened."

"I had been taking sleeping medicine from time to time, but for some reason or other this night I was so nervous the sleeping medicine didn't do me any good. I had been moving and unpacking, and my nerves were all keyed up. I was physically and mentally exhausted. I tried to sleep, but I was too tired to sleep. I guess perhaps you know how it is, Your Honor," she said, turning to the judge with a winsome smile.

The judge regarded the attractive young woman, smiled in a fatherly way, nodded, and said, "We all get overtired at times. Go on with your testimony, Miss Tanner."

"Well, I was trying to sleep, and I think I had just gotten to sleep when I was awakened by a continual sounding of the buzzer over there in the apartment across the hall. It was a low, persistent noise which became exceedingly irritating to a person in my nervous state, who was trying to sleep."

"Go on," Linn said. "What did you do?"

"I finally got up and put on a robe and went to the door and flung it open. I was terribly angry at the very idea of people making so much noise at that hour of the morning. You see those apartments aren't too soundproof and there is a ventilating system over the doors of the apartments. The one over the door of 702 was apparently open and I had left mine open for nighttime ventilation. And then I was angry at myself for getting so upset over the noise. I knew my allowing myself to get so angry would prevent me from sleeping at all, which is why I lay still for what seemed an interminable time before I opened the door."

Linn smiled, "So you became angry at the people in the hallway, and then became angry at yourself for being angry?"

Her laugh was musical. "That's about the way it happened."

"And you say you *flung* open the door?"

"Yes, sir."

"What did you find?"

"Two people across the hall."

"Did you recognize them?"

"I didn't know them at the time, but I know them now."

"Who were they?"

She pointed a dramatic finger at Perry Mason.

"Mr. Perry Mason, the lawyer for the defendant, and the young woman, I believe his secretary, who is sitting there beside him— not the defendant, but the woman on the other side."

"Miss Della Street," Mason said with a bow.

"Thank you," she said.

"And," Linn went on, "what did you see those people do?"

She said, "I saw them enter the apartment."

"Did you see how they entered the apartment . . . I mean, how did they get the door open?"

"They must have used a key. Mr. Mason was just pushing the door open and I . . ."

"No surmises, please," Linn broke in. "Did you actually *see* Mr. Mason using a key?"

"Well, I heard him."

"What do you mean?"

"As I was opening my door I heard metal rasping against metal, the way a key does when it scrapes against a lock. And then when I had my door all the way open, I saw Mr. Mason pushing his way into 702."

"But you only know he must have had a key because you heard the sound of metal rubbing against metal?"

"Well, it stands to reason . . ."

"But you only heard the sound of metal against metal?"

"Yes, and the click of the lock."

"Did you say anything to Mr. Mason and Miss Street?"

"I most certainly did, and then I slammed the door and went back and tried to sleep. But I was so mad by that time I simply couldn't close my eyes and keep them closed. I couldn't understand why, if a person had a key, he would go through all that agony of ringing a doorbell and waking me up. Why didn't they simply go in there in the first place and . . ."

"Now, never mind that," Linn interrupted impatiently, holding up his hand palm outwards, and moving it back and forth as though patting the words back into her mouth. "Never mind your conclusions, never mind your reasons, just tell the Court what you *saw*."

"Yes, sir."

"What happened after that?"

"After that, when I was trying to sleep—I would say just a few seconds after that—I heard that buzzer again. And this time I was *good* and mad."

"And what did you do?"

"I swung open the door and started to give these people a piece of my mind."

"People?" Linn asked promptingly.

"There were four people standing there. The Mr. Ralston, who has just testified, two other men and a woman. They were standing there at the doorway, jabbing away at the button, and I told them this was a sweet time to be calling on someone and making a racket and that anyway the gentleman already had company, so if he didn't answer his door, it was because he didn't want to."

"Did you at that time see Mr. Mason and Miss Street walking down the corridor?"

"No. I did not. I had my door open only far enough to show me the door of apartment 702 across the way. You see, my door opens toward the end of the corridor away from the elevator. My apartment is a corner apartment and 702 is a corner apartment. So, when my door is open, I can only see just that blind end of the corridor unless I open it all the way."

"Thank you," Linn said. "Now you distinctly saw Mr. Mason and Miss Street enter that apartment?"

"Yes."

"And close the door behind them?"

"Yes."

"Cross-examine!" Linn said triumphantly.

Mason, taking a notebook from his pocket, walked up to stand beside Shirley Tanner, but his voice was good-natured. "Miss Tanner," he said, "are you certain that you heard me rub metal against the keyhole of that door?"

"Certain," she said.

"My back was towards you?"

"It was when I first opened my door, yes. I saw your face, however, just after you went in the door. You turned around and looked at me over your shoulder."

"Oh, we'll stipulate," Linn said with an exaggerated note of weariness in his voice, "that the witness couldn't see through Mr. Mason's back. Perhaps learned counsel was carrying the key in his teeth."

"Thank you," Mason said, turning toward Linn. Then suddenly stepping forward, he clapped his notebook against Shirley Tanner's face.

The witness screamed and jumped back.

Linn was on his feet. "What are you trying to do," he shouted, "intimidate the witness?"

Judge Jordan pounded with his gavel. "Mr. Mason!" he reprimanded. "That is contempt of court!"

Mason said, "Please let me explain, Your Honor. The Prosecution took the lip prints of my client. I feel that I am entitled to take the lip prints of this witness. I will cheerfully admit to being in contempt of court, in the event I am wrong, but I would like to extend this imprint of Shirley Tanner's lips to Mr. Benjamin Harlan, the identification expert, and ask him whether or not the print made by these lips is not the same as that of the lipstick kiss which was found on the dead forehead of Carver L. Clements."

There was a tense, dramatic silence in the courtroom.

Mason stepped forward and handed the notebook to Benjamin Harlan.

From the witness stand came a shrill scream of terror. Shirley Tanner tried to get to her feet, her eyes fastened on Mason, wide, round and terrified, her face the color of putty beneath the make-up which suddenly showed as dabbed-on bits of orange.

She couldn't make it. Her knees buckled. She tried to catch herself, then fell to the floor.

10

It was when order was restored in the courtroom that Perry Mason exploded his second bombshell.

"Your Honor," he said, "either Fay Allison is innocent or she is guilty. If she is innocent, someone framed the evidence which would discredit her. And if someone did frame that evidence, there is only one person who could have done it, one person who could have had access to the defendant's apartment, one person who could have transported glasses, toothbrushes, and tooth paste containing Fay Allison's fingerprints, one person who could have transported clothes bearing the unmistakable stamp of ownership of the defendant in this case.

"Your Honor, I request that Anita Bonsal be called to the stand."

There was a moment's sudden and dramatic silence.

Anita Bonsal, there in the courtroom, felt suddenly as though she had been stripped stark naked by one swift gesture.

One moment she had been sitting there completely lost in the proceedings, trying to adjust her mind to what was happening, attempting to keep pace with the swift rush of developments. The next moment everyone in the courtroom was seeking her out with staring, prying eyes.

It was as though she had been quietly bathing and the side of the building had collapsed and left her naked and exposed to the curious eyes of the gawking multitude.

In that sudden surge of panic, Anita did the worst thing she could possibly have done. She ran.

They were after her then, a throng of humanity, actuated only by the mass instinct to pursue that which ran for cover.

Elevators were too slow for Anita's frantic feet.

Behind her was the bedlam of the crowd, a babble of voices which speedily grew into a roar.

Anita dashed to the stairs, went scrambling down them, found herself in another hallway in the Hall of Justice. She dashed the length of that hallway, frantically trying to find the stairs. She could not find them.

An elevator offered her welcome haven. It was standing with the doors open, the red light on above it.

"Going down," the attendant said.

Anita fairly flung herself into the cage.

"What's the hurry?" the attendant asked.

Shreds of reason were beginning to return to Anita's fear-racked mind.

"They're calling my case," she said. "Let me off at . . ."

"I know," the man said, smiling. "Third floor. Domestic relations court."

He slid the cage to a smooth stop at the third floor. "Out to the left," he said. "Department twelve."

Anita's mind was beginning to work now, functioning smoothly, cunningly.

She smiled her thanks to the elevator attendant, walked rapidly to the left, pushed open the door of Department 12 of the Superior Court, entered the partially filled courtroom with all the assurance of a witness coming to testify in a case.

She marched down the center aisle, gave an apologetic smile to the young woman who was in the aisle seat, crossed in front of her and calmly seated herself in the middle seat in the row of benches.

She was now wrapped in anonymity. Only her breathlessness and the pounding of her pulses gave indication that she was the quarry for which the crowd was searching.

Then slowly the triumphant smile faded from her face. The realization of what was bound to be the effect of what she had done stabbed her consciousness. She had admitted her guilt. She could flee now to the farthest corners of the earth, but her guilt would always follow her. She would always be an object of scorn and contempt.

Perry Mason had shown that she had not killed Carver Clements, but he had also shown that she had done something which in the minds of all men would be even worse. She had betrayed her friendship. She had tried to besmirch Fay Allison's reputation. She had attempted the murder of her own roommate by giving an overdose of sleeping tablets.

How much would Mason have been able to prove? She had no way of knowing. The man was uncanny with his shrewdness of perception. But there was no need for him to prove now. Her flight had given Mason all the proof he needed.

She must disappear, and that would not be easy. By evening her photograph would be emblazoned upon the pages of every newspaper in the city.

11

BACK in the courtroom, all but deserted now save for the county officials who were crowding around Shirley Tanner, Mason was asking questions in a low voice.

There was no more stamina left in Shirley Tanner than in a wet dishrag.

Shirley heard her own voice answering the persistent drone of Mason's searching questions.

"You knew that Clements had this apartment in 702? You deliberately made such a high offer that you were able to sub-lease apartment 701? You were suspicious of Clements and wanted to spy on him?"

"Yes," Shirley said, and her voice was all but inaudible to her own ears, although her eyes told her that the court reporter, stand-ing beside her with his hand moving unobtrusively over his note-book, was taking down all that was said.

"You were furious when you realized that Carver Clements had *another* mistress, that all of his talk to you about waiting until he could get his divorce was merely another bait which you had grabbed."

Again she said, "Yes." It seemed the easiest thing to say, the only thing that she could say. There was no strength in her any more to think up lies.

"You made the mistake of loving him," Mason said. "It wasn't his money *you* were after, and you administered the poison. How did you do it, Shirley?"

She said, "I'd poisoned the drink I held in my hand. I knew it made Carver furious when I drank because whiskey makes me lose control of myself, and he never knew what I was going to do when I was drunk.

"I rang his bell, holding that glass in my hand. I leered at him tipsily when he opened the door, and walked on in. I said, 'Hello, Carver darling. Meet your next-door neighbor,' and I raised the glass to my lips.

"He did just as I knew he would. He was furious. He said, 'You little devil, what're you doing here? I've told you I'll do the drinking for both of us.' He snatched the glass from me and drained it."

"What happened?" Mason asked.

"For a moment, nothing," she said. "He went back to the chair and sat down. I leaned over him and pressed that kiss on his head. It was a good-by kiss. He looked at me, frowned, suddenly jumped to his feet, tried to run to the door, staggered and then fell face-forward."

"And what did you do?"

"I took the key to his apartment from his pocket so I could get back in to fix things the way I wanted and get possession of the glass, but I was afraid to be there while he was . . . retching and twisting . . . and dying."

Mason nodded. "You went back to your own apartment and then after you had waited a few minutes and thought it was safe to go back, you couldn't, because Anita Bonsal was at the door?"

She nodded and said, "She had a key. She went in. I supposed, of course, she'd call the police and that they'd come at any time. I didn't dare to go in there then. I tried to sleep and couldn't. Finally I decided the police weren't coming after all. It was past midnight then."

"So then you went back in there? You were in there when Don Ralston rang the bell. You . . ."

"Yes," she said. "I went back into that apartment. By that time I had put on a bathrobe and pajamas and ruffled my hair all up. If anyone had said anything to me, if I had been caught, I had a story all prepared to tell them, that I had heard the door open and someone run down the corridor, that I had opened my door and found the door of 702 ajar, and I had just that minute looked in to see what had happened."

"All right," Mason said, "that was your story. What did you do?"

"I went across the hall. I went in and wiped all my fingerprints off that glass on the floor. Then the buzzer sounded from the street door."

"What did you do?"

She said, "I saw someone had fixed up the evidence just the way

I had been going to fix it up. A bottle of Scotch on the table, a bottle of soda, a pail of ice cubes."

"So what did you do?"

She said, "I pushed the button which released the downstairs door catch and ducked back into my own apartment. I hadn't any more than got in there than I heard the elevator stop at the seventh floor. I couldn't understand that, because I knew these people couldn't possibly have had time enough to get up to the seventh floor in the elevator. I waited, listening, and heard you two come down the corridor. I could barely hear the sound of the buzzer in the other apartment. I opened the door to chase you away and saw you were actually entering the apartment, so I had to make a quick excuse, that the sound of the buzzer had wakened me. Then I jerked the door shut. When the four people came up, I really and truly thought you were still in the apartment, and I was dying of curiosity to see what was happening."

"How long had you known him?" Mason asked.

She said sadly, "I loved him. I was the one that he wanted to marry when he left his wife. I don't know how long this other thing had been going on. I became suspicious and one time when I had an opportunity to go through his pockets, I found a key stamped 'Mandrake Arms Apartment, Number 702.' Then I thought I knew, but I wanted to be sure. I found out who had apartment 701 and made a proposition for a sublease that simply couldn't be turned down.

"I waited and watched. This brunette walked down the corridor and used *her* key to open the apartment. I slipped out into the corridor and listened at the door. I heard him give her the same old line he'd given me so many times, and my heart turned to bitter acid. I hated him. I killed him . . . and I was caught."

Mason turned to Stewart Linn and said, "There you are, young man. If you want to be the fearless prosecutor, there's your murderess, but you'll probably never be able to get a jury to think it's anything more than manslaughter."

A much chastened Linn said, "Would you mind telling me how you figured this out, Mr. Mason?"

Mason said, "Clements' key was missing. Obviously he must have had it when he entered the apartment. The murderer must have taken it from his pocket. Why? So he or she could come back. And if what Don Ralston said was true *someone* must have been in the apartment when he rang the bell from the street, someone who let him in by pressing the buzzer.

"What happened to that someone? I must have been walking down the corridor within a matter of seconds after Ralston had pressed the button on the street door. Yet I saw no one leaving the apartment. There was no one in the corridor. Obviously then, the person who pressed the buzzer must have had a place to take refuge in another near-by apartment.

"Having reasoned that far, having learned a young, attractive woman had only that very day taken a lease on the apartment opposite, the answer became so obvious it ceased to be a mystery."

Stewart Linn nodded thoughtfully. "Obvious when you have once pointed it out," he said.

Mason picked up his brief case, smiled to Della Street. "Come on, Della," he said. "Let's get Fay Allison and . . ."

He stopped as he saw Fay Allison's face. "What's happened to *your* lipstick?" he asked.

And then his eyes moved over to take in Dane Grover, who was standing by her, his face smeared diagonally across the mouth with a huge red smear of lipstick.

Fay Allison had neglected to remove the thick coating of lipstick which she had put on when Mason had asked Benjamin Harlan, the identification expert, to take an imprint of her lips. Now, the heavy mark where her mouth had been pressed against the mouth of Dane Grover gave an oddly jarring note of incongruity to the entire proceedings.

On the lower floors a mob of eagerly curious spectators were baying like hounds upon the track of Anita Bonsal. In the courtroom the long efficient arm of the law was gathering Shirley Tanner into its grasp, and there amidst the machinery of tragedy, the romance of Fay Allison and Dane Grover picked up where it had left off.

It was the gavel of Judge Randolph Jordan that brought them back to the grim realities of justice, transferred the courtroom from the scene of a dramatic confession to a crowded place, filled with chairs, tables and benches, peopled by puppets who were mechanically doing the bidding of justice.

"The Court," announced Judge Jordan, "will dismiss the case against Fay Allison. The Court will order Shirley Tanner into custody and the Court will suggest to the Prosecutor that a complaint be issued for Anita Bonsal, upon such charge as may seem expedient to the office of the District Attorney. And the Court does hereby extend its most sincere apologies to the defendant, Fay Allison. And the Court, personally, wishes to congratulate Mr. Perry Mason upon his brilliant handling of this matter."

There was a moment during which Judge Jordan's stern eyes rested upon the lipstick-smeared countenance of Dane Grover.

A faint smile twitched at the corners of His Honor's mouth.

The gavel banged once more.

"The Court," announced Judge Randolph Jordan, "is adjourned."

THE CASE OF

The Crying Swallow

CHAPTER NUMBER

1

PERRY MASON, tilted back in his walnut desk chair, was studying a recent decision of the state supreme court when Della Street, his secretary, opened the door from the outer office, advanced to the desk and quietly laid ten crisp one-hundred-dollar bills on the blotter.

Mason, too engrossed to notice what she was doing, continued his reading.

Della Street said, "A client sends his card."

Mason straightened in the swivel chair and for the first time caught sight of the money which Della Street had so neatly spread out.

"He said his name was Mr. Cash," Della Street explained. "Then he handed me ten one-hundred-dollar bills and said these were his cards."

Mason grinned. "So the black market begins to turn yellow. What does Mr. Cash look like?"

"He's a floor walker."

Mason raised his eyebrows, glanced at the cash. "A *floorwalker?*"

"No, no, not a department store floorwalker! I mean that he's a floor *walker*, the same as you are. He paces the floor when he's worried. He's doing a carpet marathon out there right now."

Mason said, "I don't know whether civilization is breaking down the character of our criminals or whether the black market operators haven't been in business long enough to develop intestinal stamina. The bootleggers were a tougher breed. My own opinion is that these black market operators simply haven't had time to become accustomed to the fact that they're on the other side of society's legal fence. Give them another eighteen months and they'll be as tough as the old gangsters."

"He definitely *isn't* a black market operator," Della Street said positively. "He's distinguished-looking, has a slight limp, is deeply tanned, and . . . and I've seen him somewhere before. Oh, now I have it. I've seen his picture!"

"Give."

"Major Claude L. Winnett, polo player, yachtsman, millionaire playboy. When the war came, he quit being a playboy and became an aviator, bagged a whole flock of German planes and then was captured, liberated last fall, discharged because of his wound, returned to his doting mother and . . ."

Mason nodded. "I remember reading about the chap. He got a citation or something. Didn't he get married?"

"About four or five weeks ago," Della Street said. "That was where I first saw his picture—in the paper. Then again last week a reporter for the society supplement paid a visit to the Winnett home—one of the old-time country estates with stables of polo ponies, riding trails, hedges, private golf courses . . ."

"Show him in," Mason said. "But let him know first that you've placed him. It may save time."

Major Winnett, lean, fit, bronzed, and nervous, followed Della Street into the office. The excitement and anxiety of his manner were more noticeable than his slight limp. A well-modulated voice and patrician bearing made his surrender to emotion all the more impressive.

"Mr. Mason," he said as soon as he was in the room, "I had intended to keep my identity a secret and ask you to represent another person. Now that your secretary has recognized me, I'll put my cards on the table. My wife has disappeared. She needs your help. She's in trouble of some sort."

"Tell me about it," Mason said.

Major Winnett reached into his inside pocket, took out a folded piece of letter paper, and handed it to Mason.

The lawyer opened the letter, read:

"Claude, my darling, there are some things that I can't drag *you* into. I thought I had a way out, but I guess I didn't. Our happiness was such a beautiful thing. But beautiful things are always fragile. Don't worry about anything. I am responsible, and I am not going to let you suffer because of what you have done for me. Good-by, my darling.—MARCIA"

"What does she mean by saying she's responsible and not letting you suffer because of what you have done for her?" Mason asked.

Major Winnett's manner was uneasy. "My marriage was not exactly in accordance with the wishes of my mother. I went ahead with it despite her objections."

"Spoken objections?"

"Certainly not."

"Yet your wife knew of them?"

"Women feel many things without the necessity of words, Mr. Mason. I want you to find her and straighten things out for her."

"And then report to you?"

"Certainly."

Mason shook his head.

For a moment there was silence, broken only by the faint rumble of traffic and the breathing of Mason's client. Then Major Winnett said, "Very well. Do it your way."

"When did your wife leave?"

"Last night. I found this note on the dresser about midnight. I thought she had previously retired."

"Is there any reason why your wife would have been vulnerable to what we might call an outside influence?"

"Absolutely not—if you mean blackmail."

"Then tell me why your wife wasn't free to come to you with her troubles."

"I don't know, unless it's on account of my mother."

"What about her?"

"My mother is a very unusual person. When my father died, a dozen years ago, mother stepped in and took charge. She is living in a bygone era. She has old-fashioned ideas."

"The proprieties?" Mason asked.

"Not so much the proprieties as . . . well, class distinctions, the aristocracy of wealth and that sort of thing. I think she would have been more happy if I had married someone more in our own set."

"Who, for instance?"

"Oh, I didn't say any particular person," Major Winnett said hastily.

"I know you didn't. That's why I'm asking you."

"Well, perhaps Daphne Rexford."

"You think this caused your wife to leave?"

"No, no. Not directly. My mother has accepted Marcia into the family. Whatever may have been Mother's ideas about the marriage, Marcia is now one of us—a Winnett."

"Then suppose you tell me what you mean when you say 'not directly.'"

"Marcia would have done anything rather than subject me to any notoriety because she knew how my mother felt about that. You see, Mr. Mason, we live in a large, rather old-fashioned estate surrounded by hedges, with our private bridle paths, high wire fences, locked gates, no trespassing signs, and all the rest. The more the world moves in a way that meets with the disapproval of my mother, the more she tries to shut that part of the world out from her life."

"Anything unusual happen within the last few days?" the lawyer asked, probing his client's mind.

"A burglar entered our house Tuesday night."

"Take anything?" Mason asked.

"My wife's jewelry, valued at perhaps twenty-five or thirty thousand dollars, although I don't suppose a person could get that for it. It had been insured at fifteen thousand dollars."

"Had been?" Mason asked.

"Yes, my wife canceled the insurance. As it happened, only the day before the burglary."

Major Winnett glanced almost appealingly at the lawyer.

"Canceled her insurance," Mason said, "and then twenty-four hours later the burglary took place?"

"Yes."

"And you fail to see any connection between those two facts?"

"I am certain there is none," Major Winnett said hastily. "My wife's reasoning was absolutely sound. She had carried this insurance policy and paid high premiums on it while she was living in apartments and hotels because she wanted to keep her jewelry with her and wanted to wear it. But when she married me and came to live in Vista del Mar, it seemed hardly necessary to continue paying high premiums."

"Tell me more about that burglary and why you didn't report it to the police."

"How did you know we didn't report it to the police?"

"Your facial expression," Mason said dryly.

"That was purely on account of the fact that my mother . . . well, you know, the newspaper notoriety and . . ."

"Tell me about the burglary," Mason said.

Major Winnett spoke with the rhythm of a man who is carefully choosing his words. "I am a sound sleeper, Mr. Mason. My wife is not. On Tuesday night I was awakened by the sound of my wife's scream."

"What time?"

"I didn't look at my watch at the time but I did look at it a few minutes later and as nearly as I can place the time, it was around quarter to one."

"How long had you been in bed?"

"We retired about eleven."

"And you slept until your wife screamed?"

"Well, I have, in the back of my consciousness, a vague recollection of a swallow crying."

Mason raised his eyebrows.

"You are, of course, familiar," Major Winnett went on hastily, "with the famed swallows of the Mission of San Juan Capistrano?"

Mason nodded.

"The nesting place of those swallows is not confined to the Mission. They get more publicity at the Mission because they leave on a certain day and return on a certain day. I believe that the time of their return can be predicted almost to the hour. A very unusual sense of keeping a calendar. How they are able to return year after year . . ."

"And you have some of those swallows at your house?" Mason interrupted.

"Yes. They are a nuisance. Their nests are built out of mud, and are fastened to the eaves. Our gardener knocks them down as soon as he detects the birds building, but in case one of them eludes his vigilance and the nest is built, then we don't disturb it, because the birds lay eggs very soon after the nests are built."

"Go on," Mason said.

"Well, this particular swallow's nest was located in a very unfortunate place. The main residence at Vista del Mar is a large Spanish-type house with the tile roofs and a white exterior. My bedroom is on the second floor with a projecting balcony. The tile projects out over that balcony and the birds had made their nest in such a place that if a man climbed over the balcony rail, he'd be within a few feet of the nest."

"And a man did climb over that rail?"

"Evidently that is what happened. We found a ladder that had been placed against the side of the house. The intruder had climbed up the ladder. In doing so, he disturbed the swallows. When they're disturbed, they have a peculiar throaty chirp."

"And you heard that?"

"I either heard it or dreamed that I did. My wife doesn't remember it, and she is a much lighter sleeper than I am, but I don't think I was mistaken."

"Then you went back to sleep?"

"Apparently I did. I remember hearing the protestations of the swallows and, while I was aroused from a sound slumber, I didn't thoroughly waken. I dozed off again and was soon in a deep sleep from which I was awakened by my wife's scream."

"She saw the burglar?"

"She was aroused by some noise in the room. She saw this man standing at her dresser. At first she thought I had gone to the dresser for some purpose and she started to speak to me. Then she looked over and saw that I was in my bed . . ."

"There was enough light for that?"

"Yes. A late moon was giving some light."

"What happened?"

"The man heard the motion—some sound of the bed springs, I guess. He darted out to the balcony. My wife screamed and that awakened me, but it took me a few seconds to get oriented, to realize where I was and what was happening. By that time the man had made his escape."

"And you think the swallows were crying because the man disturbed them?"

"That's right. When he entered the building, he must have climbed over the balcony rail and touched the nest."

"When did your wife cancel the insurance?"

"Monday afternoon."

Mason toyed with his lead pencil, asked abruptly, "What happened Monday morning?"

"We all four breakfasted together."

"Who's the fourth?"

"Helen Custer, my mother's nurse."

"Your mother isn't well?"

"She has a bad heart. Her physician feels it's advisable to have a nurse in the house."

"She's been with you long?"

"For three years. We consider her very much one of the family."

"You breakfasted and then what?"

"I wrote letters. My mother . . . I don't know exactly where she *did* go. Marcia went riding."

"Where?"

"Heavens, I don't know. One of our bridle paths."

Mason said, "I believe it rained Sunday night, didn't it?"

Major Winnett looked at him curiously. "What," he asked, "does that have to do with it? . . . I mean what is the significance?"

"Skip it," Mason interrupted. "What happened next?"

"Nothing. My wife returned about eleven."

"When did she tell you she was going to cancel the insurance?"

"That was just before lunch. She telephoned to the insurance company; and then she wrote them a letter confirming her action."

"Did you notice anything unusual in your wife's manner?"

"Nothing," Major Winnett said so swiftly that it seemed the answer had been poised on his tongue, waiting merely for Mason's question.

Mason said, "Well, it's ten-thirty. I want to get Paul Drake of the Drake Detective Agency. We'll make a start out at your place and go on from there. I'll leave here about eleven. Does your mother know your wife has left?"

Major Winnett cleared his throat. "I told her my wife was visiting friends."

"How will you account for us?" Mason asked.

"How many will there be?"

"My secretary Miss Street, Paul Drake the detective, myself, and perhaps one of Mr. Drake's assistants."

Major Winnett said, "I'm working on a mining deal. I can explain to my mother that you're giving me some advice in connection with that. Your detective wouldn't mind posing as a mining expert?"

"Not at all."

"You'll come to the house and . . . will you want to stay there?"

Mason nodded. "I think we'd better. And I'll want photographs and a description of your wife."

Major Winnett took an envelope from his inside pocket, extracted nearly a dozen photographs. "I brought these along. They're snapshots. She's twenty-five, redheaded, bluish gray eyes, five feet two, a hundred and fifteen, and as nearly as I can tell from checking the clothes that are left in the closet, she's wearing a checkered suit, sort of a gray plaid. It's the one that she's wearing in this picture."

Mason studied the photographs, then reached for the envelope. "All right," he said, "we'll be out. You can go on ahead and see that all necessary arrangements are made."

2

THE city of Silver Strand Beach lay in a sheltered cove on the lee-side of a peninsula. The Winnett estate dominated this peninsula, its wire fences with forbidding "no trespassing" signs stretching for some two and a half miles. The Spanish-type house, perched on the summit some five hundred feet above the ocean, commanded a view in all directions.

Mason's car swept around the last curve in the graveled drive-way, came to a stop in front of the imposing house as he said to Paul Drake, "I think the cancellation of that insurance policy is, perhaps, the first indication of what she had in mind, Paul. And I think that may have some connection with the horseback ride she took Monday morning."

Paul Drake's professionally lugubrious face didn't change expression in the least. "Anything to go on, Perry?"

"It rained Sunday night," Mason said. "It hasn't rained since. If you could find the path she took, it's quite possible you might be able to track her horse."

"For the love of Pete, do I have to ride a horse?"

"Sure. Tell the groom you'd like to ride. Ask him about some of the bridle paths."

"I can't see anything from a horse," Drake complained. "When a horse trots, I bounce. When I bounce, I see double."

"After you get out of sight of the house, you can lead the horse," Mason suggested.

"How about me?" Della Street asked.

"Try and get acquainted with the nurse," Mason suggested, "and take a look around."

Major Winnett himself answered Mason's ring; and the swift efficiency with which he installed them in rooms, introduced them to his mother, and Helen Custer, the nurse, showed that he had already made his preliminary explanations.

While Drake departed for the stables, after having expressed his spurious enthusiasm for horseflesh, Major Winnett took Mason on a tour of inspection.

Once they were alone in the upper corridors, Major Winnett asked quickly and in a low voice, "Is there anything in particular you want to see?"

"I'd like to get familiar with the entire house," Mason said guardedly. "But you might begin by showing me *your* room."

Major Winnett's room was on the south side. Glass doors opened on the balcony, from which the ocean could be seen shimmering in the sunlight.

"That's the swallow's nest?" Mason asked, indicating a gourd-like projection of mud which extended from the tiles just above the balcony.

"That's the swallow's nest. You can see that a person climbing a ladder . . ."

"Was the ladder already there?" Mason asked.

"Yes. The handy man had been doing some work on a pane of glass on the side of the bedroom. He had left the ladder in position that night, because he intended to finish it the next morning. Damn careless of him."

"In that case," Mason said, "your thief was an opportunist, since he didn't bring his own ladder."

"Yes, I suppose so."

"One who was, moreover, apparently familiar with the house. How about your servants?"

"You can't ever tell," Major Winnett said. "Particularly these days. But I *think* they're all right. Mother pays good wages and most of the help have been with her for some time. However, she *is* rather strict at times and there is a certain turnover."

"You own virtually all of the land on this peninsula?"

"Quite a bit of it, but not all of it. In a moment we'll go up to the observation tower and I can show you around from there. Generally, we take in about three-fourths of the peninsula. There is a strip out on the end where the county maintains a public camp ground."

"The public can reach that camp without crossing your estate?"

"Yes. Our line runs along by the grove of trees—beautiful oaks that offer a place for picnics. Picnickers are always scattering papers and plates around. We try to persuade them to go on down to the public camp grounds on the end of the peninsula."

"So anyone who came out here at night would have been definitely a trespasser?"

"Quite definitely."

"And having taken that risk, must have had some specific objective in mind, and would, therefore, if he were at all prudent, have arranged some manner of reaching his objective?"

"Yes, I suppose so."

"Therefore," Mason went on, "your burglar must either have been someone who knew that the ladder was here, or else it was an inside job."

"But how could anyone have known the ladder was here?"

Mason said, "If you can see the camp and the picnic grounds from here, it is quite possible that someone in the camp or picnic grounds could see the house."

"Yes, the house is quite a landmark. You can see it for miles."

"And perhaps a man, looking up here about dusk and noticing that a ladder had been left in place, would have decided it might be worthwhile to climb that ladder."

"Yes, I suppose so. However, Mr. Mason, I can't see that there is the slightest connection between the theft of my wife's jewelry and her disappearance."

"Probably not," Mason said.

They finished their tour with a trip up a flight of stairs to the place which Major Winnett described as "the tower."

Here was a belfry-like room, fifteen feet square, with plate glass windows on all sides. In the center, a pair of eighteen power binoculars attached to a swivel on a tripod could be turned and locked in any position.

"In times past," Major Winnett explained, "when there was more merchant shipping up and down the coast, we used to enjoy looking the boats over. You see, these binoculars can be swung in any direction. Now I'll point them toward town and . . ."

"Just a minute," Mason warned sharply, as Major Winnett reached for the binoculars. "They seem to be pointed toward that grove of trees. If you don't mind, I'd like to look through them."

"Why certainly. Help yourself."

Mason looked through the powerful prismatic binoculars. The

right eye showed only a blur, but the left showed a shaded spot under the clump of big live oaks where the road crossed a mesa before dipping down through a little canyon to again come into view as it swung out toward the picnic and camping grounds on the extreme tip of the promontory.

"There's no central focusing screw," Major Winnett explained. "You have to adjust each eyepiece individually. Perhaps . . ."

"Yes, so I see," Mason said, removing his eyes from the binoculars.

"Here is what I mean," Major Winnett went on. "You simply screw this eyepiece . . ."

Mason courteously but firmly arrested the Major's hand. "Just a moment, Major," he said. "I want to look at that right eyepiece."

"Someone must have been tampering with it. It's way out of proper adjustment," the Major said.

"The left eyepiece is at zero adjustment. I take it that means a perfectly normal eye," Mason said, "whereas, on this right eyepiece, there is an adjustment of negative five. I take it those graduations are made so that a person can remember his own individual adjustment for infinity and adjust the binoculars readily."

"I suppose so. The figures represent diopters."

"And an adjustment of negative five certainly blurs the entire . . ."

"That can't be an adjustment," the Major interposed. "Someone has idly turned that eyepiece."

"I see your point," Mason said and promptly turned the eyepiece back to zero. "There," he announced, "that's better."

It was now possible to make out details in what had before been merely a patch of shadow.

Mason swung the binoculars to the picnic ground, and could see quite plainly the masonry barbecue pits, the tables and chairs. Beyond them, through the trees he caught a glimpse of the ocean.

"A beach down there?" he asked.

"Not a beach, but a very fine place for surf fishing."

Mason swung the binoculars once more toward the clump of trees and the wide place in the road. "And you say people picnic there?"

"Occasionally, yes."

"From that point," Mason said, "one could see the house quite plainly with binoculars."

"But the binoculars are up here."

"Not the only pair in the world surely."

The Major frowned. Mason turned the glasses on a moving object, saw a magnified image of Paul Drake walking slowly along a bridle path. The short, somewhat cramped steps indicated that his brief experience in the English riding saddle had been more than ample. The detective was leading the horse, his head bowed as he plodded along the bridle path.

3

MASON waited until he saw Major Winnett leave the house, walking toward the stables. Then the lawyer quietly opened the door of his room, walked down the corridor to Winnett's bedroom, crossed the balcony and climbed to the rail.

The entrance of the swallow's nest was too small to accommodate the lawyer's hand but he enlarged the entrance by chipping away bits of the dried mud with his thumb and forefinger.

From the inside of the nest came faint rustlings of motion. An immature beak pushed against Mason's finger.

The parent swallows cried protests as they swooped in swift, stabbing circles around the lawyer's head, but Mason, working rapidly, enlarged the opening so that he could insert his hand into the nest. He felt soft down-covered bodies. Down below them, his groping fingers encountered only the concave surface of the nest.

A frown of annoyance crossed the lawyer's face. He continued groping, however, gently moving the young birds to one side. Then the frown faded as the tips of his fingers struck a hard metallic object.

As the lawyer managed to remove this object, sunlight scintillated an emerald and diamond brooch into brilliance.

Mason swiftly pocketed the bit of jewelry, drew back from the fierce rushes of the swallows. He dropped to the floor of the balcony and returned to the bedroom.

Back in the bedroom, he made a swift, thorough search of the various places where small objects might be concealed. A sole leather gun case in the back of a closet contained an expensive shotgun. Mason looked through the barrels. Both were plugged with oiled rags at breach and muzzle.

Mason's knife extracted one of the rags. He tilted up the barrels, and jewelry cascaded out into his palm, rings, earrings, brooches, a diamond and emerald necklace.

Mason replaced the jewelry, inserted the rag once more and put the barrels back in the leather case, returned the case to the closet.

Preparing to leave the room, he listened for a few moments at the bedroom door, then boldly opened it and stepped out, retracing his steps toward his own room.

He was halfway down the corridor when Mrs. Victoria Winnett appeared at an intersecting corridor and moved toward Mason with stately dignity and a calm purpose.

"Were you looking for something, Mr. Mason?" she asked.

The lawyer's smile was disarming. "Just getting acquainted with the house."

Victoria Winnett was the conventional composite of a bygone era. There were pouches beneath her eyes, sagging lines to her face, but the painstakingly careful manner in which every strand of hair had been carefully coiffed, her face massaged, powdered, and rouged, indicated the emphasis she placed on appearance, and there was a stately dignity about her manner which, as Della Street subsequently remarked, reminded one of an ocean liner moving sedately up to its pier.

Had she carefully rehearsed her entrance and been grooming herself for hours to convey just the right impression of dignified rebuke, Mrs. Victoria Winnett would not have needed to change so much as a line of her appearance. "I think my *son* wanted to show you around," she said as she fell into step at Mason's side.

"Oh, he's done that already," Mason said with breezy informality. "I was just looking the place over."

"You're Mr. *Perry* Mason, the lawyer, aren't you?"

"That's right."

"I had gathered from what I read about your cases that you specialize mostly in trial work."

"I do."

"*Murder* trials, do you not?"

"Oh, I handle lots of other cases. The murder cases get the most publicity."

"I see," she said in the tone of one who doesn't see at all.

"Nice place you have here," the lawyer went on. "I am very much interested in that observation cubicle on top of the house."

"It was my husband's idea. He liked to sit up there. Didn't I hear the swallows crying out there?"

"I thought *I* heard them too," Mason said.

She looked at him sharply. "We try to keep them from nesting here but occasionally the gardener fails to see a nest until it is completed; then we don't disturb the nest until after the young birds have hatched. They're noisy and talkative. You can hear them quite early in the mornings. I trust they won't disturb you. Are you a sound sleeper, Mr. Mason?"

They had paused at the head of the stairs. Mrs. Winnett apparently did not intend to go down, so Mason, standing poised on the upper stair tread, used strategy to terminate the interview.

"My friend, Drake, is looking over the horses, and if you'll pardon me I'll run down and join him."

He flashed her a smile and ran swiftly down the stairs, leaving her standing there, for the moment nonplussed at the manner in which the lawyer had so abruptly forestalled further questions.

4

In the patio, Della Street caught Perry Mason's eye, gave him a significant signal and moved casually over to the driveway where she climbed into the car and sat down.

Mason walked over. "I think Paul Drake has something," he said. "I'm going down and look him up. He's just coming in on the bridle path. What have you got?"

"I can tell you something about the nurse, chief."

"What?"

"In the first place, if a woman's intuition counts for anything, she's in love with the Major—one of those hopeless affairs where she worships him from a distance. In the second place, I think she has a gambling habit of some sort."

"Races?"

"I don't know. I was up in the cupola just after you were. There was a pad of paper in the drawer of the little table up there. At first it looked completely blank. Then I tilted it so the light struck it at an angle and could see that someone had written on the top sheet with a fairly hard pencil so it had made an imprint on the bottom sheet. Then the top sheet had been torn off."

"Good girl! What was on the sheet of paper? I take it something significant."

"Evidently some gambling figures. I won't bother to show you the original at this time but here's a copy that I worked out. It reads like this: *These numbers* on the first line, then down below that, *led;* then down below that a space and 5″5936; down below that 6″8102; down below that 7″9835; down below that 8″5280; down below that 9″2460; down below that 10″1320."

"Anything else?" Mason asked.

"Then a line and below the line, the figure 49″37817. That looks like some sort of a lottery to me. I learned Mrs. Winnett has been up in the cupola lately and since *she'd* hardly be a gambler, I assume the nurse must have written down the figures."

Mason said thoughtfully, "Notice the last three numbers, Della, 5280, 2640, 1320. Does that sequence mean something to you?"

"No, why?"

Mason said, "5280 feet in a mile."

"Oh, yes, I get that."

"The next number, 2640 feet, is a half mile, and the last number, 1320 feet, is a quarter mile."

"Oh, yes, I see now. Then that double mark means inches, doesn't it?"

"It's an abbreviation of inches, yes. What does this nurse seem like, Della? Remember I only barely met her."

"Despite her muddy complexion, straight hair, and glasses, her eyes are really beautiful. You should see them light up when the Major's name comes up. My own opinion is this nurse could be good-looking. Then Mrs. Winnett would fire her. So she keeps herself looking plain and unattractive so she can be near the Major, whom she loves with a hopeless, helpless, unrequited passion."

"Look here," Mason said, "if you've noticed that within an hour and a half, how about Mrs. Victoria Winnett? Doesn't she know?"

"I think she does."

"And hasn't fired the nurse?"

"No. I think she doesn't mind if the nurse worships the ground the Major walks on but doesn't presume to raise her eyes to look at him, if you get what I mean."

"I get it," Mason said thoughtfully, "and I don't like it. Wait, here comes Paul now."

Drake, walking stiffly, joined them.

"Find anything, Paul?" Mason asked.

"I found something," Drake conceded, "and I don't know what it is."

"What does it look like, Paul?"

"In the first place," Drake said, "you can easily follow her tracks. She took the lower bridle path. After the first quarter mile, there's only one set of tracks going and coming. They were made when the ground was soft and they go down to a road and a gate that's locked. I didn't have a key but I could see where the horse tracks went through the gate and down onto the road, so I tied up my horse and managed to squeeze through the fence."

"Any tracks around those trees, Paul?"

"An automobile had been parked there," Drake said. "There must have been two automobiles. That's the only way I can figure it out but I still can't figure the tracks right."

"How come?"

Drake took a small thin book from his pocket. "This is a little pocket book which gives the tread designs of all makes of tires. Now an automobile was in there that had some fairly new tires. One of the wheels was worn too much to identify but I identified the track of a right front wheel. Then the track of the other front wheel and the other hind wheel and . . . well, there I bogged down, Perry."

"What do you mean?"

"Of course, you have to understand it's a little difficult trying to get those tracks all fitted into the proper sequence. They . . ."

"What are you getting at?" Mason said.

"Hang it, Perry, I got *three* wheels."

"And the fourth was worn smooth?"

"Not that—what I mean is, Perry, that I got three wheels *on a single side.*"

Mason frowned at the detective. "*Three* wheels on a side?"

"Three wheels on a side," Paul Drake insisted doggedly.

Mason said rather excitedly, "Paul, did you notice a circular spot in the ground, perhaps eight or ten inches in diameter?"

"How the deuce did you know that spot was there?" Drake demanded, his face showing bewilderment.

Mason said, "It was made by the bottom part of a bucket, Paul. And the three tracks on each side were all right. That's the way it should be."

"I don't get it."

"A house trailer," Mason explained. "An automobile and a house trailer were parked under the trees. The waste water from a trailer sink is carried out through a drain to the outside. A bucket is placed there to catch the water as it runs off."

"That's it, all right," Drake admitted, then added morosely, "I'm kicking myself for not thinking of it myself, Perry."

Mason said, "It now begins to look as though Marcia Winnett had kept an appointment on Monday with someone in a house trailer. And that seems to have been very much a turning point in her life."

Drake nodded. "On Monday—that's a cold trail, Perry."

"It's the only one we have," Mason pointed out.

5

MASON, studying the tire tracks, said, "It was an automobile and a house trailer, Paul. The round place which marks the location of the spout bucket can be taken as being approximately in the middle of the trailer. You can see over here the mark of an auxiliary wheel attached to the front of the trailer to carry part of the weight while the trailer was parked. That enables us to estimate the length of the trailer."

Drake said, "The trailer must have been backed in between these trees, Perry."

Mason started prowling along the edge of the fence. "Took some clever handling to get it in there. Let's look around for garbage. If the trailer remained here overnight, there are probably some tin cans . . . potato peelings, stuff of that sort."

Mason, Della Street, and Drake separated, covering the ground carefully.

Abruptly Della said, "Chief, don't look too suddenly, but casually take a look up there at the big house on the hill. I think I saw someone moving in the glassed-in observation tower."

"I rather expected as much," Mason said, without even looking up. "However, it's something we can't help."

Drake exclaimed, "Here it is, Perry, a collection of tin cans and garbage."

Mason moved over to where Drake was standing. Here the water from the winter rains, rushing down the ditch at the side of the road, had eddied around one of the roots of the big live oak and formed a cave which extended some three feet back under the roots of the tree.

Mason, squatting on his heels, used two dry sticks to rake out the articles.

There were three cans which had been flattened under pressure, some peelings from onions and potatoes, waxed paper which had been wrapped around a loaf of bread, an empty glass container bearing a syrup label, and a crumpled paper bag.

Mason carefully segregated the items with his sticks. As he did so he kept up a running fire of conversation.

"That flattening of the cans is the trick of an old outdoor man," he said.

"Why flatten them?" Della inquired.

"Animals get their heads stuck in cans sometimes," Mason said. "Moreover, cans take up less room when they're flattened and require a smaller hole when they're buried. This little garbage pit tells quite a story. The occupant of the trailer must have been a man. Notice the canned beans, a can of chili con carne, potatoes, bread, onions—no tomato peelings, no lettuce leaves, no carrots, in fact, no fresh vegetables at all. A woman would have had a more balanced diet. These are the smallest cans obtainable and . . . hello, what's this?"

Mason had pulled apart the paper bag as he talked. Now he brought out a small oblong slip of paper on which figures had been stamped in purple ink.

Della Street said, "That's a cash register receipt from one of the cash and carry grocery stores."

Mason picked up the receipt. "And a very interesting one," he said. "The man bought fifteen dollars and ninety-four cents' worth of merchandise. There's a date on the back of the slip and this other figure refers to the time. The groceries were bought at five minutes past eight on Saturday morning. It begins to look, Paul, as though this is where you take over."

"What do you want me to do?" Drake asked.

Mason said, "Get a room in the hotel at Silver Strand Beach. Open up something of an office there. Get men on the job. Get lots of men. Have your men buy groceries. See if the printing on the slip from any cash register matches this. If it does, try and find out something about the single, sun-bronzed man who purchased fifteen dollars and ninety-four cents' worth of groceries at five minutes past eight on Saturday morning. A sale of that size to a man just a few minutes after the store opened might possibly have attracted attention."

"Okay," Drake said. "Anything else?"

"Lots else," Mason said. "Della, where's that slip of paper, the copy you made of what you found in the observation tower?"

Della ran to the glove compartment, brought back the square of paper on which she'd made the copy.

Drake looked at it, said, "What is it, Perry?"

"Stuff Della found in the observation tower. What do you make of it?"

"Some sort of dimensions," Drake said. "Here's this number 8 inches and 5280 feet, 9 inches and half a mile, 10 inches and quarter of a mile. What's the idea, Perry, why should the inches run 5, 6, 7, 8, 9, 10, and . . . ?"

"Suppose they aren't inches?" Mason said. "Suppose they're ditto marks."

"Well, it could be."

"Then what?" Mason asked.

Drake said, "Then the numbers could have something to do with a lottery of some sort."

"Add them up," Mason said dryly.

"The total is already here," Drake said, "49″37817."

Mason handed him a pencil.

Della Street, leaning over Drake's shoulder, was the first to get it. "Chief," she exclaimed, "the total isn't correct."

"I knew it wasn't," Mason said. "I didn't know just how much it was off, however. Let's find out."

Della Street said, "The total is . . . Wait a minute, Paul, I'll get it . . . 45″33113, but the total that's *marked* there is 49″37817."

"Subtract them," Mason said. "What do you get?"

Della Street's skillful fingers guided the pencil as she hastily wrote down numbers, performed the subtraction. "4″4704," she said.

Mason nodded. "I think," he said, "when we get this case solved, we'll find the important figure is the one that *isn't* there. Bear that figure in mind, Paul. It may turn up later."

6

PERRY MASON took the steep stairs to the observation tower two at a time.

There was no one in the cupola. The binoculars, however, had once more been swung so that they were pointing to the grove of trees where the trailer had been parked. Mason placed his eyes to the binoculars. The left eye showed a clear vision, the right was blurred.

Mason bent over to study the adjustment on the right lens, saw it was set once more at negative five, then he changed the focus on the binoculars.

As he did so, he heard motion behind him and straightened abruptly.

Mrs. Victoria Winnett was standing in the doorway. At her side was a slender brunette in riding clothes whose face showed startled surprise. Mrs. Winnett's face showed no expression whatever.

"I hardly expected to find *you* here," Mrs. Winnett said to Mason and then turning to the young woman at her side said, "Miss Rexford, permit me to present Mr. Perry Mason, the lawyer."

Daphne Rexford favored Mason with a smile which went only as far as her lips. Her eyes showed an emotion which might have been merely nervousness, might have been panic.

Mason acknowledged the introduction, then said, "I'm fascinated with the view you get from here, Mrs. Winnett."

"My late husband spent much of his time here. The place does hold something of a fascination. Daphne loves it."

"You're here frequently?" Mason asked Daphne Rexford.

"Yes, I study birds."

"I see."

"But," she went on hastily, "since you're here I'll postpone my bird study until some other time."

"On the contrary," Mason said, "I was just leaving. I wanted to get the lay of the land."

"He's working with Claude on a mining deal," Mrs. Winnett hastened to explain to Daphne Rexford. "There's a mining engineer with him. And Mr. Mason has his secretary. You'll meet them if you're over for dinner tonight."

"Oh, thank you, but I . . . I don't think I can make it for dinner tonight. If Claude's going to be busy . . . Where's Marcia?"

"Visiting friends," Mrs. Winnett said dryly. "*Please* come."

"Well, I . . . I should . . ."

Mason said as she hesitated, "Well, I must get down and hunt up my client. After all, I must earn my fee, you know."

"I feel quite sure you will," Mrs. Winnett said with a certain subtle significance. "Come, Daphne, dear. Draw up a chair. What was it you were saying about swallows?"

Daphne said hurriedly, "Oh, there's a meadow lark! I think there must be a nest down by that bush. I've seen that same lark so many times in that exact position . . ."

Mason quietly closed the door, walked down the stairs.

Major Winnett was in the drawing room. He looked up as Mason crossed toward the patio. "What luck?" he asked.

"Progress," Mason said.

Major Winnett's lips tightened. "Can't you do better than that? Can't you give me something definite? Or are you just running around in circles?"

"A good hound always runs around in circles to pick up a scent."

"Then you haven't anything definite yet?"

"I didn't say that."

"You intimated it."

Mason slid his right hand down into his trousers pocket, abruptly withdrew the diamond and emerald brooch he had taken from the swallow's nest.

"Seen this before?" he asked, extending his hand.

Major Winnett stiffened for a moment to rigid immobility. "It looks . . . Mr. Mason, that certainly is similar to a brooch my wife had."

"One that was stolen?"

"I believe so, yes."

"Thank you," Mason said and slipped the brooch back into his pocket.

"May I ask where you got that?" Claude Winnett asked excitedly.

"Not yet," Mason told him.

The telephone rang sharply. Major Winnett moved over to the library extension, picked up the receiver, said, "Hello," then turned to Mason. "It's for you."

Mason took the telephone. Drake's voice said, "We've got something, Perry."

"What?"

"That oblong slip of paper from the cash register. We've located the store. The girl that was on duty remembers our party. We've got a good description now. With that to go on, we had no trouble picking up his trail in a trailer camp. He registered under the name of Harry Drummond."

"There now?" Mason asked.

"Not now. He pulled out early yesterday morning. I've got men covering every trailer camp anywhere near here. We should pick him up soon. We have the license number and everything. And here's a funny one, Perry. There's a jane looking for him."

"You mean . . . ?"

"No, not the one we're interested in, another one. She's brunette, snaky, young and tall and she was asking the cashier about him earlier in the day. Had a good description. Wanted to know if such a man had been in."

"Are you located there in the hotel?"

"Yes. I've fixed up an office here and have half a dozen men out on the job, with more coming in all the time."

Mason said, "I'll be right up."

"Okay, be looking for you. Good-by."

Mason heard the click at the other end of the line but did not immediately hang up. He stood holding the receiver, frowning at the carpet.

Abruptly he heard another sharp click and the telephone bell in the library extension gave a little tinkle.

Mason dropped the receiver into place, turned to Major Winnett. "I take it," he said, "you have several extensions on the phone?"

"Four," Major Winnett said. "No, there's five. There's one up in the observation tower. I almost forgot about that."

"Thank you," Mason said, and then added after a moment, "so did I."

7

PAUL DRAKE was talking on the phone as Mason entered the suite of rooms Drake was using for headquarters. In an adjoining room Della Street, a list of numbers at her elbow, was putting through a steady succession of calls.

"Come in, Perry," Drake said, hanging up the receiver. "I was trying to get you. We're getting results fast."

"Shoot."

"Our party is a man thirty-eight years old, bronzed, wears cowboy boots, a five-gallon hat, leather jacket, Pendleton trousers, rather chunky and has a wide, firm mouth. The license number of his automobile is 4E4705. He's driving a Buick automobile and has quite an elaborate house trailer painted green on the outside with aluminum paint on the roof. Up until Saturday morning he was in the Strand Trailer Camp. He left Saturday, showed up again late Monday night, pulled out again Wednesday morning and hasn't been seen since."

"How did you get it?" Mason asked.

"Just a lot of leg work."

"Give me the highlights."

"We located the store that has that cash register—the only one in town. Cash register gives the time and date of sale, the amount of the items and the total. This sale was made shortly after the store opened Saturday morning and the cashier remembers the man's general appearance. She particularly remembered the cowboy boots. We started covering trailer camps and almost immediately picked up our trail."

"What are you doing now?"

"I've got operatives scattered around with automobiles covering every trailer camp, every possible parking place for a house trailer anywhere in this part of the country. We're working in a constantly widening circle and should turn up something soon."

Mason took out his notebook. "The number is 4E4705?"

"That's right."

"Then our mysterious observer in the observation tower made a mistake in addition. Remember, we were looking for a number 4"4704. The first number must have been 4E4705 and ditto marks were beneath the E. The real total then should have been . . ."

He was interrupted by a knock on the door, a quick staccato knock which somehow contained a hint of hysteria.

Mason exchanged glances with Drake. The detective left the desk, crossed over, and opened the door.

The woman who stood on the threshold was twenty-seven or twenty-eight, a tall brunette with flashing black eyes, high cheek bones and an active, slender figure. A red brimless hat perched well back on her head emphasized the glossy darkness of her hair and harmonized with the red of her carefully made-up lips.

She smiled at Paul Drake, a stage smile which showed even, white teeth. "Are *you* Mr. Drake?" she asked, glancing from him to Mason.

Drake nodded.

"May I come in?"

Drake wordlessly stood to one side.

His visitor entered the room, nodded to Perry Mason, and said, "I'm *Mrs.* Drummond."

Drake started to glance at Mason, then caught himself in time, and managed to put only casual interest in his voice. "I'm Mr. Drake," he said, "and this is Mr. Mason. Is there something in particular, Mrs. Drummond?"

She said, "You're looking for my husband."

Drake merely raised his eyebrows.

"At the Strand Trailer Camp," she went on nervously. "And *I'm* looking for him *too*. I wonder if we can't sort of pool information?"

Mason interposed suavely. "*Your* husband, and you're looking for him, Mrs. Drummond?"

"Yes," she said, her large dark eyes appraising the lawyer.

"How long since you've seen him?" Mason asked.

"Two months."

"Perhaps if you want us to *pool* information, you'd better tell us a little more about the circumstances and how you happened to know we were looking for him."

She said, "I'd been at the Silver Strand Trailer Camp earlier in the day. The man promised me that he'd let me know if my husband returned. When your detectives appeared and started asking questions, he took the license number of their car, found out it belonged to the Drake Detective Agency, and . . ." She laughed nervously and said, "And that is where I started to do a little detective work on my own. Are you looking for him for the same reason I am?"

Mason smiled gravely. "That brings up the question of why you're looking for him."

She gave an indignant toss of her head. "After all, I have nothing to conceal. We were married a little over a year ago. It didn't click. Harry is an outdoor man. He's always chasing around on the trail of some mining deal or some cattle ranch. I don't like that sort of life and . . . well, about two months ago we separated. I sued for divorce."

"Have you got it yet?"

"Not yet. We had an understanding about a property settlement. When my lawyer sent my husband the papers, he sent them back with an insulting note and said he wouldn't pay me a red cent and that if I tried to get tough about it, he'd show that I didn't have any rights whatever."

"Why?"

"I don't know."

"And you want to find out just what he means by that?" Mason asked.

"That's right. And now suppose you tell me what *you* want him for. Has he done something?"

"Is he the type that would?" Mason asked.

"He's been in trouble before."

"What sort of trouble?"

"A mining swindle."

Drake glanced inquiringly at Mason.

"Where are you located?" Mason asked Mrs. Drummond.

"I'm right here at the hotel. And don't think they're the ones who told me about Mr. Drake's being here," she added hastily. "I found that out by . . . in another way."

"You spoke of *pooling* information," Mason said suggestively.

She laughed and said, "Well, what I meant was if you find him, will you let me know? And if I find him, I could let you know. After all, he shouldn't be difficult to locate with that trailer, but

I want to catch him before he can get out of the state. If I can find out where he is, I have—some papers to serve."

"You have a car?" Mason asked.

She nodded, then added by way of explanation, "That is one thing I salvaged out of our marriage. I made him buy me a car, and that's one of the reasons I want to see him. The car's still in his name. He agreed to let me have it as part of the property settlement, but in his letter to my lawyer he said he could even take the car away from me if I tried to make trouble. Does either of you gentlemen have any idea what he meant by that?"

Mason shook his head and Drake joined in the gesture of negation.

"Perhaps," Mason suggested, "we might work out something. You see, even if your assumption is correct that we are looking for your husband, we would be representing some client in the matter and would naturally have to discuss things with that client."

"Is it because of something he's done?" she asked apprehensively. "Is he in more trouble? Will it mean all his money will go for lawyers again, just like it did before?"

"I'm sure I couldn't tell you," Mason said.

"That means you won't. Look, I'm in Room 613. Why don't you ask your *client* to come and see me?"

"Will you be there all during the evening?" Drake asked.

"Well . . ." She hesitated. "I'll be in and out. I'll . . . I'll tell you what I'll do. I'll keep in touch with the hotel and if there are any messages, I'll be where I can come and get them."

She flashed them a smile, moved toward the door with quick lithe grace, then almost as an afterthought, turned and gave them her hand, glancing curiously through the open door of the adjoining room to where Della Street was seated at the telephone. Then she gave Mason another smile as the lawyer held the door open for her, and left the room, walking with quick nervous steps.

Mason closed the door, cocked a quizzical eyebrow at Paul Drake.

"The guy's wise," Drake said. "That means we haven't much time, Perry."

"You think he was watching his back trail?"

Drake nodded. "She's an alert little moll who knows her way around. This man Drummond has done something that he's trying to cover up. He left her to watch his back trail. She hypnotized the man who runs the trailer camp and then when my man showed up in an agency car . . ."

"But how about her asking questions at the cash-and-carry, Paul?"

Drake snapped his fingers. "Shucks, there's nothing to *that*. That's the way she builds up a background for herself. After all, she . . ."

The telephone interrupted. Drake picked up the receiver, said, "Drake talking . . . Okay, let's have it . . . When? . . . Where? . . . Okay, stay on the job . . . We'll be right down."

Drake hung up the receiver, said, "Well, that's it. We've got him located."

"Where?"

"Little down-at-the-heel trailer camp in a eucalyptus grove about three miles from here. Not much of a place, auto court cabins in front and, as an afterthought because there was lots of room, the owner strung up some wires and advertised trailer space in the rear. The conveniences aren't too good and it's patronized mostly by people who want to save two bits a day on the regular parking rate. The chief advantage is lots of elbow room. The grove consists of several acres and if a man wants to walk far enough to the bath and shower, he can pick his own parking place for the trailer."

"Any details?" Mason asked.

"One of my men just located it. The trailer came in yesterday night. The man who runs the place was busy selling gasoline at the time, and the driver of the car called out that he'd come back and register later. He tossed the man a silver dollar and the man told him to park any place he wanted to where he could find a plug for his electric connection."

Mason said, "Let's go. Della, you stay here and run the place. We'll telephone you in half an hour or so."

They drove down to the trailer camp in Mason's car. Drake's operative, lounging casually in the door of one of the auto cabins, gave the detective a surreptitious signal, and pointed toward the adjoining cabin.

Registering simply as "P. Drake," the detective rented the vacant cabin, then settled down with Perry Mason. A few moments later, Drake's operative came across to join them.

"Ever met Pete Brady?" Drake asked Mason.

Mason shook hands, said, "I've seen him once or twice before around your office."

"Glad to know you," Brady said to Mason, and then to Drake, "I'm not certain but what the guy who runs the place is getting a little suspicious. I asked too many questions."

"What's the dope?"

"The trailer's out there attached to the car. So far, I haven't had a glimpse of the man who is in it, but it's the license number of the car we want okay—4E4705."

"Let's take a look around," Mason said.

"You'll have to take it easy," Brady warned. "Just sort of saunter around."

"How about the gag of buying a trailer," Drake asked. "Have you used that?"

Brady shook his head.

"We'll try that," Drake said. "You can wait here for a while. What's the guy's name who runs the place?"

"Elmo, Sidney Elmo."

"Did he see you come over here?"

"No. I waited until he was selling gas."

"Okay. Stick around. I'll go tell the bird that we heard one of the trailers here was for sale. He won't know anything about it. That gives us an opportunity to go sauntering around looking them over."

Five minutes later when Drake returned, Mason joined him and they walked slowly out past the line of somewhat dilapidated cabins into the eucalyptus grove. Late afternoon shadows made the place seem cold and gloomy. The ground was still moist from the rain and the drippings of the trees when ocean fog enveloped that portion of the country.

"There's the outfit," Drake said. "What do we do? Go right up and knock and ask him if it's for sale?"

Mason said, "Let's try one of the other trailers first. We can talk loud enough so our voices will carry over here."

"Good idea," Drake said.

"Take this one," Mason suggested.

The two walked over to the small homemade trailer Mason had indicated. It was parked about a hundred feet from the green trailer. Electric lights showed a well-fleshed woman in her late forties cooking over the stove. On the outside, a man was taking advantage of the failing light to tinker with the bumper on the trailer. There was an Oklahoma license plate on the car.

"This the outfit that's for sale?" Mason asked.

The man looked up, a long thin mouth twisted into a smile. He said with a drawl, "I ain't saying yes, and I ain't saying no. You want to buy?"

"We're looking for a trailer that we heard was for sale here."

"What sort of a trailer?"

"We just heard it was a good one."

"That's the description of this job all right."

Drake interposed, "You're not the man who spoke to the manager of the Strand Trailer Park and said he wanted to sell, are you?"

"Nope. Fact is, I'm not particularly anxious to sell. But if you wanted to buy it, I'd be willing to listen."

"We're looking for a particular trailer that's for sale," Mason explained. "How about that green one over there? Know anything about it?"

"No. It just came in last night."

"Don't suppose you've talked with the people who own it?"

"I ain't seen 'em. They haven't been around all day."

Mason said, "That looks like it. Let's go over there, Paul."

"Take it easy," Mason said as they approached. "Ever use a house trailer, Paul?"

"No. Why?"

"The steady weight of the trailer has a tendency to wear out springs. So most trailers are equipped with an auxiliary wheel which can be screwed into position when the trailer is parked."

"There isn't any here," Drake said.

"That's just the point. Furthermore, no spout bucket has been put out under the spout. And to cap the climax, the cord hasn't been connected with the electric outlet."

"What are you getting at, Perry?"

By way of reply, Mason knocked loudly on the trailer door. When there was no response, the lawyer tentatively tried the knob.

The door swung open.

There was still enough afternoon light to show the sprawled figure lying in stark silence on the floor. The dark pool eddying out from under the body showed little jagged streaks of irregularity, but its ominous significance could not be misjudged.

"Oh-oh!" Drake exclaimed.

Mason stepped up and entered the trailer. Carefully avoiding the red pool, he looked down at the body. Then he bent over, touched the high heeled cowboy boot, moved it gently back and forth.

"Been dead for some time, Paul. Rigor mortis has set in."

"Come on out," Drake begged. "Let's play this one on the up-and-up and notify the police."

"Just a minute," Mason said. "I . . ." He bent over, and as he did so a shaft of light struck his face.

"What's that?" Drake asked.

Mason moved slightly so that the beam of light struck his eye.

"That," he announced, "is a hole in this trailer, directly in line with the window of that Oklahoma trailer. Light from the window over there where the woman is cooking comes through the hole in this trailer. The hole could have been made by a bullet."

"Okay, Perry. Let's notify the police."

Mason said, "First I want to find out a little more about that Oklahoma trailer."

"For the luvva Mike, Perry, have a heart! You're in the clear on this one—so far."

Mason, moving cautiously, left the trailer. He hesitated a moment when he stepped to the ground. Then he carefully polished the doorknob with his handkerchief.

"That's removing evidence," Drake said. "There are other prints there besides yours."

"How do you know?"

"It stands to reason."

"You can't prove it," Mason said. "The murderer probably wiped his fingerprints off the door just as I did."

Mason walked back to the trailer with the Oklahoma license. The man, still bent over the bumper at the rear of the trailer, seemed to be working aimlessly, stalling for time. The position of his head indicated an interest in what had been going on over at the other trailer.

"That the one?" he asked as Mason approached.

"I don't know. No one seems to be home."

"I ain't seen 'em leave. They couldn't go very far without their car."

"Seen any visitors over there?" Mason asked casually.

"Not today. There was a young woman called last night."

"What time?"

"I don't know. We'd gone to bed. Her headlights shone in the window and woke me up when she came. I sat up in bed and looked out the window."

"See her plain?"

"Yeah—a redhead. Checkered suit—trim looking package."

"She go in?"

"I guess so. She switched off her lights and I went back to sleep. Woke me up again when she left. Her car backfired a couple a times."

Mason glanced at Drake. "I'd like to find these people."

"I think there's only one—a man. He drove in last night and had quite a bit of trouble backing the trailer around. You take one of these big trailers and it's quite a job to park it. You try to back up and everything's just reversed from what it is when you're backing just a car. We went to bed pretty early and sometime after I'd got to sleep this other car came up. What really woke me up was headlights shining in my window. I looked out and seen this woman."

"Remember what sort of car she was driving?"

"It was a rented car."

"How do you know?"

"From the gasoline rationing stamp on the windshield."

"Your wife didn't wake up?"

"No."

"How long have *you* been here?" Mason asked.

"What's it to you?"

"Nothing."

"I thought not," the man said, suddenly suspicious, and then after a moment added, "You're asking a lot of questions."

"Sorry," Mason said.

The man hesitated a moment then, by way of dismissal, turned back to the bumper.

Mason glanced significantly at Paul Drake. Silently the two walked away.

"Okay, Paul," Mason said in a low voice. "Get Della on the phone. Tell her to put operatives on every drive-yourself car agency within a radius of fifty miles and see if we can find where the woman rented the car. When we spot the place, I'll handle the rest of it."

"I don't like it," Drake said.

"I don't like it myself," Mason told him. "But the young woman who called there last night was Marcia Winnett."

"And her car backfired," Drake said dryly.

Mason met his eyes. "Her car backfired, Paul. And in case it ever becomes necessary, remember that the only person who heard it said it was a backfire."

Drake nodded gloomily. "Not that *that* will do any good, Perry."

"It keeps us in the clear, Paul. You don't rush to the police to report that someone's car backfired."

"When you've discovered a body, you do."

"Who knows we've discovered any body?"

"I do."

Mason laughed. "Back to the hotel, Paul. We'll try and trace that car. And just to be on the safe side, we'll see where Mrs. Drummond was last night."

8

THE last task Mason had given Paul Drake turned out to be simple. Mrs. Drummond had been trying to locate her husband in the near-by trailer camps all the evening before, and she had arranged with a police officer who was off duty to accompany her.

Locating the rented car in which the girl in the checkered suit went to the trailer camp was another matter.

Despite all of Drake's efficiency, it was nearing eight o'clock when his detectives uncovered the lead Mason wanted. A man who operated a car rental agency in one of the coast cities, some twenty-five miles from Silver Strand Beach, had rented a car to a young woman who wore a checkered suit and who answered the description of Marcia Winnett.

Drake looked up from the telephone. "Want my man to try and pick up the trail from there or do you want to do it, Perry?"

Mason said, "I'll do it, Paul. And just to be on the safe side, let your man think that that isn't the trail we want."

"Okay," Drake said, and then into the telephone, "Describe her, Sam. Uh huh . . . uh huh, well, that's not the one. Keep working. Cover those other agencies and then report."

Drake hung up the phone. "Want me to come along, Perry?"

"Della and I'll handle it," Mason said. "Start calling your men in. Let them feel it turned out to be a false lead. And you'd better start checking on Mrs. Drummond, Paul. I wouldn't like to have her show up right now."

Drake nodded, said solicitously, "Watch your step, Perry."

"I'm watching it. Come on, Della."

The man who operated the car rental agency which had furnished a car to Marcia Winnett was not particularly communicative. It took diplomacy to get him in the mood to talk. Even then he confined his information to bare essentials.

He had never seen his customer before. She gave her name as Edith Bascom. She said her mother had died and it was necessary for her to use a car in connection with handling the estate. She was registered at the local hotel.

"Do you check on these stories?" Mason asked. "Or do you just rent cars?"

"Sometimes we just rent cars. Sometimes we check."

"What did you do in this case?"

"Cars are scarce now," the man said. "We checked."

"How?"

The man picked up a daily paper dated the day before and indicated the obituary column. Mason followed the man's finger to the stereotyped announcement of the death of Mrs. Shirley Bascom and the statement that funeral arrangements would be private.

Mason said, "I guess that covers it all right."

"What's your interest in it?"

"I'm a lawyer."

"I see. Well, she's okay. Rather upset on account of her mother's death, but a nice girl. You'll find her in the Palace Hotel, two blocks down the street."

"You checked on that?"

"I told you cars are scarce," the man said. "I checked on it."

It was but a matter of routine for Mason and his secretary to get the number of the room which had been assigned to Edith Bascom. Two minutes later Mason was knocking on the door.

There was no answer. Mason tried the knob. The door was locked.

Mason made a swift survey of the hall, stooped and held out his hands. "Step on my hands, Della. Take a quick look through the transom."

She braced herself with a hand on his shoulder, caught the lower ledge of the transom and peered through.

Mason, with his right hand on her hip, steadying her, felt her body stiffen. Then she was scrambling to get down.

"Chief," she said in an ominous whisper, "she's stretched out on the bed. She's . . . terribly still."

"Lights on?"

"No, but the shade is up and there's enough light coming in from the electric sign in front to make out the form on the bed."

Mason said, "There's a spring lock on the door . . . Better take another look, Della. See if she's breathing and . . . hold it. Here comes a chamber maid."

The chamber maid who wearily approached was aroused only momentarily from the lethargy of overwork by the bill Mason pushed into her palm.

"My wife and I seem to have left our key downstairs. If you could let us in, it would save us a trip down . . ."

"It's against the rules," she said, then added tonelessly, "but I guess it's okay," produced her passkey, and clicked back the latch on the door.

Mason boldly pushed open the door, stood aside for Della to enter, then followed her into the dimly lighted room, and closed the door behind him.

Della Street crossed over to the woman lying on the bed, as Mason groped for her pulse.

"She's alive!" Della Street said.

"The lights," Mason said crisply. "Pull the curtains first."

Della Street jerked down the shades, ran over and switched on the light.

Mason glanced at the bottle of sleeping tablets by the side of the bed, picked up the newspaper on the floor, glanced at it.

"She must have taken them yesterday," Della said. "We'll need a doctor and . . ."

"This afternoon," Mason interrupted curtly. "This is a late edition of the afternoon paper."

He dropped the paper, shook the sleeper, said, "Towels, Della. Cold water."

Della Street grabbed towels, turned on the cold water in the bathroom. Mason slapped Marcia Winnett with cold towels until the eyelids flickered open.

"What is it?" she asked thickly.

Mason said to Della Street, "Run down to the drugstore, Della. Get an emetic. Have room service send up some black coffee."

"How about a doctor?"

"Not if we can avoid it. Let's hope she hasn't had the tablets down long enough to get the full effects. Get an emetic."

Marcia Winnett tried to say something but the words were unintelligible. She dropped back against Mason's shoulder.

Mason calmly started removing her blouse. Della Street dashed from the room, headed for the drugstore.

Thirty minutes later Mason and Della Street assisted Marcia Winnett from the bathroom. There was a dead, lacklustre look about her eyes but she could talk now, and the coffee was beginning to take effect.

Mason said, "Concentrate on what I'm telling you. I'm a lawyer. I'm retained to represent you."

"By whom?"

"Your husband."

"No, no, he mustn't . . . he can't . . ."

Mason said, "I'm *your* lawyer. Your husband retained me to help you. I don't have to tell him anything."

She sighed wearily, said, "Let me go. It's better this way."

Mason shook her once more into wakefulness. "You went riding Monday morning. You talked with a man in a trailer. He made demands on you. You had to have money and have it at once. You didn't dare to ask your husband for it."

Mason waited for an answer. She made none. Her eyelids drooped and raised as if by a conscious effort.

Mason said, "You went back to the house. You canceled the insurance on your jewelry because you were too conscientious to stick the insurance company. You arranged to have some repairs made to a window on the side of your bedroom so a ladder would be handy. You got up in the night, went out to the balcony, and dumped your jewelry into the swallow's nest. Then you started screaming."

Her face might have been a wooden mask.

Mason went on, "You had waited until Tuesday to stage the burglary. You knew that it would be too obvious if it happened Monday night, the day you had canceled the insurance. Wednesday morning you found an opportunity to get most of the jewelry out of the swallow's nest. There was one piece you overlooked. Now then, suppose you tell me what happened after that."

She said, with the drowsy calm of one who discusses a distant event which can have no personal bearing, "I wanted to kill him. I can't remember whether I did or not."

"Did you shoot him?"

"I can't remember a thing that happened after . . . after I left the house."

Mason glanced at Della Street, said, "If I'm going to help you, I have to know what hold that man had on you."

"His name is Harry Drummond. He was my first husband."

"You were divorced?"

"I *thought* I was divorced. There were reasons why I couldn't go to Nevada. I gave him the money. He went to live in Nevada.

"From time to time he sent me reports of how things were coming. Twice he asked for more money. Then he wrote me the divorce had been granted. He was lying. He'd gambled the money away. There never had been a divorce."

"When did you find this out?" Mason asked.

"Monday morning," she said. "He was clever. He'd kept in touch with me. He knew I rode down along that bridle path. He parked his trailer there. Mrs. Victoria Winnett doesn't like to have people camp there, so I rode down to ask whoever was in the trailer to please move on down to the public camp grounds."

"You had no idea who was in the trailer?"

"Not until Harry opened the door and said, 'Hello, Marcia. I thought it was about time you were showing up.'"

"What did he want?"

"Money."

"And he threatened you with—what?"

"The one weapon Claude couldn't stand, notoriety."

"So you promised to get him money?"

"I promised to get him my jewelry. He had to have money at once. He said someone was putting screws on him for cash."

"You were to meet him there when?"

"Wednesday morning."

"So you manipulated this fake burglary on Tuesday night after canceling your insurance on Monday. Then you took him the jewelry. Did he ask you how you had managed to secure the jewelry?"

"Yes. I told him the whole story. I told him it was all right to pawn it because the Winnetts wouldn't report the burglary to the police."

"And then what happened?"

"I can't remember."

"What can't you remember?"

"I can't remember a thing from the time . . . from the time Harry took the jewelry. He made some sneering remark, and I remember becoming very angry and then . . . then my mind went entirely blank."

"Did you have a revolver with you when you went down to the trailer Wednesday morning?" Mason asked.

"Yes."

"Where did you get it?"

"From a bureau drawer."

"Whose gun was it?"

"I don't know. I think it was . . . Mrs. Winnett's gun—pearl handled. I thought I might need some protection. It was a crazy idea. I took it along."

"Where is that gun now?"

"I don't know. I tell you I can't remember a thing that happened after I gave him the jewelry and he made that sneering remark."

"Did he make some further demands on you? Did he tell you you had to meet him at an isolated trailer park last night?"

"I don't know. I can't remember."

"*Did* you meet him there?"

"I can't remember."

"Did you," Mason asked, "rent an automobile from a drive-your-self agency about two blocks down the street?"

Her forehead puckered into a frown. "I seem to have some faint recollection of doing something like that, but I . . ." She shook her head. "No, it eludes me. I can't remember."

Mason said impatiently, "Why don't you come clean? You were clever enough to read the obituary notices and pretend to be the daughter of a woman who had just died. I'm trying to help you. At least tell me what I'm up against."

"I don't know. I can't remember."

Mason motioned toward the bottle of sleeping tablets. "And you thought you could take this way out and it would help?"

"I don't know. I guess I must have been . . . perhaps I was nervous. Perhaps I hadn't been sleeping at all and I just took too large a dose. I can't remember."

Mason turned to Della Street. "Willing to take a chance, Della?"

She nodded. "Anything you say, chief."

Mason said, "Put her in a car. Take her into Los Angeles. See that there's plenty of money in her purse. Take her to a *private* hospital. Under no circumstances give *your* name or address. Put on the rush act. Tell the first nurse you meet that this woman accosted you on the street and asked you to help her find out who she was. That you think it's a racket of some sort; but that she seems to have money and if she needs any assistance, the hospital is the place where she should be able to get it. Then turn and get out of the door fast."

Della nodded.

Mason turned to Marcia Winnett. "You heard what I said?"

"Yes . . . I . . . you mustn't take chances for me. I know that I must have killed him. I can't remember the details, Mr. Mason, but I killed him. I *think* it was in self-defense. I can't remember."

"I know," Mason said gently. "Don't worry about it. Remember you're a widow now. Don't get your memory back, and the next time you see me remember I'm a stranger. I'm going to try to help you. Get started, Della. Drive with the window open. Let her get lots of cold air. Get her to a hospital."

"How'll *you* get back?" Della asked.

"I'll have one of Drake's men pick me up."

Della looked at Marcia with cold contempt. "If you ask me," she blurted indignantly, "this act of hers . . ."

Mason gently closed one eye in an owlish wink. "Take her to the hospital, Della . . . and be sure you get out from under."

9

THE gravel on the driveway caused the wheels to slide as Mason slammed on the brakes. The car skidded at a sharp angle and Mason didn't even bother to straighten it out. He snapped off the lights and the ignition, leapt out and headed up the steps of the Winnett mansion, pushed open the door, and strode into the drawing room unannounced.

Mrs. Victoria Winnett and Daphne Rexford were lingering over liqueurs, talking in low voices.

Mrs. Winnett's smile was distantly friendly. "*Really,* Mr. Mason," she said, "you're rather late—for dinner."

The lawyer merely nodded, glanced at Daphne Rexford.

Mrs. Winnett reached for the bell. "I presume I can get you something," she said. "But after this, if you don't mind . . ."

"Let the food go," Mason said. "I want to talk with you."

The finger which had been touching the bell remained motionless. She said, "*Really,* Mr. Mason," in a voice that indicated a polite rebuke.

Daphne Rexford hurriedly arose. "If you'll excuse me, I have a telephone call I want to make . . ."

"Sit down, my dear. After all, I can't permit this human tornado to come bursting in on our tête-à-tête with . . ."

Mason caught Daphne Rexford's eye, jerked his head.

She made a feeble attempt at a smile and left the room.

"Really, Mr. Mason," Mrs. Winnett said, her voice now quite cold. "My attachment to my son is such that I am willing to make all allowances for his friends. Even so . . ."

She let her unfinished sentence carry its own meaning.

Mason drew up a chair and sat down. "Where's the Major?"

"He was called out about twenty minutes ago."

"You're fond of Daphne Rexford, aren't you?"

"Of course."

"Was she in the observation tower Monday?"

"Really, Mr. Mason. I'm not on the witness stand."

"You're going to be," Mason said.

"I'm afraid you've been drinking."

"If you think this is a joke," Mason said, "just keep on stalling. Time is precious. The officers may be out here any minute."

"Officers?"

"Officers. Cops. Bulls. Detectives. Plain-clothes men. Newspaper photographers. Walking around here with their hats on, throwing cigarettes on the rugs, taking flashlight pictures with captions— 'Society Leader Insists on Innocence.' "

That last did it. Mason saw her wince.

"You're a good poker player, but you can't bluff now. This is a showdown, Mrs. Winnett."

"Just what do you want?"

"To know all that you know."

She took a quick breath. "I know some trouble has developed between Marcia and Claude. I think that Marcia has left him. I hope she has."

"Why?"

"Because I don't feel that they are destined to be happy together . . ."

"No, I mean why has she left him?"

"I don't know."

"Make a guess."

"I can't."

"You know something about what happened on Monday?"

"On *Monday?* No."

"Was Daphne in the cupola on Monday?"

"I think she was."

"Did she come to you and tell you anything about what she saw either Monday or Wednesday?"

"Mr. Mason, you're being impertinent!"

Mason said, "You've found out something about Marcia. You thought she had involved the family good name, and took it on yourself to try and avoid notoriety. Your attempt backfired. I'm trying to find out just how badly it backfired."

"You can't prove any of these things you're saying, Mr. Mason."

"That," Mason said, "is only because I haven't the facilities at my command that the police have. The police may prove it."

"They won't," she said coldly. "I have told you absolutely everything I know."

Mason pushed back his chair, started for the door which led to the patio, then abruptly whirled, tiptoed swiftly back to the drawing room door, and jerked it open.

Daphne Rexford, plainly embarrassed, tried to pretend she had just been approaching the door. "Heavens," she said laughing, "I thought we were going to have a collision, Mr. Mason. You seem in a hurry." She tried to push easily on past him.

Mason barred her way. "You were listening."

"Mr. Mason, how *dare* you say anything like that?"

"Come in," Mason said. "Let's have it out. Let's . . . no, on second thought, I think I'll talk with you alone. Come on."

Mason took her arm. She drew back.

Mrs. Winnett said, "Mr. Mason is completely overstepping the prerogatives of a guest. I dislike to ask him to leave in my son's absence, but . . ."

Mason said to Daphne Rexford, "Police are going to be swarming over the place before midnight. Do you want to talk to me or do you want to talk to them?"

Daphne Rexford said over her shoulder to Mrs. Winnett, "Good heavens, Victoria, let's humor the man! I'll be back within a few minutes."

Without waiting for an answer from Victoria Winnett, she smiled disarmingly at Mason and moved away from the drawing room. "Come on, where do you want to talk?"

"Over here's good enough," Mason said, stopping in a corner of the library.

Daphne Rexford stood facing him. "What," she asked in a low voice, "are the police going to be investigating?"

Mason met her eyes. "Murder."

"Who . . . who was killed?"

"Let's talk first about what *you* know," Mason said. "You're the one who has the trick right eye. Mrs. Winnett has been covering up for you."

"I'm afraid I don't know what you mean."

"Whenever you look through the binoculars," Mason explained, "you have to move the right eyepiece quite a distance in order to see clearly, don't you?"

"What if I do?"

Mason said, "*You* were the one who was watching Marcia on Monday. What did you see?"

"Nothing. I . . ."

"Were you here Monday? Were you in the observation cupola?"

"I believe I was." ·

"You're over here quite a bit?"

"Yes. Victoria and I are great friends. She's an older woman, of course, but I like her. I like what she stands for and . . ."

"And like to be near Major Winnett and see as much of him as you can?"

"Certainly not," she said indignantly.

"We'll let it go at that for the time being," Mason said. "Now, about Monday, what did you see?"

"Nothing. I . . ."

"You were up in the tower?"

"Yes. I go there quite frequently. I study birds, and I write poetry. I can get inspiration up there, and . . ."

"And keep an eye on Major Winnett's wife when she's around the grounds, I suppose?"

"Mr. Mason, that's unfair and untrue."

"All right. You saw her Monday. What did you see?"

"I . . . nothing."

Mason said, "You saw her go into that orange trailer that was parked down in the trees. You watched her . . ."

"It wasn't orange. It was green."

Mason grinned at her.

"All right," she said. "Don't think you're trapping me. I just happened to notice Marcia riding, and then I saw a house trailer parked in the trees."

"Did you see her go in?"

"I saw her tie up her horse and walk over toward the trailer. I wasn't interested. I returned to the poetry I was writing."

"How long was she in there?"

"I don't know."

"Why did you watch her?"

"I didn't watch her. I was looking at birds."

"You had a pencil and a pad of paper up there with you?"

"Yes, of course. I told you I write poetry. One doesn't write on the walls, Mr. Mason. I keep pencil and paper in the drawer of the table up there."

"You used the binoculars to get the license number of the automobile. You marked it down, didn't you?"

"No."

"When were you up there last writing poetry?"

"Why . . . why, today."

"Do you go up there every day?"

"Not every day, but quite frequently."

"Have you been up every day this week?"

"I . . . I guess I have. Yes."

The telephone rang a sharp, strident, shrill summons.

Mason waited, listening, heard the butler answer it. Then the butler walked with unhurried dignity across the library to the drawing room, said something to Mrs. Winnett. She arose and went to the telephone. Mason heard her say, "Hello, Claude darling . . . Yes, dear . . . he's here . . . I'm afraid, Claude, that there has been some misunderstanding. Mr. Mason's activities are hardly such as one would connect with a mining matter. He has shown quite an interest in what Marcia . . ."

Mason walked over, gently pushed her aside, took the receiver from her hand, and said into the telephone, "Okay, Major, I've got it now. Get out here at once."

Major Winnett's voice was harsh with anger. "Just what do you mean, Mr. Mason? I'm afraid that you and I . . ."

Mason interrupted. "Your mother is trying to protect somebody. Daphne Rexford is trying to protect somebody. There's only one person I can think of whom they'd both go to such lengths to protect. That's you. If you get out here fast, we *may* be able to beat the police to it."

"What do you mean?"

"You know damn well what I mean," Mason said and hung up.

10

MAJOR WINNETT'S limp was more noticeable as he moved across the drawing room to confront Perry Mason. "I don't know exactly what's been going on here," he said angrily. "I don't know what prerogatives you have assumed, Mr. Mason. But as far as I'm concerned, our relationship is ended."

Mason said, "Sit down."

"I'm waiting to drive you to town, Mason, in case you don't have a car. If you do, I'll go with you to your room and you can pack up."

Mason said, "As nearly as I can put things together, you had previously discovered the trailer parked down in the trees. You were suspicious. You went up to the observation tower and saw Marcia go to the trailer and then later on saw the car and trailer go away. You took down the license number of the car. You looked up the man who owned that car. After that you kept a pretty close watch on what was going on.

"You didn't say anything when Marcia canceled the insurance on her jewelry and then had such an opportune burglary. You were very careful not to call the police because you knew the police would tab it as an inside job. You let your wife think it was because your mother didn't want any notoriety but you got the jewelry and hid it in that twelve-gauge shotgun. After that you kept a pretty good watch on your wife. Where did you get the jewelry?"

"Mason," Winnett said coldly. "In case you don't leave this house at once, I'm going to call the servants and have you put out."

Mason brushed aside Major Winnett's angry statement with a gesture. "You'll have to hire more servants, then," he said, and then went on. "When the trailer came back on Wednesday and Marcia went down there the second time, you decided to investigate. When you got down there, you found you had a fight on your hands. You killed Harry Drummond. Then you locked up the trailer, came back to the house, and waited until dark. Then you took the trailer with its gruesome evidence of murder, drove to a trailer camp . . ."

"Mason, watch what you're saying. By heaven, I'll throw you out myself!"

"Parked the trailer," Mason went on, as smoothly as though Major Winnett had said nothing, "but only after some difficulty; then got out and went home. Then you felt it would add an artistic touch to have two shots fired so the *time* of the killing could be definitely fixed. So you went back, sneaked in to the trailer park, stood in the dark *outside* the trailer and fired two shots in the air.

"You didn't realize that Marcia had been following you, and when she heard those shots she naturally thought you had killed Drummond out of jealousy, decided that she loved you too much to let you take the rap, and so skipped out. That's the reason you didn't go to a detective agency to get someone to try to find your wife. You wanted a lawyer who specialized in murder cases, *because you knew there was going to be a murder case.*"

Major Winnett snapped his fingers. "A lot of half-baked theories!"

"You see," Mason went on, "you made a couple of fatal mistakes. One of them was that the first shot you fired missed Drummond and went clean through the trailer leaving a hole in the double walls that clearly shows the direction taken by the bullet. When you parked that trailer in the automobile camp under the eucalyptus trees, it was dark and you didn't take the precaution of noticing where a bullet fired under such circumstances would have hit. That was a mistake, Major. As it happened, the hole in the trailer was lined up absolutely with the window of an adjoining trailer.

"At first the police will think the shot *might* have been fired from the other trailer. Then they'll make a more careful investigation and find that the direction of the bullet was the other way. Then they'll *know* that the murder wasn't committed there at the trailer park. There's another little thing you hadn't thought of. At the time you moved the trailer, the body had been dead for some time but the pool of blood hadn't entirely coagulated. Near the center of the pool there was blood that was still liquid. It spread around when the trailer swayed from side to side in going over irregularities in the road. That is what gives the pool of clotted blood the peculiar appearance of having little jagged streamers flowing from it."

Major Winnett was silent and motionless. His eyes were fixed on

Mason with cold concentration. The anger had left his face, and it was quite plain the man's mind was desperately turning over Mason's words.

"So," Mason went on, "you knew that when police started to investigate, they would find the dead man had been Marcia's first husband. You knew they would then start looking for her. When they found that she had skipped out, you knew what would happen. And so, you came to me."

Major Winnett cleared his throat. "You made a statement that Marcia had followed me. Do you have any evidence to back that up?"

Mason said, "It's a logical deduction from . . ."

"That's where you're wrong. Come to my room, I want to talk with you."

Mason said, "You haven't much time. The police have found the body. They're going to be out here looking for Marcia as soon as they have completed an identification and checked up on the man's history."

"All right," Winnett said, "come with me. Mother, you and Daphne pretend you haven't heard any of this. I'll talk with you later."

Major Winnett led the way to his room, opened a portable bar, took out a bottle of Scotch.

Mason refused with a gesture, then when Winnett had poured out a drink, the lawyer reached over and poured half of that drink back into the bottle. "Just enough to give yourself a bracer," he warned, "not enough to give you a letdown afterwards. You're going to be talking with the police pretty soon. Start talking with me now."

Winnett said, "I didn't know Marcia went to visit the man in the trailer on Monday. I did know that Marcia went to the trailer on Wednesday."

"*How* did you know?"

"I was watching her."

"Why were you watching her?"

"Someone told me she had been to the trailer on Monday."

"Who?"

"My mother."

"What did you do?"

"After she left the trailer on Wednesday, I went down there to see who was in the trailer and see why my wife was having a rendezvous."

"What did you find?"

"I found the man dead. I found Marcia's jewelry spread out on a table in front of him. I realized what must have happened. I saw that one shot had gone into the man's heart. One had apparently gone past his head and into the wall of the trailer."

"All right," Mason said sarcastically, "it's your story. Go ahead with it. What did you do then?"

"I took Marcia's jewelry, I locked up the trailer. I came home. I waited until after dark, then I moved the trailer to a trailer camp I knew of, where I parked it. I got out and left the trailer and walked to where I had parked my own car earlier in the day. I had driven home before I realized that I could completely throw the police off the scent by letting it appear the murder had been committed late that night in the trailer camp. So, I returned, stood near the trailer, fired two shots into the air, then ran to my car and came back home. I thought Marcia was in bed. But when, after a couple of hours, I went up, I found she wasn't there, that she had left that note. That's why I came to you. I wanted your help. That's the truth, so help me."

Mason said, "You wrote down the license number of that automobile. Later on you tried to cover it up by adding some words and some figures. Then you added the total . . ."

"Mr. Mason, I swear I did not."

"Who did then?"

"I don't know."

"Someone wrote down the license number of the car," Mason said, "4E4705, then tried to camouflage it by working in a number of other figures and writing at the top *These numbers called*—but a mistake was made in the addition. I . . . wait a minute . . ."

Mason stood motionless, his eyes level-lidded with concentration.

"Perhaps," Major Winnett suggested, "it was . . ."

Mason motioned him to silence, then, after a moment, picked up the telephone, dialed the hotel where Drake had established an office, and when he had Drake on the line, said, "Hello, Paul, Perry talking. I think I've got it. There wasn't any mistake in the addition."

"I don't get it," Drake said, "the total should be 49″37818. Actually it's 49″37817."

"And that figure is right," Mason said. "The number we want is 4E4704."

"But the license number was 4E4705."

Mason said, "What happens when you have two cars? You are given license numbers in chronological order. Look up license number 4E4704. You can start your search in room 613 there at the hotel. Make it snappy."

Mason slammed up the telephone receiver and nodded to Major Winnett. "We've got one more chance. It's slim. The next time you go to a lawyer, don't be so damn smart. Tell him the truth. Where's your mother's room?"

"In the other wing at the far end of the corridor."

"And the nurse's room?" Mason asked. "That must be a communicating room?"

"It is."

Mason said, "Let's go."

Helen Custer, answering their knock, seemed somewhat flustered. "Why, good evening, I, ah . . . is there something . . ."

Mason pushed his way into the room. Major Winnett hesitated a moment, then followed. Mason kicked the door shut.

"Police are on their way out here," Mason said to the nurse.

"The police? What for?"

"To arrest you."

"For what?"

Mason said, "That's up to you."

"What do you mean?"

Mason said, "Playing it one way, it's blackmail. Playing it the other way, it's being an accessory after the fact on a murder charge. You'd better take the rap for blackmail."

"I . . . I . . . why, *what* are you talking about?"

Mason said, "I've practiced law long enough to know that a man should never torture clues to make them point in the direction he thinks they should go. When that column of figures added up to 49E37817 and I thought it should have been 49E37818, I assumed a mistake had been made in the addition. It wasn't a mistake. You marked down the number *Cal* 4E4704. You wanted to preserve that number but you didn't want anyone to think that it had any significance so you added the words at the top. *These numbers* and then inserted *led* after the *Cal*, so that made it read, These numbers called. Then you added other numbers after that number and then totaled the sum. Now then, you probably have less than five minutes to tell us why you wrote down 4E4704."

She glanced from Mason to Major Winnett. There was dismay in her eyes. "What makes you think I . . ."

Mason took out his watch, said, "If the police get here first you'll be an accessory after the fact. If you use your head, you *may* be able to get by with a rap for attempted blackmail."

"I . . . I . . . oh, Mr. Mason. I can't . . ."

Mason watched the hand ticking off the seconds.

"All right," she blurted. "It was yesterday morning. I was looking for Mrs. Victoria Winnett. I thought she was up in the observation tower. I went up there. She wasn't there. The binoculars were adjusted so they pointed down to that grove of trees. I just happened to look through them and saw the trailer. A light coupé was parked beside the big Buick that was attached to the trailer. A man and a woman were having a struggle of some sort. The man tried to strike her and the woman reached into her blouse. I saw the flash of a gun, then another flash. The man staggered back and the woman calmly closed the door of the trailer, got in her car and drove away.

"Through the binoculars I got a look at the number of her automobile. It was Cal 4E4704. I wrote it down on a piece of paper, intending to tell the police. Then . . . well, then I . . . thought . . . I . . ."

"What did you do with the piece of paper?" Mason asked.

"After a moment I realized that perhaps I could . . . well, you know. So I changed the focus on the binoculars back to . . ."

"So what did you do?" Mason asked.

"I didn't want that number to seem too conspicuous. I had written Cal 4E4704, so I wrote down other things, just as you said."

"The first number you wrote on a single sheet of paper that was on the table and not on the pad. When you wrote the rest of it, you had placed the paper on the pad."

"I . . . I guess I did."

Mason pointed to the telephone. "Ring up police headquarters," he said, "tell them what you saw. Tell them that it's been bothering you; that you thought you should have reported it to the police but that Mrs. Winnett is so opposed to any form of publicity that you didn't know just what to do; that tonight you asked Mrs. Winnett about it and she told you to telephone the police at once; that the reason you didn't do so before, was because the trailer was gone when you looked again and you supposed that the man hadn't been hurt and had driven the trailer away."

"If I do that," she said, "then I . . ."

"Then you stand about one chance in ten of beating the rap all around," Mason said grimly. "Don't do it, and you're stuck. What did you do—actually, I mean?"

"I looked up the license number. I found that the car was registered in the name of a Mrs. Harry Drummond. I located her and while I wasn't crude or anything . . . I wanted to open up a beauty shop and . . . well, she agreed to finance me."

Once more Mason pointed to the telephone. "Get police headquarters. Come on, Major. Let's go."

Out in the corridor Major Winnett said, "But how about my wife, Mason? How about my wife? That's the thing that bothers me. That . . ."

"And it damned well should bother you," Mason said. "She must have seen you driving the trailer Wednesday night and followed you to the place where you parked it. She went in, found Drummond dead and thought you had been trying to avenge the family's good name. You can see now what happened. She gave Drummond money to get a divorce. He told her he'd secured one. She married again. Drummond made the mistake of also marrying again. When the blow-off came, his second wife threatened to prosecute him for bigamy unless he gave her money. The only way he had to get money was to put the heat on Marcia. She was too conscientious to ask you for money or to try and stick the insurance company for money, so she staged a fake burglary, cached her jewelry in the swallow's nest, then turned over the jewelry to him. When the second Mrs. Drummond came for her money, all her husband had to offer her was jewelry. She thought it was hot. That started a fight and she shot him. And probably shot him in self-defense at that."

"But how am I going to explain—about moving the body?" Major Winnett asked.

Mason looked at him pityingly. "You're not going to explain one damn thing," he said. "What do you think you have a lawyer for? Get in my car. Leave the nurse to put the police on a hot trail."

11

It was nearing midnight when Perry Mason and Paul Drake walked into metropolitan police headquarters with a description of Marcia Winnett and a series of photographs.

"Of course," Mason explained to Sergeant Dorset, "the Major doesn't want any publicity. She had a spell of amnesia several years ago. He's afraid it *may* have returned."

Sergeant Dorset frowned down at a memo on his desk. "We've picked up a woman who answers that description—amnesia—a hospital telephoned in the report. How does it happen *you're* mixed in the case, Mason?"

"I handle the Winnetts' business."

"The deuce you do!"

"That's right."

Dorset regarded the memo on his desk. "The county teletype says a man named Drummond was murdered. Mrs. Winnett's nurse saw it all, phoned in a report. She had the license number of the murder car, Drummond's wife's."

"Indeed," Mason said, his voice showing courteous interest, but nothing else. "May we take a look at this amnesia case now? The Major is very anxious."

"And," Dorset went on, "when the county officers picked up Drummond's wife, she swore that not only was the killing in self-defense, but that the nurse had been blackmailing her. The nurse called her a liar. Mrs. Drummond's confession puts her in a poor position to claim blackmail. I understand the county is so pleased with having cracked the murder case they're washing their hands of all the rest of it."

Mason glared at Sergeant Dorset. "Will you kindly tell me what all this has to do with Major Winnett's wife?"

Dorset sighed. "I wish to hell I knew," he said, and then added significantly, "but I'll bet a hundred to one we never find out now."

Mason said, "Come down to earth. That murder case is county. The sheriff's office wouldn't like a city dick sticking his nose in."

Dorset nodded. "And by the same sign the way you've arranged it, the amnesia case is city and the county men won't mess around with *that*."

He regarded the lawyer with a certain scowling respect.

Mason said very positively, "I don't see what the murder has to do with all this if the sheriff's office has a solution and a confession, but one thing I do know is that if you have Major Winnett's wife here she's suffering from a nervous ailment and if you make it worse with a lot of fool notions, you'll wish you hadn't. Do I get her now, or do I get a *habeas corpus?*"

"Hell, you get her now," Dorset said disgustedly. "I can't help feeling that if I knew everything you'd been doing in the last twelve hours I'd get a promotion; and if I try to find out, I'll be back pounding pavements. Damn it!"

He picked up the telephone, said into the transmitter, "Send that amnesia case number eighty-four on the night bulletin up to my office."